DOOR NUMBER THREE

PATRICK O'LEARY

TOR®

A Tom Doherty Associates Book
New York

DOOR NUMBER THREE

Copyright © 1995 by Patrick O'Leary

Edited by David G. Hartwell

A Tor Book
Published by Tom Doherty Associates, Inc.
175 Fifth Avenue
New York, N.Y. 10010

Tor Books on the World-Wide Web
http://www.tor.com

Tor® is a registered trademark of Tom Doherty Associates, Inc.

ISBN 0-312-85872-8

First edition: December 1995

Printed in the United States of America

0 9 8 7 6 5 4 3 2 1

To Kelly Dona

Acknowledgments

A book can't grow up by itself. My warmest thanks go to those who nurtured it: my wife, Claire; Ken Ethridge; my friends in the Detroit Writer's Group; Kathryn Cramer; my agent, Susan Ann Protter; David Hartwell, for the wisdom, guidance, and support that made this story possible and probable; and, of course, you the reader, without whom this book would have no place to live.

—P.O.

"The Dream itself is a texture woven of space and time inside which we find ourselves."

Robert Bosnak,
A Little Course in Dreams,
A basic handbook of Jungian dreamwork,
Translation 1988, Shambala Publications, Inc., Boston, Mass., p. 7

"Dreams are sort of suspended in time. They don't have any tenses."

Gregory Bateson,
Steps to an Ecology of Mind,
1985, Ballantine Books, N.Y., p. 51

Prologue

We burned the Time Machine in Hollywood.

Now if life were a movie, that would have killed the sequel right there. But, of course, life has endings. Real endings. Some of them are happy. I don't know why I choose to begin here, but, at the time and in that Capital of Sweetened Dreams, it seemed to bring a much-needed closure to the craziest year of my life. A year that, summarized, sounds desperately unbelievable, even for a tabloid headline:

> I FELL IN LOVE WITH AN ALIEN, DISCOVERED THE
> SECRET OF FORGOTTEN DREAMS, SAVED THE EARTH
> FROM WORLD WAR III, AND KILLED MYSELF

As you can imagine, I was tired.

My new friend Saul and I stood in the gray basement of a decrepit studio warehouse and watched through the round amber porthole of the incinerator as his invention took on the flames: the distinctly low-tech-looking pallet that had sent us both across the bridge of dreams into the future. Like Rosebud, I thought. It didn't take long to burn, maybe five minutes before the whole contraption crumbled into ashes.

It seemed unreal as it happened, and it still does now, as I remember. How strange that something as fixed as the past can surprise us, as if we'd never been there. The way the Intolerable Sinatra of my childhood, braying archly on my dad's Motorola, transformed when I turned forty into the epitome of soul: a thrilling, artful interpreter of middle-aged angst: "How little we know . . ." That's one of the casualties of Time Travel: continuity. Having stepped out of the flow of time, it seems I've lost the benefit of hindsight. And I find myself in the peculiar position of constantly revisiting my past only to discover it is occupied by a stranger whose behavior is totally unpredictable. It's sort of the opposite of déjà vu.

Let me try to explain.

No, that's asking too much. Let me just improvise.

I don't need the Time Machine anymore.

I "Blip."

Usually backward.

As I was typing those five lines I "Blipped" five times into my past. I was a boy looking at his reflection in the bottom of a dark well. I was a young man dreaming of an NCAA basketball final—passing off the winning assist—as I lay drooling in a hammock. I was a drunken teenager falling backward off an oak tree, about to break my arm, watching the bare winter branches soar away from me. I was two and crying in my playpen. I was seeing my strangest patient Laura for the first time: a silhouette coming toward me down the hall to my office, the dip and sway of her hips. Finally I logged back into my now; the page I am typing swam before my eyes, and as I pulled it into focus, I saw a red bird dancing on the keyboard between my hands, tilt-

ing his head and cocking an eye at me as if to say: You back?
I was back.

Welcome to the Wonderful World of Time Travel.

Sounds as harmless as daydreaming, doesn't it?

Think again.

What if your past was just as surprising to you as your future? What if you didn't just recall your memories but actually relived them as they happened? Your "now" body is put on hold, and you actually inhabit the bodies of your former selves. What if the whole process was involuntary? You could be called away at any time; you could be gone for hours, days, even weeks—and when you return you pick up when you left off, as if no time had passed. What if after every time-blip you carried back with you the separate physical impressions of each time, but jumbled all together—body memories that swim and clash along your nerves in a sickening gumbo of sensation:

**CoolDampWell/BasketballSkin/Dream/Drool/Falling
Terror/Tears/Full Diapers/Beautiful Woman**

Do you see why we burned the Time Machine? It's not an experience I'd wish on anyone, even an enemy.

So, in some ways, this story is as much news to me as it is to you. I'm like an amnesiac watching a slide show of the highlights of his life—the official markers of our memories—birthdays, vacations, graduations, weddings, funerals (but we don't take pictures at funerals, do we?). So if you read, My Dear Reader, to find out what happened next, I write to find out how it all began, to retrace the zigzag route I took to get here, this unlikely future where I live, this new world that's probably as improbable to you as the past is to me. Remember how permanent the Berlin Wall seemed a year before it fell?

The past, I think, is very much like a forgotten dream, a whole realm of experience that resides in all of us. It happened. We can't deny it. The experience, if not always the memory, survives. But where? Where do we carry it? What unconscious fears and hopes had their birth in those dreams we have forgotten? What treasures lurk in that hidden place, waiting to be unearthed? I've learned on this journey backward to myself that we carry worlds within us, worlds that bind and burden us with invisible threads of gravity, forcing us to orbit them, secret worlds that are, in fact, though we won't admit it, the source of our identity.

When the Time Machine was starting to roast I felt a sudden unexpected swelling in my throat—a bubble of memory rising to the surface.

"You okay?" asked Saul, the tiny bald man standing next to me smoking a cigar.

I looked at him. "I was remembering something I hadn't thought of in years."

"Yeah. Time-blipping does that to ya. Scrapes the barnacles off yer hull."

"It's like it happened yesterday."

"I know. A cruddy memory?"

I nodded. "I was eighteen. Sitting in the den watching a fire. My dad came home early, or I was up late. Anyway, he didn't expect to see me. And he did the strangest thing. He sat down next to me on the couch. Started telling me these"—I swallowed—"things. Like how proud he was of me. How he bragged about me all the time at the dealership. He said he called me his 'Smart Boy.' He said he was glad at least one of his boys was going to finish college."

Saul cocked an eyebrow at me. "What's so cruddy about that?"

"You don't understand. I could smell the gin on his breath."

The little man shrugged. "Wouldn't be the first time a guy hadta get juiced to, you know . . ."

"No," I said. "That's not it. He was nervous. Guilty. He was taking me into his confidence. So I wouldn't be tempted to tell my mother." I saw I wasn't making sense. "He'd been sober for five years. She'd threatened to leave him if he took another drink. He was buying me off."

"Oh."

"He told me everything a son wants to hear from his father. And he didn't mean a word."

We looked at the flames for a moment. I didn't know then about the things fathers find impossible to say, the tragedy of the things they leave unsaid; I do now.

"Maybe," Saul said gently. "Or maybe it was something else."

I was always making the stupidest faces around Saul. I think he enjoyed it. "Something else?"

Saul lifted his pudgy index finger and launched one of his trademark non sequiturs, which I have come to appreciate as the daily bread of Time Travelers. He bellowed it out and sent the whole basement echoing. "Pay no attention to that man behind the curtain!"

I couldn't help but laugh. Having successfully broken my mood, Saul opened the incinerator's hatch and let loose a blast of heat into the basement. I flinched and saw inside nothing but glowing coals and cinders.

He slammed it shut and a rogue sliver of ash drifted into a shaft of sunlight and settled on the red dome of his head. I reached down and gently brushed it off, leaving a gray smear on his forehead. It felt like the final order of business on the agenda, the concluding chapter of our ordeal, the last leg of a journey of which, had I been warned, I doubt I would have taken the first step. And, believe me, I was more than ready to click my heels together and get back to Kansas, or in my case, Detroit. I was determined to do absolutely nothing for as long as it took to reassemble my shattered psyche. I wanted home, normalcy, anything ordinary. After a dizzy year on the roller-coaster that had become my life, I wanted off.

"Well, it's over," I said with a sigh.

The little man Saul looked up at me with scorn, as he was in the habit of doing when I made some obviously stupid remark. I ought to have known better by then that once time has been shuffled you never know what's going to come up.

"Doc," he said, shifting his stogie to the opposite side of his mouth like a carnival barker and looking back into the fire and the ashes, "you ain't seen nothing yet."

As usual, he was right.

That night "The Changes" began. And The World As We Knew It became The New World.

One

When we were still on speaking terms, my mother once asked me, "How on earth will you ever know if you've cured anyone?" It was a loaded question to ask a psychology major. It encompassed entire realms of parental disapproval: a sly challenge to my pride, a devout Catholic's skepticism for any form of secular salvation, an implied reprimand for my abandoning my "vocation"—I had just left the seminary—and, of course, an Irish mistrust of a world without suffering.

Our arguments were the ideal initiation into my profession. From them I learned that the crucial element of conversation is the unspoken, the deftly avoided chuckhole that words swerve around—which dictates by denial, deception, and omission the path and shape of human conflict. She taught me to keep a lookout for the invisible choreography we all dance when we think we're merely talking. It took me years to decipher the astonishing levels of guile in her words. In that sense, she was my first analysis. She taught me that nobody is who they appear to be, and nobody says what they really mean, especially if they love you.

So I answered her, or the implied question I felt I could return with the most spin. "It's a *science*, Mother. Doctors know when their patients are cured. *I* will know."

"Well," she said with a forgiving sigh, "I've no doubt you'll learn from your failures."

I always wondered whether Mom's benediction should be formally recognized, take a place on the wall of my notoriously ragged office. All my clients comment on it, my idea of interior decoration: Leave it where it falls. It's an habitual sloppiness I no doubt developed as a declaration of independence from a childhood home obsessed with cleanliness, which, as you know, is next to You-Know-What. I'd get it notarized and framed and mount it above my scummy aquarium next to my diplomas: an Official Certificate of Failure. I could put it on my business card: John Donelly, B.S. in Psychology, Master of Social Work, A.C.S.W., Licensed Therapist, Lapsed Catholic, Failure.

All of which is a roundabout way of saying: This is the story of my greatest failure. Laura came into my life in the spring of 1990. To say she was the most unusual client I've ever worked with would be an understatement of vast proportions. To say I didn't cure her is laughably beside the point. In fact, she did for me exactly what I'd always hoped to do for all my clients: she changed the way I thought, felt, and lived forever. She split my life into two neat historical periods: Before Laura and After Laura. She was not just the only client I've ever fallen in love with, she was the only client I ever wanted to kill.

I was in my fifth year of private practice. An appropriate description of therapy: practice. It's a craft at which I always feel like an apprentice, an amateur in the process of learning. Therapy is the jazz of sciences: free-form, unscored, and largely improvised. Amidst the rare sweet passages when everything syncs up and harmony prevails, there are a lot of bum notes. No wonder people regard it with suspicion, and rank it for discomfort somewhere between dentistry and plumbing.

Usually people seek me out only after reaching some state of critical mass: a job lost, divorce, depression, abuse, addiction. They come with sharp hurting eyes, or bewildered pleading smiles; they come bitter or blaming, or full of polite reassurances that they have no idea why *they're* here; it's really their *spouse* that has the problem.

But by far the worst off are the ones who come benumbed, unaware of their torment, at best able to admit that their lives have become unmanageable. I brace myself for them. I don't tell them that they have to work back to the point where it hurts again; if I did they wouldn't stay. And I want to help them, perhaps more than they want to be helped. For I know them well: people who choose survival and cheat themselves out of life, people who squelch their grief and block out any chance for joy. I've been to that dark place and I tell them: there's a way out. I tell them joy and suffering are not mutually exclusive, they flow from the same valve. Close that valve and you may not hurt as much, but neither will you shine.

How many people have entered my office, sat opposite me in the blue overstuffed chair, the Kleenex box beside them, the clock in my line of sight (not theirs), sat down with the mess of their lives and waited for me to work a miracle? They expect me to do something to them. They charm or chat and tell me lots of delightful stories, until at last they use up their routine, and like a newscaster who has finished his report too soon, they feel the great emptiness of the clock, the beating heart, the imperfect, unscripted human gap that aches to be filled with the only terror that heals: the terror of being ourselves. How we suffer to avoid it.

It is this reluctance that forces people into the most artificial encounters: two strangers alone in a room, talking about the most intimate troubles. Friends specialize in acceptance. Families in saving face. Neighbors in keeping up appearances. The clergy in moral absolutes. So to the therapist falls the lot that no one else will take: confrontation. Which is why most people see me only as a last resort. They'd prefer to search in the light for something lost in the dark.

I listen; I talk; I encourage, and together we build a trusting place: a halfway house between the inside and the outside of themselves, a safe place where the issue is Reality. Often I find myself moved by their struggles and the little offerings of courage they make me (not yet aware they give it to themselves).

What flavor of shrink am I? Well, I use a sort of smorgasbord of methods. My discipline derives from Depth Psychology, the discoveries of Freud and his devotees; I believe in the contents and structures of the human unconscious, the benefits of dream analysis. Hell, I believe in whatever works, from Prozac to primal screams. The fact is individual problems require individual treatment, not theories. Having said that, I admit that the heaviest emphasis in my work is on the theories of Carl Jung (a mental genuflection here). While I'm not strictly a "Jungian," and I have no official certification in that area, I do try to practice what he preached. And I am continually amazed by the efficacy of his ideas in my daily work. I've seen too much synchronicity, witnessed too much of the human shadow, seen over and over the healing guidance of the psyche, to doubt the breathtaking depth of Jung's insights. There are many useful tools available to shrinks. Jung's, however, in my opinion, seem to cut deeper, heal stronger, and salvage more real growth from real trauma. In my experience, he works. End of commercial.

If I'm due any credit for this healing, it's only because I have a gift. A reflexive hypervigilance I learned as a survival tactic to get through my childhood. An early warning radar system I used to gauge my mother's moods, dodge her disapproval, maneuver my way through a maze of mysterious and unspoken demands. I can actually read a person's disposition at a glance—a very neurotic holdover from my youth that serves me well in my profession.

Or, it did until Laura. I simply could not "read" her. And though her story was incredible, it contained no obvious patterns of disturbance, no subtle hints at the dark secrets that normally take months to uncover, no sense of self-deception or guile, and no clues as to what this striking, well-adjusted person was doing in my office on a cold May afternoon. I couldn't even hazard a guess at her ethnic background: this tall dark-haired woman with the brown skin of a Native American, the green eyes in the almond shape of an Asian, and an elongated English face and chin. Surely the genetic uniqueness alone might have enticed me into believing this creature (I keep calling her that) was "otherworldly" in some sense. But all I saw was a young woman with grace and calm and that unusual beauty you see in the offspring of mixed races, like the soft curly hair and golden skin of African/Caucasian children.

Her voice was deep. I remember thinking she had a cold, but it never got higher in the thirty-some sessions we had together. She told me she would see me once a week. She agreed to my fee of seventy dollars for a fifty-minute hour. Then she fixed me with her penetrating green gaze and said she had only one condition. I was to tell no one. No one.

A husband? Relatives? I asked. She shook her head. Not even the clinic's psychiatrist? (I explained his approval was required by law when prescribing sedatives.) No one. What about emergencies? She smiled and shrugged. Surely she understood that for insurance purposes I had to keep a record? I saw then a fierceness, something that boiled behind her eyes as she bent forward in the blue chair. No one. Not my supervisor. Not my co-workers. Not my friends. Not my mother. Not "my mate." No one. There would be no insurance problems. She would pay cash.

"Why the secrecy?" I asked, trying to ease the tension. "Of course our sessions will be in total confidence. But I might, for instance, want to consult a colleague who could shed some helpful light on your problems. There'd be no need to mention your name."

"I have no problems," she said with a sad smile.

"Laura," I asked reasonably, "if you have no problems . . . then what do you need me for?"

She nodded, accepting the logic of it. Then I saw her bracing herself for a difficult truth. "They gave me one year. In that one year I have to convince one sane person that I'm telling the truth. If I can do that . . . I can stay."

An emigration problem? Was her visa going to expire? Sane person? "Stay?" I asked.

She did not answer, but her eyes shivered slightly as they pleaded and spoke words too full of longing for language. And in that first brief breach in her calm I saw how much this meant to her. Then she regained herself and continued. "So I guess . . . I need you to believe me. My only problem is time. I've only got a year. Eleven months, actually."

I noted she put an odd twist on the word *Time,* as if it meant something quite different to her. "What do you mean, 'only one year'?"

"That's when they return for me."

"Who?" I asked.

I doubt I can express the impact her answer had on me. My intuition should have registered a eureka—for certainly this was the simple heart of the matter. Instead, all my trusted instincts told me the impossible: she spoke the truth.

"Who is coming?" I repeated.

"The Holock," Laura replied.

"Hoe-lock?"

"Creatures," Laura said, like someone who didn't expect to be believed, "from another world."

In the long silence that followed, I flashed on *The Song of Bernadette,* the film about the young girl from Lourdes with the visions of Our Lady. Jennifer Jones is radiantly innocent: disarming her host of inquisitors, the professional skeptics of the government and church, quoting Mary as claiming to be "the Immaculate Conception." It was an idea theologically problematic and way beyond the comprehension of such an unschooled peasant girl. Then I thought about the recent appearances of Mary in Yugoslavia. In a small country church, people kneel and stare for minutes at a point on the wall, enraptured by a vision no one else sees. Then, on cue, the devoted begin the Lord's Prayer in chorus at the exact point where they are bidden to follow: ". . . who art in Heaven . . ."

So why not "aliens"? Jimmy Carter himself saw a UFO. So did John Lennon. So have thousands more. Carl Jung said flying saucers are a Modern Myth, a "psychic reality," a technological mandala symbol that the unconscious, yearning for "wholeness," projects upon normal reality: if you stare long enough at a floor of checkerboard tiles your mind will begin to form various geometric patterns upon their randomness—that way. How we long for meaning.

And no wonder. I have plenty of firsthand knowledge of the starved casualties of the mechanistic materialism of our western culture, which will gladly give us a paycheck so long as we don't expect clean air or water, quiet, a sensible tempo of living, or the luxury of knowing why we are alive. Something is out there. Or in here. And, surely, not *all* these witnesses are hoaxers or gullible, losers or Californians.

"Aliens?" I asked, making sure.

"That's right."

A long pause. I started moving my hands, as if the words had to be juggled into sense. "The aliens . . . told you . . . if you can convince me . . . then . . . you can . . . stay?"

She nodded.

"Stay on earth," I clarified.

She nodded.

Oh boy.

I coughed. "Let's move back a bit. Tell me, where were you born?"

"In another world."

"Your mother and father . . . ?"

"I don't have a mother. I have two fathers. My earth father, I never knew. They tell me he was from Detroit. And my alien father was a Stillner. That's something like a conductor on a train." She paused. "His name is Sukamon." A longer pause. "I called him Suki." She tilted her head and smiled. "Do you always twirl your hair like that?"

"Does it bother you?" I asked.

"No. I like it. It's sort of childlike. May I call you John? Or do you prefer Doctor?"

"Doctor, John—whatever," I replied.

A long, long pause.

"You're wondering why I chose you."

I was. It wouldn't take a clairvoyant to guess that.

"I saw your lecture on 'Dreams and Memory.' I thought you were intelligent, sensitive."

"Thank you," I replied.

She smiled. "I'd never heard dreams compared to plumbing. Or, for that matter, psychosis compared to constipation."

"It's just a pet theory of mine." I shrugged. I'd been wondering for years if, as the latest research in the field indicates, dreams are critical to memory storage, then why do we forget so many of them? My lecture suggested, somewhat humorously, that maybe they are the equivalent of RAM (Random Access Memory): they serve their function, then empty themselves; they operate as a holding tank that flushes when we log out (wake up). We haven't learned to Save them, maybe because dreams are an organizing Process, not a Content: a Dewey decimal system of the mind. This could explain why they feel both meaningful yet evasive, orderly yet jumbled, richly symbolic but coded. Put it another way: Imagine trying to make sense of a play if you could only read the stage directions and not the actual dialogue: "Curtain, King Enters Stage Right, Distraught, Whispers to Himself, Lights Candle, Explosion Off," etc. So, my theory suggested, maybe dreams are the index, not the text. It was received with amusement by the audience, which, I suppose, was all it deserved. I was flattered that she'd enjoyed it.

"I liked what you said: 'An open mind is the best assurance of sanity.' I wondered if you practiced what you preached."

I liked her deep voice: it seemed to vibrate in her chest before it spilled out—there was something comforting about it. And she smelled unlike any woman I'd ever known. It wasn't perfume. It was the scent—it sounds absurd—of a wild animal. But what struck me most in that first session was her enormous composure. She had complete self-possession. Not the insulated smugness you sometimes see in real psychos. No pretensions whatsoever. She had that bearing certain people have about them who have endured ultimate degradation and terror. Some concentration camp survivors are said to have it: an eerie aplomb; the knowledge that "Nothing you can do to me could ever be worse than what I've already endured." Certain Native Americans have it. Laura had it.

"I try very hard to have an open mind," I said.

"Good. And you agree to my condition?"

I thought a moment. I did not yet comprehend how difficult this would be. "Of course."

She looked at me for a second, then pulled off her blouse. She wore no bra and her breasts were tan and full. I gasped at what I saw. Her nipples were brown and square. Perfect brown squares.

"Laura, please," I said.

"I wanted to show you something you'd never seen before. I thought, perhaps, this would make it easier for you to believe me."

It was to be the first of many such surprises. The shock was so great I dropped my cigarette and it rolled into the folds of my chair. I had to get down on my knees, tear off the cushions, brush off the orange cinders, and dig out the butt. I was glad for the distraction. I didn't want to imagine the kind of surgeon and procedure that did such a thing to a woman's body. I suppressed an urge to gag before I settled back to see she had covered herself again. I lit another Salem. I cleared my throat.

"Who did this to you, Laura?"

"It wasn't an operation. I was born this way. Your genes have a fractal organic structure. Their genes are crystallike. You merge the two and you get . . . strange hybrids. Did I embarrass you? I'm sorry." She smiled, as if flashing were a mischievous habit she hadn't quite broken. "I won't do it again."

Two

The image of two squares on those lovely breasts stayed in my mind for weeks and kept me awake long into many nights. One morning, at breakfast, I was staring into my coffee mug, my thoughts repeating Laura's absurd statements the way a computer stubbornly rejects unfamiliar commands. "Stillner? Folded Space? No Feminine? Green Jell-O Atmosphere? Memory Films? Suki? Ten Dimensions?" How, oh, how, was I supposed to make any sense of this?

"You're doing it again," Nancy informed me from the kitchen. Staring into my coffee, she meant: I do that when I can't leave a case at the office. Nancy was the woman I'd been living with for a year, the bright and orderly woman who hadn't quite left me.

"What?" I mumbled. "Oh. Sorry."

"Who is it this time?"

"Nothing. Nobody. What?" She was smiling. "Just a patient."

"Tough nut?" she asked, checking her hair in the mirror by the sink.

"Listen. Let's not talk about it, okay?"

"Okay," she said.

"Thanks. Really, it's no big deal."

"No problem," she said, standing.

I looked back at my coffee mug.

"Pretty?" she asked.

"Very," I answered before thinking. I looked up. She wasn't smiling. "The truth is, Nancy, I want to talk about it but I can't."

"Can't?" This was her cross-examination routine. She'd bear down with surgical precision until the flaw was exposed.

"I made a pact. Sworn to secrecy."

"Is that routine? What if you have to discuss her problems with the clinic's doctor?"

I laughed dryly. "She has no problems."

She reached over the table, hooked her pinky into my index finger, and jostled it a bit. It was the last tender gesture she ever gave me, but I was too preoccupied to notice. "Are you all right?"

I looked at her. I really did want to talk. "Have you ever seen a UFO?"

She snorted and asked, "Is this a trick question?"

"No. Lots of sensible people have."

She narrowed her eyes at me.

"I didn't mean it that way." It was a code word I used on her when I'd get mad: *sensible.* As in dry. As in unimaginative. As in "Must everything you say be perfectly logical, you're making me crazy!" Who was it that said the things you fall in love with are the very things you later find unbearable? "Really!" I insisted, "that wasn't a crack."

There was a tenderness and worry in her face that she seldom allowed herself to show, and remembering it, I remember why I once loved her. "What is it, John?" she asked.

"I'll tell you someday. Not now."

She left the room and I went back to staring at my mug. Diagnosis. Diagnada. Diagnihil. Suki. Ten Dimensions. A Wheel that looks like a Tube. In and Out. Out and In. Jell-O Atmosphere? Jell-O? Dear God.

Then I remembered a dream.

Or rather: a fragment of a dream I had forgotten. And, strangely, it felt like an old dream: not from the night before, but weeks, maybe months, ago. I wasn't sure of the order of events—whether this was the beginning of the dream, the middle, or the end—but I remembered being in a police lineup, sweating under bright lights in a white room that smelled of Jell-O: lemon-lime.

"Turn to the right," said a deep female voice over a hidden speaker.

There were a dozen of us. We did as we were told. I saw then we were all naked. I seemed to remember a long row of nude men carrying Dixie cups of urine, waiting in line for various tests, bending over and spreading our cheeks to let a doctor inspect us en masse for hernias. I concluded this was my draft physical: we were being inducted. We stood there in the steamy white-tiled room, our fists clamped before our privates, waiting to be judged fit for military service.

"Turn to the left," she ordered.

We obeyed.

"Number Three . . . step forward."

There was a pause as I squinted against the glare, trying to make out the dim figures behind the dark glass windows on the opposite wall.

"Number Three?" she repeated.

For some reason, I realized she meant me, and stepped up quickly, a tad embarrassed.

"Name?" she requested.

"Doctor John," I replied.

"Full name, please."

I was already off to a bad start. "Doctor John Donelly," I told her with a wince.

"Age?"

"Forty."

"Religion?"

"None." This was not quite true. I was actually somewhere in the middle on the God Issue. But I recognized the question as Binary and had rounded off to the nearest answer.

"Sexual preference?"

"Brunettes," I replied, thinking of the color of Nancy's pubic hair.

"Stereo or mono?" she clarified.

This gave me a fit of anxiety: a question I hadn't studied for! I could feel her waiting for me, and after a baffling analysis of the terms, I realized—what the fuck—I had a fifty-fifty chance of being right, so I told her, "Mono."

"Last sex?" she asked.

My mind raced. I was never any good at dates. But this had been a sore point between Nancy and me.

"What's today?" I wondered.

"The first day of the rest of your life," she answered. There were stifled guffaws from the Interrogator's Room.

"Five months ago, at least," I calculated.

"War?"

"No thanks."

A muffled discussion went on behind the glass, as if someone were holding their hand over the microphone. Then her question came: "Are you a coward or are you a pacifist?"

"Yes." I was proud of that answer.

"Confirmed," a man's voice said.

"Heroes?" she asked.

"Yossarian. Van Morrison. Lennon. Jung. Monk. Greene—"

"That's a color," she interrupted.

This untracked me. I was going to name someone else, someone important. It was right on the tip of my—the guy with the beard. The Dead Jew. They put him on baseball cards and statues. Played with the Lambs. Woodmaker? Was that it? No. Something about love. His father loved him. His mother slept with another man. Damn, it was maddening! Why had she interrupted?

"One last question. Take your time. Take all the time you need. It's a trick question."

It was nice of them to warn me. I waited. But the question never came. I took this opportunity to imagine she was naked behind the glass and we were looking at each other. I imagined she was beautiful. Her voice certainly was. I looked down in horror to see I had an erection. There was no way to cover this discreetly. I felt mortified in a way I hadn't felt since junior high: betrayed by my manhood, in the showers after gym. I've always been self-conscious about my body. I'm built like Bobby Jones, the old forward of the Philadelphia Seventy-Sixers: pale, long, and knobby. I wanted to get out of the spotlight as soon as possible. What was taking her so long?

"Yes?" I asked.

"Yes?" she echoed. "That is your answer?"

"No!" I protested.

" 'No' is your answer?"

I was getting flustered. "Could you repeat the question, please?"

She repeated the question. "Have you read the Blue Book? Have you read the Blue Book?"

I was terribly confused. That was two questions. Was *that* the trick? Did I have to answer twice? The Blue Book? I must have read it. Hadn't everyone read at least one blue book in their lives? Or were there two books and both of them blue? This was not a fair test.

"I need more time," I whimpered.

"Thank you. You may join the others."

Relieved, I turned to take my place in line, thinking on the whole it hadn't gone so badly. That's when I noticed that every one of the suspects was looking my way.

And they were all me.

"Yes," the woman with the deep voice concluded. "He's the one."

That's all I remembered of the dream. The memory was vivid—I could even identify the woman's voice as Laura's, though somewhat distorted. The problem was: I could have sworn I'd had that dream *months* before I met Laura. How was that possible?

The phone rang and my ever-punctual roommate answered.

"It's for you, Walrus!" Nancy called from the next room. Walrus was the affectionate nickname she had dubbed me on our first date, a play on my resemblance to the Dead Beatle, especially his glasses. But in the last few months it had acquired acerbic and mocking overtones—having to do with my perpetual tardiness. Somehow, Nancy had gotten the idea that the walrus was the slowest creature alive and—well, it's a long story.

As I picked up the receiver I saw out the window a gray gull rummaging through the open Dumpster in the corner of the blacktop parking lot behind our apartment. Ugly birds. It was one of those phone calls that should have burned itself into my memory. I remember it was my brother Hogan on the line. I don't remember much else.

But I do recall, after I hung up, my leg had fallen asleep, my ear was sore from the receiver, and Nancy's voice: it seemed to come from a great distance, another time zone, acquiring volume the closer it came, like a train, swelling and ebbing like the song of a humpback whale. I don't even think I heard her until the third time she called my name.

"John? John? For god's sake, John, what is it?"

"Huh?" I mumbled. "Oh. My mom. Looks like I have to go see her."

She sighed, relieved, and began her morning ritual: systematically stuffing the many pockets of her brown briefcase with legal pads, documents, law books. "I thought you guys had an agreement," she said to the open bellows of her briefcase, feeding it like a hungry pet with the work she had been taking home regularly as a distraction from our last bitter months together.

"Agreement?" I said, dazed. "When did Mom and I ever agree on anything?"

I knew she wasn't about to let *that* go: Nancy surrendered nothing. And by then all we had in common was our arguments, the only leftovers of our love. We clung to their thin threads in those difficult months, hoping, I guess, that even if we couldn't salvage our love, we could part with the illusion that we hadn't lost something valuable. We had merely stopped an argument.

She turned her attention from her briefcase, flung her short brown hair over her shoulder, and faced me. "You told me," she said, laying out the evidence for the jury, "you see each other only when there are no alternatives."

"She's dying," I said. "There are no alternatives."

If I had been less shell-shocked I might have appreciated what happened next. For it was the only time Nancy ever apologized to me. It's a strange human habit we resort to when we hear someone has lost something precious. I'd always thought it was an odd way of sharing pain: claiming to be responsible for something you didn't do. But in the following weeks I was to hear it over and over, and was surprised to learn: it actually helped.

"I'm sorry, John," said Nancy.

Three

It wasn't hard to keep my mind off Mom. Laura proved to be a great distraction, like an aching tooth I couldn't resist bothering with my tongue. She was no longer just another patient. She had become my private obsession, a maddening code I was determined to crack, for my sake as much as hers. For what had begun as a mere mystery became in short order a descent into hell.

How could Laura sit there in my office, playing with my dusty plants, her eyes taking in the clutter of full ashtrays, stacks of unfinished paperwork, cockeyed paintings, towers of Styrofoam cups, and casually recount the most horrifying stories without betraying any emotion?

About her father: "All I know of my Earth Father is a brief Memory Film they took of him. His face was paralyzed as they did things to his body. Like somebody in a dentist chair. He was bald. He wore sock suspenders. He drooled."

About her rape: "You couldn't equate it with rape. They were like children playing adult games. They took turns with me. Using various types of phallic instrumentation. Metal was the worst; plastic the least objectionable. It was really quite amusing. They were so dedicated they even tried to simulate the noises of intercourse. But their voices made everything sound birdlike and comical."

About her toys: "They never got the dolls right. They managed the eyes and the mouth, but the hair was a batch of wire that sliced my fingers if I held it too tightly. They didn't know how important the skin was. They don't understand touch."

About her captors: "It was like they were born without an organ or a sense. Imagine trying to understand music if you didn't have ears. They're so clumsy. If they want you, they grab you. They'll grip you by the shoulder and have no idea it hurts until you scream. And then they're terrified of you again and put you in the Dream Room for days."

Or this: "They sleep forever. They have a gift for stillness. Sometimes I wondered if I was moving too fast for them, and they just couldn't see me. You know, like the wings of a hummingbird."

Like the wings of a hummingbird. Every session she bombarded my mind with these detailed, utterly strange stories. She told them offhandedly, as if they happened to everyone. But neither her casual tone nor the oddness of it all buffered the horrors she described. They wrenched me as I listened. And the more Laura told of her captivity, the more I dreaded her release. For if, as I was certain, her aliens were just a "shield memory" guarding her psyche against a repressed trauma—what unspeakable reality did her fantasies hide?

I'll never forget a boy I counseled. A seven-year-old who had spent all of his life in a box in a basement. A dark box. Fed through a slit. Finally his parents were found out. One committed suicide, one was committed. He was a timid boy with eyes that seemed to be constantly adjusting to the light. He used to give me little tentative grins and he was always grateful and surprised for any attention I gave him. My job was to counsel him through his first year of foster care. Even though he lacked the basic skills of other children his age, he was an eager student and he made quick progress. We were doing great after six months: laughing, learning, painting pictures, singing songs. He was fine until one day he figured out that other children were not raised the way he was: in the dark. The horror of that knowledge, which I had the privilege of granting him, so overwhelmed the boy that—how can I say this?—he *crumbled* before my eyes. He would never speak to me again. I couldn't blame him.

For weeks I'd been struggling with Laura's diagnosis. My professional tools were sharpened. My handy little blue book, the standard AMA DSM3R—the reference guide/bible of therapists—was well thumbed and useless. I'd been up and down my Decision Tree like a monkey looking for fruit—tracing the symptomology of Laura's condition. I'd gotten nowhere. Nothing but dead ends and lopped-off branches.

In the frustrating inner debates that were to be my daily crucibles in my diagnosis of Laura, I always cast my roommate Nancy as the Cross-examiner. Actually Nancy was something of an expert on the insanity plea—it's how we first met: in court. I'd been flattered when I was asked to testify as a substitute expert witness when my boss had gotten food poisoning. She nailed me to the stand. It was such a humiliating experience that I never volunteered again. And ever since then, whenever I mull over a particularly slippery diagnosis, Nancy becomes my mental accomplice/adversary.

"Borderline?" she asked, cocking an eyebrow.

"No," I said firmly.

"Garden-variety character disorder, then?"

"Hell, everyone can be diagnosed as a character disorder..."

"Mood disorder?"

"She has no moods as far as I can tell."

"Depression? Elevation? Manic? Expansive?"

"No to all."

"Personality disorder?"

"Perhaps."

"Impaired occupational functioning?"

"She's blissfully unemployed. Independently wealthy."

Nancy smirked. *"I always suspected the rich were crazy. It's a comforting thought. Presence of delusions or hallucinations?"*

"Of course."

"Ahh. See psychotic decision tree ... Delusions for at least one month?"

"Yes."

"Prominent auditory or visual hallucinations?"

"Secondhand, not prominent. But if memories of being raised on an alien planet count, I'd say: yes."

"Delusional disorder, then? Schizoid?"

"Yes. No." (A mental sigh.) "She's too fluid to be schizoid."

"Fluid?"

"Schizophrenics are incredibly concrete. You ask them 'How do you feel?' They answer, 'With my hands.'" I rubbed my forehead. *"Still, that's the right neighborhood. Look up Schizotypal."*

Nancy cracked open the little blue handbook and proceeded. *"Okay. By the book."* She read aloud, *" 'Schizotypal ... Patient exhibits not less than four of the following ... 1. Long-term Peculiar Ideas of reference?' "*

"Yes."

" '2. Odd Beliefs *or magical thinking: i.e.: Telepathy,
sixth sense, others can feel my feelings, etc?' "

"*Yes.*"

" '3. Unusual Perceptual Experiences, *e.g.: illusions,
sensing the presence of a force or person not actually present
(e.g., 'I felt as if my dead mother were in the room with
me')?'*"

"*Jesus. It says that? Definitely yes.*"

" '4. No Close Friends or Confidants *(or only one)
other than first-degree relatives?' "*

"*Not sure. First-degree? That sounds like Mom.*"

Nancy snorted. "Who's the patient here? You or her?"

"*Sorry. Go on . . .*"

" '5. *Eccentric Behavior:* Unusual Mannerisms?' "

"*Absolutely," I said, twirling my hair.*

" '6. *Inappropriate or* Constricted Affect, *e.g. silly or*
Aloof?' "

"*Yes.*"

" '7. *Suspiciousness or Paranoid Ideation?' "*

"*How about a world invaded by aliens?*"

"*How about it?*"

"*Let's say: yes.*"

"*All right, then. '8. Bizarre Delusions (i.e.: involving a*
phenomenon that the person's culture would regard as totally implausible?' "

"*Bingo," I said, without any satisfaction.*

*Nancy applauded with a conviction I envied. "Well,
that's it! Textbook schizotypal. Sounds open and shut to
me."*

"*Maybe it's the wrong door.*"

"*You're being difficult, John.*"

"*I'm being honest. Something stinks somewhere and I
can't smell it out.*"

"*Don't get Jesuitical. We're obviously looking at an*

imbedded delusional system rendered ineffectual by a recent stress. Right?"

"Right. But . . ."

"Rank your stressors, please."

"Both acute and enduring. On the 1-to-6 scale, I'd put her at 7—off the scale. Beyond catastrophic."

Nancy slapped the blue book shut. "Post-Traumatic Stress, then?"

"Yes, but to a degree and for a duration I've never seen before. We're talking heavy denial, deep repression . . . probably shield memories. She's like a dreamer haunted by a nightmare she doesn't remember. And doesn't want to."

"Rape? Sexual abuse? Incest?"

"Or worse. It actually frightens me to imagine the root of such a consistent, integrated airtight delusion. What scares me more is how together she seems."

"She's functional?"

"God, that's an ugly word. But it's true. She's anything but traumatized. She's not falling apart. She's coping just fine. Which makes me wonder . . ."

"Yes?"

"She could be lying. She could be toying with me. Maybe she just likes the attention. Maybe she's just a spoiled neurotic woman who can afford to act out some strange weekly ritual with somebody gullible."

"But you don't believe that, do you? Why?"

"She says she needs me. I believe it. I feel it. But I haven't any idea of why she needs me. And I doubt even she knows what triggered her delusional scheme. I suspect it's a lifelong defense mechanism."

"You're not happy with your diagnosis?"

"Schizotypal? It's perfectly plausible. That's what bothers me."

"You know, if there's an organic basis for this . . ."

"I know. It'd be unethical to treat her psychologically if she has a brain tumor."

"You've ruled that out?"

"Not entirely. It's too early to tell."

"What do you think?"

"I don't know."

"What do you believe?"

I shuddered. "I believe she's telling the truth."

"What do you hope?"

"I hope she's lying."

"What are you going to do?"

"Exactly."

There's a famous story about a psychiatrist who treated a brilliant physicist who harbored an elaborate fantasy: he was the lord of a distant planet. For years, while maintaining a productive career and betraying nothing of his private obsession, he had been mapping out, in extraordinary detail, a history of this alien planet: their customs, languages, geography, politics, etc. In order to gain a foothold in his neuroses, the shrink joined him, questioning the discrepancies in this labyrinth of inspired yet illusory logic. Eventually, under this Socratic empathy, the patient was able to see through his delusion. But a funny thing happened along the way: the doctor continued lapping the patient (so to speak) long after he had pulled into the pits. So seductive was this fantasy realm that the shrink found himself thoroughly enchanted, perfectly unable to leave the charmingly concocted landscape. His patient had to talk him out of it.

That didn't happen to me. I became entranced with the patient, not the fantasy. But after each session with Laura, I would be spent, my head pounding, my shirt soaked through. Finally I had to switch her appointment to the last of the day: I was useless to anyone after her. I wanted to harm her captors. I'd get so worked up I'd have to catch myself and remember that there were no captors. All of this was impossible. Without foundation. An elaborate fantasy. But in those long hours, I suffered with her.

And I settled on a tactic: surrender my disbelief, treat Laura's "aliens" as I would the characters in a play. I was thinking of Jung's breakthrough, when he approached the figures of his unconscious "as if they were real people." Not haunting dreamfolk, not imaginary figments, not abstract symbols of his complexes, not ghosts or demons or angels, but real people. Jung understood that our psychic realities are just as real as the external world. But only by believing in this cast of players that inhabits us all, only by recognizing their "autonomy"—one of Jung's more revolutionary discoveries, which few seem to take seriously— only then do we become aware of the enormous influence they exercise upon our waking lives.

If you find yourself scoffing at this idea, consider how comfortable prejudices are to bigots. How it would never occur to them to question their racial superiority. That's how we feel about the authority and command of our ego, our conscious self. It is an assumption so integral to our perception we cannot see it for what it is. Yet the evidence is literally all around us. Have you ever driven a freeway— say, a familiar route you've taken every day—and found yourself emerging from a daydream with no memory whatsoever of the last twenty miles? Were you quick to pat yourself on the back for your highly developed motor skills? Or were you just a little shocked that you could unconsciously command a vehicle through such a multitude of judgments and choices? Who drove the car those twenty miles?

So I pretended to believe. They say faith can happen that way: that it is possible to go through the motions of belief and, eventually, some inner transformation takes the soul. I wish it were that simple. Her words entered me deeply and found home in the places within that have no need of logic. But my mind held back, aloof, unconvinced. And in our months together I gave her my ears, my skills, my concern, and yes, my love. I shared her anguish, her lonely tragic tale. But as the distance between us grows, and I daily feel the wake of her absence, I sometimes think of her as a character in a book that was never published, a private manuscript abandoned and discarded, never to be shared. Today I am left holding a mystery so unfathomable that I can only express it in absurd terms. She did not need my help, my belief, or even my love. The stakes were much higher than that. She was offering me an option inconceivable: she wanted me to end the world.

Four

I'd put off visiting my mother at the hospital for as long as I could. It would be a reluctant "reunion" for both of us—we hadn't been on speaking terms for years. And I told myself that it couldn't be as bad as my brother Hogan had implied on the phone. Hadn't he said something about tests and treatments and her condition being serious but not critical? The doctors still had hope. The doctors had said to hope for the best. Hogan talked a lot about hope. It took me a week to realize how ominous that sounded.

Finally I couldn't put it off any longer. I had been summoned to see my mother: she was asking for me. She was a formidable woman, a devout Catholic, a proper lady who still retained the trace of an Irish brogue. You did not cross her with impunity. Imagine a grade-school teacher who knew precisely how to shame you and you'll get an idea of the stature she held for me, even then. I couldn't see her without feeling a reflexive urge to duck, never knowing when the verbal blow was coming. Growing up, my brother and I—and to a lesser degree, my father—lived in a constant state of readiness for her detonations: ever watchful, gauging her moods out of the corners of our eyes. She had the ability to make our lives hell; she knew it and she used it.

"One," she would say, ever so calmly, which meant you'd better stop whatever you were doing right now.

"Two," she'd say after a moment, in that chilling voice that echoed in the kitchen, which meant you'd better drop everything, run to her, wait for her, acknowledge her, listen to her, and, of course, obey her, without question or hesitation.

She never got to "Three." We knew better. Or rather, we knew we didn't want to find out what happened when she got that far. "Three" was the point of no return, the door we never dared open.

Yet, the truth is, for most of my childhood, I was her perfect boy, her favorite son. I could do no wrong, which meant I would do whatever she wanted. I can still recall the day she put on her white gloves and walked me to the parish rectory to inform Father Riker that I wanted to be an altar boy. This was news to me, but if it pleased her, I had no objections. The priest, however, was a little taken aback when my mother suggested I learn the responses in both English *and* Latin. He said, with some sympathy in my direction, that this was entirely up to me. But since Vatican II, the vernacular was the norm—and English would be enough. Suddenly they were both looking at me. I could feel a lot was hinging on my answer. I knew it had something to do with being on my mother's side, living up to her expectations. I didn't know that my identity was being abducted.

"I'll learn both," I said.

"Father," my mother said, beaming as she pulled taut the cuffs of her gloves and made ready to go, "I think we have a vocation in the making!"

For the next eight years I belonged to her. I was young enough to find this thrilling. On every birthday I received two cards from my parents. My dad's always held a mint silver dollar for my coin collection. My mom's usually contained a religious sentiment and was always signed: "You Are God's Gift To Me, Mom." I became a head altar boy, serving twice on Sundays. I earned my Catholic merit badge from the Boy Scouts: "In Altare Dei." I met all sorts of priests and became something of a mascot. At her side I studied the lives of the saints and sent away for pamphlets on various religious orders. A "vocation" was very exotic to a twelve-year-old: the cassocks, the rituals, the incense, the esteem of men, the obedience of children, the subtle flirtatious attention of middle-aged women like my mother. It all seemed very special. Girls were not an issue yet.

While enjoying the privileges of a devout boy I was also cultivating a self-righteousness that was socially suicidal. It's a wonder I wasn't lynched, for there's really only one cardinal sin in childhood and one commandment that every kid knows: Thou Shalt Not Tell. I told on everybody. Candy thieves. Liars. Test cheaters. Vandals. And when I told on Pablo Petrozzi for stealing a bike, and he beat me up, my mother tended my wounds with pride and read me the story of the Boy Martyr who hid the illegal host beneath his shirt, next to his heart, clutching it so fiercely he would not let it go until the Roman centurions had beaten him to death. It was years later that I recalled with genuine surprise: during all the time I lived within her Obedience, I was rarely ever touched by my mother.

I think the breach started at Sacred Heart Seminary High School in my sophomore human development class. Father Hopper was attempting to explain, with great sensitivity and reverence and detachment, something no one in the class knew anything about, including him: the physical act of love. It was mostly words, and as long as it was words, it was fine. There was no danger. But he made the mistake of jettisoning the jargon of Reproduction and, for a moment, raising his hand above his desk, as if he were trying to retrieve an invisible helium balloon before it rose beyond his grasp, to the ceiling. I can still recall the distant besotted expression on his face.

"He caresses the woman's breast," he said.

A silent bomb had exploded in the classroom, and every boy was paralyzed by the concussion. We'd known about breasts. Giggled about them. Joked and strutted with the confidence that only ignorance can provide. But in that electric moment the reality of breasts, specifically, the fondling of them, by the hand of a man or a boy, became very real. And every one of us registered on some level that this was something Father Hopper would never know anything about.

Girls became an issue. And the ephemeral rewards of a vocation couldn't stack up. I dated; my mother was concerned. I fell in love; my mother looked wounded. I went steady; my mother did not approve. And in my senior year, when I broke the news that I would not be going on to the seminary college, but transferring to Wayne State: a public university, my mother was livid and stopped doing my laundry.

For the years that Mom and I were a duo, my father was strictly my younger brother's territory. Their communion was as wordless as ours was chatty; Hogan and Dad had transcended the realm of language. They'd golf, they'd fish, they'd fix things, side by side, in silence. They even assembled a pool in our backyard, without words or directions. I'd watch them roughhouse in it all summer long; I'd never join in—partly because I didn't feel welcome, but mostly because I was terrified of water. My mother told me I nearly drowned when I was five and she saved me. I don't remember any of it. But I never learned to swim.

Now, my dad was a talkative guy and a crackerjack salesman. But when he came home from his car dealership and changed out of his suit, his vocabulary seemed to vanish: he and Hogan communicated by grunts and gestures, which they seemed to understand telepathically. He knew when Dad was hungry; Dad knew when Hogan was bored. Hogan knew when Dad was depressed; Dad knew when Hogan needed a game of catch. Every night Hogan would bring Dad a fresh Stroh's from the fridge just before his bottle was empty. Dad would let him have the first sip. Then they'd watch TV: Dad in his La-Z-Boy lounger, Hogan prone on the floor beside him, chuckling in unison with the laugh track—jumbo and junior versions of the same model: blond, crew-cut, T-shirt, khaki pants, white dockers. And when Dad was snoring in his chair, his bottle hanging from his loose wrist, Hogan would snatch it and take it to the kitchen.

"Dad's a drunk," I said one night in the bedroom we shared until we were teens.

"Nahh," Hogan replied. "He just likes his beer."

"Mother says there's a commandment about that."

" 'Mother says'," Hogan mocked. "If I was married to her, I'd drink, too."

"Hogan, that's hateful." It was my mother's word for any genuine feelings she deemed inappropriate.

"No, it's not. I love Mom."

This was true. At an early age Hogan had developed the ability to feel two opposite things at the same time, or at least very close together. He could love someone capable of the most thoughtless cruelty. Me, for instance. He forgave without a second thought, maybe because he expected so little of people. I, on the other hand, had all sorts of standards, and they were all my mother's.

"I love Dad," I admitted. "But he doesn't love me."

It seemed safer to say it in the dark. If the light was on I might have cried. For the plain fact was: Dad and I never connected. He was a sweet man, a kind man, a good provider, but he couldn't feign an interest in my life or concerns. For Dad, religion was Sunday Mass, literature was *Field & Stream,* fun was golf and fishing—which bored me violently. Even when I acquired a taste for basketball, he couldn't bring himself to watch the games on TV. "They never miss!" he claimed, bewildered. "Where's the sport in that?" I recall when Hogan was injured in the Class A championship football game in his senior year of high school. Dad and I were in the stands and saw the whole thing. The late hit, his son squirming on the field, carried off on a stretcher. Dad wept openly, without shame, and I remember wanting to trade places with my brother, for that one moment, to feel that broken leg and know my father was suffering.

"That's crazy!" Hogan said. "What do you mean he doesn't love you? He bought you that *Sports Illustrated* subscription two Christmases ago!"

We were quiet for a moment. I was thinking about the yearly Swimsuit Issue that had stunned me into my first erection.

"That was for both of us," I corrected.

"See?" said my little brother. "He doesn't play favorites."

I was twenty-three when Dad had a massive heart attack on the eighth green. I recall sitting beside his hospital bed, listening to him snore, unable to guess what he wanted from me. His death was hard on both of us. But for Hogan it was a clean break: a sharp grief that hurt and healed quickly—there was no unfinished business. I was depressed for months, haunted by the ghost of a man who'd always been around, but never present. It was difficult to let go of something you never had.

When Dad died Mom shifted her allegiance to Hogan, who, after an embarrassing fling with the Peace Corps in Africa, became a respectable car salesman, taking over the Mazda dealership, temporarily disrupting the family decorum by marrying a nun. But it was a happy union and Angela soon won my mother over with grandchildren, who came in the correct Catholic fashion: quickly and unplanned.

I've never been able to dislike Hogan despite his salesman's tendency to flatter and cajole. He always had an irresistible smile. And marriage had mellowed him into the kind of guy who carries a pot belly around like an apology. He had a shy way of looking just over your shoulder when he spoke as if he were revealing too much of himself. Conventional down to his bones, he tried so hard to fit in, to do the right thing, to smooth over any conflict—he was really quite a lovable mug. No wonder Mom preferred him.

She and I finally parted ways over the Vietnam War. Though I was, by then, an ex-seminarian, I was still a fervent believer. I was also a psychology major, nineteen years old, and, most importantly, "1-A." A patriotic immigrant, my mother was humiliated by my decision to apply for conscientious objector status. I was shocked that she was ready to sacrifice me for her principles; she was appalled that I would sacrifice her love for anything. It wasn't simply a disagreement. This breach was a matter of character; it meant one of us was wrong.

She gripped the arms of her pink rocker, held me with her still blue eyes, and, for the last time for years, called me by name.

"John . . . I have no respect for a man who will not fight for his country." That was how she put it.

"There's nothing respectable about war, Mother," I replied coolly. "Especially this war. And I have no desire to become a respectable corpse, no matter how proud it might make you."

That was the final straw. I had moved beyond the orbit of her influence and approval to that chilly place reserved for relatives who had slighted us, friends who had disappointed us, acquaintances who talked funny, parishioners who wore the wrong clothes, people who had no dignity, experienced nervous breakdowns, got divorced, or joined Protestant churches: in short, anyone who had somehow not lived up to her impossible standards.

There would be holidays and birthdays, family funerals and weddings, but they were strained affairs; my mother and I would have nothing to say to each other. There was none of the easy laughter, the unspoken affection and approval. No longer would we roll our eyes at the silliness of people outside our circle of two. No longer would we gossip of the antics of this priest or that. No longer would we relish the fine points of theology and tradition, as we had in my high school days at the seminary, talking for hours around the yellow kitchen table about the oppression of Catholics in Ireland, about how many miracles it took to be a saint, about every facet and degree of sin.

When you let someone get that close to you, when you let them get inside you, as I was inside my mother and she was inside of me, when you've let them touch your secret places, where you are most wounded and needy, it's quite a shock to discover they're your enemy. And part of you recoils in revulsion, as if to say, "I touched that?" Perhaps all hatred is a psychic variation on the gag reflex, that rare, exclusively human trait that alerts us to the most intimate violations of our boundaries, which ultimately says: "I am not that; that is not me; get it out of me!" Of course hatred, like love, must be taught. Unfortunately, hatred seems to be the easier lesson. I learned it well. I had a great teacher.

It took us years to negotiate a comfortable distance and truce. We regarded each other warily, as strangers whom we had once made the mistake of trusting. It had been twenty years since I had moved out of her home and left the trap of her approval, but I could still feel her critical eye, and the power of her disappointment. She was like a limb I had cut off, which hounded me with its absence, clinging to my spine through phantom nerves.

I called the hospital to check on visiting hours with the reluctance of a man submitting to major surgery, as if I were the patient not she, as if I were the one who was threatening to die.

Five

On my way to the hospital I brooded over my last session with Laura. I brooded about archetypes. Anything to keep my mind off the inevitable scene with Mother that would happen whether I wanted it to or not.

I recalled an experiment on subliminal influences they once did at a train station. Most of the terminal was quiet and calm. But on one peculiar stretch of floor, for no apparent reason, people trotted. They found that this section was more pliable than others—that people, in fact, bounced on the floor. Instruments were able to detect an oscillating rhythm created by the springing boards underfoot—a beat, if you will, inaudible to the conscious ear. People were falling into step, oblivious to the fact that they were keeping time, as you might unknowingly tap your foot to an irresistible pop song.

Jung's archetypes are something like that. Unconscious choreography. I could only assume that somehow Laura had been overwhelmed by her unconscious: possessed by her archetypes. My task then became making her aware of her identification with these figures. Understand the patterns of the neurosis and you will render them impotent. Get to know the ghost and he evaporates. In retrospect I am appalled by my arrogance, and I cringe recalling how I humored her.

"Why are they so elusive? Why the hide-and-go-seek? Why don't they just land on the White House lawn and sign in?"

She sighed as if she had expected a more challenging cross-examination. "They're tourists. They take snapshots, eavesdrop on the natives, soak up some scenery. They don't care to fraternize. All they want is souvenirs. They're on vacation—you know, see strange and distant lands."

"You're joking now."

"Only a bit," she said, examining the beige carpeting of my office. She might have been counting the stains; I'm a notorious spiller. "The fact is you are not the most interesting creatures in the universe. They don't care that much about you. They see you in terms of what you can offer *them.* As you regard the primitive cultures you exploit."

An amusing explanation. A little self-righteous, maybe, but not your standard "They're-such-superior-beings-they-don't-deign-to-etc." And it was very odd the way she capsulized their culture with the detachment of a world traveler. Apparently she owed no allegiance to them, or, for that matter, to us. She did not consider herself either human or alien. She was very clear about what *she* was: Something Other. I recalled the scorn and rejection inflicted upon the Vietnamese/American children our G.I.s left behind. They belong to no one. I began to understand her isolation.

"Anyway," she went on, "would you stop and introduce yourself to a bird? Would you take the time to teach it your language? Would it sit still for you? What if its language was based on cultural assumptions that were untranslatable? Or suppose they repulsed you? What if you couldn't look at them without gagging? Perhaps it's simply a case of different tribes who have nothing to say to each other. One eats meat. One eats meat-eaters." She was clenching and unclenching her fists. "You call them 'elusive.' Such egotism! What you really mean is, 'How dare they ignore us!' "

"You've made your point," I said sharply. It wasn't the last time I found myself feeling defensive on behalf of our species. In fact, whenever Laura went off on one of these diatribes it was very strange how I felt compelled to make excuses. I had become accustomed to being the Outsider, the skeptical critic of Modern Values. How odd to have that role usurped from me, to be cast as the Defender of the Status Quo.

"The truth is," she continued, "they haven't got time. Their visits average between a week and ten days. That's just the halfway point of an exhausting journey—a round-trip takes a third of a lifetime. So naturally only the youngest volunteer for the outlying assignments, because only they have the stamina. As you might expect, the young are the most narcissistic. They're much more curious about their own experiences and speculations than yours. It's very simply a matter of time. And fear."

"Fear?"

"That surprises you?" she asked, rearranging herself on the blue chair.

"Well, yes. I mean, I understand we're not the most benign species."

She looked at me as if I'd just said Hitler was not the wisest leader on earth. "Do you presume a superior intelligence—no, call it a more technologically advanced intelligence—would be above the terror of self-extinction? Would consider nothing threatening?"

"But how on earth could we threaten them?" I asked.

She said nothing for a moment. "After all," I added, "you do have those nasty ray guns."

"Ray guns? Oh, you mean laser pistols. Zappers. Phasers."

"Don't you?"

"You mean, 'Don't they?' "

I nodded.

"Weaponry is peculiar to Earth. There is no evidence that any other species uses objects for self-defense or aggression."

I rolled back a few feet in my chair, the wheels squeaking noisily on the worn beige carpet. "I find that amazing."

"Listen, tools are tools. Weapons require a different mind-set. You have to want to conquer. You have to have something to defend. Perhaps you even have had to evolve from a hunting culture."

"Don't they eat?"

"Sea plants. And . . ." She hesitated. "They are cannibals. They eat their dead. It's all very hygienic and ritualistic and not at all as grotesque as it may sound to you."

"What if someone prefers not to be eaten?"

"I said they eat their *dead.* I didn't say they murdered their meals."

This turn in the conversation was giving me the creeps, so I changed course.

"Why saucers?"

She rolled her eyes. "That's just how they appear to you."

"What are they, then?"

"Tubes. You only see a slice of them and you think they are sideways. No. Your sideways is their up and down. Think of a kid in an empty tire rolling down a hill—something like that. Don't ask me how they do it. Their engineering's too complex for me."

"What propels them?"

"They are stationary. They move space, they don't move in it. It just looks that way. Actually, *move* is inaccurate. They *fold* space."

"Fold?"

"Think of a Slinky. Or the curls of lasagna. Or the way they fold up the American flag. Same flag, same colors, same volume. But compressed."

"I'm confused. You said tubes, but then you talked wheels."

She moved to my desk and plucked the straw out of a Hardee's cup left over from lunch the day before. Then she moved to my aquarium. "They're both. Look down the end of the straw; it's a wheel."

"I see."

She dipped the straw into the water and my guppies scattered. "Now imagine a two-dimensional universe."

"Like a piece of paper?"

"Right. Or the flat surface of the water. Just the surface, mind you. What do you see when I stick a straw in?"

"In two dimensions? A circle."

"Or a wheel. Or a saucer. Our dimensions overlap on the surface of the water."

Intriguing. I asked coyly, "How many dimensions are there?"

"They used to think: only six. Their two and your four. But recent discoveries in mathematics suggest as many as ten."

"You said our four?"

"Up and down, back and forth, to and fro, and, of course, time."

"Oh. And their two?"

"In and out, and out and in. Hard to imagine?"

I must have been scowling. I scowl when I'm at a loss.

The more details she supplied, the more uncomfortable I became. I'm sure a better mind than mine could have torn her delusions to shreds. I could only throw feeble questions at her and watch the answers boomerang back at me. I felt the impact of every absurdity, every fresh astonishment. Once or twice I felt as if I were enjoying the privilege of a lucid dream, one in which it is possible to control the plot: to read signs, converse with the odd personages, ignore the laws of physics and float upward to observe toads eating chocolate flies in the art deco lounge of a golden zeppelin. But how exhausting was this dreamland! I wiped the sweat from my upper lip and noticed the clock. I was grateful the proceedings were called on account of time. "Time." Ever since Laura, I've never been able to use that word without including mental quotation marks.

"We'll have to stop now."

Usually after several sessions I've already confirmed my preliminary diagnosis. No such luck with Laura. I'd find myself staring at her fingernails as she counted into my hand three crisp twenty-dollar bills and a ten. She had painted them purple and against the grain: short, horizontal brushstrokes. As an immigrant might imperfectly mimic the fashion of a native. Or a little girl might adopt the rituals of her mother. Or the obvious.

At times I felt like a carnival roustabout—those deft torturers who orchestrate the speed, incline, and momentum of their personal hells—a grubby knobman who'd been suddenly sucked into the vortex of his Tilt-a-Whirl, helplessly watching as he circled again and again past the controls—his only hope of getting off. A strange analogy, I know. But it was a strange situation. What could I do? How could I stop this ride?

Sometimes, as I write this, I see her face. Not the calmness and composure she wore so effortlessly in my office in those first sessions. But the fragile beauty that erupted months later when we made love. It was during a thunderstorm, and in the pale flashes of light I glimpsed her startled green eyes as they looked up into mine, the pupils fixed and narrow. She was afraid. I will never forget that. After a year of hard-won trust, in that moment when two can be as close as possible, when the pleasures of our bodies seemed to obliterate our differences, we were completely foreign to each other. We were strangers. It didn't matter that I loved her. Her eyes were terrified. They seemed to stare at me from both a great distance and an uncomfortable proximity. Close: as if she were caught in the cage of a wild creature with whom she had stumbled into a dangerous confidence. Distant: the way fish will sometimes stare up through the clear ice, at the faces of the giants in their heavens. That, more than anything, hurts when I remember it. After our love, we lay coiled around each other, counting the seconds between the flashes of light and the inevitable thunder, our voices whispering the same numbers in the dark. She turned to me then and laid her hand gently on my face.

"I have lied to you," she said.

Six

Hogan met me in the hall outside Mom's hospital room. "What took you, John?" he asked, checking his watch.

"I stopped for these."

"Jesus. Flowers. Why didn't I think of that?"

"How you doin', Gun?"

"Good. You missed Angie. She was just here with the girls. Where's Guatemala?"

You expected such detours from Hogan. The apparent matter at hand was always a distraction from more pressing issues. "Central America, I think."

"She's got this crazy idea of moving to a mission down there."

"Really?"

"I don't even speak Spanish! And I just got a second on the house!"

"What about the kids?"

He looked stunned. "I hadn't thought of that! That's a good one!"

"Maybe it's just a stage," I said. I could never resist teasing him.

"Do you think so? Like one of those midlife sex-drive things? I read about it in the Digest."

Hogan fancied himself an expert judge of character, by which he meant: Men. But he always consulted me as a resource with vast insight into that peculiar species: Women. Never mind that he never took my advice.

"Probably."

"I sure hope so. I hate Spanish."

"How's the Lady?" I nodded toward her door, through which a game show could be heard: "Wheel of Fortune" or "Family Feud."

"It's bad, Johnny. You better brace yourself."

"She's not in a coma?"

"No, but she's yellow as a walleye. Her bile backed up. Christ, she looks like somebody buttered her."

"How could it happen so quickly?"

"Doctor said she's been real sick for months. Just like her, not saying a word to anybody. Keeping on with the altar society until she couldn't even hold a chalice in her hand." He bent closer as if he were sharing a secret. "It's gone to the spine. It shouldn't be too long." For a moment we looked at our feet. "She's been asking about you." I looked up to see he was struggling to say something. "Listen, don't take this wrong, but are you thinking about apologizing?"

"For what?"

"Well, you know. Just in general."

"No," I said frostily. Catholics have a thing for forgiveness. To me it's always seemed a false priority. I've seen too many battered wives, abused kids, neurotic offspring who are only too glad to forgive their enemies, especially if they love them. But forgiveness comes cheap. It's healing and understanding and growth that are costly, that reawaken the agony of the past.

He waved his hand as if I had misunderstood. "It wouldn't have to be sincere. You know, just to buck her up a bit. Cry, even."

"Cry?"

"Listen, what's more important? Your pride or her peace of mind? I know it's none of my business, and Angie told me to shut up about it, but, you know, this is the bottom of the ninth."

"Not the sports analogies, Hogan."

"I'm not putting you down! That varsity stuff was ages ago."

"Hogan. I wasn't talking about—"

"—all I'm saying is think about it. It could *help* her, for Chrissakes! Oh," Hogan interrupted himself. "This must be Nancy!"

But I turned to find Laura in a turquoise sundress walking toward us down the hall with a broad smile.

"Nancy?" asked Laura.

Hogan looked at me and reappraised the situation. "Yeah. Yeah. Nancy . . . your *lawyer.*"

"Hogan, this is Laura." I almost said "a patient," then "a friend," or "I met her at the office"—finally I said nothing. She shook Hogan's hand and I could tell he was rotating his former judgment of me as a guy who went for bookish types. For a moment I thought he was going to slap me on the back.

Hogan went to scrounge up a vase for the flowers, and I took Laura out of the hall, into an empty waiting room. I remember thinking it was the first time, in the few months she had been seeing me, that she ever looked "real." Her dress was so bright it made her green eyes glow. Her breath smelled like she had just finished a fudge sundae. She stood beside me, full of purpose and intent, as if she belonged there, a striking woman, very dignified, very alive.

That is what I saw; what I felt was annoyed.

"What are you doing here, Laura?"

"I came as soon as I heard," she said with obvious concern.

"Heard? How could you have heard?"

"Does it matter? How *are* you?"

"It matters," I said evenly. I couldn't imagine that my secretary had talked out of turn. But who else?

She sighed. "I know a doctor here. We had an appointment. I was walking past the reception desk when I heard someone ask for the room number of 'Rose Donelly.'"

"But how could you know that was my mother?"

She folded her arms and tilted her head as if she were dealing with an unreasonable child. "I *didn't* know. Not until I saw you."

She's lying, I thought, surprised at how surprised I was. After all, hadn't I assumed that, on some level, she was "lying" to me during every session? Why did it shock me now? Maybe because she had included me into her deception?

"Must have been my sister-in-law," I offered, more for my sake than hers. But, again, her reaction made me uncomfortable. It seemed too foolproof.

"I don't know," she said a little impatiently. "I didn't see her."

"Listen, Laura," I finally said. "Thanks for your concern. I'll see you tomorrow at the usual time."

She seemed surprised. "You don't want me here?"

She was one of those people who compelled you to use their name in a sentence. "Laura . . . I haven't even seen her yet." She had no reaction. "We can talk tomorrow." Again that blank face. "Is there something wrong?"

She looked straight at me and said, "I can help."

"Laura . . ." I began, then noticed she was waiting for me to catch on. "Help? How?"

"The pain," she said. "I know a way. But it's tricky."

"I don't think that would be appro, pa, pa," I stuttered. "I mean, things are complicated enough . . ." For a moment I forgot the decorum of a doctor/patient relationship and just said what was on my mind. "Dammit! Why did you come?"

She smiled and shook her head as if the answer were obvious. "I came because I love you."

This was news to me. I couldn't think of anything to say. Not a damn thing.

"Let me see her," she pleaded.

It had gone too far. I put on my best paternal doctor's face and said sternly, "Laura, this is impossible. You're my patient. You're not a relative, or a friend. I appreciate your concern. Truly. But I must ask you to leave."

She looked wounded.

"Please," I said.

I watched her eyes go quiet. She turned and walked down the hall and strode around the corner out of sight. As her footsteps receded I noticed a fat man with a crew cut in a blue suit leaning against the wall, watching her legs. I noted then that I had made a conscious effort in my sessions with Laura to avoid looking at her legs. At the time I didn't take this insight as a warning—as I should have—but as evidence of my innate self-control.

My first impression of the room was: an Egyptian crypt. My mother looked like a tiny mummified Cleopatra in a pink fluted nightgown. Her whole body seemed to be plated with gold—an ugly tarnish that made her look like an overdone museum display. She would have objected to the arrangement. I hadn't seen her face without makeup in years—there were enormous dark circles around her closed eyes. An IV hung like a strand of spiderweb to her wrist. Her golden toes peeked out of the blanket that covered her legs. I watched her for a minute. Had I ever seen her sleeping before? Had she always been this small? She had once carried herself like some great bird: clearing the air before her with smooth, broad strokes of wings, her chin high, her eyes wide and critical—a woman attending to her life with perfect posture, even when she did the housework. Now she resembled a collapsed loaf of bread. I recalled how I used to sit at her feet as she silently said her rosary. With her free hand she'd twirl my hair. I recalled I had once adored her. When I turned off the murmuring game show on the wall-mounted TV, she opened her eyes.

"You!" she said. She had called me that for years, as if I were still a source of constant betrayal. As if one day I would return transformed, and I would be recognized and called by name.

I covered her bare toes with the blanket and stood at the foot of the bed. "Hi, Mom."

"I heard Hogan say something about flowers."

"Yeah, I brought you some lilies."

"Lilies. How nice."

Christ. Even the whites of her eyes were gold. "How are they treating you, Mom?"

"The doctors are very considerate. But the nurses are inefficient. They can't seem to clean things properly."

"Are you . . . comfortable?"

"No," she said with a weak smile.

I nodded. Dumb question. There was the inevitable silence while we both had to decide how far this would go.

She shifted under the sheets. "I'm glad your father doesn't have to see me like this. I feel like such a burden."

It bothered me that she always called him "your father." Never Robert. Always: Your Father. As if he didn't belong to her. As if he were *my* problem.

"Can I get you anything?" I asked.

She shook her head slightly. "Father Otto gave me communion today. We said a rosary. Such a nice young man. There's something holy about him. Something untouched." She looked at me and, realizing I wouldn't understand, she added, "Angela says the girls are praying for me." She looked out the window.

"Well, of course," I said.

"Somehow it makes me feel funny. To think of them including me in their good-night prayers like your father. Like I'm already a saint."

I knew by "saint" she meant nothing presumptuous. It's merely what a lucky dead Catholic becomes. But I hoped we'd get off the subject. Talking religion with my mother was always a precarious venture. At any moment she could be affronted.

"I won't ask if *you're* praying for me. So don't worry."

"I don't do that anymore. You know that, Mom."

She sighed and looked out the window. "I don't see how a child of my body could throw away his faith so lightly."

You mean YOUR faith, I wanted to say. YOUR rules, YOUR laws and superstitions. That's why Hogan never learned empathy. He adopted your myopia about the world. THE church. THE faith. THE truth. It would never occur to you that someone else could see it differently. That's betrayal to you. If she was making a deathbed plea for my conversion, I was going to walk out.

"Still," she sighed, "your father was very fond of you." Apparently this was a taste she had outgrown.

"We could have been strangers for all we knew about each other."

For a moment, I thought she looked frightened. But it passed and I told myself I was seeing things.

"You never understood him," she continued. "He was a very generous man. He wanted the best for Hogan and you."

That was the order, all right, I thought. "Why are we talking about Dad?" I asked testily.

"I don't know. I dreamed about him last night. Or today. I don't remember. He had a funny red sweater. He was very cruel. I told him I would not be spoken to that way."

"John?" A low voice called from the doorway.

"Christ!" I mumbled as Laura came in.

"John, it's urgent. Can I speak to you?"

We whispered at each other in the doorway.

"I asked you to leave!"

"She's dying."

"I know that!"

"I mean she's dying now. I have to touch her," Laura insisted.

"You . . . ? Laura, this is going too fast for me."

"There isn't time!" she said, rushing past me into the room. "Mrs. Donelly? My name is Laura."

My mother was frowning. "Young lady, you interrupted us. The least you could do is apologize."

"Mom," I said, angry and embarrassed.

"I'm sorry, Mrs. Donelly. This won't take a moment."

I could not believe what happened next. Laura flipped back the covers and began to reach her hand up my mother's nightgown. If she could have, my mother would have leapt out of bed and slapped her, but she could only twist to one side.

"Just a second, Laura!" I snapped, reaching for her arm. In a move so quick it startled me she pushed me in the chest and I fell back several steps and bounced off the wall. For a moment I was dazed by the impact and shocked by her strength, then horrified when I saw her hand was on my mother's belly, stroking it in circular movements. I could see her thin golden legs.

"Stop that! Why are you— WHAT are you doing to me?"

"It's a simple procedure to make you more comfortable."

"You're not a nurse! You don't work here!"

"I'm trying to help," said Laura, her face fixed in concentration.

"Laura, please!" I strode toward her.

"Get her out of here!" my mother demanded.

"Just another moment!"

My mother stared at me in rage. "Stop her!"

I grabbed Laura's shoulder and she elbowed me in the gut. I went down hard. As the air left my lungs and the room swirled about me, I could hear my mother squirming on the bed, making noises in her throat. For a horrible moment I watched the steel wheels shimmy to and fro on the linoleum. Then there was an abrupt silence. When I managed to stand, I saw a scene of unexpected serenity. My mother was tucked in again; she wore a calm, easy smile. Laura was stroking her forehead.

My mother whispered, "My dear sweet girl! Wherever did you come from?"

"Far away," Laura replied, removing her hand.

My mother examined her. "Do you love my son?"

"Very much."

"Does he love you?"

"Not yet."

My mother rolled her eyes. "That boy will be late for his own funeral. Give him time. He'll come around."

So sudden was her change of mood that for a moment I was dizzy. Someone had switched channels from a murder mystery to the cheerful resolution of a hospital drama. I was rubbing my stomach, wondering how bad the bruise would be, when I realized Laura had taken the same route to achieve two opposite results: comfort and pain. I moved beside her and recognized that wild smell that had haunted me ever since our first meeting. My mother looked up at me with an expression I had never seen on her face before. Her eyes seemed full of light.

"It stopped. She stopped it. How does she do that?"

"I don't know."

"Where's Hogan?" she asked.

"He'll be back," I said.

She squinted over my shoulder and said weakly, "Young lady, will you excuse us? There's a family matter."

Laura smiled and touched my mother's hand. "I have to go anyway." Then, noticing I was still stroking my stomach, she winced and added, "Sorry. I'll see you tomorrow?"

I nodded, dazed into what was to be a familiar state of befuddlement, one that I always eventually arrived at with Laura. What, I wondered, had I gotten myself into?

My mother watched her leave and said, "Such a pretty girl. Could you . . . ?"

I scooted down the bed. "Yeah, Mom?"

"I want to tell you something."

Her hand was dangling over the side of the bed, so I took it and held it lightly. I couldn't recall the last time we had touched. Her skin was shockingly cold.

"Closer," she said.

I leaned down.

"Closer," she said.

I nearly put my ear against her mouth when an odd thought occurred to me: What if she bit it off?

She took a deep breath and whispered, "I'm sorry, John."

I couldn't move. My ear was warm from her breath. The words seemed to change the atmosphere of the room, like a sudden shade on a blazing day. When I looked into her face, it took me a half a minute to see she was no longer there.

I met Hogan coming down the hall, his concentration fixed on the vase of white lilies he held before him. When he saw me, he said, "What? God! What?"

I was going to say, "She's dead." But for some reason, I said, "She apologized."

Hogan looked at me for a long moment. "I missed it, didn't I? She's gone, isn't she?" I nodded and he took me into his arms. Part of me imagined what we looked like: two grown men embracing, one holding an arrangement of flowers. Then in his clumsy, lovable way, he said the right thing. "She hurt me, too, Johnny."

Why did I begin to cry? I was thinking of all the years I was the favored son and Hogan could do no right. The smug glee I felt whenever he was compared to me, against me, against my achievements, against my obedience. He had worked fiercely to attain the approval that was bestowed on me so freely that I never felt its worth. I knew how difficult it was for him to say anything critical about Mother. It was a concession to my feelings that touched me deeply. Especially coming from a man so insulated from empathy—whose innate denseness made the motives of others forever a mystery.

Again I noticed the huge fat man with a crew cut and a baggy blue suit still lingering in the white hall. I saw him put what looked to be a cellular phone into the pocket of his suit coat: some sort of plainclothes security guard, I supposed. My younger brother spoke sharply to him, "What are you looking at? This is a hospital! People are supposed to cry in hospitals."

Seven

If all this seems disjointed, I apologize. My thoughts bounce a lot. My memories, too. And as I've said, since Laura, "Time" has become a more fluid and paradoxical concept for me. I simply don't recall the events of that year I spent with Laura in any neat order. I doubt that if I put them chronologically they would make any more sense. So if I've let the cat out of the bag by admitting I had sex with a "patient," let me say this in my defense: I've never done anything like that before or since. The fact is, by the time we became lovers our relationship had gone well beyond therapy. I had stopped seeing her as a patient—in both senses. By then, I knew she wasn't crazy; I knew she didn't need my help. I did not know what she really was until it was too late, and, more to the point, I didn't know I was in love with her. The fact is that after several months of these intense, delightful, shocking, mind-boggling, frustrating sessions, she no longer felt like a patient, she felt like a rival—as if *I* were the one who needed to be convinced of the futility of his coping scheme.

I mean, how was I to handle a woman who could re-count a cannibalism myth as if it were a children's fable!?

"There once were two fathers who argued about their son," she began. "The first father thought, The child is mine. I carried him. I birthed him. The child is mine.

"The second father thought, How can you think that? I gave you the seed. I named him. And I have taught him the word. The child is mine.

"Their son was very sad to listen. And he thought, You are my fathers. I am your son. There is enough for every-one.

"Finally the fathers came to an agreement. They decided the only fair thing to do was to share the son equally, to split the child in half, to eat him one bite each in turn so neither would have the advantage. One would have the head and torso. The other the hips, legs, and feet.

"And the son thought, You are my fathers. I am your son. There is enough for everyone.

"So they ate their son. One father started at the feet. The other at the head. They finished in the middle. And when they were done they found they had no son to argue over. They both had the same share of nothing.

"And when the family learned about this agreement, both of the fathers were Left Out. And from that day on it was decided that every son should eat his father when he died."

After she had told me this story Laura burst into gig-gles. I watched horrified as she sat convulsing in the blue chair, holding the back of her hand to her mouth, her cheeks turning bright red. Eventually she sighed and com-posed herself. "Don't you get it?" she asked, puzzled. "It's *funny*."

Several weeks of this, and *I* was going a little crazy. Zero progress. No evident pathology. No insight into her "problems." I began to feel incompetent. Every therapist will at times doubt his abilities. But it's usually a specific insecurity.

I began to feel like a fraud.

"A frog?" Nancy bellowed over the hiss of the shower, echoing and distorting my phrase. "You feel like a frog?"

"Right!" I laughed, sitting on the can, watching her silhouette through the opaque curtain. "And she's a princess."

The shower stopped and she slung back the curtain and eyed me. "Honestly, the things your mind comes up with." She didn't have to say anything else. I could by now very easily imagine the editorial comment she was making to herself. "How can this man live with such untidy thoughts? Or, for that matter, why do I?" I watched her towel herself dry, thinking how myopic we are about the rituals we adopt. We think everyone does it our way. I would never rest my leg on the side of the tub to dry it, as Nancy did. But then, I would never make an issue of it, as if there *were* a right way.

Nancy used to think nothing of touching up after me. I'd clean the house and she would retrace my footsteps, rearranging books, moving furniture as if I had *almost* got it right—not quite. She was in the habit of criticizing concerts—I mean right in the middle of them. She'd cock her mouth to one side and say "Flat." She seemed incapable of enjoying a moment without evaluating it. "This steak is good, but it's just a little . . ." It was that distance, that detachment—all right, that composure—that doomed us.

She had a big thing about honesty. She hated my tardiness. "You and your talk about reality," she stung me once. "The only way *you* can cope with Reality is by being late for it!" She constantly chided me for my memory lapses: "That's not how it happened at all!" And she was appalled to learn I allowed my patients to call me "Doctor." It never bothered me, especially as it seemed to comfort them. But to Nancy, it was a breach of ethics. "You're a *therapist*. A counselor with a master's in social work. There's a BIG difference!" I can hear her saying, "I'm just being honest. I thought you admired my honesty. Don't you want me to be *honest*?"

"No," I'd say. "I want you to *indulge* me. Say my efforts couldn't be improved upon—no matter how much it compromises your precious integrity. Lie, goddammit, lie! Tell me I'm the best. Tell me no one appreciates my true genius. JUST ONCE GIVE ME YOUR UNQUALIFIED APPROVAL!!" She couldn't. She was maddeningly sensible. That's why I fell in love with her. That's why, in the end, I couldn't stand being in the same room with her.

Likewise in my sessions with Laura, I began to resent how inept she made me feel. Just when I thought I had a bead on her, she'd skitter away like a cat. She'd tell me stories that sounded symbolic, but only made sense as truth, and even then they were absurd! I kept waiting for a slip, a fumble, anything to catch her in a lie. She kept cataloging these ridiculous "facts" that I couldn't disprove. Laura's "reality" seemed totally consistent—so consistent that I began to think she'd done something unspeakable, and her whole therapy was an attempt to establish a foolproof alibi. I couldn't admit that she was telling the truth. That would mean a wholesale revision of human knowledge. It was easier to suspect I was a failure, a fraud.

Not surprisingly, I chose to project the "fraud" outside myself. (There are limits to the amount of self-honesty one can take.) I recall thinking: "Laura is a complete charlatan, a compulsive, wildly inventive liar." But how could I separate the truth from the fiction? Laura was real, even if her story wasn't. Her distress was palpable, even if it sprang from fantasy. I wasn't going to argue away her delusion with words, or define it out of existence. I needed proof.

So I changed tactics. I became, for all practical purposes, a private investigator. It started when she left her purse in my office after her appointment. Deliberately or not, it gave me a great excuse to pursue her, to get a glimpse of her life outside our four walls. I didn't have to open it; it was unsnapped. I could see it was full of chocolate: Hershey bars. Sugar addiction? Hypoglycemia? She was driving me nuts! I wanted physical evidence. I wanted the mystery to stop. I wanted to know.

I followed her. I watched her hitchhike down Eight Mile Road, a notorious strip for prostitutes. Prostitution? Was that it? She got a ride to EastLand Mall and stopped at Waldenbooks. I saw her running her finger down the spines of paperbacks in the psychology section: Motherhood, Fertility, Baby Care. I thought: she's lost a child, that's it.

What if she had seen me? What would I have said? I had the uneasy feeling that she would know why I was there. But I also had a strong alibi: her purse. She stopped at a pharmacy, picked up a prescription, paid cash from her pocket, and left. I was following her outside the mall when it hit me: prescription. She has a doctor! A condition! Evidence!

The pharmacist had thick lenses that doubled the size of his dark eyes and a dark beard that looked like an armpit.

"Excuse me," I said. "I'm Mr. Johnson. Laura's husband? I wonder, could you check her prescription?"

"Sorry?"

"Was it refillable?"

He plucked a white paper off a spindle. "No, no refill. One hundred capsules is more than a month's supply."

"Her doctor asked me to keep an eye out. She sometimes asks for more, and I get a little concerned—well, you understand."

He stared at me, then like a good bureaucrat, reverted to the rules. "It's right here. Stewart's the one doctor with handwriting I *can* read. One hundred capsules. Generic Valium."

So much for composure, I thought sadly. When I turned to leave I saw a huge man in a baggy blue suit examining the condoms. I could have sworn he was the same guy I saw at the hospital after Mom died. Small world.

There were three Dr. Stewarts in the phone book. Two were surgeons. I called up Henry Ford and asked for him by name. A nurse answered.

"Psych."

"Dr. Stewart, please."

After a few beats . . . "Stewart here."

I introduced myself and, when I mentioned Laura, he agreed to meet me for lunch the next day. He seemed genuinely curious, which didn't surprise me. Anyone who knew her must have been caught in her spell. What *did* surprise me was how much he looked like me: we could have been twins. We even ordered the same meal: ham and Swiss on rye with an iced tea.

"I had no idea Laura was seeing someone else," he began. How oddly that phrase should have rung on my ears—but it didn't.

"How often do you meet?" I asked.

"Once a month. Strange girl. She's been through a lot."

"Yes, I know." But did he?

"But at least she's put on some weight. You wouldn't have recognized her. Yellow. Malnourished. Babbling."

"Did you ever examine her?"

"Of course." He looked at me. "Oh, you mean her nipples? She showed you?" I thought I saw the briefest hint of a smile before he continued with an abrupt frown. "Disgusting stuff. Like to wring that surgeon's neck."

"When did you meet her?"

"It was . . . April. I was smelt fishing off Pointe Peele. There was a huge commotion down the shore. Some Canadian fishermen had caught her in their nets. Scared the bejesus out of them. When I walked up they were cutting her out. She was golden in the light of the lamps; her body caked with sand. Smelt flopping all around her. Amazing. I thought she was a floater."

"Drowned?"

"Almost. I gave her CPR and she coughed all the water out of her lungs. I still remember when she opened her eyes. Gave me the creeps."

"Why?"

"Damned if I know. Ever get the feeling like you slipped into a dream? Very odd."

"Suicide?" I asked.

"Probable. You know the undertow off the point is deadly. That's not what she said though." He smiled. "She said she had gone swimming."

"A little cold for that, eh?"

"Really." He snorted. "And they never found her clothes. I didn't buy it. She was in bad shape before she hit the water. Malnutrition. Jaundice. Hypothermia. Shock. Diabetes mellitus. Lucky lady."

"What do you make of it?"

"I thought she was Botticelli's *Venus* risen from the sea."

We laughed, then he continued, shaking his head, obviously puzzled. "Her muscles were contracted yet atrophied, as if she'd spent a long time cramped up in the fetal position. So I thought: kidnapping. Some maniac tied her up and stowed her in the trunk of a car. I suspected organized crime."

Stowed in a trunk, I thought. Like a kid in a tire. "Any evidence of rape?"

"No."

"So what's your prognosis?" I asked.

"What's yours?"

"I haven't the foggiest."

"Me neither. Except that she's gone through a severe trauma and she's made a remarkable recovery."

"How'd you get her across the border?" I wondered.

"She said she had an uncle in Detroit. They released her into my care, and I followed her ambulance all the way to Henry Ford."

We were silent for a while. The mystery was heavy.

"Brain tumor?" I asked casually. It was my last resort.

"Nothing to indicate it. She's perfectly fit. Some minor anomalies, but . . ."

"Anomalies?"

He asked, "Have you noticed her eyes?"—as a biology student might refer to a lab specimen. "The pupils are constant. No adjustment to light. She has trouble in the dark, I bet. Tell you the truth, she refused the full battery of tests. Religious reasons."

I sensed he was making small talk now. Or rather I sensed there was something he wasn't telling me. I gave it a shot.

"Did she ask you to marry her?"

He couldn't conceal his shock. "Did she tell you?"

"No," I said. "She asked me, too."

Eight

I don't know how Laura and I got on the subject of marriage. But I recall we treated it lightly—one of those pleasant therapy detours when both parties need a break from the work at hand. And again, I had written off her flirtation as a typical patient's transference with a therapist. This was, I thought, normal, healthy, and temporary—an inevitable stage we had to work through. It threatened neither of us— so I thought. She proposed a week after the incident at the hospital, after my mom died. Everyone at the clinic was amazed that I didn't take some time off. I told them I was fine. I said I needed the distraction. I was lying; I had put my mother on hold.

"Why not marry me?" Laura asked. "Some might consider me a real catch. I'm beautiful. I can be kind. I'm very intelligent."

"Yes," I said. "But can you rub your belly and pat your head at the same time?"

She looked at me. I kept forgetting how unpredictable her sense of humor was. She had no trouble with verbal puns. But some of the more obvious jokes sailed right over her head. Apparently she had mastered the language but not the subtle cultural presumptions behind it that make things funny.

"That's a joke," she said.

"Right."

"You haven't answered my proposal."

"Laura," I teased, "we were talking about sex. You're a little off the subject, aren't you?"

"Fine," she said. "I'll tell you about my first time, if you tell me yours."

As a rule, I don't share my private life with patients unless they ask. I was aware that she was trying to provoke me. In fact, she had been flirtatious from the very start. This should have bothered me more than it did. "Is that really necessary?" I asked, stalling.

"I think it's only fair."

I actually thought about it for a moment. I wonder if our initial sexual experiences imprint a pattern upon us that we ritually reenact for the rest of our lives, perhaps in a futile attempt to recapture that moment of pure discovery. For, on thinking of it, it occurs to me that every encounter since that delicious first one has been initiated by the woman.

"Are you embarrassed?" Laura asked innocently.

"Absolutely." I chuckled as the memory swept over me. I was nineteen. She was a secretary at the hospital where I was a janitor. We'd been working late. She asked if I could help her get a file from the top shelf of her closet. (A transparent excuse—she stood a head taller than me—but it worked.) I was on top of the stool when the closet went black. She had shut the door. I was amazed when I felt her hand on my ankle, her whisper reassuring me that nobody would catch us: we were all alone. She was a bold girl. She undid my tie, loosened my jeans, and I was shocked when she began to whisper a stream of bawdy suggestions. They sounded, to my young ears, like the prophecies of angels.

Maybe we were tantalized by the prospect of someone discovering us: some old geezer gazing on our nakedness with shock and gratitude. I don't know. But something special happened. It was dark in there. So our bodies had to be imagined. And I think our dimensions swelled. I know our words became more mysterious than they could have been in the light; the smells, the tastes more sensual. Strange. It's not a visual memory at all. I recall how crowded the closet was: bumping into stuff, fumbling around, the musty smell of envelopes. The details aren't important. It was the dark. Touches in the dark.

I looked up at Laura, and caught myself emerging from a vortex of memory, blushing at how exposed I felt. And I knew I'd been stupid to contemplate sharing such a private moment with a patient. "Let's just say: she was a sweet girl."

"Sweet." She smiled. "You have no idea how ironic that is."

Perhaps it was the residue of the erotic memory. Or maybe I finally, consciously, allowed myself to feel how attractive I found her. But for a few long seconds I was lost in sexual desire. My stomach actually fluttered. I had to force my gaze away from her body, even her face, for it was as if a veil had been rent and I had been given a glimpse of a woman's true beauty. It shook me. I mean, I'm just as liable as the next man to arousal, but *this,* this was Major League Perpetuation-of-the-Species time. I'd never felt that way about a patient before. Worse yet, I was pretty sure she knew exactly what I was going through. That sort of peculiar attunement that happens between shrink and patient when real work is being done became a very fragile bridge over a deep, dangerous gorge. I felt as if I were about to fall to my death. I'm embarrassed to admit that I wrote it off with the feeblest of excuses. I had fallen in love before; this was obviously Lust. I could handle it.

Yet it took all my will to muster up a casual, "Your turn."

She crossed her legs Buddha-style on the blue chair. And she never took her eyes off me during her story. There was something confrontational, almost hostile, in her stare. I felt that on some level she was saying: That was a nice little fairy tale; this is the Real Thing.

"Okay. My turn. I was twelve. They knew enough about human biology to waste no time on me until I had begun my period. They wanted a sample. You know, first specimen born in captivity?"

"How were they going to accomplish that? Sperm samples?"

"No, they weren't interested in breeding humans. They wanted cross-species pollination. They wanted another one of me."

"But you said you had *two* fathers. To get another one of you wouldn't they just repeat the process?"

"They wanted a boy."

"I'm totally lost."

"Gender is always determined by the father, right? They had their girl—me. They wanted a boy. They wanted a mate for me. Get it? They tried very hard to make it happen."

"How?"

"Their physiology is such that they can manipulate the shape of their bodies."

"You told me," I said. *Shape Changers* she'd called them. One of her more implausible statements.

"Like certain lizards can lose their tails and grow back a new one. Something like that, anyway. So they took turns.

They erected imitation penile extensions and poked around in me. And yes, in case you're wondering, they *do* ejaculate. They tried various lubricants to facilitate the process. That was the only kindness involved, if you can call it that. They were excited when the first one withdrew his member and found it bloody. It went quickly after that. One after another. Oh, I forgot. It was on a table, like an operating room. Everybody watched when they weren't going at it. It was not by any definition pleasurable."

I was getting sick. "How many?"

"Hundreds. I went to sleep. When I woke they were still at it only they had progressed to instruments and mimicking the noises of sex. They were very literal about the mechanics involved." You've heard the next part: plastics, stainless steel, etc.

She paused and I looked down to find I had two cigarettes burning in the tray. "You were twelve," I said.

"Yes."

There was nothing in her green eyes, no emotion whatsoever. Until I asked, "Have you ever made love to a man?"

"No. I've read a lot about it. Seen a lot of Memory Films."

"How did all this make you feel?"

She tilted her head and squinted at the ceiling. "It was odd. They barely touched me at all in the first twelve years of my life. Then, suddenly—all this physical attention. In a curious way I felt important. And relieved." She was tracing circles on her bare ankles. "The skin has needs and appetites just like the rest of your body. They never understood that. That's partly why they let me return. They're working on adding the tactile to their Memory Films. So far they've perfected sights and sounds, but touch—that's a complete mystery to them." She shook her head and smiled. "It's ironic in a way: master craftsmen, mechanical wizards, machinists, engineers—they really are a race of tinkerers. And they have no insight into touch. Maybe because they're so mentally attuned they need physical distance to preserve their privacy. You know: Good fences make good neighbors. I don't really understand it. I waited for years with this gnawing unnamed hunger. And, whenever they came close, I got excited, anticipating. Never happened. I used to watch the Memory Films and play the fights and the kisses over and over. I could never get enough. It was years before I understood what it was all about. Touch. The hunger for a simple human touch."

I was crying. I got up and walked across the room. I looked down at her and laid my hand on her cheek. Her face was very cool in my palm. During this whole time she never stopped looking at me. Until that moment.

"Like this, you mean," I said.

She closed her eyes.

We were months into her therapy when it occurred to me that Laura never mentioned her dreams. An absence notable because they're usually an important tool in my work. When I finally asked her, she shrugged. She said she didn't dream now.

"Now? You mean: you don't remember them?"

"I mean I don't have them. Not here."

"Laura . . . everyone dreams . . . an average of six dreams, two hours of REM a night." I held out my hands. "Everyone."

She smiled. "I'm not everyone."

And we never mentioned it again.

We didn't have to. For weeks I'd been having more than enough strange dreams for the both of us. And, stranger still, I'd remember them. I usually forget all my dreams. But these were as rich and vibrant as memories: the smells, sounds, sights were uncannily vivid. We've all had recurring dreams. I had a recurring character. A young boy around ten in a baggy red sweater. He kept turning up on the periphery of my dreams: a presence out of place, having no significance to the action. But insistently there. I got the feeling he was waiting for me to do something. In the morning I'd only recall fragments of imagery, but he remained very clear in my memory: a startling cameo appearance that stole the show.

In one dream, we passed each other on escalators: I was going up, he was going down. Once I saw him in a huge supermarket as I waited for my number to be called at the deli. He was pulling a fistful of red licorice from a barrel. I recall how appropriate his heavy red sweater seemed in the arctic chill coming off the meat racks. He had unlaced black and white sneakers that seemed a leftover from my childhood: Red Ball Jets. His hair was unkempt, as if it hadn't been combed or washed in weeks.

He was everywhere: in my erotic dreams, in my escape dreams, in my trapped dreams. It got to the point that I went to sleep wondering where he would show up next. We never spoke and we only made eye contact once, but there was an instantaneous rapport, as if we were old friends. I was in line at a drive-in bank and he smiled at me: a sweet, sad smile.

The day after Laura asked me to marry her I decided to follow him. But, so typical of dreams, once I began the pursuit he became elusive. He was always just around the next corner, teasing me like a mosquito you can hear but can't swat. I spotted him across the chicken coops at Eastern Market. Then he passed me as I waited at a People Mover station: his breath frosting a circle on the tram's window.

Finally, I sat down exhausted on a concrete slab in Hart Plaza and looked at the Detroit River. When I turned around he was playing under the fountain, alone and soaked, jumping up and down in the spray. I approached him; his back was turned to me. As I came close he stopped and turned around. His wet bangs dripped water in tiny rivulets down his face. He looked at me for a long time. Then, as if it were the most natural thing in the world, he took my hand and led me to an ice cream cart.

"Popcycle," he said, mispronouncing the word, and I bought him a raspberry one shaped like a rocket ship. He ate voraciously, sucking it up. His lips were stained red afterward. As we sat in the top row of the empty amphitheater, we watched a blue balloon rise and coast past the Hotel Pontchartrain, up and up until it was just a dot against the lighter blue sky.

"Who are you?" I asked.

He squirmed as kids do.

"Where are your parents?"

He looked at me. No answer.

"Who do you belong to?"

"Let me see your timepiece," he said. He examined my digital watch, pressing all the buttons.

I was getting tired of being patient. "What are you, a ghost?"

"I'm no spook," he said. "Spooks can't dream."

"Why are you here?"

His whole attitude changed. He looked up at me with wonder and joy, as if something had been unlocked.

"That's it!" he said. "That's the right question!" He sighed. "I thought you'd *never* ask it." He crossed his legs and faced me. "Thanks for the treat, Doc."

"You're welcome." And, again, as in dreams, for no appropriate reason, I was filled with a great sadness—so abruptly that I felt it didn't belong to me, but that someone else's feelings had overflowed. I thought: Would someone please tell me what's happening? I'm counseling a woman from the stars. My lover won't speak to me (by this time Nancy and I were well into our breakup). I'm getting migraines. The Pistons are losing. I'm being followed by a boy from— And I knew. I knew exactly what he was and where he was from.

"You're one of them. You've come back."

"Right," he said.

"But why? Why are you here? Why me?"

"Here's the thing," he said, then interrupted himself to touch my arm. "You got a lot of hair," he remarked, surprised. Then he continued. "I figured it out. When you're a baby, they put you in the Dream Room. There's nothing to do there but sleep and dream—'cause, when you're awake, it's like—real boring. No pictures. No Memory Films. Nothing on the walls. They wait for you to start thinking of something. They like pictures. Dream pictures they like best. Like this one. But they can't record them, see? They can only make Memory Films. Once in a while I get to see my mother. But not for long. And they don't let us touch each other or anything. They don't like that. So we just talk. And she told me about you. And I wanted to meet you."

Very little of this made sense.

"You have to get mad at them before they listen. And then maybe they let you watch the Memory Films. And that's how I learned about baseball and Elvis. Ever seen him?"

"Just in films."

"Me, too. Elvis is my man. He sure can sing."

"He's dead," I said tactlessly.

He stared at me wide-eyed; his mouth hung open in a drooping crescent. "Dammit! You mean it!?"

"Yeah. Sorry."

"Damn!" he said, punching his tiny fist into the concrete. He fiddled a moment with his Popsicle stick, then said "So, anyway, I came back to tell you it's really lousy. I mean *lousy*. No fun. Nothing to do. And I been through all the Memory Films twice." He stared at me meaningfully. "And I don't think it's a good idea."

"What?"

"You're my only way out, see? So just forget it," he said, wiping the air with his hand and scowling. "Why you want to touch a woman like that, anyway?" He got up. "I gotta go. You're waking up." He began to jog away. I ran after him.

"Won't do you any good," he said. "You can't catch me." And just like that he was ten feet ahead of me.

I ran again, caught up, and tackled him. I squeezed his leg. I had this idea that if I could pinch him, I would know he was real and not a dream. He looked at my fist clenching his leg, then into my face.

"That's what they do," he said.

"Goddamn you!" I cursed. "Who are you?"

"I'm gonna be your son." He shrugged.

I sat down in the grass.

"But it's not worth it, Dad," he continued with a wobbly smile. "I don't . . . I don't want to be *anybody*. Not there."

I closed my eyes. I couldn't bear the look on his face. When I opened them, he was gone. And I woke up wrapped in a cocoon of sheets.

One phrase from that dream kept resounding in my head for hours. And it haunted me because every time I remembered it, it meant something different.

"Why you *want* to touch a woman like that?"

"Why you want to *touch* a woman like that?"

"Why you want to touch a *woman* like that?"

"Why you want to touch a woman like *that*?"

Nine

I probably should have canceled my next appointment with Laura. It happened to fall on the day after Nancy and I broke up, and I was in no shape to be of help to anyone. Nancy had moved out a month before, but we hadn't broken the habit of seeing each other—maybe because neither of us had options. We had stayed up late; Nancy was determined to "hash things out." We were talking. Then we were arguing. Then she threw something at me. A clock or a book, I'm not sure which. It was dark. I'm embarrassed to admit how much glee I took in her losing her cool. It was the climax of a long boring series of "You always do that!" "You never do this!" "If you really loved me, you'd accept . . ." "I'm sick and tired of all of your . . ." "Can't we have a reasonable conversation without your bringing up . . ." Our arguments had become a carousel of repetitious gripes. Like a wheel spinning in a ditch: lots of energy, no progress. Stuck.

Nancy is, as I've noted, a remarkably sensible woman. This is just fine when you're buying furniture or figuring your income tax, but it is damned annoying just about any other time. It's very difficult to live with someone who is always correct, whose every opinion is impeccably reasoned, whose every judgment is final. Nancy never believed in a subjective universe. She was very tolerant of anyone else's aberrant point of view.

But I suppose we choose the mate who most compensates for our shortcomings. Loners will marry hams. Opposites attract. It's one of those true clichés. So, if I've trashed Nancy, it probably says more about me than her. I've a tendency to operate in a purely emotional mode. I put a lot of stock in my intuition. This leads me to express rather whimsical notions with great fervor, like my theory of dreams as RAM. People often look at me out of the corner of their eyes, as if to say: Who is this guy and what the hell is he talking about? Nancy never learned to live with my quantum leaps of logic, my hunches. "I'm glad you don't gamble," she'd say, laughing through her nose. "You really believe that underdogs eventually win!"

I should have known Laura and I were on thin ice when we started talking about Sex and Sin. Because whatever motives she had for coming to me, seduction was primary. Sadly, victims of child abuse often gravitate toward such relationships with their therapists. I knew the dangers involved; I had read about them. But I felt it was a remote concern. You know, the smug way you regard a sin you've never been tempted to commit.

"So, they don't have sin there?" I asked.

"Sin presumes a higher law. An objective morality. They're much too practical for that."

"They feel no remorse about snatching people?"

Once again she shrugged off my naïveté. "No. Why should they? They need them. They're not so much different from you. Except it never occurs to them that their actions need justifying. They may lack an arbitrary morality, but they are not hypocrites. Manifest Destiny. Subdue the Earth. My Country at all costs. All for the Motherland. Need I go on?"

"Some would say guilt is the only true symptom of a civilization."

She curled her lips contemptuously. "That's like saying failure is the only true symptom of success."

"How can you dismiss the way they treated you?"

"How do abused children regard their parents?" She gave me a steady look. "Aren't they usually pretty loyal to them?"

"True," I admitted.

"I don't take it personally," she went on, flinging her hair over her shoulder. "It has nothing to do with me. I've been through all that. They're different. When they hurt you, it's because it hurts, not because they intend it to. I find that more tolerable than your species's habitual hypocrisy. See, if you are to understand them, you must take them for what they are. They are not your worst nightmare come true. They are nowhere near as horrendous as your good Christians, your loyal Nazis, your selfless Marxists. They are children."

I had put up with this for months. I had put on a pleasant, empathetic face. It was a struggle to keep it up now—I was exhausted from last night's argument. For a long moment I looked at the permanent coffee stain on the beige carpeting at my feet. It suddenly pissed me off. Why hadn't the cleaning lady taken care of that? What do we pay her for, anyway? Is it too much to ask that somebody do their job right? I found myself shaking.

"I think you're full of shit," I barked. "I think you're brimming with rage and for most of your life you've had no one to pin it on. You survived by learning to expect nothing from your captors. That worked, but it didn't erase your needs. And when human needs are ignored or denied or abused, there is *rage*. You can't sit there and tell me you have no feelings about your experience. That you've dealt with it very nicely, thank you. That's bullshit and you know it! So now you've got a convenient target, and you're glad to dump all that rage on our species. That's understandable. But you're smart enough to know what psychodrama you're acting out. Face it, Laura! You're an abandoned child. A child who cried in the dark for a lifetime. And nobody came. Nobody cared. Nobody did anything to rescue you."

"You don't know that," she said evenly.

"Don't sit there and tell me you feel nothing but understanding for the people who snatched you from any semblance of a natural, healthy life. Because, GODDAMMIT, it's a CROCK! You wouldn't feel so free to turn up your nose at our 'species,' as you so smugly call it, if you didn't have a full arsenal of anger to draw upon. Or didn't you know that righteousness is one of anger's favorite masks? So please! Stop the bullshit about how inferior we are to a culture that, by all your facts, is fascist, sociopathic, cannibalistic, and wouldn't know a joke if it kicked them in the shins! Humor. Maybe that's the only evidence of a civilization, not guilt. In any case, I'd prefer a roomful of hypocrites to a saucerful of your little green drones!"

I had held off on that outburst for a long time. I didn't regret it for a minute. And it was not without forethought. I was trying to crack her impervious shell. But, if I'm to be really honest, there's always the temptation to act out the unconscious or repressed feelings of your patient, to express what they find inexpressible. It's called stealing their catharsis. You see this a lot in marriages, where one mate will rage on behalf of the tolerant, forgiving spouse.

"You've got a boner," she said, looking at my crotch with a smile.

"SO FUCKING WHAT!"

"One of us seems to be enraged. And it's not me."

"I don't believe you," I said coldly.

How strange that that remark and not my rant should trigger her tears. But it did, and she cried silently for the rest of the session. She used no Kleenexes. The tears streamed down her face, on to her blouse. She didn't look at me until it was time to go. "But you must believe me," she said. "You simply must."

We bantered back and forth for months. We'd gone over the physics, the mysteries—we did four whole sessions on the UFO phenomenon. I had tried every way I could think of to dismantle her delusion. I coaxed, teased, debated, empathized, berated, doubted, accepted, ridiculed, scoffed, cross-examined. I hadn't managed to open up the slightest crack.

She would not allow her life to be revised or reinterpreted. It was *her* story, not mine. And it was the most heartbreaking story I've ever heard. I hear her voice repeating it sometimes, usually when I'm alone. For that, more than anything, is what her tale is about: being alone. I doubt any of us have experienced anything like her isolation. I shudder remembering it.

"They snatched my father in 1947. They say he was drunk, peeing in a dark Detroit alley. They paralyzed him. Brought him onboard. Took sperm samples. Brain wiped him and dropped him back where they found him. Suki was young then. He injected himself with my daddy's sperm and knew immediately he was fertilized. He carried me to term all the way back. He was old when he deboarded. I was born blue, they tell me. They don't have blue there."

She smiled. "I know what you're going to say. In the

same time span, he aged years and I aged nine months. How is that possible?"

"Something like that," I agreed.

She shrugged. "I don't know. Maybe they age more quickly than you. Perhaps they experience time differently, or humans react differently to space travel, or maybe Suki's 'womb' kept me in some state of suspended animation. I can't help you over this one." She started stroking the dusty leaves of one of my neglected plants beside the chair. "They say I was very sick for the first years of my life. I couldn't adapt to their atmosphere. I was isolated for long periods. Fed through tubes. It took them a long time to calculate a formula I could be nourished by. They said I wouldn't open my eyes until I was one. When I did I cried for days. They said my favorite toy was a doughnut-shaped *kolnok;* I'd chew on it, gurgle at it. They said I was very quiet after my first year. I slept a great deal. I recall none of this, of course."

Laura's recollections seemed warmer when they became firsthand. "My first memory was Suki's face. Let me try to describe it. It was long like mine. Very narrow. The eyes were green, the skin rubbery and white. No wrinkles whatsoever. A small pinched nose right above a thin slit, which is the mouth: no lips to speak of, no teeth, a longish white tongue. When he spoke his mouth barely moved. It was a beautiful face. I could look at it for hours. He didn't want to be touched, but he'd let me look into his eyes as much as I wanted."

She pointed all her fingers to her eyes. "That's where they are most eloquent. Their pupils dilate rapidly depending on their moods. My pupils are fixed. You've noticed?" I nodded. "Humans have only a primitive understanding of facial expressions, although it's true that some of your best salesmen have an unconscious working knowledge of these eye gestures."

I thought of my brother Hogan, the car salesman. I had a hard time imagining that his success was due to such hyper-perception; I always thought it was his gift for evoking pity.

"Eye gestures?" I asked skeptically.

"It's an essential part of their language," she said. "They don't talk much—maybe they're out of practice. They prefer telepathy to the spoken word."

Oh, God. Telepathy. Mind readers. Great. Just great.

"Did *you* learn telepathy?"

"No. I'm not capable of sending. I can only receive. That's a big difference between me and humans. You can send or receive."

"*We* can communicate telepathically with each other?"

"Not with each other. With them. In fact, you do it all the time." She smiled at me.

"We do it all the time?" I asked.

"Yes."

I thought for a moment. "Am I doing it now?"

"No, of course not. You're talking to me now."

Sometimes I could have smacked her. "So how do we know when we're doing it?"

"You don't. You haven't any clue. And you've been doing it forever."

"All right, I give up."

"When you dream."

I sighed. Another one of her irrefutable claims: the only witnesses are sleeping! How many times had she led me down these blind alleys?

"Well, I've never seen a white-skinned alien in my dreams. And I bet there are millions more like me."

"Okay," she said. "Let's do this slowly. Have you ever had a dream that was so real, so credible, that it felt like you didn't make it up?"

"Often," I replied. Especially lately.

"That's a clue. Telepathy isn't just words. In fact, it's mostly not words but images. That's how they talk. That's how they're linked to your world. Dreams are the door." She sat up straight, eager to explain. "Think of the paralysis of a sleeper in REM. Stillness, right? That's when space can be folded. You could do it, too, but you're years from the applicable sciences and the essential revolution in your concept of reality. And the strangeness of dreams, the odd logic, the impossible geography, leaps of time, the associations that only make sense within the dream—that's *them*. That's how *they* think. Even the thoughtless brutality—that's them, too."

"But the images are variations on *our* world, not theirs."

"That's because they're speaking through your imagination, your tongue. It's a translation. They can't impose their vision on you; they can only infiltrate and fiddle with your imagery. They don't create, they direct."

"You're saying all our dreams are plays based on their scripts?"

"Not all. Some. They dress up in your images, but the action is co-created between you. And—this is crucial—it's not scripted. It's improvised."

"What are they trying to tell us?"

"Nothing. They have nothing to say to you. And vice versa. They're playing."

"Playing?" Was she putting me on, or was I too stupid to get it?

"Sure. Most dreams are frivolous, aren't they? Remember, this is a race preoccupied with order, efficiency, making things work. How might they behave if they had a vacation—which they don't. Wouldn't they want to loosen up a bit?"

"Dreams are their vacations?"

She lifted her eyebrows and gave me an impish smile. "Right."

Something occurred to me. "If they're in our dreams, are we in theirs?"

"No."

"Why not?"

"They don't dream. That's why they need you."

"They *need* us?"

"Yes."

I thought: Don't dream. "Spooks can't dream."

Have you ever wondered if madness is a disease you can catch by exposure to the insane? Many times after our sessions I'd walk out of the clinic and be struck dumb. I would stand still for a minute and just look around me. The more familiar I became with her reality, the stranger ours looked. Things we take for granted became alien to me, as if I'd skipped fifty years into the future and could see the irony of all the assumptions of our past. Traffic lights are red, yellow, and green. We pay money to park our vehicles. There is only twenty minutes of news every day. Healthy women are considered chubby and repulsive. The most hallowed creatures on our planet are men who play with various types of balls. BALLS! I mean, think about it. Our sky is BLUE. It's usually blue. Did it ever occur to you that no other planet in our solar system has a blue sky? Our singular atmosphere creates the effect. And that's how everything began to appear to me. An arbitrary effect. A chance coincidence of forces. No longer was it The World. But just one of many possible worlds.

Reality had begun to look as strange as the pet section at

Kmart. I kept seeing this image of a gerbil locked up in a sawdust-strewn cage, quivering with fear, surrounded by an incomprehensible menagerie of species: green chameleons, manic parrots chirping, snow-white cockatoos, bubbling aquariums full of darting rainbow guppies, filigreed angelfish—what could a gerbil do but go mad? Enclosed by an invisible force field, exposed to the inspection of giants, subject to the intrusions of a huge claw that plunges down from above like the hand of God, which can snatch your companions away without any warning, to God Knows Where. What an unbearable combination of claustrophobia, paranoia, and exposure. Who wouldn't go mad? Perhaps that's how Laura felt on some level: surrounded by the chaos of our melting-pot world, where ghettos rub shoulders with mansions, crack houses with Baptist churches, Asians with Blacks with Arabs with Caucasians. This is a damn strange planet. Or, maybe, just maybe, the analogy applies to me. Maybe my comfortable world view was shattered by the possibility of an alien culture that could only make sense on its own terms. Sometimes listening to her I felt as if she had fractured something essential to my makeup, and it would never be repaired. A fissure of doubt that rendered fallible my most fundamental convictions. Was I breaking down? Or was she finally convincing me? It never occurred to me to ask the obvious: Was I falling in love?

Ten

Ironically enough, one of my last dealings with the normal world, before I began my descent in earnest into the unknown, was a Halloween costume party. It was a yearly event for classmates and co-workers of mine who had at one time or another worked at the Home: our quaint term for the Hospital for the Criminally Insane. Over time the get-together had come to include spouses and lovers, but generally, the same faces took on a variety of new facades every year. The game became guessing who everyone was. There were angels at the party. A marine drill sergeant. A magician. A ninja. A "space bitch," as one concoction of foil and silver was dubbed. One man came as "himself," which is to say, he wore no costume: the most flagrantly egotistic disguise or the most provocative postmodern statement of the evening. I came as an Old Testament prophet. There was an endless loop of Motown records—that strange combination of tame juvenile sentiment over an extraordinarily complex arrangement wedded by an irresistible beat seemed quite appropriate for such a night of dualities.

One of the few faces I couldn't recognize was a pale diminutive woman who wore black gloves with studs at the knuckles and a very tight black leather dress: an S&M madam. As we shook hands she smiled and we registered a mutual whisper of attraction under the small talk. Throughout the night I found something comforting about her high voice: a lovely flute dancing above the murmuring conversation, wild laughter, tinkling glasses, and buttoned-up Motown soul. I was given to believe that her costume was the most outrageous of the evening.

"I gotta hand it to Adrian," someone began.

"The quietest lady on staff dresses up like that!"

"She's pulling it off, though. Like it was perfectly natural."

"She's not like that, eh?" I said. "For a moment there I thought she was my type."

"Ah! The shrink is rebounding!" teased an old colleague.

"She's too shy for you, John. You'd be lucky to get two words out of her."

"Is she a doctor?" I asked.

"Nurse's aide."

"Really? Who'd she come with?"

My friend smiled. "She came alone. Like you."

The glimpses I caught of her as the party progressed confirmed my interest and her mystery. She always seemed to have a caramel apple in her hand—I wondered if it was part of her costume. I couldn't imagine her changing bedpans and sheets, turning patients, or pushing laundry carts. She seemed more intelligent than that.

After the magician mimed "Mack the Knife" and was given a standing ovation, I heard her urgent whisper coming from the kitchen. A fat man dressed as a clown had

Adrian pinned against the fridge, his arms on either side of her face.

"Come on," he said.

"Roy, you're drunk," she replied pleasantly.

"Come on, just a little one for the clown."

Her eyes met mine over his shoulder and I understood her request. Leaning against the fridge, I smiled at him and said, "Ice."

He looked at me for too long. His pancake was running and sweat beaded on his ball nose. "Later," he said, turning back to Adrian.

"But I'm thirsty," I persisted.

He swiveled his head about so quickly I thought it might do a complete rotation. Then his eyes made a slow cantering assessment of me, starting at my toes.

"So get a drink," he said.

I held out my hand. "John Donelly. Nice costume."

"Fuck off, Moses," he replied.

"Listen, friend," I said. "Let me get you some coffee. How do you take it?"

By now he had forgotten Adrian and she slipped away. He ambled toward me, looking out from under his painted eyebrows: a crazed Bozo spewing a cloud of liquor breath. "I'm not your friend."

"Hey. I'm John. You're Roy. That's a start."

He smiled and swung at me. I ducked, but it caught me flush above the ear. I went down seeing stars.

"Get the message, friend?" he said, towering over me.

I had an ant's-eye view of his floppy shoes. "Christ, that hurt."

He chuckled and turned around. I could see Adrian between his striped baggy pants. I watched her foot rise and soundly punt the space between his legs. He fell to his knees, clutching his crotch; the air came out of him with the sound of an electronic drum, then he fell on his face.

"I hate clowns," Adrian said sweetly, stepping over him.

The host arrived and began apologizing to everybody. I sat up and heard water running in the sink. Then Adrian was pressing a damp dish towel of ice cubes to my head. I winced and looked at her tiny breasts. How pale she was!

"Sorry to get you involved," she said. "He's an asshole."

"I gathered that."

When she pulled back the towel it was red. "Uh-oh," she said, looking at my scalp. She pressed the skin around the cut with her fingers and I felt a tear and yelled, "Christ!"

She flinched as if my skin had shocked her. "Sorry. That bastard cut you."

Through clenched teeth I asked, "How bad is it?"

She looked again and clicked her tongue on her teeth. "Honey, I think we're talking stitches here."

What I get for playing cowboy. She helped me to my feet. *Honey*—I didn't mind her calling me that. I noticed she was leading me with a firm grip on my arm. "Where are we going?" I asked.

"Hospital. Here. Hold this." She handed me the ice pack, then wrapped a fresh towel around it.

"Hey, that's not necessary. I can make it."

"Your car a manual or automatic?"

I looked at her. "Manual. Why?"

"Unless you're a stunt driver it'll be hard to hold that ice pack and shift."

"Oh. Right. Listen, just call me a cab."

"Nonsense. I got you into this. Give me your keys."

We made a grand entrance at Emergency: Moses and the

Leather Woman. We sat and chatted for about half an hour. For some reason, we talked a lot about birth control. Odd way to flirt, I thought. But what the hell—she is a nurse. Then they took X rays, and led me to a draped cubicle, where they shaved and stitched the side of my head. On the way home I had a whale of a headache. She accepted my invitation in, gave me a shot of whiskey and an aspirin, and watched me fall asleep on my La-Z-Boy.

I recall waking, or seeming to wake, or maybe a short glimpse of a dream. The TV was full of blue snow; its light threw everything in the room into dramatic relief. I seemed to hear a low hissing sound. Had the volume been turned down low or had someone left their sprinkler on overnight? In the corner of the room Adrian lay on the couch. She had peeled down the front of her dress and was doing something to her body. I couldn't turn my head but my eyes strained toward the corners. In the blue haze I could have sworn she was touching herself, plucking her breasts with her long talonlike fingernails. The memory excites me until I recall the image of her stretching her nipples higher and higher like taffy, until her breasts hung several feet above her chest like closed umbrellas. Then I knew it was a dream and I closed my eyes.

In the morning I stumbled toward the smell of coffee. Adrian sat at the kitchen table eating a DoveBar.

"He has risen," she greeted me.

My head felt like a handball had been sewn under the skin, right above the ear.

After my first sip of coffee, I spotted the clock on the kitchen counter and mumbled, "Christ! I'm late! I gotta call the clinic."

"You sure swear a lot."

I restrained myself from the "So what?" I was forming and said, "Does it bother you?"

"I just don't find cursing necessary. I wonder why others do."

This fastidiousness didn't jibe with the worldly woman I had gotten to know the night before. But I made a note to watch my language around her.

"Isn't it a little early for ice cream?" I asked.

"Does it bother you?" she mocked. I should have known better than dumping that therapist's cliché on her. It seemed to trigger a crossness, like the undertow of malice you sometimes hear between couples who've been married too long. I managed to say, "Thanks for taking care of me," though at that moment I didn't feel particularly grateful.

"Likewise," she said, licking chocolate off her lip and gazing away.

"You didn't look like you needed that much help, the way you put out that clown."

"Oh, that's just something I picked up from the orderlies—how to control the ward, how to squelch an incident before it starts."

"Why'd you call *me* over, then?" I surprised myself with the anger I felt. Where did that come from?

"I had to distract him."

I realized then I had felt used right after she crotched him. "Glad to be of service," I snapped.

She gave me a cool look. "I did say I was sorry." She stood up, took a massive bite of her ice cream, and dropped the stick in the trash.

Following her to the door, I tried to make amends. "Adrian? Stay for breakfast."

She opened it and looked at me. "Another day, maybe."

"You gotta go?"

"I work tonight. I need my sleep."

"I'll drive you to your car."

"The clown drove it over last night. He was apologetic."

I spotted my next-door neighbor, Mrs. Jordan, in her bathrobe, bending down to pick up her paper. I imagined what she must have thought of the scene: man with bandaged head, dominatrix strutting away toward her red Miata.

"So?" I called.

"So call me," she replied.

I watched her drive off. When I turned to go inside I found Mrs. Jordan inspecting me. "What happened to you, John?"

I picked up my paper. "Limbo accident," I muttered and stepped inside.

Eleven

A few weeks later I got a phone call.

"Jesus, Johnny! I thought you disappeared!"

"Hogan?"

"What the hell's wrong with you? You drop Nancy. You hurt your head. You don't tell anybody!"

He meant: "You didn't tell me."

"I was going to. I've been having phone problems." A host of them, in fact: strange clicks when I answered, bad reception on local calls, and, sometimes for no apparent reason, my connection would be cut. It was a convenient excuse, but true nonetheless.

"*Phone* problems?" he asked. "What the hell's that mean?"

"It's sort of complicated. Anyway, you knew Nancy and I were on the outs. I told you at the funeral we hadn't touched each other for months."

"What? Does somebody have to *die* before you talk to me?"

I thought about that. "Who told you about my head?"

"None of your business!" he replied grouchily. "All right, your secretary. I must have given her a dozen messages."

They were all on my desk: a pile of green slips that each read "Hogan." I felt a twinge of guilt when I realized that he could have used my company these past months. Hell, I was all the family he had left. It was a burden I didn't feel up to.

"I mean, I'm having a hard time with Mom's death, too," he said. "But I can't just up and leave my kids and drop the dealership. I mean, what would Dad say?"

"Hogan, calm down. First of all, I don't have any kids. Secondly, it's got nothing to do with Mom." Not entirely true, that. "Thirdly . . ." What was thirdly? Dad was dead?

"Thirdly? That's not even a word!"

"Well, you know what I mean."

"No, I don't! That's why I'm calling!"

"Everything's fine, Gun. That's all that matters."

There was a long pause. "Johnny, this is important. We gotta go through Mom's drawers."

"What?"

"Her belongings. I been putting it off 'cause I couldn't bear facing all those pictures and stuff. I know our schedules are impossible, but I need your help. I haven't even put the house up for sale."

"That's right!" I replied. "We better shut off the utilities."

"There's no hurry on that," he said. "I need the lights."

He needed the lights? "You shouldn't have to take care of all of this yourself, Hogan."

"I don't mind."

"Well, let me find a real estate agent, and you can take care of the utilities and furniture."

Hogan seldom raised his voice, so I was shocked when he yelled, "Geez, John! I can handle it!" It sounded like he was doing breathing exercises.

"Hey, Hogan? Are *you* all right?"

There was a pause. "I'm coping," he answered sadly. "But I tell ya, I'll be right in the middle of closing a deal and I start to cry. I feel like a goddamn fool. I'm crying all the time, Johnny."

"That's because it hurts."

"That's what Angie said. Is this normal?"

"Perfectly."

"I thought maybe I was, you know . . ."

"No, not at all." I didn't tell him how I was dealing with Mom's death: poorly. I had tried to put it out of my mind. And whenever it threatened to emerge, I'd get good and drunk on martinis. I knew this was stupid. I knew I'd have to face those feelings sometime. I wasn't ready.

Hogan took a couple of deep breaths. "I didn't know it was possible: to hurt like this. My whole body has a headache."

"It'll hurt for a while," I told him with an expertise that felt phony as hell. "The tears will stop. But grief takes time. Does anything help?"

He thought about it for a moment. "Sex."

"Yeah?" I hoped he wasn't going to go into details.

"And don't laugh. After we close I go sit in the cars in the showroom. Nobody can see me in the dark. I sit and listen to the radio and smell the factory. New cars are very peaceful."

"Sounds like you're coping just fine, Gun."

"Well, what are you gonna do? I dream about her a lot. What's that mean?"

"Maybe you miss her . . ." I offered.

"Yeah. I do. She keeps saying the same thing over and over."

"What?"

"I want more grandchildren."

After I hung up, I thought of something Laura had said. "Dreams are the door." I've often wondered why we take dreams so lightly. Is it because they're so commonplace we forget how mysterious they are? Or are they unsettling reminders of a reality beyond our control, doors to a deeper, more frightening realm? In any case, I have a professional suspicion of the conspiracy of silence that surrounds dreaming, for I have learned that that which is taboo, unspoken, unacknowledged, often exercises the most subtle tyranny.

So part of me was intrigued by Laura's description of the Holock's ritualistic approach to dreams. ". . . After Suki's face I remember the Dream Rooms. There's only a few thousand of them. They're domes. The walls are lima-bean green and they have the texture of sharkskin. They appear to be very smooth; they even glisten. But when you touch them they're rough like sandpaper, almost prickly. And they're wet, like most everything is there. It's all underwater, right? Except the water is like Jell-O.

"In the Dream Rooms there's perfect silence. Nothing to do but sleep and dream. You sleep on the floor, or the walls, or the ceiling, and it's cool. I don't think I knew it was a room for many years. You never got hungry there, so they never had to feed you. Nutrients were pumped into the air, a rich mixture that smelled like fish, and when you breathed it felt like you were swallowing pockets of cloud—like a cool humid day here—you could feel the moisture seeping into your lungs."

She took a playful swipe at my cloud of cigarette smoke

rolling past her. "I'd see the Holock every day, curled up like fetuses, absolutely still, eyes wide open, a green cloud quivering around them. There was a drumming sound. Actually, it was more a mechanical drone than a drum. That's how they do it. They stay for days, switching from one dream to the next when the dreamer wakes. It's such a pleasure that they had to regulate it. One is allowed six days in the Dream Room after every twelve. Otherwise, I think, they'd do it all the time. It's rather narcotic for them. 'The Dreaming,' as they call it, was forbidden me. I mean, I could dream, but I couldn't share your dreams. They wouldn't teach me the technique—they regard it, if it's not too strong a word, as sacred.

"I never felt alone in the Dream Rooms. Somehow I always knew they were watching me, outside somewhere, watching. The only way to get out was to dream. And, once I filled my quota, the wall would unzip and a hand would reach in and signal me to follow."

She crossed her legs and yawned. "They can watch your memories as well. They simply access another channel on the same wavelength, so to speak. They upload them when you sleep."

"In the Dream Rooms?"

"No. Memory Films are like television—entertainment. Every dwelling has one on the wall. They're voice-controlled. You adjust for date, country, sex. They enjoy speed watching, which is exactly like fast forwarding. There's a lot of tedious trivia in every memory. Meals, for instance. They can go through a lifetime of memories in a day. Most of their documents about your world are filtered through your memories. This led to some discrepancies. They thought, for instance, all women were buxom. They were surprised to find that the masculine memory had exaggerated their size."

I smiled in spite of myself.

"The world outside the Dream Rooms and the dwellings is one long green dream. They live in clear—I guess you'd call them plastic—domes and bubbles. Everything's transparent. You can see through every wall, for miles and miles: bubbles everywhere. Like when you dive into water?"

"I never learned to swim," I said.

"Really?" She looked shocked.

"Yup. There's a family tale about me falling in a pool or something when I was five, my mom pulling me out by the hair. I don't remember it. But that's probably why water has always frightened me."

"I could teach you!" She seemed excited by the idea. "We could go to the Y."

"No thanks," I replied, which disappointed her. I think she was just trying to plant the image of her in a bikini in my mind. It worked. "Why is everything transparent?" I asked.

"They have no privacy," she replied. "It's not in their vocabulary. Everyone is open to inspection. They figure if there are no secrets there are no dangers. It's a strange part of their makeup: their paranoia. They have no natural predators. Their existence is regulated, insulated, as safe as anything you can imagine. Yet they fear. They keep no secrets. That's a part of your world that intrigues them so much: how cut off you are from each other. Your separateness."

"Like joggers with their headphones," I offered. "In their own private world."

She seemed to be remembering, looking far away. "Your music puzzles them. They cannot duplicate it and they can't sing or dance, but they have an immense curiosity for its structures and dynamics. They're especially intrigued by rock and roll. Elvis, Chuck Berry, Jerry Lee Lewis, Buddy Holly. They were amazed when I pointed out that all the songs rhyme. They can't do that. They regard it like a riddle, a zen koan. At best they appreciate the beat, the clockwork regularity."

"What did they think of disco?"

"What's disco?"

"Come on!" I insisted. "Tight pants, high heels, tribal thump."

She looked at me.

"You never heard of the Village People?"

"Who?"

"Well, they used to be very big."

"As big as the Big Bopper?"

"Big Bopper? What, were you raised on 'American Bandstand'?" Then I had an odd thought.

"How about Crosby, Stills, Nash and Young?"

"What's that? A law firm?"

"Procol Harum? The Grateful Dead? Moby Grape? Jefferson Airplane?"

"Jefferson Starship. I've heard of them."

"John, Paul, George, Ringo."

She stared at me.

"I want to hold your hand."

She brightened up. "Okay!"

"Laura," I began. "The Beatles. The Fab Four. Liverpool."

"I must have missed it."

This was a serious rotation of my head. Life without the Beatles!

"John Kennedy," I said.

"Is this like a word-association test?"

I continued. "Ask not what you can do for your country. *Ich bein ein Berliner*. Dallas. Pink Jackie. Oswald. Tipitt. Ruby. John-John. Oh Christ! You don't, you don't, you don't expect me to believe that, do you?"

"Believe what? You're not making a lot of sense."

"Who's president now?"

"Which country? No, I'm just teasing. George Bush, right?"

"Now we're getting somewhere." I relaxed a little. "And before him?"

"The actor. And Nancy."

"And before him?"

She looked at me. She shook her head. "I don't watch a lot of news."

"Hitler?" I studied her.

"Him I know."

"Hiroshima."

"Of course."

Whew. "Truman."

"The buck stops here."

"Eisenhower."

"I like Ike."

"Then what?" I asked.

"Then what what?" she countered.

I sighed. If she was playing with me I was ready to bop her. I searched my memory banks for the fifties. "Davy Crockett."

"Killed him a b'ar when he was only three. Ever been to Disneyland?"

"Shut up," I said. "John Wayne."

"That'll be the day."

"Nancy Sinatra."

"Frank's wife?"

"Woodstock."

"Wait a second. That's a yellow bird in the comics, right?"

My alien had missed the sixties. And the seventies. A convenient lapse of memory? Enforced amnesia? I covered my face with my hands.

She took pity on me. "Listen, I think I know what you're after. Let me make it simple for you. I know nothing much of what's happened since around 1959."

"Why?"

"That's when they sent me back. The trip took about thirty of your years."

"Hold it," I said, lighting another cigarette. I had her now. And I didn't want to let on. This was IT. "The trip took thirty years?"

"Yes."

"You said you were in utero the whole voyage there."

"Right."

"Nine months one way. Thirty years back?" I looked at her. I could barely contain myself. I had broken the code. Just let her try to wriggle her way out of *that!*

"I can't explain."

"You can't."

"I told you . . . I don't understand it. You want me to guess? Okay. Perhaps the trip there is faster than the trip here. You know, uphill and downhill? Perhaps they age one way, and I age the other. Anyway, it's just time."

She made it sound like a stop sign she hadn't seen. I think this is when I started to get mad. I'd just taken my best swing and hit nothing but air. "How old are you, anyway?"

"In your years, I'm forty-two."

"Come on! You're not a day over thirty."

"I'll take that as a compliment, knowing how obsessed you all are with age. I am forty-two."

"A well-preserved forty-two."

"Thank you. The trip has some beneficial side effects."

"Got any kids?" I asked suddenly.

She eyed me. "No."

"Ever want any?"

Her face grew very solemn. "Every day."

"You must be in a hurry, then." I was thinking of a boy in a red sweater.

She said nothing.

"Your biological clock is catching up with you." I looked at the clock. "But, then again, it's just time."

Her eyes got a little scary. But I couldn't stop.

"Is that a glimmer of anger?" I taunted. "Oh, I forgot. You're more *evolved* than that. Of course, it helps if you lead a medicated lifestyle." Shut up, I said to myself. Why are you saying this?

"Medicated?" she said, warily.

"Oh, you know. Some of us are so primitive we need to stomp on our emotions with mood-altering drugs. Takes the edge off. Gives us an aura of peace of mind."

She said nothing.

"What's your dosage, Laura?"

"What?"

"How many Valium do you take a day?"

She looked hard at me. "You went through my purse that day?"

"I didn't have to. You just *happened* to leave it open so anyone could see what's inside: an empty prescription and a fistful of Hershey bars."

"You had no right."

"You want to tell me about it? Your condition? You know, it might actually *help* me do my job. It might really be *useful* for me to know what my patient is going through on this planet."

She said nothing.

"Start anywhere you like."

She said nothing.

"Okay." I held a finger to my lips. "A suggestion. A question, actually." A pause to consider how to put this in exactly the right way. "What's with this candy bar shit?" I asked.

"Why are you angry?" she said.

"I'm angry? I'M angry? Oh, that's right. I'M the one who's been abused. I'M the one in denial! I'M the one with TWO FUCKING FATHERS!!"

She stood up and made for the door. I stood and blocked her way. "Wait." I held up my hands and took a deep breath. Nice going, Doc. Textbook professional decorum. "I'm sorry. I—I lost it. I didn't get much sleep last night and I'm running on fumes. I'm sorry."

She regarded me silently. I couldn't tell if she was sad or furious. "Laura?"

"What?" she said, looking at the floor.

"You want to work with me? Then, please, *work* with me! Don't pretend the only reason you come here is because I turn you on, or you're on some abstract mission for your little green men." I tried to catch her eye. "Let me help."

She looked up. "What do you want from me?"

"The truth."

Definitely furious now. "You mean . . . all *this*"—she indicated my office—"all this *time* . . . And you don't *believe* me?"

I couldn't pretend anymore. "No," I said sadly.

She hit me. I didn't see it coming. I'd never been struck so hard by a man, much less a woman. I fell on top of my desk. She grabbed me by the collar and I swear to god this tall, thin woman LIFTED me off the ground WITH ONE HAND. She held me there for a second. Stars shot in my eyes. When I was able to focus on her, she said: "Then believe THIS."

I don't remember what happened next. When I woke up it was dark and my jaw was purple and swollen. I expected never to see her again.

Twelve

Good Fucking Riddance. Who needs this bitch, anyway? She cracked my jaw! Thirty weeks together and she cracked my jaw! I stewed about it for days. When she sent me three twenties and a ten in an envelope, I tore them up into little pieces. Only later did it strike me strange that these new bills, like all her others, bore the signature of the U.S. treasurer under Eisenhower: Ivy Baker Priest—a leftover tidbit from my days of coin collecting.

When I had discharged enough bile and gained enough perspective to realize I'd come within an inch of professional suicide, I did the only sensible thing: I had a panic attack at three A.M. How was I capable of misjudging a patient like that? Why hadn't I seen her violence coming? Why had I trusted her? Why did I let her flirt with me? Why did I still, even after her attack, feel like I was failing her? I realized, with horror, that I was making excuses for her in the same way the abused wives I had counseled blamed themselves for their husbands' assaults. I decided I needed a break.

I went on my first vacation since graduate school. Spent two weeks near Traverse City. The isolation of northern Michigan after the tourist season was exactly what I craved. I read a lot. I slept. I listened to a lot of Van. I treated myself to a lot of silence. You can't imagine how delicious silence can be after years of sitting and talking/listening/talking/listening. I made a lot of fires. Celebrated Thanksgiving by getting drunk and taking a long walk in the woods. I saw three gray deer standing on top of a rise. They couldn't see me. I wanted nothing to do with flying saucers. I felt really duped for getting into all that. I had had it with mysteries and the Great Unknown and I resolved never to get swept up in anything like that again. Leave it to Enquiring Minds. Not once for two weeks did I even think about Laura—that was after seven months of thinking of little else.

When I returned to work, I felt ready to conquer. There was a bounce in my step and a twinkle in my eye. It lasted until I went through my mail. One of the envelopes had no return address. It was heavy and smelled funny. I held it for a long time. Somehow I knew it was from her. I had Pandora's box in my hand and I debated long and hard about opening it. Did I really need this? I rubbed my jaw. It was still sore from the hairline fracture.

Dear John,

Since you probably won't ever see me again, I thought I ought to tell you the rest of the story . . .

No, no, no, no, no, no. Don't do it. Don't. I twirled my hair. I smoked a cigarette. I had to read it.

It was a strange experience, seeing her sharp and eloquent mind expressed in the handwriting of an adolescent

girl. Loops and flourishes filled the robin's-egg-blue statio-
nery. And you know how some girls put little circles over
their *i*'s? She *squared* them.

*I can hear you saying with your persistent skepti-
cism: this Stillness Thing—I don't get it. So I'll try
again. First, the Holock were Dream Hopping centu-
ries before they discovered they could apply a similar
technique to folding space. They didn't really get it
right until about one hundred of your years ago.
Think of a merry-go-round. You don't actually
change your position on the horse, but the whole
thing goes around.*

*Or think of Heraclitus and his river of "Univer-
sal Flux": you can't step in the same river twice. So
imagine if you wanted to go upstream against the
current, you'd have to fight against a lot of momentum, right? You'd have to expend more energy than
the current against you just to make any headway.
But, if you lie down in the river, the part of the river
you want to get to would eventually flow down to
you. You don't move; the river does. The trick is to
maintain stillness against the current.*

*Space-Time is like that: constant motion. You
can't beat the current. That's the constant speed of
light. You can't gather enough momentum to push
beyond that—unless you're Buck Rogers. So if you
can't beat it, you join it. You learn to maintain your
position. It's a strategic stillness. And it has parallels
in some of your Eastern meditation. But they're just
riding the current wherever it takes them. They
don't know how to step In or Out. That's the Holock's specialty.*

But I've never done it. It was different for me in

the Dream Room. I'd just go to sleep listening to that
dull drumming sound. I'm told that they can travel
into past or future dreams. Suki said that when you
leave the Dream Room you feel as if no time has
passed, as if you had just checked in. But you feel im-
mense relief and refreshment. Like I said, I never
knew that. They never let me try. But I found out
they don't have the same control over memories that
they do over dreams. That makes sense. They're co-
creators of dreams. They're spectators of memories.
But, on the other hand, they're collectors of memo-
ries. They haven't yet found a way to record dreams.

I put down the letter. Why couldn't they record them?
It seemed illogical, and yet, it resonated with part of me,
like a forgotten dream that leaves an impression without
leaving a content. Like the fossilized footprint of a Nean-
derthal in the mud. It felt like a clue.

When I was five, Suki taught me how to swim.
They're amphibious, as I am, in case you're wonder-
ing, so we needed no scuba equipment. An ocean sur-
rounds their entire planet (or "place," as they call it).
It is bathed in green light and very warm. There's
never any night. Just a constant green glow as the
sunlight passes through the Jell-O. The topography is
crystallike—great castles of crystal looming up to-
ward the surface and stretching downward into
darkness. They are superstitious about the atmo-
sphere above the water, so they never go up. They
say anyone who has gone to the surface does not re-
turn. It's called "Left Out." (I'll explain in a mo-
ment.) Their dwellings are about midway between
the surface and the bottom, on a plateau that spreads

*out for miles and miles—it would take you a week to
walk from end to end.*

I stopped reading again. The image of little Laura and
this white ghost swimming hand in hand played in my
mind. I recalled the time she invited me to come swim with
her at the Y.

*There are only two other species on the planet.
Both are snakes. Both are blind. One is a small black
thing about the size of my middle finger. The other is
what you might call a dragon. It's long and white
and has sharp teeth. They range from about ten to
thirty feet. The dragons live off the crystal forma-
tions; they chew them like rock candy. The little ones
live off the excrement of the white ones. Every day
you can see a school of them, swimming behind the
long ones, nabbing at their tails, like a black swarm
of locusts. Neither species is a threat to the natives.
They're something like your birds.*

*I've said their sideways is your up and down. I
meant it. So you must imagine their metropolis of
bubbles resting on its side. They literally walk sideways. Your up is to their left, your down is to their
right. Which is why they experience a sort of vertigo
in your dreams; they keep wanting to tip things over.
It may account for some of the weird shifts in P.O.V.
you sometimes get in dreams. To them, you look at
the world cockeyed. Their planet's gravity is such
that, located where they are in the sea of Jell-O, they
can choose to walk on whatever surface they like. So,
in your terms, ceilings become floors; they can lie
down on walls; they think nothing of having conversations head to head, with their feet planted on oppo-*

site floors. Except, remember, they don't talk—they send.

Which accounts for the silence of their world. They can hear perfectly well. They just prefer "Picture Talk," as they call it, to "Mouth Talk." Their voices are very unattractive; they sound like screeching birds even when they whisper, so the benefits of "Picture Talk" are clear. Over time, as they came to rely on telepathy, their ears shrank, so now all that's left are two little concave depressions on the sides of their heads, little swirls like a spiral staircase or a cutaway view of a nautilus shell.

They have an odd myth about how they learned telepathy. It says a lot about their culture, as any myth does. But first, understand that in their mythology, "Left Out" is the same as the underworld in your myths. They have no equivalent of "Heaven," unless it's your Dreamland. Left Out is where someone goes who is different, who doesn't follow, who is not "In the One," as they put it. It's where someone goes to be alone. Hell, in other words.

The legend goes that one day a Holock heard a strange music. It came from beyond the Shlom (the sea). He left the Home and swam away. And when he left out, he found a Great Mother floating on the Shlom. (That's what they used to call the dragons. They were once as huge as your dinosaurs, and they are the only thing feminine on the planet.)

She sang to him and he came close enough to touch her tail. She stopped singing and said:

"Who touches me?"

"I am a Holock. Sing to me."

"I cannot see you, come closer."

And the Holock swam closer.

"Here I am."

"Still I cannot see you, come closer."

And the Holock swam closer.

"Here I am."

"I can smell you, but I cannot see you."

So the Holock swam all the way up to the Great Mother's head.

"Here I am. Please sing to me."

The Great Mother said, "Put your ear to my mouth that I may sing."

And the Holock put his ear to the Great Mother's mouth.

"Sing to me, Great Mother, for your song is (there is no equivalent word) and I have come a long way to hear it."

She bit off his ear and the Holock swam away in terror and hid for many days until his ear was healed . . .

I stopped again. This story had a familiar ring to it, as if I'd heard it before. But I couldn't place it. Something about ears. I was beginning to feel uncomfortable, though I couldn't say why.

But one day he heard the music again. And he could not resist its (that word again). So he swam beyond and came to the Great Mother's tail.

"Sing to me, Mother, for I cannot live without your song."

"Come closer, for I cannot see you."

So the Holock swam closer.

"Closer. I can smell you, but I cannot see you."

So the Holock swam to the Great Mother's mouth. And he was very afraid to lose his other ear.

So he said, "Mother? I will not come as close as your mouth without your promise that you will not eat my one good ear."

"But ears are my favorite," said the Great Mother.

"But, if you eat my only ear, I could not hear your music, and I would die."

And the Great Mother said: "If you will let me eat your last ear I will give you a great gift. You will hear my music without your ears. It will live in the space between your ears and my song will be with you forever."

So the Holock put his last ear close to her mouth. And the Great Mother devoured it. And he came back to The One with no ears. He told everyone his story, but they would not believe him. Neither his fathers nor his sons would listen. And they shut him in a far room to be rid of his wild tales.

Now it happened that after a time The One began to hear something strange. It was the sound of weeping. And it filled their lives as they made and learned, and they could not be rid of it. At last someone said it sounded like the cries of the Holock who had Left Out. And they went to his chamber, and sure enough, the Holock lay weeping on the ceiling. And they scolded him for all the noise. And he said he had no music anymore, and that the Great Mother had lied to him and he was going to die. But he quieted, and they thought that was that. But the sound did not stop. They heard the Holock's weeping every day. So they decided the only solution was to eat the Holock and be done with the noise. So they did. And for a time things were quiet.

Then one day they heard a strange humming—

some called it music, some called it weeping—and it filled the Home. Then they began to hear words. Then came pictures. Soon all The One could hear the thoughts of the Holock beside them. And that is how they learned "The Listening."

If that was their one story about the Feminine, you can imagine how they regarded me. They wouldn't come close to my mouth. I realized later they were afraid I'd bite them . . .

I couldn't read anymore. I felt like I'd been kicked in the chest. I had to do something—what could I do? I couldn't just walk away without knowing that someone was taking care of her. Even if *I* couldn't help her, she *had* to be helped—she had to be hospitalized. I could call Dr. Stewart. I couldn't commit her, but he could. At least if she was seeing *him,* I could let her go. I could do that.

I must have been transferred six times before someone would talk to me. It was the director of personnel at Henry Ford Hospital.

"Dr. Stewart is dead," he said.

"I'm so sorry."

"Were you a friend?"

"An acquaintance, actually. But what a shock. He seemed healthy enough."

"You haven't read the papers?"

I got chills as soon as he said that.

"I've been on vacation."

"Dr. Stewart was murdered in his home about two weeks ago."

I couldn't speak for a moment. "When exactly?"

"Two Thursdays ago. In the evening."

Oh God, I thought. The same night she slugged me.

"It was fairly gruesome," he went on. "He was such a fine doctor. I can't imagine him having enemies."

"Do the police have a suspect?" I managed to ask.

"No. It's a complete mystery."

After I hung up the phone I had the purest flight impulse I've ever felt. I wanted to get on a plane, leave the country, change my identity. I wanted to drop off the face of the earth. A psychopath had fallen in love with me.

I took refuge at a friend's house. A cop whom I'd helped through a crisis—he'd been a crack addict for three months. He's straight now, though he lost his marriage during Recovery. He said he could find out who the investigating officer was on the Dr. Stewart case. When he told me the guy's name was Jack Kiefer, he looked like he had just sucked on a lemon.

"Problem?" I asked.

"He was my sergeant for five years. Tough bastard. Lived with his mother. Pity that poor lady."

I met Detective Kiefer at a Big Boy's on the east side. After my usual apologies for being delayed, he began.

"You say she assaulted you the same night."

"That's right."

He asked me some specifics about times, my injury, Laura, and jotted them down in a little notebook. His face was full of pockmarks, his skin was greasy, and he smoked even more than I do. He was still scribbling when he said, "You look big enough to handle a woman."

"Ever tried to cuff somebody on PCP?" I snapped. "Or a psycho?"

He smiled. "It was a cheap shot. Sorry." He tapped his pencil on his notebook. "This case is wearing on me. You're my first lead—I guess I oughta be a little grateful."

"I'd be grateful if she was caught. She's incredibly

strong." The image of a muscular trapeze artist came to mind, but I doubted he would appreciate the analogy.

"How well'd you know Stewart?"

"I met him once."

"Did you know he was a 'friendly doctor'? Good bedside manner?"

"What are you saying?"

"He made it with several patients."

"How'd you find that out?"

He smiled. "His wife told us. Seems they had an understanding."

"Sounds like a lame alibi."

"We're working on it."

"And his patients?"

"Actually, all the women have fairly fond memories of the doctor. A lot of them attended the funeral." He laughed and I made a mental note to let him pick up the check. When he saw I didn't share the joke, he said, "Revenge is another angle. We're working on it."

"How did he die?"

"They were pretty discreet in the press. His neighborhood has some bigwigs who'd like to keep their property values intact."

"How?" I repeated.

"Cause of death was a broken neck. But he was mutilated before."

"Before? You can tell that?"

"Sure."

Nice job, I thought. Interesting people.

He lit another cigarette and asked, "You sure there's no records on this girl?"

"Henry Ford Hospital might have some. I don't have any."

"Why is that?"

"A private agreement," I replied.

"Sounds fishy."

"It sounded less so at the time."

"Listen . . . I've got your number. I got hers. We'll let you know."

"Please do. I'd like to know when the coast is clear."

"Scared you pretty good, did she?"

Was he taunting me? "Yes," I said evenly. He stood up and was reaching for the check when I asked, "Mutilation?"

He eyed me. He sat down and looked around the restaurant. A grandma was wiping some ice cream off the chin of a toddler. "You want details, eh? Docs like details."

I swallowed. "If I'm a target, I'd like to know."

"Fine," he said. "Someone bit off his ears."

I closed my eyes for a moment.

"And his dick," he said smiling.

Thirteen

If this were a mystery story, now would be the time to take off the masks and reveal the true murderer. Laura, of course, was not an alien child by any means. She was born in Iowa. She was sexually assaulted throughout her childhood by an albino step-uncle who swore he'd kill her if she ever told anyone. He still loomed large in her mind, and her fear was so primal, having its genesis at such an impressionable age, that she doubted her safety, even today. Thus the secrecy. She had grown up in various mental institutions and had been, at regular intervals, administered psychotropic drugs—thus the hallucinations. The Dream Room was actually a padded cell. Dr. Stewart was only the latest in a long line of abusive caretakers. Her rescue was her imagination. It provided her the only possible refuge from a horrific existence. Very simply, her life was a tragic cycle of abuse and psychosis, victimization and escape. She was a damaged creature and well beyond any help I might have to offer her. It sounds almost cruel to say I wished it were all true. I concocted this plausible theory at four-thirty in the morning after a night spent in a state of near panic. It helped.

For a while, I hid out at my friend Greg's flat. I painted his kitchen to keep my mind off things, and to feel useful. But I knew that I would have to resume my practice soon—my patients depended on me, and I wasn't about to let them down, no matter how threatened I might feel. Reluctantly, I went back to my routine at the clinic. But every day I expected the knock, the phone call, the familiar silhouette in my doorway. I rehearsed what I would say to her. I read and reread her letter:

> *So Memory Films. The Dream Rooms. The snakes. The bubbles. The Listening. The Jell-O. What have I left out? Oh, of course, their precious machines. First of all, there's no comparison to things mechanical in your world. They coo and dawdle over them, with the same irrational affection you have for your domesticated creatures. They rely on them for everything. Making meals, cleaning, teaching—everything. They'd be lost without them: their precious pets. I recall being jealous of them, growing up. I even broke a few in anger—and boy, I caught it for that. Weeks in the Dream Room for that.*
>
> *I wish you could see the view from my window. There's a fair in the parking lot of the mall across the way. I can hear the cacophony of the different carnival songs that accompany the rides. But all I can see is the upper half of a Ferris wheel—why do you suppose they're called that? Sometimes someone screams, usually a young girl. But it's somehow not alarming: more like a squeal of delight. I guess they know eventually the ride will stop and they can get off.*

I suppose I should come clean about the candy issue, as it seems to be troubling you so. Candy is the drug, not Valium. Remember my constitution is similar to yet different from yours. Sugar, and especially candy, has the calming effect on me that Valium would have on you. The valium will stimulate me into Alpha Stasis. It's how I intend to get back. And, though I know you'll find this hard to swallow, I'm not talking about suicide. I would have killed myself long ago if I really wanted to. But I want to live. I want to stay. And I want to stay with you.

The rest is just stories. I can fill in the blanks in person. That is, if you'll ever see me again. You will, won't you? You must. You're my last hope.

Love,

Laura

P.S.: You haven't told anybody, have you?

P.P.S.: Burn this letter.

My answering machine at work had a cryptic yet obvious message that night. "This is me. I must meet you. You're in danger. I'll be at—" At least it was in public.

I was smart enough to let my cop friend Greg drive me and wait in the car. He insisted on bringing his gun, which actually did more to exacerbate my anxiety. She had chosen to rendezvous at Border's Bookstore in Southfield—a large, cozy favorite of Detroit book lovers, with lots of comfortable crannies to sit and browse in. As it was a weekday afternoon the place wasn't crowded, and she was easy to spot. She sat on one of two wooden chairs beside a potted plant in the literature section under—as I recall—Wells. She wore a bright blue jumpsuit. She was reading a paperback. I watched her for a moment, checked to make sure my friend was outside, then approached.

She put down her book and greeted me with a warm smile. "Hello, John. How are you?"

"Fine." I sat down. "Been waiting long?" I asked hopefully.

"Not really. How's your jaw?"

"Healing."

"I would have included an apology in my letter, but I thought you deserved one face-to-face."

"Thoughtful of you."

"So do you want to hear the rest of the story?" She acted as if we had been interrupted five minutes ago, and could resume our relationship with a few formalities.

"No."

She looked crestfallen. "No?"

I wanted a cigarette badly. "Not without some ground rules."

"I'm not going to hit you again, if that's what you mean."

"How do I know that? Why should I trust you?"

"Well," she said, looking away sadly. "Trust."

She was quiet until I said, "Look. I'm not going to subject myself to a situation where I'm not safe."

"Safe?" Now she looked disappointed.

"If you ever strike me again, our relationship will be terminated." I could have put that better.

"I understand. And I agree."

"Secondly: I want to know what you've left out. I want your address—your real one, not the bogus one you gave me. I also want the name of someone I can contact you through. A reference, if you will." I'd been thinking of that scene from the movie *The Day the Earth Stood Still,* where the alien, Michael Rennie, fixes the mathematical equation on the chalkboard of the earth's leading astronomer: tangible proof of a higher-developed mind. "And I want to know the formula of your planet's crystals. As well as your definition of pi. I want a sample of your blood. A photograph. And I want you to talk to the police about Dr. Stewart."

She showed no reaction to my demands. "The police?"

"You'll have to give them an alibi."

"You're my alibi," she said with a smile. "I was with you when he was murdered."

"You can prove that?"

"The police can. I've already talked to them." She pulled a bookmark out of her paperback and wrote down her address. She said she didn't know about her planet's crystals. The value of pi was universal. Her blood type was O-positive, and I could check it, if I wanted, in her hospital records at Henry Ford. Then she got coy about the photograph. "Do you think I'm a vampire and it won't develop?"

"Very funny," I said.

"All right. I'll give you a photograph on one condition: you destroy it after you've seen it. And you show it to no one."

I agreed. Recalling this, I register a small bitter tang of triumph. I had lied. I had no intention of destroying the photo; I still have it.

"What about the reference?" I prodded.

She wrote down a phone number in that peculiar style of hers: squaring every zero. "Saul is a friend. He may not want to talk to you. Depends on his mood. He's a sweet man who occasionally helps me out."

"Is that where you get your money?" I asked. This had bothered me for a while.

"Yes."

"Will he vouch for you?"

"I think so." She began rubbing her forearms as if she were chilly.

"Why, Laura? Why haven't you told me all this before?"

"No one must know," she almost whispered. "The slightest leak could be hazardous."

"Why?"

"I only have one chance. They don't want this to be public knowledge. They're afraid."

"Of what?"

"You. All of you. Discovery."

"What could we possibly do to harm them?"

She hesitated. For a moment I thought she was checking to see if anyone nearby was listening. A dog barked in the distance. "You could take away your dreams," she whispered.

"How could we do that?"

"I can't elaborate."

Yet another mystery. Would they never cease? The dog barked again and Laura craned her neck, looking out the window for it.

"You said I was in danger?"

"You are, as long as you're tempted to tell anyone."

"But how could they find out if I did?"

"The Memory Films. They see everything." The dog was barking violently now and it seemed to be distressing her. She frowned and asked, "Do you have a pet?"

"A pet?"

"Like a cat or a dog? Or anything . . ."

"Goldfish. Why?"

"Never mind," she said. "Fish don't count. Worry about people. All it would take is someone other than you thinking about me and my story."

"I've told no one."

"You must have told Dr. Stewart."

"Yes. We talked about you, but I— What's the matter?" The color had left her face. She looked like she was going to faint.

"You shouldn't have. That gave him a dangerous memory."

"A *what?*"

She swallowed hard. "That's why they killed him. I thought I warned you. You can't tell anyone. Even the most innocent remark." She shuddered then looked intensely at me. "I'm not playing games. I'm not being paranoid. They will find out. There's no hiding it."

The idea that I might have catalyzed the doctor's death filled me with dread. "But I told him nothing about your past! Nothing!"

"It doesn't matter. They've set the rules: one sane person. No one else. That's all I need. One sane person who'll believe me. Then I can stay." She looked at the carpet. "I think the only reason they let me go was because they didn't think I could do it."

I thought about this for a long moment. When I looked up she locked eyes with me. "John, I swear to you. I am what I say I am. If they feel you can't be trusted, they may kill you. You've not told anyone else, have you?"

"No," I lied, wondering about my friend. And the detective.

She got up to leave. "If you must talk to someone, talk to Saul. They wouldn't dare touch him."

As she was turning to go, she smiled with a sudden cheerfulness that felt creepy. "Think of it as a secret. You can keep a secret, can't you? Saul says that's the difference between Big Boys and Little Boys. Big Boys can hold a secret; Little Boys always drop it."

As I watched her leave, I remembered my mother had once said almost the same thing to me. We were wrapping Christmas presents, and she wanted to make sure I didn't tell Dad about his gift. I don't remember what the gift was. I wanted to tell Laura: It's a good thing my memory is so lousy, because I've made a career of exposing secrets. It's what I do for a living.

I was going out the door when I saw him again. The crew-cut fat man in the baggy blue suit. He was getting into a car.

"Hey!" I shouted, running toward him.

He pulled out of the parking lot fast in a nondescript gray Plymouth.

"Hey!" I yelled after him.

Damn! He was following me!

I was shaky when I joined my friend in the car, so you can imagine how relieved I was to hear him say, "I saw her. The tall ugly broad in the red dress, right?"

"That's Louise, all right," I said. "But don't worry. I'm never going to see her again."

Any notion I had that Laura's "reference" was going to clarify matters faded the moment I called the man who turned out to be the most bizarre detour in this convoluted tale: Saul. Saul was just another peel in the ever-unfolding, never-revealing onion. I will say this about him: he was fun. Over the phone his voice sounded like a character from an old movie: muffled, affected, arch. He reminded me of Edward G. Robinson. He even said "nyaaah" once or twice.

Nyaah, he didn't want to talk to me. Nyaah, he didn't want to talk about any girls. He gave up girls long ago. Was I a Catholic? When was my last confession? Where did I stand on birth control? In this, our first of many "conversations"—that somehow doesn't do justice to these flights of either senility or shrewdness—I often held the yammering receiver away from my ear and looked at it as if it had some obscure purpose far beyond my comprehension.

"What kind of a name is that—'Donelly'?"

"It's Irish."

"You said you weren't Catholic."

"I'm not. Saul, all I want is a few minutes—"

"Well, yeah, TIME, you know. Time's the thing. Time's a-wasting. Time is money. Time waits for no man. For a race that knows shit about Time, you sure do talk about it a lot."

Was I going to have to put up with another cultural critic?

"How much you charge an hour?" he asked.

"None of your business."

"I used to charge a couple of hundred for lunch. And they paid. Believe me, they paid. They knew what Saul Lowe was worth."

"If you could just see your way to—"

"Time or money's not the issue anymore. I've played that game. Ask Wanda. Ask Rudi. Ask Lenny. Ask Duke. Ask the princess—"

I missed the last six names—I was looking at the phone in my hand, whining like an alarm. When I listened in again, he was talking to somebody in the room.

"Imish! Imish, you get away from that alligator!"

"Saul?"

"Goddamn Cardinals! Greedy sons of bitches!"

"Saul?"

"Listen, all I'm asking is if you're OPEN to the idea . . ."

There was a long pause before I realized he was talking to me. "What idea?"

"God!" he said. "What other idea matters?"

"I don't follow you."

"What are you? Dense? I'm talking about the Almighty!"

"Oh," I said. "*That* God."

"You don't have to be specific, mind you. Every culture has a vision. Except those goddamn Baptists and their tambourines. You think God likes tambourines?"

I wasn't about to answer that one.

"But maybe that's just me. I don't know. I'm just saying you gotta get Under the Mercy. You need protection? You get God on your side."

"I see."

"You see? I give you a bulletproof vest and you say 'I see'?"

"Saul. What the FUCK ARE YOU TALKING ABOUT!"

His change in tone was so abrupt it startled me. He sounded suddenly very sane. "The Holock. What else are we talking about?"

"You know about them?"

His laughter wheezed out of the phone and led to a prolonged coughing fit. "Yaaah, you could say I know about them! Or didn't the princess tell you?"

He could only have meant Laura. "She didn't mention it."

"Well. Maybe we should have a talk, then. You are swimming in deep water if you're not Under the Mercy." It was a cliché that had always made me nervous. "You say you don't pray?"

"Not since I was twenty-two."

"Whew! You're gonna be a tough nut. But you'll come around. See, the Holock don't fuck with you if you say your prayers."

It was, perhaps, the most original appeal to faith I have ever encountered.

"Well, let's talk about it."

"Okeydokey," he said. "Bring me some orange juice. FRESH—none of that astronaut shit." He chuckled to himself. "Boy—you are in for the ride of your life!"

That night I met the Dream Boy again. I recall waking up (this seemed to cue the credibility of what followed— who *wakes* into a dream?). I was in my bedroom, which seemed normal, except for the fact that I was still sleeping at Greg's flat. The Dream Boy in the red sweater was perched on the post at the foot of my bed, like one of those flagpole-sitters you see in old newsreels. His arms were wrapped around his knees and he was smiling.

"You!" I said, sitting up.

"I can't stay long," he said.

"What do you want?"

"The crystal's formula is ——." He was either talking gobbledygook or mathematics; I understood none of it.

"I have to write that down," I said, rising from the bed. I noticed the room smelled like Jell-O. Lemon-lime.

"You can't," he said. "It's a secret. You can keep a secret, can't you?"

"I don't have a pencil."

"You wouldn't tell anybody, would you?"

"I'm a doctor," I lied indignantly. "I have a code."

"They don't like me talking to you. If they catch me, I'll get poked."

"Poked?"

"It hurts," he said.

I stepped over to him and reached out to touch his arm.

"Don't!" he said angrily.

"I'm sorry."

"Don't ever touch me." His voice was threatening.

"I'm sorry."

"Don't tell anyone."

"It's too late," I said. "The detective knows."

He scowled at me. "The greasy man who masturbates?"

Why did his description sound so logical? "Yes," I answered.

"That was a mistake."

"I know."

"Anyone else?"

I was about to answer when I saw something in his eyes. The pupils were dilating rapidly, like a mouth saying "Oooooh! Ahhhhh!"

"Anyone else?" he repeated.

Fear—raw and mindless—flooded through my body. Maybe it was the way he perched on the post, like a bird of prey; maybe it was the eyes, or the tone of his voice—I couldn't have been more frightened if I had found a tiger in my room. I knew then this was not the boy I'd met before, but some horrible presence masquerading in that fragile body. Laura had said they were "Shape Changers." Instinctively, I began a prayer from my youth: "Bless us, O Lord, and these thy gifts, which we are about to receive . . ."

"Stop it!" he barked.

"—from thy bounty—"

"STOP!" he screamed.

"—through Christ Our Lord. Amen."

All at once the law of gravity slipped back into the dream; the boy tumbled off the post, landing hard on the floor at my feet. He smiled up at me with rage and hatred. "Say hi to Saul. He'll remember me." I blinked and he was gone.

I woke with that vicious grinning face stuck in my mind. It stayed there for days. And it came back whenever it wanted to.

Fourteen

After that dream I began to suspect there was an anonymous player lingering in the wings of this drama I had stumbled into. Laura sounded convincing about Dr. Stewart. That meant someone else had killed him. An assassin. The Fat Man? One of Them? I decided to call Detective Kiefer to see if there was a less terrifying culprit. He sounded different. I heard none of the swagger or slime.

"Mr. Donelly?" His voice sounded puzzled.

"Yes, you remember . . . we had lunch?"

"I don't recall. Are you sure you're talking to the right man?"

"Come on! The Stewart case?"

"The Stewart case is closed."

"You have a suspect?"

"A confession. She's in a mental institution now. Maybe you ought to talk to my chief."

"Did you talk to Laura?"

"Who?"

I exploded. "Jesus Christ! What is going on?"

He hung up on me. I called his boss and got the low-down. Case closed: signed confession. Berserk ex-patient out for revenge. No mystery. I mentioned Laura to him and he said yes, he remembered her. Her story checked out. My interview with Detective Kiefer cleared her. My secretary had confirmed the appointment times. Autopsy confirmed time of death. No connection. She was a friendly witness.

I called a friend at the Home. He told me I could see the murderer if I wanted; she liked talking to strangers. On the drive over I was surprised to find my stomach rumbling. All my thoughts were interrupted by suggested detours: I had to pick up this, I needed that. Like a guardian angel tugging at my sleeve, whispering in my ear: "Come away. We don't belong there. We gave that up years ago." It had been so long since my last visit that I'd forgotten how much I dreaded going anywhere near the Home.

Working with the criminally insane does something to you. They don't just affront your standards of decency; it's more subversive than that. They challenge your offhand belief in the equilibrium of the universe. It still amazes me I survived four years: two as a janitor (while I got my degree) and two as a counselor. My tour of duty as a maintenance man was courtesy of the U.S. government: an "alternative service" offered me by the Selective Service Board, once my conscientious objector status was approved. I took on my position with a sort of messianic humility. I had fancy illusions of Daniel in the lion's den.

I should have known I was in trouble when I felt the need to get a "theological grasp" on the experience. Love wasn't working, see. I hated the prisoners. I had to rationalize my repulsion for the objects of my charity: "Humans are moral. If they weren't, they wouldn't perceive evil as such an anomaly, they wouldn't experience it as alien; it wouldn't be news. That's why my flesh crawls every time I see that child rapist. That is why I want to run whenever I look in the eyes of that animal mutilator. That is why I'm so frightened I can't even pee straight."

My fragile barricade of faith and pacifism was no match for the Home. I began to see these inmates as normal. They looked normal. They played normal chess. They told normal jokes. Some had pictures of their families on their walls. I began to wonder: Had their acts driven them to this state, or had their state driven them to these acts? Were they the outcasts of a society whose standards they had betrayed or the scapegoats of a sick civilization? Perhaps they suffered under an inner compulsion—serving some obscure evolutionary purpose or psychic compensation—to act out the darkest fantasies of their collective. I began to think of evil not as exceptional, not an abstraction I could condescend to (like the Pentagon), not even as "just human." To my horror, it started to look like another facet of God.

One night I was mopping the halls when I saw a priest in black sitting on a bench in one of the waiting rooms. Waiting for a conference, no doubt. It wasn't unusual, to see a clergyman there. But this was two in the morning. He was reading *Time*.

"Do you mind?" I asked, indicating the floor and my bucket on wheels.

"Not at all," he said smiling, and swung his feet up into the lotus position.

I was by now quite fluent with the mop, having mastered the Möbius/infinity swirl you use for the best results. I was almost finished when the priest asked me a question.

"Have you noticed? The serial killers?"

I stopped and leaned on my mop. I couldn't read his expression.

"All their faces are the same," he said.

"What do you mean?"

"They all have the trace of a child. Impish. Innocent.

Like part of them hasn't grown up. They remind me of people who have lost their faith. They're missing something."

"I never noticed," I replied. "You must be new here."

"Yes."

At last: someone to flaunt my experience for. "It takes a while," I assured him and we introduced ourselves.

"Is it me or is there a smell?" he asked.

"There's a smell." It had taken me weeks to adjust, too. I still couldn't identify it. Sometimes I thought it was something burning. Other times I thought it was something sweet. Like burning sugarcane.

"Have you ever wondered about people who lose their faith?" he asked. "What do they replace it with?"

"Not really," I replied.

"I think they replace it with an explanation for suffering. It's my experience that most people leave the church because of suffering. A child dies. A parent stays in a coma. A friend is murdered."

It seemed to be a problem he'd given a lot of thought to. I put the mop in the bucket and leaned against the wall. His skin was puffy and red; his hair was curly, gray. The blood vessels on his cheeks had burst.

I replied, showing off. "That's the price of free will, isn't it? Suffering?"

He smiled, surprised. "You're a Catholic!"

I nodded.

"That's sound theology. But what I mean is: people can bear awful pain as long as they feel it has meaning. Sometimes I think they'd rather have an explanation than be out of pain. They can accept it as a punishment, or an accident, or a test. But people feel betrayed and enraged when God allows the innocent to suffer. It's as if a parent had dropped them."

"That's the Mystery of the Cross in a nutshell."

He started to laugh. A long, sad laugh. "I'm sorry. I couldn't help myself. It's just that I could hear those Catholic capitalizations as you spoke. As if we could order the world into meaning by punctuation alone. But you're absolutely right. That is the Mystery: How the Torture of God's Innocent Son could be construed as the Ultimate Act of Love."

"So?"

"Well, don't you see? The presumption. Why do people expect such things? And why this yearning for justice and love? It's like they've put all the expectations that their parents couldn't live up to onto God. As if there were two possible answers to the Question of Suffering. Two doors: Free Will . . . or No God. They forget the trapdoor."

"Trapdoor?"

"Strange God. A God inconceivable. As bizarre to us as an octopus is to a bird."

I was curious. "For example?"

"Maybe he is to reality what we are to dreams." His eyes widened and he licked his lips, an academic relishing an eccentric line of reasoning. "Maybe we are his dream. Maybe he's a boy having a nightmare and that's what reality is. That's why his relationship to us is so passive. That's why he has no control over us. Maybe he's as brutal and thoughtless and warm and loving as any child. Maybe he needs us to wake him up."

"You're a Jesuit, aren't you?" I asked.

"No," he said. "I'm a resident."

Then he showed me he was handcuffed to the arm of the bench.

"Child molesting—in case you're wondering," he said, blushing.

The Home became my initiation into new mysteries that replaced old certainties. It's where I lost my faith, my virginity, took up cigarettes, and found my true vocation. I had forgotten its distinct, powerful presence, but my body hadn't, and was saluting it with anxiety, as you would approach sacred ground: respectfully, with the suspicion that you could be altered.

The murderer and I talked for fifteen minutes through thick bars in a white room that smelled of pine. She was a young woman with disheveled hair, dressed in a nightgown under a pale blue robe. She never stopped smiling. An armed guard stood at my shoulder through the whole interview.

"Are you a doctor?" she asked through the bars.

"Yes." It seemed a harmless lie.

"Are you somebody important?"

"No."

"I've seen you before?"

"No. Did you kill Dr. Stewart?"

Her smile broadened. "It's a good story. No ears. No dick. *He, he, he, he.* They typed it on a piece of paper."

"Did you kill him?"

"I signed it, didn't I?"

"Did you?"

"He said he loved me. He said I was beautiful. He said I needed his help."

"He did that to several women. He was a bad man."

"Yes. He deserved to die. So on the night of the crime I gained entrance to the victim's house, mutilated his body, and broke his neck. Did you see the paper? It's a good story."

"Did you do it?"

"I must have. He deserved it."

"Why did you sign the confession?"

For a moment, she became absorbed in the ceiling. "It's very nice here. Very clean." Then she smiled slyly at me.

"You're not a doctor. You're the Egg Man." Her expression softened into a heartbreaking sincerity. Her chin trembled. "I love you. I have always loved you. Could you take me to a Tigers game?"

"Sure," I said.

"Do you love me?"

"Sure." Funny thing is, part of me meant it. Such a sad, broken creature. She flicked her greasy tangled hair with nervous fingers.

"I'm going to be beautiful again," she said with a wide smile. Then she added something that stopped me cold: ". . . Now that the dreams are over."

"The dreams?"

"They've stopped. It doesn't hurt anymore."

"Your dreams have stopped?"

"No—only the bad ones. I only have good ones now."

"That's good," I assured her. A trickle of sweat ran down my ribs. "Why do you think they stopped?"

She began stroking the bars with her hands. Her wrists were tiny; I couldn't imagine them breaking anything, much less a neck.

"Because I signed."

"The confession?"

"They stopped as soon as I signed."

I swallowed hard. "Your bad dreams stopped?"

"Yes."

"They stopped when you signed the confession?"

"Yes." She stared at me for a long minute, looking for something no one had ever given her. "Do you love me?" she asked again.

"Of course." I smiled.

She lightly touched my hand through the bars. "Why doesn't it help?"

I was still shaking hours later when I had an unexpected

visitor at the clinic, the last person I wanted to see at six o'clock on a Friday night: Detective Kiefer. But there he stood in my doorway, in gray jogging sweats, looking like Jimmy Swaggart. He wore wraparound sunglasses.

"Secretary said you were through for the day."

"I am." I started putting papers into my briefcase, hoping he'd get the hint.

"I need to talk."

"So you remember me now?"

"Let me explain. I couldn't say anything over the phone."

"Why not?"

"Can I sit?"

I indicated the chair and he sank wearily into it. He wore a cheap wristwatch, which he kept playing with. "Mind if I smoke?"

I handed him an ashtray. He took a long drag that burnt his cigarette halfway down. A cloud of smoke swirled slowly above his head for the rest of our conversation. He seemed a much diminished figure on the blue chair, silhouetted against the venetian blinds. He looked like an alcoholic in his first week of recovery: fuzzy, uncertain in his movements, shy—like you could blow him over.

"Detective Kiefer?" I began. He seemed to drift away before my eyes.

"I need to talk."

"You already said that."

"I mean, I need to talk to a professional."

"Therapy?" This wasn't the same man I'd had lunch with.

"Yeah. How much?"

"My schedule is full at the moment. But I could recommend someone."

He shook his head; his face turned bright red, as if he were holding his breath. "You. Only you."

"Take it easy," I said. "Let's talk. I've got some time."

"Thanks," he said, nearly sobbing.

"Jesus, Detective, what happened?"

"Lot on my mind. Leave of absence. Needed time. Hard to talk."

"Relax," I said. "There's no hurry."

"I've done some bad things. I've got to tell someone."

You'd be surprised how many therapies begin like this: with a confession. And how seldom these "sins" turn out to be the heart of the matter. Usually they're a patient's attempt to plea-bargain to a lesser charge. But admitting your mistakes is often like a man caught in a mudslide admitting he's filthy. Sin, I've discovered, is not the bottom; it's only a door into deeper darknesses. We are so ready to brand ourselves criminals, and so reluctant to see ourselves as victims. "Go ahead," I said.

"I was in Nam. Intelligence. Did you . . . were you ever there?"

"I got out on a CO. Mopped the floors at a mental hospital for two years. It's actually how I got into this business."

"CO? Huh. Was a time I woulda called you a coward. Not now. I think there's a lotta cowards in uniform. They don't fight 'cause they're brave. They fight because they're afraid what'll happen if they don't. What their buddies will think. I was decorated. But I was scared as any grunt. You heard of search-and-destroy missions?" I nodded. He smiled. "We used to go on search-and-avoids." He took another drag and stubbed out his smoke. "You know what Intelligence means?"

"I think so."

"Think again. There's two kinds of *I* men. One pushes paper. The other kills."

"You were . . . ?"

"I killed. We used to take VC up in a helicopter. Interrogation. Three at a time. Ask the first one a question. If he doesn't answer—out he goes. They always fell the same way—pumping their legs and waving their arms. We'd do 'em one at a time. The first two were decoys. We already knew the third one was the one who had the answer. He usually came around. We even had a joke about it. 'How do you get a VC to talk?' " He took off his sunglasses. " 'You teach him to fly.' "

I know by experience I am no help to a patient for whom I don't have at least a little bit of empathy. It may sound corny, but it's quite practical: healing needs love. I never would have expected to feel anything but repulsion for this man. Yet, as dusk settled behind him, and his silhouette darkened, he began to resemble a reluctant witness who spoke under the protection of anonymity: his voice cracking, the fear palpable in the way he glanced about, fidgeted and fiddled with his watch. Unexpectedly, a sort of sympathy rose between us. We might have been two travelers lost in the same wood, sharing a fire and a silent understanding of the dangers in the surrounding night.

From this point on, he never stopped crying.

"I've been having dreams."

My stomach tightened. "Dreams?"

"Yeah. Bad ones. I mean, awful ones. I never used to dream much. Anyway, I never remembered them in the morning. I've had 'em ever since I saw you. I didn't think there was any connection. Then I had this, this one—"

He wept silently for a full minute. "I'm going nuts. I swear to god," he whimpered.

"Tell me, Detective."

He lit another cigarette. "How about just Jack?"

"Fine, Jack."

"What's it mean when you have a dream and it's . . . so *real* it doesn't feel like a dream?"

"It could mean a lot of things. Often, something important is trying to be heard."

"Trying to be heard?" he asked with fear.

"The unconscious has insight and knowledge we're not aware of. If the information is crucial enough to our well-being, it usually manages to break through. Especially if we try to repress it."

"I don't know. I don't think *this* was my subconscious talking."

"Why?"

He grew more uncomfortable. "I haven't slept in three days. I'm afraid of the Gook."

"The Gook?"

"He was the last VC I killed. After him, I couldn't throw anybody out of a helicopter anymore. He was young. Just a kid. He smiled at me all the way down."

"I read somewhere that means they're frightened."

"What?"

"Smiling."

"Oh." He grunted. "I wondered what they were so happy about." He snatched a Kleenex, blew his nose, and balled it up in his fist. "I hadn't thought about him for twenty years. A week ago I started to dream about him. At first he had nothing to do with the dreams. Just stood off to the side somewhere. Then he started following me. Then talking to me. Now every night . . ." He shuddered.

"What does he say, Jack?"

"He keeps talking about this Laura lady. It's always the same. Every night, we're in the helicopter. My hands and feet are tied with licorice—goddamn red licorice. And he's, like, interrogating me. I can hear the rotor. I can see the treetops outside the Huey. And he just smiles and smiles and asks me . . ." Choking sounds came out of his throat.

"What, Jack?"

" 'Where's Laura? Tell me about Laura. Have you seen her tits?' " He laughed mirthlessly. "And I can't answer. I mean, nothing I say is good enough. Christ, I only met the broad once! I mean, we talked for ten fucking minutes! 'I don't know!' I say. 'Who gives a fuck about Laura?' But that's not good enough for him. He wants answers I don't have!" He wiped his nose on his sleeve. "I'm the decoy, see? I'm just someone he's pushing around so they can break the real one."

I was shaking inside. But I put up my best front of calm for him. "Who's the real one, Jack? Who are they after?"

"I don't know!" He looked up to me like a beaten puppy. "Can I ask you a question?" I nodded. "What the fuck's a Holock?"

I almost came out of my chair. "Where'd you hear that word?" I whispered in horror.

"Nowhere!" He flung the tissue on the carpet. "Never heard it before in my life. But he keeps saying it like I'm supposed to know. He just stands there in that crazy red sweater and keeps asking me: 'Who are the Holock? Tell me about the Holock. What do you know about the Holock?' "

Fifteen

It was a bitch trying to find Saul's house. I kept circling around a few blocks north of Cobo Hall, but all I could see were empty lots, boarded-up businesses, a Catholic church, and run-down homes with the wrong addresses. I had just about given up when I saw a tall priest in black coming down the steps of the church. He walked briskly and seemed to grow older the closer I got to him. I figured he knew the neighborhood, so I stopped and waved him over. Sure, he knew Saul. Everybody knew Saul. Just park over there and knock on the rectory door.

When I got to the door I turned and caught a glimpse of a gray car turning the corner. Me and my shadow: the Fat Man, again. What was he? An old boyfriend jealous of all the attention I'd been giving Laura? Had he stalked Dr. Stewart as he was stalking me? Or was he some government agent hunting down UFO witnesses? Some top-secret CIA heavy? Maybe they've reopened that old Air Force Project Blue Book? Blue Book? I thought. Why does that ring a bell? I was getting paranoid. I told myself to cool it.

The door buzzed open and a small black secretary with

Brillo-gray hair led me through a large old house that must have been pretty impressive in its day: dark woodwork, lead-glass windows, elaborate light fixtures, and carved banisters. We walked to what appeared to be a room above a garage that had probably once held five cars.

"You a priest?" she asked.

"No."

She smirked. "They keep saying they're gonna send somebody to help out Father Ed. He's retired and his ticker's bad, so he's only good for one Mass on Sundays. But they never do. Vocations," she added with a meaningful look. "You're not the guy from the *Wall Street Journal?*"

"No."

"A doctor?"

"Yeah."

She pointed to a small door at the top of some steep stairs, then looked at the plastic bottle in my hand with suspicion. "What's that?"

"Orange juice."

"Umm." She stuck her tongue in her cheek and nodded. "I thought so."

My knock was answered by a shout: "Whaddya want?"

"It's Donelly." When no one answered, I added, "I brought the juice."

That must have been the password, for the door snapped open and Saul said, "Yer late."

"I got lost."

I slipped in and he slammed it shut. "I gotta be careful. Imish wants out."

"Imish?" I asked.

"Right," he said, leading me into a large room with an arched ceiling. Two cloudy windows overlooked the Lodge freeway. There was an unmade bed in one corner, a gro-

tesque crucifix above it: lots of blood. Ashtrays everywhere: full of butts. One wall was covered with books.
Theology. Engineering. Economics. A long rug with frayed
edges ran the length of the room. A sink and kitchen area in
one corner next to a door I presumed to be the john. There
was the smell of coffee that had been simmering for hours.
And cigarettes. Suddenly, a flash of red swooped down and
sent me ducking.

"What the—!"

"Goddamnit, Imish! You got the manners of a jay!"

I saw a red cardinal perched on the rafters. Then his gold
cage hanging in the corner—the door open. Saul relieved
me of the orange juice and moved to the kitchen area. "Siddown, siddown," he said. "I'll fix that bird. I'll put pepper
in his juice. Teach 'im to treat guests that way!" He pulled
out a saucer and poured the juice into it. The bird glided
down and landed on his shoulder. "Man brings your favorite, and you dive-bomb him. I oughta lock you in the bathroom for that. Don't you give me that look! You know you
been nasty." I watched them from the couch. The old man
talking to the bird on his shoulder. "Coffee?" he shouted,
and, after a moment, I answered, "No thanks." It was to be
a pattern in our conversations: I could never tell if he was
talking to the bird or me. And I usually guessed wrong.

As he moved about the kitchen in his purple quilted
robe, his slippers lisping, Saul reminded me of a miniature
Scrooge: he stood five feet at the most, his body was
chubby, his bald head shone like a tomato, and his eyes, set
deeply under thick white brows, were tiny pools of ink. He
was pouring coffee when I noticed an old magazine in the
corner of a bookshelf: *Business Review.* On the cover was a
black-and-white photo of the Man Himself, thirty years
ago. He was still bald, but his hair and eyebrows were jet
black. His gaze was steady. The headline read: "Saul Lowe.

Entrepreneur of the Year." Beside it was a small print of the *Mona Lisa*, which, for some reason, reminded me of Laura.

Saul must have seen me looking at it, for he said, "Leonardo. Now that was a Thinker. Wrote backward. Designed a cannon. Helicopter. Did ya know he invented the parachute?"

"No, I didn't."

"Then he invented an airplane." He gave me a meaningful look over his shoulder. "See what I mean?"

"Not really."

"Fuckin' Italian. Draws a parachute. Twelve years later draws an airplane. Kinda like inventing a saddle before you've ever seen a horse."

"Oh," I said, wondering if this were true. "First the parachute . . . then the plane."

"You got it." He smiled, took a sip of coffee, and winced. "So, you slept with her?"

"Mona? I never touched her."

"Now we're getting somewhere!" he said jubilantly. "Chaos. Relativity. Quantum. They're all connected. You gotta ride the flow. Find the link. Make the leaps. Intuition. Fourth force. Leonardo knew. When's the last time you got laid?"

"You first."

He didn't hesitate. "Nineteen forty-eight. Holiday Inn. Room 56. Wanda. Had a spider tattooed on her butt. After that I swore off women."

"Why?"

"Too much energy. Can't pray with a boner. Prayer's more important. You'll see what I mean. So you never touched the princess?"

I scanned my memory. I seemed to recall this was his nickname for Laura. "No."

"But you want to . . ."

I was extremely uncomfortable. "She's an attractive woman, yeah."

He held up a hand. "Hey. You're a man. A man's got needs. I'm not objecting to it. It might be a good idea. I'm just curious."

"It's not really your business, Saul."

"You're right about that. I'm retired now. I did my stint. Guess how much I'm worth."

"I couldn't care—"

"Go on, go on, go on."

"A million."

"Geez, you're not very smart, are you? Well, how would you know? I been out of circulation since the Incident." He sipped his coffee. "I lost most of it investing in dream research in the fifties. I was once the richest man in New Jersey—if that means anything. I had fifty pairs of shoes. My own driver." He pulled out a blue handkerchief and blew his nose loudly. His eyes were teary when he continued. "I was into everything: patents, real estate, show business." He caught my look. "You think I'm crazy?"

"The thought has occurred to me."

"Com'ere, com'ere, com'ere." He led me to a tiny altar in the corner. A stitched white cloth hung over a small chest. Two devotional candles. A portrait of Pope Pius XII. A rosary made of blue beads. He flipped back the cloth to reveal a small steel safe. He turned the combination lock, twisted the handle, and opened the little door. "Look," he said.

I squatted down. It was full of money, stacked wall to wall. He reached in and pulled out an egg. "What the hell?" he said, looking at it, then slipped it into the pocket of his robe. "You wanna guess how much is here?"

"Thousands?"

"Try nine hundred thousand seven hundred and thirty-five dollars."

I whistled and he seemed to enjoy my shock. "You want any?"

I stood up. "No thanks."

"You sure?"

"Yeah. I'm fine."

"You want an egg?"

"Thanks, no."

"Well," he said slamming the door and twirling the lock. "Don't say I never offered."

We went back to our seats and Saul pulled out a small blue book with gold letters on the cover. He tossed it over to me. *THOMAS AQUINAS' 12 PROOFS OF THE EXISTENCE OF GOD.* "Smart guy."

The pages were full of underlining and notes in the margins.

"Keep it," he said.

"Thanks," I said, putting it in the pocket of my sport coat.

"Imish likes you." He smiled, looking past me. I turned to come face-to-face with the cardinal. It stood on top of the couch, cocking its head at a curious angle. "He's a greedy bird, but we can't all be perfect."

I looked at Saul. His eyes danced as if he had just lobbed a joke over my head. I looked at the bird. He winked. At that moment if someone had told me I was dreaming I would have believed them. "Saul," I said, rubbing my forehead with my fingers. "Can I ask you a question?"

"Shoot."

"What the fuck have I gotten myself into?"

He pulled the egg out of his pocket, held it up to the light, and squinted. "Marvelous. Perfect. You like eggs?"

I sighed. "Sure."

"You look uncomfortable. Relax. I'm getting to it." He seemed pleased when I pulled out a Salem and lit up. He was already smoking. "You're what—forty? You've been around. You probably think you've dealt with some serious shit in your life. Shrinks hear a ton of it, eh?"

I nodded.

"You've been playing junior varsity, Son. This is the big leagues." It was one of Hogan's favorite sports analogies. In fact, I got the uncanny feeling that, somehow, Saul *knew* this.

He smiled and flicked an ash on the floor. "Okeydo-key, Doc. I'm gonna tell you a story. In five minutes you're gonna think I should be locked up. In ten minutes you're gonna wish you never met me. In fifteen minutes you're gonna be so scared you won't want to leave here. But now you gotta make a decision."

Somehow the room had gotten hot and the egg had disappeared from his hand. He smiled and spit it out of his mouth; it dropped into his lap. He began to play with it. "You can walk out that door with a fond memory about a fat little man with a little red bird and a lot of money. Party talk. *Reader's Digest* stuff. Unforgettable character." The egg disappeared again. He smiled and spit it out again. I laughed. "That's one choice. Or you can stay for the duration. The whole hitch. One or the other, you can't do both.

"If you stay—two things could happen. You could die. Or you could change the world. If you go—I got a enve-lope with ten thousand dollars cash for you. It's yours if you keep your mouth shut. I mean SHUT!" He slammed his fist on the arm of his chair, raising a cloud of dust. He stood and walked over to me. Suddenly, he was a little frightening. "I mean, cut your fucking tongue out. No hints. No anonymous letters. No juicy memoirs. I mean, if you ever so much as drop a clue to a living soul—you will be killed." He smiled. "Those are the choices. The money. Death. Or Door Number Three." The egg was in my hand. I didn't know how it got there. "You look like a smart man. What I wanna know is . . . are you a brave man?"

"That's not for me to say."

"Ever tried to break an egg in your fist? Go on, go on. Try it." I squeezed the egg with all my might. I couldn't break it.

"Some things look wimpy. But they're made of strong stuff. So what are you made of, Doc? Take yer time. Think about it. Imish? Bring the man a Camel."

The red bird flitted past my ear and lighted on a side table, where Saul's smokes were. Gripping the pack with one claw, it pulled out a cigarette and shuffled it into its beak. In a flash it landed on my shoulder and began to jab it at my mouth. I opened and bit down. Saul produced a lighter. I took a long drag on a brand of smokes I hate. Change the world, die, or shut up for ten thousand bucks—not bad options.

The egg felt warm in my hand, hatchable. All those months I'd been waiting for some tangible proof. Something I could lay my hands on. I never would have guessed that a little fat man, his red bird, and an egg would tip the scales. But insight comes in strange ways. Little ways. An apple falls on your head. Water rises as you settle into a tub. C. S. Lewis took a bus to the zoo. On the way home he became a Christian. I don't know if it was the egg trick, or the bird, or the thick blue cloud of smoke that hung in the room like the aftermath of an explosion. In a blink of time I knew that my world had irrevocably changed. I don't know how I knew, but I did. The fear came later. But at that moment all I felt was a breathless elation that before I had only associated with falling in love.

"I'll do it," I said.

Saul laughed and said, "A sucker born every minute."

Sixteen

So there I was, sitting on the couch in Saul's rectory, the cardinal Imish perched on my shoulder, as Saul revealed the mysteries of the Holock.

"The Holock aren't just Dream Sharers," he began. "They're Dream Eaters. They suck 'em up like candy. That's why we can't remember most of our dreams. They've been eaten. They're a race of dream junkies. Now, what's the worst thing an addict can think of? Withdrawal, right? They discovered that our dreams stopped at a certain time. No more dreams. Like somebody had hung up on 'em. That scared them shitless. Someday they were gonna run out of candy! So they started working on a travel program based on their knowledge of dream-hopping. When they had the technology, they began to send out missions."

"Wait. Wait a second, slow down." It took a moment to process all this. Even then it didn't make sense. I asked him to repeat it. He did. "Missions?" I finally said. "For what purpose?"

"To learn how to dream. They tried everything. They couldn't do it. Then around the turn of this century they began to take specimens. Hoping to clone their own race of humans. Like pets, you know. If they couldn't master dreaming, they'd settle for the next best thing: they'd each have their own pet that they could 'Dreamfeed' off of. Problem was, the specimens couldn't survive the journey. Sperm wouldn't last. Blood and skin cells died. Zygotes withered. Those humans that *did* survive couldn't adapt to the Jell-O environment. Cross-pollination was a joke, until Laura. And they've never been able to duplicate her. They still don't know how she happened." He chuckled and shook his head—as if he did know "how she happened." "So they'd struck out. Then they found something worse."

"What?"

"Their forefathers."

"Huh?"

"For the longest time I wondered how the Holock could read our future dreams. It was too simple for me to see. The Holock exist in the future—our future. They're Time Travelers, not Space Travelers. Do you follow?"

I shook my head.

"They discovered they *lived* on planet Earth. Our dreams stopped when we stopped. Our last war will be their genesis."

I was staggered by the impact of what Saul was saying. "They're not really aliens?"

"Bingo!"

"So this whole 'alien' scenario is . . ."

"A cover-up. A shuck. Well-orchestrated propaganda. They don't want us to know the truth. 'Course, they'll evolve so differently from us they may as well be aliens."

I covered my face with my hands.

"Hey! That's just the first act!" He continued: "So their priorities changed. Forget about losing their dream fix; they found their entire *existence* depends on a nuclear holocaust.

No problem, right? Bound to happen. But then they found a loophole in their destiny. One possible past that could cancel their future existence before it started. They were able to narrow it down to one era, one country, one year, one man."

"One man?" I asked.

"Sure. Hey, Oswald changed everything with one bullet."

"This man . . . will be an assassin?"

"You could say that. But he won't kill anybody. He will assassinate an idea."

"An idea?"

"You got it. Our civilization suffers a mass delusion— it's so ingrained that we can't even see it, like visual fluoride. Maybe it started when we lived in caves and our survival depended on fear. You know, when we were other creatures's food. Then tribes learned to protect their hunting grounds. Then we moved into cities; trade and specialization made us more dependent on other cultures. So we pulled back our boundaries into what we owned: our property and possessions. We cast the idea into a more wholesome form: competition. The marketplace became the battlefield. Marx tried to turn things around, but all he did was set class against class. The workers are pure, the owners are evil. Today we got the Military-Industrial Complex: the perfect marriage of competition and destruction. America sets aside twenty-five percent of its budget for war. We call it 'defense'! Why? Because the human race believes that war is inevitable. Think about sports."

"Sports?" What *was* he talking about?

"Ever notice how few sports allow the possibility of a tie? They got a handy little concept called OVERTIME." Saul's laughter bellowed through the room. "That's my personal favorite: OVERTIME!" He realized I wasn't laughing, stifled himself, and continued. "The point is: we need a Winner; we need a Loser. We need to have an Enemy. That's the idea that will be banished: *There must be an Enemy.* Part of us NEEDS an Enemy. No earth system, whether it's economic, political, religious, or recreational, is free of this Enemy idea. It is a cultural presumption we call Common Sense. And we cling to it. Because it was once so central to our psyche, so necessary for our survival. But it doesn't work anymore. I mean, we literally need each other to survive. Everybody loses or everybody wins."

"It sounds too simple," I said.

"It is simple. That's why we can't see it. We got a lot at stake in this concept; you don't lose a survival instinct overnight. But if someday we realized that the nightmare is over, the monster is a myth—we'd be forced to change ourselves in drastic ways."

"Would we?"

"Hey—insight transforms the world. We stopped burning witches when we understood they were women. We stopped selling slaves when we realized they were human. Someday we may stop treating kids like property. We may even stop raping women. All it takes is one idea," he said, tapping his index finger on his forehead. "The Enemy's in here."

"Jung said something like that," I remembered. "Our enemies are a projection of our darkest selves. What we can't face in ourselves we put on someone else. We project our fears."

Saul nodded. "But what happens when we lose the object of our fears? How does a species deal with an extinct predator? Doesn't it still maintain its hyper-vigilance? We have always had an enemy. We have depended on fear for survival. The Enemy has gone, but the fear remains."

"But, Saul. Terrorists. Fanatics. Racists. The drug cartel. Crime is not an illusion. Can you really say there are no enemies?"

"Let's take those one by one. Terrorists and fanatics are fighting other terrorists and fanatics—how could they behave like monsters unless they were cornered, fighting the terror of the Great Satan? Drugs, when they don't make you paranoid, help you escape your fear. Racism is learned—a reflex scapegoatism based on illogical fear. And how much crime comes from empty bellies and poverty? If we're so sincere about protecting ourselves and rehabilitating criminals, why do we send them to Schools of Crime? We're training them, we're not healing them—creating a whole subclass of criminals we can fear, fight, and banish. The key is not eliminating the Enemy, but the fear."

I tried to picture a human being free of fear. I couldn't. I may just as well imagined a lake without water. "It sounds impossible."

"Of course it does! It's a revolution in your conception of reality that hasn't happened yet! Automobiles were impossible in the eighteenth century. Try explaining relativity to a nineteenth-century scientist! We're talking revolution, here. And not the political or technological kind. The next revolution will be in the realm of consciousness."

"Some New Age Utopia?" I frowned. "I can't imagine it."

"But we have to," said Saul solemnly. "Imagining a Utopia is our responsibility. Are you getting this? The Holock need us to believe in an Enemy. So they're invading our dreams and terrorizing us with staged kidnappings. They want to spread this primal fear: THERE IS AN ENEMY. Their message is simple: ARM YOURSELVES."

"But why the secrecy?"

"They understand terror. They make nightmares, don't they? They know fear lurks in dark corners, the unexplainable, the unknown. So they use guerrilla tactics."

"But why wouldn't they just take over?"

"They don't want to rule."

"They don't?"

"Nyaah. They don't want to bring in a new order; they want to maintain the old. Their existence depends upon us destroying ourselves."

All this was getting creepier and creepier. Maybe because I knew it was leading to something. "You spoke of 'one man.'"

"That man is you. Your fate will determine whether or not the Holock survive."

"Me?" I asked.

"You."

"How?"

"Sometime this year you will have a child. The Holock know your descendant will bring about a revolution in consciousness. A whole new paradigm. A whole new world. The Enemy will be gone."

"They've seen this?"

"Yup. You're gonna be a daddy. Let me be the first to congratulate you!" Saul smiled and let the idea sink in.

"Jesus," I blurted, "why don't they just kill me? Wouldn't that solve their problem?"

"No. You WILL have a child. They cannot prevent that. They can only try to control it."

I thought of one of the first things Laura ever said to me: "I only have a year."

"Laura!" I said.

Saul nodded. "They sent Laura back to carry your seed. She said they gave her two options: Bring your daughter back to them so she can't spread her infection. Or stay here and bear you a son."

"A son?"

"Right. A son won't do it. A daughter will."

"Why is Laura doing this?"

"They promised her a child. A daughter there. Or a son here. You can't imagine what that means to her. To have the company of your own kind in the zoo she was raised in alone."

"Maybe I can imagine," I said. "But what if I have a bastard? What if Laura's not the mother?"

"That's why they sent a backup: to keep watch. They don't trust anybody working alone. See, they usually work in pairs. One on the inside, one on the outside. The Dreamer and the Waker."

"What?"

"You got the Dreamer. The licorice kid?"

"Oh."

"Dr. Stewart got the Waker."

"His killer?"

"Yup."

The Fat Man, I thought. It had to be the Fat Man. "The Waker and the Dreamer," I repeated. He nodded. "What's Laura then?" I asked.

"Laura's Door Number Three," Saul said with a laugh. "But feel free to ask her yourself." He looked at the phone. I looked at the phone. The phone rang and startled Imish, who flew to the top of the bookshelves and began nibbling on a rubber alligator that lay there.

"Hey, Princess. No. No. Yeah. He's here. Yeah, right here. Of course he wants to fuck you. Hey, that's not my problem. Here, you tell him." Saul handed me the phone with a snicker.

"Laura?" I began.

"I'm worried," she said. "I start ovulating soon. This could be our last chance."

"For what?"

"To get me pregnant, of course."

I looked at the receiver in my hand. "Laura, suppose I don't *want* to get you pregnant?"

"You don't have to *want* it. It is going to happen."

Saul was trying to hide his giggles in the corner.

"I don't have a choice?"

"Of course you have a choice! I thought Saul told you. You're going to get me pregnant. You haven't mated with anyone else, have you?"

"No." I was thinking about Adrian after the Halloween party. We could have, but didn't.

"So what's the problem?"

At this point I started to lose it. The room felt like a sauna. My heart was pounding like a snare roll. "Goddamnit, I'M the problem. First, you're my fucking patient! That may mean nothing to you, but I could lose my career over it. Secondly, I don't FEEL like making love to you!"

"Liar!" shouted Saul with glee.

Laura sounded dismayed. "You don't?"

"Well, I mean, I LIKE you just fine. I find you very attractive. But that's no reason— I mean, Christ! I don't fuck STRANGERS!"

"I thought you knew me better than that!"

"Is this some TIME thing?" I said angrily. "The Holock are in a possible future. I'm in a possible past. My child will come from a possible PRESENT." I wiped my brow. "This whole thing is fucking impossible! I don't sleep with someone because it's my DESTINY." By now Saul was hysterical in his chair, pounding the arms, raising more dust. "Do I . . . ?"

Simultaneously, Laura on the phone and Saul in his room answered, "Yes."

"Fucking humans," Saul laughed. "Don't know shit about time."

I hung up the phone. I walked over to Saul, who was still sniffling with mirth. "Do you know what I'm going to say next?"

Saul smiled. "I got a good idea."

"I want to wake up." I leaned down to say it to his face. "This is a very bad nightmare. And I want to wake up right now. I want to get out of my bed, mix myself a dry gin martini, turn on 'Letterman,' put my feet up, and relax. I've been under a lot of stress. I've been imagining things. You're not real. Laura's a bad dream. Dr. Stewart is a man I've never met." I started reciting a litany of numbers. "It's nineteen-ninety. The Pistons are in third place. I charge seventy dollars an hour. My bedroom has one window. There are two socks under my bed. My dad had a heart attack ten years ago. His last words to me were 'Have fun.' Saul, please. Please let me wake up. Don't keep me in this dream, or I'm going to lose my mind!" I was leaning over, holding the arms of Saul's chair, closing my eyes as tight as I could.

"Sorry, kid. No can do."

I opened my eyes. Saul was staring up at me with a sad, rueful smile.

"I'm not dreaming?" I asked.

"Sorry," he said, lighting another Camel. "You should have taken the money. I warned you about Door Number Three."

I stood up and let out a big sigh. Then, on a whim that to

this day I can't explain, I held out my index finger as if I were pointing at something. "Imish?" I called. And just like that the cardinal lighted on my finger, looked up at me with one eye, and gurgled. I couldn't believe how light he was. "You're real, aren't you, Imish? You stupid bird."

Seventeen

Following that pivotal meeting with Saul, my life changed in considerable and unexpected ways. In the span of two weeks, all my patients left me. Most said they were cured and were grateful for my help. A few said they couldn't take any more. A few asked to be referred to another therapist. One moved in with me: Detective Kiefer. Or rather, we both moved into "Saul's rectory," as we came to call it. I felt like a man who had lost his job and returned from the office to find his house had burned to the ground, his family had moved to another state, and none of his friends recognized him. I felt like a stranger in my own life. Saul had said something like this would happen. "Not to worry. Not to worry. The details are handled. Get into the big picture."

Hogan and I finally got our schedules arranged so we could meet at our mother's house to take stock of her possessions. It wasn't something we looked forward to. How strange to go back to your childhood home. To recognize the smells, the telltale scars on the furniture where this toy or that had been thrown. The upstairs air grate where Hogan and I used to keep vigil whenever our parents had a party: thrilling to the coarse and indecipherable chatter of adults under the influence of cocktails. My past was cataloged in the brand names of my youth: the case of Stroh's still stashed in the back hall. The milk chute where Hogan got stuck and had to be greased with Fleischmann's to get him out. The stairwell that smelled of Murphy's Oil Soap. The scent of Lemon Pledge under the dust that coated everything: a condition that would have mortified Mom.

It was depressing going through belongings that belonged to no one. Hogan wanted to give her jewelry to Angie. We split up the pictures. I'd forgotten how many shots there were of Hogan in his football uniform, Hogan with his trophies. I found my First Communion photo. There I was: an eight-year-old with a starched collar and slicked-back hair, holding a white rosary wrapped around a white prayer book with a golden cross embossed on the cover. You poor fuck, I thought. And came as close to feeling my grief as I had yet. Though I wasn't sure whom I was mourning: the mother I lost or the child I used to be. I wasn't ready for this. I put away the picture.

I was going through her dresser when I came upon a shocking bit of wardrobe: handcuffs wrapped in a black lace frill. I must have looked at them for a minute. I wanted to throw them away, or hide them from Hogan. The implications were staggering. A well-hidden aspect of our parents' sexuality? A romantic memento she had kept after my dad's death? An affair with someone on the parish council? Though reasonable, none of these possibilities seemed credible. Sensuality wasn't in my mother's vocabulary. I caught Hogan looking at me in the mirror.

"Do you know what these are?" I asked.

"Sure."

"Do you think Mom . . . ?"

"Christ, no!" He walked over, took the cuffs from my

hand, and held them to his nose, closing his eyes. Then he dropped them in the drawer and shut it.

"Don't worry. It's not Mom's."

"You don't think Dad . . . ?"

"You got a sick mind." He looked guiltily at me and shrugged. "It's a friend of mine's."

I looked at him a long time. He might have been blushing. "Right here?" I looked around the room. "On Mom's bed?"

"Well. No," he said. "Not all the time."

I started twirling my hair. "I had no idea you and Angie were . . ."

"There's nothing wrong with me and Angie," he said, slicing off the suggestion with his hand. "It's just . . ."

"Just what? Christ, do I have to tell you what you're risking?"

"I know. I know. I can't help it, Johnny." He looked at himself in the mirror. "She makes me feel smart."

I didn't have the heart to tell him how many of my clients had done the same thing: funneled their loss of a loved one into an affair. Actually, it's fairly natural behavior, a primal reaction to extinction: propagate. "How'd you meet her?"

"I sold her a Miata. Don't worry. It's nothing serious. Adrian knows I'd never leave Angie."

"Adrian?" I repeated.

"You'd understand if you ever met her."

"Adrian what?" I asked.

He told me and I shook my head. "She's a nurse's aide, right?"

"So?"

"I know her. I met her at a party."

"You know her?" He sat down on the bed, biting his lip. "This is too weird." I could tell he was thinking: another hand-me-down. That old competitive thing we used to have between us. "Johnny, you didn't sleep with her or anything?"

"No," I replied, thinking: Thank God!

"I need a beer," he said.

I went to the fridge and found a six-pack of Stroh's and a half-eaten DoveBar. I opened the freezer. It was stuffed with ice cream. Dark chocolate. Milk chocolate. Strawberry. There must have been twenty DoveBars in there. I recalled her DoveBar breakfast the night she stayed over at my place. That's Adrian, all right, I thought.

My brother was on my mind when Laura and I met for our first appointment at the rectory. If anyone found out about his affair, it could ruin him—especially in the tight-ass circles he was so proud to run in. Why would he take such a chance? A happy husband with a great wife, a devoted father with a dozen pictures of his family in his office, a success, a respected man in the community, a paragon of his parish, an ex-football hero: it didn't compute. The only precedent for it was his mysterious pilgrimage to Africa. His decision to volunteer for the Peace Corps was as uncharacteristic as his affair. He was not a risk-taker. They used to call him a "coachable" athlete. Nobody understood why this predictable middle-class kid tossed off his college football scholarship to go teach English to Toureg children in Niger.

Hogan said the best thing about Niger was his Jeep. He still misses it: a desert-brown, topless runabout, a classic design that hadn't changed since World War II. It was really the only way to get around the Sahara, unless you had a camel. He had gotten used to tooling down the dusty byways, waving at the tall, stately Toureg warriors who rested under the date trees, watching the children dash into tents to hide whenever his dust cloud appeared on the horizon. Once he saw a turbaned man chasing an ostrich around a makeshift corral.

The natives had warned Hogan about the floods from the spring runoff; when the snow-capped mountains around Agadez melted, sending wild treacherous rivers down their slopes. He hadn't taken it seriously: these were superstitious primitives who talked to trees and worshiped their dead ancestors. So he only got annoyed not alarmed when his Jeep leaped into a dry riverbed, flattened a rear tire, bent the rim, and stripped one of the lug nuts. It was a bitch to get off. He ended up cursing in frustration, bashing away at the nut with a tire iron, the hollow clangs ringing off the steep mountain cliffs a football field away.

He finally got it off. And as he tightened the final nut on the spare, Hogan thought he heard the static hum of telephone wires in winter. He grew homesick: for his friends, for his mother, for the Lions, for Michigan autumns, fresh apple cider and warm doughnuts that steamed when you bit them. Then there was a strange light that dappled the side of his Jeep with color. He looked over his shoulder and got a faceful of cold brown water that slammed him hard against the fixed wheel.

"Christ!" he yelled, and got a mouthful of sand. The wave pulled the tire iron out of his hand and his legs out from under him. He clung to the tire. Then his hand slipped and he was dragged under, scraping his elbows on the sandy bottom. Reaching up, he grasped the front bumper and pulled his head above the frigid gushing water. But his boots were heavy as anchors, tugging and stretching him out like an undertow, pulling him under again. His arms began to ache, from the cold and from the current. He knew if he let go he would drown. Holding the bumper tight with one hand, he grabbed the grille with the other, and, with an enormous effort, hoisted himself drenching onto the dusty hood of the Jeep. His clothes made a hissing sound on the hot metal—"the most beautiful sound in the world," he told me.

When he had caught his breath he sat up and found himself in the middle of a rushing river. The wave had already traveled a couple hundred yards beyond him; the water had risen to tire-level and the Jeep looked ridiculous. "Jesus," he said, "I thought they were exaggerating!" He looked upstream and saw a small black something rolling over and over in the brown river, coming toward him. He watched it. If he just reached out he could almost grab it. He did.

It was slippery like a fish. The small black something. The black body. The black naked baby. Its eyes were closed. He'd caught it by the ankle.

Hogan was not proud of his first impulse—he wanted to throw the child back in. His next impulse was even more puzzling, for he hadn't prayed in years. He said the Our Father in French—not with great hope, but more as a man who has just caught a live grenade in his hand prays it is a dud.

He heard hysterical cries and saw a dripping Negress in a soaked red sheet running barefoot down the bank. She held her head in her hands. Her teeth chattered. To Hogan, she looked like a monster as she stood and screamed nonsense at him thirty feet away.

"Stay back!" he yelled in French, over the rush of the river.

The child lay cold in his arms. He noticed it was a boy. He looked at the mother. The mother looked at the child. Hogan looked at the child. Hogan looked at the mother.

"I'm sorry," he yelled in French. Then in English he whispered, "There's nothing I can do."

The child opened its eyes wide, looked into his face, and

threw up in his lap. Then it cried and cried and the mother fainted and the water rolled on and on.

An hour later the current had calmed and Hogan and the child were great friends. He had been amusing it with his gold Class-A championship ring. Finally, Hogan slung it over his shoulder, waded through the knee-deep water, and presented the mother with her child. Her mouth made a silent O. Then she hugged the baby and walked away scolding it. Over her shoulder the child gave Hogan a shy wave.

At the time he went to Africa, I thought he was trying to one-up me: "You're a conscientious objector? I'm a missionary!" But when I discovered the real reason, I had to admire him. He was pursuing a girl, a French exchange student he met in his first semester of college, a girl who got engaged three months after his arrival in Africa—to another man. Hogan was never the same after that. He passed the remaining two years in a haze of hangovers and short-tempered lessons, growing daily more disgusted with the obvious cunning and stupidity of third-world people. He said he thought he married a chief's daughter one night, but he was drunk and the contract didn't seem binding. Once, when he was full of gin, Hogan chased an ostrich into the night, got lost, and returned the next morning with his teeth chattering and the beginnings of bronchitis. This led to a medical discharge.

After Africa, Hogan's smile became quicker, his handshake firmer, and he fit very nicely into the dealership staff. He knew how to handle customers; he took to salesmanship with an abandon that made Dad very proud. And he became a staunch Catholic.

Mom got a lot of leverage out of his Africa Disaster and the hangdog depression he carried for several months afterward—she took great pleasure in forgiveness, especially for sins of the flesh, from which she was no doubt exempt. She once said to me: "Enjoy it while you can; the Bible says there's no sex in Heaven." She had imagined a promiscuity in my life that had never happened. She could not abide anyone enjoying what she had given up.

The only time I ever saw my mother happy—not bravely sacrificing for everyone else—was when she danced at the Irish/American League. She'd never miss a jig or reel: circular music of great precision—music that personally drives me nuts. It is the Soundtrack of Repression. Manic constricted rings of melody with no breathing room allowed—a music brimming with passion but forbidden to spill it. It is the Anthem of the Super Ego, the Catholic Church, the grand Irish Tradition of grown men living with their mothers, husbands despising their wives, idolizing their moms, boozing themselves into impotence, Venerating the Virgin, because it is unthinkable that GOD should be born from the Original Act of Sin. It is the most neurotic music I know. And the dancers look like puppets. I used to watch my mother dance, allowing herself a prim smile, as if she were getting away with something, arms glued to her sides, hands clenched into fists, bouncing up and down, up and down, as if she were dancing in a closet.

Hogan's conformity was like that.

These were my thoughts when Laura came for her appointment. It took us a while to get used to the rectory office; intimidating pictures of cathedrals and dark wood paneling surrounded us. It felt oppressive, tidy, and smelled of celibacy: that unreal doll-like scent of men without women. I sat behind a huge mahogany desk with drawers that were empty but for a purple stole and a few candles. It felt awkward having the desk between us.

"What are you smiling about?" she began.

"Was I? I was thinking about Hogan."

"He seems a sweet man."

"He is. He's taking Mom's death hard." I told her about him sitting in new cars to relieve his grief. We both laughed.

"Sounds reasonable," she said.

"Sure. His whole life revolves around cars. He met his wife trying to sell her a car. And his mistress."

"Really?"

"Really. What's weirder is I know her. She works at the Home."

"The Home?"

"That's what we call the Hospital for the Criminally Insane. In Pontiac. The strange thing is: I think of her and I think of Hogan and I can't put the two together. I can't imagine them in bed. Actually, she's more *my* type."

"What's she look like?"

"She's pretty. Pale. Long features, like you. But Adrian's just a little thing."

Laura sat very still. "Her name is Adrian?"

"Right. What's wrong?" I asked as her face seemed to stiffen.

"Did she ever hurt you?"

"What?"

"Did you ever see her hurt *anybody?*"

"Actually, she floored the guy with a kick in the pills."

"The pills?"

"Balls," I said.

"Did you ever see her eat candy?"

"Laura, what is this—an interrogation? I met her at a Halloween party. She met my brother. Now they're boinking. These things happen."

"Did she sleep with you?"

"Ah, not that it's any of your business," I said huffily, "but no. She did stay the night, though."

"Call Hogan," Laura urged.

"Why?"

"He's in danger. Tell him to come here."

"What?"

"He's got the Waker."

"Laura?" I laughed. Then I saw the image of Adrian sucking on a DoveBar at eight in the morning. The steaming freezer full of ice cream. I remember wondering how she could consume so many calories and keep her shape. I recalled that at the Halloween party she always held a caramel apple in her hand. I saw the image of that drunken clown falling on his face in front of this tiny woman. Then I remembered my dream of Adrian stretching her tits.

"Ice cream," I said. "Does that qualify as candy?"

Laura looked at me. "That's the equivalent of a good joint."

I called Hogan's house—nobody home. Feeling sick to my stomach, I called my mom's number. He answered, his voice cracking.

"Gun? It's Johnny. We gotta talk."

"Christ, you scared me! Nobody calls here."

"Are you alone?"

"Yeah, I'm early. She'll be here in an hour."

"Tell him to get the hell out!" Laura warned.

"Don't move," I said. "I'll be right there."

"Whatta ya wanna do that for, Johnny?"

"Hogan, GODDAMNIT, listen. Adrian is not who you think she is."

"What's that supposed to mean?"

"I'll explain when I get there." I hung up.

"What are you gonna do?" Laura asked.

"Go get Jack. Tell him to bring his gun. I gotta think."

Laura was at the door when she turned, walked back, and handed me her usual fee: three twenties and a ten. "Rope," she said. "You'll need rope."

Eighteen

Jack prayed the whole trip over. In their short time together he had come under the sway of Saul, and was given
to crossing himself and carrying a flask of holy water in the
breast pocket of his sport coat, right next to his Marlboros.
Saul dubbed him "our resident detective." He waited in the
van when I made a stop at the hardware store. There was an
awkward moment when I couldn't explain to the helpful
salesman what sort of chore I needed the rope for.

"What took you?" Jack asked when I made it back to
the car.

"I had no idea there were that many kinds of rope."

"We're gonna be late," he scolded.

Some time later he noticed I was trembling. "What's the
problem, Doc?"

"Jack, I don't even know what we're gonna do."

"Are you kidding? We're gonna kill her."

And that settled it. Once the words were spoken it became easier to deal with. But all the way over an old version
of myself berated me with the righteous platitudes of my
conscientious objector period. "There are no just wars!

Nothing can justify the taking of human life! If Christ were alive today, can you imagine him pushing the Button? The military is a dehumanizing school for killers! Did you forget that well-rehearsed speech you fed the draft board review? They bought it: those potbellied vets asking you questions about Hitler and ski-masked psychos attacking your kids with machetes. Maybe you're just chicken. Maybe that's why you mopped floors for two years at the Home. Remember the acrid smell of ammonia? You used to think: that's the smell of a clear conscience. You wore that job like a medal. Janitor. Super Janitor. The Man who wouldn't compromise. Boy, you really put one over on everybody, didn't you?" The voice was distant, ineffectual, like the memory of someone who used to matter a great deal. I was surprised at how easily I could pass it off.

"Laura says she's very dangerous," I said.

"So am I," he replied with a grim smile.

There was a lovely late-winter sunset as we walked up to my mom's house. The air was chilled. The bare trees glowed in the sunlight. Jack wanted to know the layout of the house. I told him. It was one of the few homes in the area, a big lot that bordered on farmland. As we walked up the steps to the porch I recalled hiding under it, eating a stash of Three Musketeers—leftovers from my birthday party.

Adrian was all smiles when she answered the door. "Hi, guys! Come on in!"

Jack and I exchanged glances and stepped inside.

Hogan was sitting at the kitchen table. Adrian sat down opposite him.

"Who's this?" asked Hogan.

I made the introductions and Jack and Hogan shook hands.

"What's in the bag?" Adrian asked. Perky as a high school cheerleader.

Jack shrugged.

I laughed a bit too loudly. "Adrian! You can't imagine my surprise when Hogan—"

"Said we were lovers?"

"Geez, A.D.!" Hogan admonished.

"No, that's all right," I said. "It's just, as you can imagine, it's a HELL of a coincidence."

"Is it?" she said, smiling.

Hogan scrunched up his face, then said, "Johnny, I told A.D. you were coming over to get some of Mom's stuff."

There was a pause. "Right!" I said. "Come on, Jack. It's in here." And we went into my mom's bedroom. I started opening drawers and stuff—making noise. "Calm down," Jack whispered. My heart was doing somersaults. Things were not supposed to happen like this. I had imagined setting a trap: a quick blackjack to the back of the head or something. Jack reassured me. "It's okay, Doc. Now we just improvise."

"How's your head?" Adrian called from the next room.

I wasn't sure at first whom she was talking to. I stepped into the doorway of the bedroom and asked, "What?"

"Your head, John. How's your head?" She was holding Hogan's hands across the table.

"Fine." I replied. "That was months ago, you know."

"I know."

Hogan interrupted. "Flipped me out when he told me. Imagine you two guys knowing each other."

"Yeah," said Adrian smiling. "Imagine."

Was I the only one who could feel the malevolence of this small young woman? If Laura sometimes reminded me of a wild creature, Adrian felt like a predator: a poisonous snake coiling around my brother. It made me sick to see her touching his hands. I am not proud of my reaction: I decided it was time to leave. To let Hogan fend for himself. Try another day. But then Hogan, in his own dumb way, spoiled everything.

"So, Johnny. What did you mean about Adrian?"

"Ohhh, you know," I said stupidly.

"What'd he say, sweety?" asked Adrian.

"Something about you not being who I thought you were."

Adrian never stopped smiling. Her eyes swiveled back to me and held me fast. It felt like being caught in the gaze of a hungry tiger. "That's a very provocative thing to say, John."

"I—I just meant that, you know, the medical profession. It attracts certain, uhhh, sensitive, caring types." I was moving my hands too much. "And I just thought, well, I could be wrong, but— Well, Hogan is not, I mean to say . . ."

"Why, John! You're shaking," said Adrian.

I looked at her and saw the mirth in her eyes. I had seen that look before in the faces of many inmates at the Home. Men who had done horrible things to women. A boy who had beheaded his mother. A woman who used to dress up in men's clothes and rape little girls with— Stuff nobody wants to know about. I had seen that look once too often. It's why I left the Home. I swore then I would only deal with victims. I never again wanted to see eyes that fed off the terror in others. She sat there with her innocence and danger and touched my brother's hand and, suddenly, my horror transformed into anger.

"Ahh, fuck it. Jack?" I called. "Let's do it."

"Way ahead of you, Doc." He stepped into the room with his gun drawn.

"What is this!?" Hogan stood up.

"Sit down, Hogan!" I barked.

"Like hell I will."

Then Adrian whined, "Baby, don't let them hurt me!"

I think Hogan grew a few inches right on the spot. "I don't know who your friend is, Johnny. But he better settle down."

Jack wiggled his gun at Hogan. "Mister, you're the one who's got some settling to do. You were told to sit."

Maybe Jack's tone reminded him of an old coach for, all at once, he sat down.

"Oh, Hogan!" said Adrian.

He looked up at me with pure outrage. "And you said everything was fine."

I walked to the kitchen, reached inside a drawer, and pulled out the long knife my mom used to slice rack of lamb. Then I opened the freezer and took out a box of DoveBars. I tossed one onto Adrian's lap. "Have some."

Her whole face was stifling something powerful. It looked like her skull was squirming under her skin. Hogan watched horrified as she removed it from the box, undid the foil wrapper, and stuffed the whole bar into her mouth and swallowed. She placed the stick on the table. "Happy?" she said.

I tossed her a bar. "Have another," I said.

She repeated the ritual, only this time she ate it slowly. Savoring the bites.

Hogan said, "I'm sorry, baby. He's gone crazy."

"Big Man," Adrian replied through a mouth full of ice cream. She finished the bar and looked at me again, her eyes sleepy and lidded. I tossed another on her lap and she ripped it open and started taking big bites.

Jack began to say the Apostles' Creed.

"Look at her, Hogan," I said. "Sweet Adrian. Sweet-tooth Adrian. Is this the woman you fell in love with?"

"You're a bastard, Johnny! So she's got a sugar problem! So what!?"

I tossed another bar at her. "Eat it, Adrian," I said.

"Strawberry," she said, like a kid at a birthday party.

Hogan's dismay grew as the sticks started lining up on the table. She put them in a neat row. Her mouth had a ring of chocolate around it, like smeared lipstick after a kiss.

"I'll never forgive you," said Hogan, his face red with fury.

"Aw, shuttup, dickhead," said Adrian.

"Adrian! This man has a gun on me!" Hogan protested.

"It's not a sugar problem," I said. "Is it, Adrian?"

"Go fuck yourself," she said between bites. She swayed in place, rocking to a tune that played in her head.

"They like sugar, Gun. Don't you, Adrian? It's their drug."

"What is this shit?" Hogan hissed.

"Listen to the man, Junior. And learn," Jack added.

"Tell him where you're from, Adrian."

She started to giggle, like a doper after the weed hits. "I am FROM THE FUTURE!" she intoned in a mock-solemn voice that broke into sniffles.

"Tell him what you are."

She saluted Hogan from across the table. "I am a HO-LOCK!"

Hogan slammed his fist on the table. "Am I the only sane person in this room!?" He stood and held out his hands, like a priest saying, "Let us pray."

"Johnny," he began, "you've had a loss. I've had a loss. But I didn't go bananas. I went to work. I got back in the lineup. I didn't let my appearance go to hell. And I didn't start hanging around with gangsters." He nodded at Jack, who was still praying.

"He's a cop," I said.

Adrian slid down in her chair in a fit of laughter.

"It's stress, Johnny. Angie told me all about it."

Adrian gave a low growl, presumably at the mention of Hogan's wife.

"Now, I'm gonna ask you guys to leave here before this gets out of hand."

Jack stopped praying to point out, "He's stupider than you said."

Adrian was almost on the floor with laughter.

"All right, Officer!" Hogan fumed. "Show me your badge."

The rest happened in a flash. It was like watching Isiah Thomas in slow-motion on my VCR. The artistry of basketball is seldom visible in real time; it looks too easy. It was an ordinary play. Isiah is dribbling at the top of the key, his teammates are spreading out, clearing the lane. The opponents are shifting their attention between him and the man they're guarding. In slo-mo, I watch amazed as Isiah waits for the moment when each of the players turns his head away, simultaneously. Only then does he make his move. That instant of neglect was all he needed. Two points.

"Okay, smartass," Jack said, glaring at Hogan, then reached into his back pocket.

"The rope," I said, turning to Jack.

Immediately Adrian had an arm around my neck and the knife was skidding across the kitchen floor.

"I'll kill you!" said Jack, bracing his gun in both hands and aiming at Adrian's head. Hogan nailed him with a punch across the jaw.

As Jack slumped against the wall, Adrian gave a cheer of surprise. "Way to go, baby!"

Hogan allowed himself a swagger as he started looking around his feet. "Now where'd that gun go?"

"Hogan. Run," I said.

Adrian started licking my ear while Hogan got down on his hands and knees.

"Hogan," I pleaded, looking at Jack out cold, sitting against the wall. "Get the fuck out of here, you stupid fool!"

"Think you're so goddamned smart," he replied. "Trying to run my life. Telling me who I can sleep with. Rope! What were you guys gonna do, kidnap me?" Adrian was biting my ear now. I had a hard time breathing: her forefinger and thumb pinched my throat.

"Hogan!" I wailed.

Adrian began whispering in my ear. "Lucky for you, John, I can't kill you. But I sure can make you wish you never fucked with me. You find the gun, sweety?"

"Nope," Hogan answered. "Wait. There it is! Under the couch."

He reached his arm under and was hunting for it when Adrian did a stage whisper, the way drunks do, unaware of how loud they are. "You ought to know better, Doc. I'm a kamikaze. Dropped behind enemy lines. I've got nothing to lose." It was so unreal: Hogan hunched down, his butt up in the air, Jack sitting against the wall with his mouth open, a tiny girlish voice whispering obscenities in my ear. "You should've fucked me, Doc. *I'd* have given you a night to remember." She hissed in my ear. "I blew that horny toad Stewart and when I got him good and hard and squirting, I chomped off his little love muscle. You should have heard the noise he made."

Hogan stood up, holding the gun by the barrel. "What's that you're saying, A.D.?"

"Nothing, baby. Now why don't you just kill that naughty cop?"

"What?" said Hogan.

"DO I HAVE TO DO EVERYTHING MYSELF!?" Adrian yelled, then burst into a laugh that reminded me of Jack Nicholson.

"Hogan, GODDAMNIT, RUN!" I yelled.

Adrian jabbed me a good one in the ribs and I howled.

"Why don't you just zip it, Doc?"

Still leaning against the wall, Jack groaned.

"Adrian," Hogan began, "that's my brother. There's no need to flaunt your karate on him."

"He's a comedian, isn't he, Doc? You just plug him in and out come the jokes."

"What are you talking about, babe?"

"Shuttup, Hogan." She bit my ear again. "Pay attention, Doc. Maybe I can't kill you, but I can show you a few tricks you'd never think up in your wildest dreams." She rabbit-punched me on the leg and I howled again.

"Hey!" Hogan objected.

She caught me as I fell and held me like a bag of groceries. The pain was awful; it felt like she had reached inside my leg and pulled something out.

"Don't worry," she explained with annoyance. "It's not broken. That wouldn't have hurt as much." She giggled.

Hogan stepped forward, puzzled. "Adrian? This is my brother! Why are you doing this?"

"For the love of God, Hogan! Get out of here!" I managed to yell. Adrian slapped me hard and I flew against the wall.

"You shuttup, too!"

"Adrian!" Hogan was stuck in a dream he couldn't believe.

"You people!" she said. "You think you're SO tough. You don't know what tough is. Try going two weeks without a dream. Try sitting thirty years in a fetal position. Try not going crazy. Try listening to a race that talks and has nothing to say."

My leg and head were throbbing. "Hogan, please," I murmured.

She bent down and picked up my head by the hair. "We got your mudda, Doc. Now we're gonna squeeze your family. Maybe you better start porking your sweetheart so we can get this show on the road." She licked her lips and smiled. "I understand you got some nieces. They're gonna have some *real* memorable dreams. Or should I pay them a personal visit?"

She laughed in my face, the way drunks go nose to nose with you, invading your space, her breath warm and full of chocolate.

Then her head exploded.

When I opened my eyes Hogan was crying. The gun was shaking in his hand. He dropped it, stepped over Adrian's body and threw up in the sink. Then he ran water and splashed his face. Adrian lay spread out on the kitchen floor looking up at the ceiling. Black blood began to pool at the back of her head.

Hogan looked out the window and said, "She was talking about my kids."

He turned around and bent over to address her eye to eye. "Nobody fucks with my family."

I managed to sit up. My face and shirt were splattered with her blood.

Jack woke up, saw the body, and said, "Praise the Lord!"

Nineteen

It was four A.M. and I couldn't get clean. I tried all kinds of soap. I even went down to the rectory's laundry room—a dark place that smelled of wet lint—and held my hands in a bucket of roman cleanser. They turned pale white, puckered, and stunk. I was taking my third shower when I started to cry. I sat down and cried for about twenty minutes. It was like my whole body wanted to get rid of some poison, squeeze every last drop of it out. My sobs were like dry heaves. I didn't leave until the hot water ran out.

I couldn't sleep, so I put on my blue robe and checked in on Jack next door. He was snoring up a storm on his bed, his Bible cracked open on the table next to his alarm. His shoulder holster and gun hung on the knob of his bathroom door. It was a sparse room: a desk, lamp, chair, and bed. Something you might see in a college dorm, except for the portrait of Mary above his bed, looking anemic as usual. Jack slept on his back, posed like he was climbing a wall. He seemed none the worse for wear.

I wondered how Hogan slept that night.

The rectory was too quiet. I needed noise, conversation,

anything but the images that wouldn't leave my head. I didn't want to sleep and risk a dream that night. I went downstairs to the ample bar in the dining room—priests get all kinds of liquor as Christmas presents. Not very intelligent gift-giving, considering the rate of alcoholism in the clergy. I poured myself a Scotch on the rocks, pulled out Thomas Aquinas, and sat down to read. Theology is great for insomnia.

Strange cold abstractions about the Idea of God. The Prime Mover. The Uncaused Cause. The Source of Perfection. Who'd want to believe in a God like that? I had yet to grasp the fervency of Saul's faith. Sure, I supposed it offered him some comfort—and Jack's bad dreams had stopped since his "prayer life" had begun. But was it true? I had never been able to make that leap back into the fold once I had left it. I had abandoned a faith that regarded life as a crossword puzzle someone had already figured out and left us to fill in the blanks. The world grew more mysterious the older I got. I mean, *World War Three* hinges on whether or not I have sex with a woman I hardly know? What kind of world is this?

I was stirring the cubes in my glass with a finger when I heard a strange noise. I stood up. It was a rhythmic thump. Three thumps. Then silence. I put down my glass. Three thumps again. I walked out into the hall. I could tell the sound was coming from around the corner, near the back stairs. I forced myself to tiptoe toward the noise. It got louder. Thump, thump, thump. I picked up Saul's umbrella from its stand, sliding it up and out. I'm glad nobody saw me: limping down the corridor like some mad musketeer. Thump, thump, thump. I peered around the corner and saw the source of the sound. It was Imish. The dumb bird was banging his little head against the window.

"Don't do that!" I scolded. "You'll hurt—"

I scared the shit out of him. He flew straight up into the ceiling, cracked his head, and fell to the floor. I knelt down to pick him up and he gave me a dizzy, accusatory look. I rubbed his crown and gently smoothed his feathers. I could feel his little heart thundering away.

"Hey, take it easy, little guy. What's got you so riled?"

I stood up, still cradling him in my arms and rubbing his scarlet head.

Then I saw the face at the window.

I screamed and Imish did another beeline for the ceiling. I was limping down the hall as fast as I could when I realized the face looked awfully familiar.

I went back, turned the corner, saw Imish standing on the floor shaking his head. And Laura laughing at the window.

"Real funny!" I snapped.

She made hand motions, saying she couldn't hear me and to open the back door. When I let her in, she was still laughing. She followed me back to the living room. I took a long drink to steady myself and glared at her as she sat down on the couch. By now she was trying very hard not to laugh.

"If you could have seen the two of you! Imish shooting up into the ceiling, you hobbling away like Quasimodo!"

I replied with a sarcastic "Ha, ha, ha."

"I *am* sorry. I didn't mean to scare you."

I took another drink.

"So how'd it go?"

"Peachy," I said.

"Uh, why are you limping?"

I took another drink. "Golfing accident," I said.

She nodded. She inquired about everyone's health. She smoothed the coverlet on the couch. I noticed she was wearing a blue dress, her favorite color. We looked at opposite walls for a time. I freshened my drink. I turned on the cable news. The usual. Car bombs and diets. Nuclear waste and Cher. We watched about a half hour of it. Then I said I had to go to bed.

"Maybe I shouldn't have gotten you into this?" she asked.

"Maybe," I said with a false smile.

"I didn't choose you, John."

"So what?" I replied.

"And I didn't have to fall in love with you."

"You wanna know how it went?" I asked. "I'll tell you. My brother, who hasn't hurt a soul since his college football days, blew somebody's brains out today. I know; they were all over me. He killed a woman he loved a day ago. He's gotta live with that. And she wasn't even a woman. Christ! She wasn't even female! Then we had to wrap this— this thing that looked like a human being in Glad bags, stuff it in my mom's Oriental, and tie it with rope. It just fit in the back of Jack's van. I had to mop up the most foul-smelling mess I've ever seen and rinse everything real good so there were no traces. So I'm on my hands and knees scrubbing the brains off the wall with Lysol and I'm thinking, 'Mom's gonna kill me if she sees her kitchen like this.' Then I had to dig up one of my dad's old shirts 'cause mine was definitely not cleanable. We burned it.

"Jack and Hogan by now are great friends, talking about Africa and stuffing the DoveBars down the disposal—try that sometime. Then the problem of getting rid of the Miata arises. We sit around the kitchen, which by now smells like a hospital ward, and we discuss it. Do we dump it in the river? Bury it? Hide it in the garage till things blow over? Hogan says something brilliant about repainting it. The CAR, you see, was a real problem. Forget the BODY. We gotta do something about the car. So Hogan gets this brainstorm about a friend of his who does repo work and Jack puts the nix on that, saying 'No way, José. We can't involve outsiders.'"

I crushed a few ice cubes between my teeth and continued. "Finally, Hogan volunteers to drive it to her house. His alibi is that he sold it to her, she's got some complaint and drops it off for him to fix. He gives it a test drive and finds nothing wrong and returns it to her apartment. Sounds good, right? So we meet him there and pick him up and first thing he says is 'Christ, her glove box was full of M & M's!' So we're all laughing in the van with the body in the rug and Jack says he knows a great landfill out in Romeo that'll do the trick, but we better do it after dark. So we're all famished and we stop for Dunkin Donuts. Smart thinking. We're sitting on those stools three minutes and a scout car pulls up. Two cops sit down next to us at the counter. I'm shaking like a leaf and Jack mentions some of his harder cases and Hogan's telling us about the time in Africa when his Jeep got caught in a runoff flood. And he saved a black baby from drowning and ever since that day St. Christopher has had a 'special meaning' for him. Then they get to talking about God. And Jack asks about women priests. And Hogan says, 'The Bible's a good book, but there's too many names.' And I'm looking at the cops, shaking my head like, 'Do you *believe* these guys?' So we end up at the dump and we get stuck 'cause we're driving without lights and there's a soft shoulder. We manage to get the rug out and stuff it under some garbage when what should come down the road but a car. Two kids looking for a spot to make out.

"So we stand out there, freezing our buns off, Jack and Hogan going on and on about infant baptism, confirmation, Salvation by Deeds or Faith, and this old Ford Galaxy is creaking and bouncing on its springs. And I swear to God that Hogan sells Jack a Mazda 626. Right there in the land-fill.

"At last the young lovers leave and by now Hogan's sneezing up a storm. We all decide we better 'lie low' for a while. Hogan's line. Jack's up for another hour hosing down the van. Literally hosing it down in the garage. I end up reading Aquinas and drinking Jameson's. That's where you came in. That's the kind of day I had."

Laura said nothing for a long while. I gave a huge yawn and leaned my head against the back of the chair. I must have dozed off, for the next thing I knew she was taking the glass from my hand. She led me upstairs to my room, locked the door, got me undressed, and took me to bed.

We were making love when I saw Imish perched on the curtains. Every time I looked at him he was looking at us. I got the impression that he didn't approve, that he was standing watch over me. Usually he was very jumpy, flit-ting about the room. But now he was silent and still as a stuffed bird.

Twenty

We were lounging on the bed, spent from sex, our bodies purring. Laura's sweet scent (not a metaphor) was heavy in the air. It was one of the surprises of her body: all the juices tasted sweet. She was not an accomplished lover, but she had a curiosity, an eagerness and an eloquence with touch, as if she had thoroughly imagined every move. She lay on her back, her head at the foot of the bed propped up by a pillow, her brown hair strewn about her face. Her body was wonderful: the color of dark sand, smooth and hairless, full of burnished dips and mounds, rising and falling like a desert rippled by waves. The squares of her nipples seemed very natural now. My eyes traced them lazily with that odd detachment you feel when sated, amazed that you have no hunger for something so beautiful. I had expected more anatomical surprises than I found. The most noticeable was the charming absence of a belly button. Her hand lay on my leg, flicking the hairs back and forth. We kept passing each other silly smiles that bordered on laughter. I was sitting up, smoking. Imish was flying figure eights above us.

"Your body's so different," she said.

I had to laugh at that.

"It is!" she said. "The way your hair grows in one direction, like a cornfield." She let her hand run down to my feet. "And your toes are so hard."

"Calluses," I said.

"You smell salty." She breathed deep and exhaled. "And I love the way your—"

"Don't!" I protested weakly. "You'll kill me."

"All those veins and ridges, and *this* . . . like a little toadstool." She held it and looked at me. "It's much bigger in the Memory Films."

I chuckled. "I bet."

"I liked it in me."

I closed my eyes and groaned. It almost hurt to remember the pleasure.

"No more?" she asked, amused and disappointed.

"Not tonight," I sighed.

"Why do you call it 'fucking'?"

I giggled. "Geez, I don't know. You want me to guess?" "Sure."

"Onomatopoeia. The sound of it. The tongue-clicking noise—like something plunking into water."

She nodded. "It's a wonderful sound."

Imish was circling the room now, his wings making tiny helicopter sounds.

"What's his problem?" I asked.

"Maybe he's happy," she answered.

We watched him for a minute. If you lived in Saul's rectory for a few weeks, you got used to the bird being around, flitting in and out of rooms, fetching smokes, lighting on your shoulder while you read. There was something homely and reassuring about his presence, a little bit of strangeness that kept at bay the greater strangeness of the world around us.

"So how long have you known Saul?"

"Since I was five."

"How could that be?" I wondered.

"He never told you?"

I shook my head.

She smiled, remembering. "He was my imaginary friend. One morning I woke up and he was there. I couldn't see him, but his voice was in my head. It felt like a candle between my ears. This warm little voice that called me 'Princess.'

" 'Morning, Princess. What's cookin'?'

"I thought I was dreaming. I didn't answer him right away.

" 'Are you the Boogie Man?' I said. It was something they used to threaten me with. 'You better be good. Or we're gonna go get the Boogie Man.' They didn't explain. But it scared me. Which I suppose was the point.

" 'Nyahhh,' he laughed. 'I'm just a man.'

" 'What's a man?' I asked.

" 'You don't know nothing, do ya, Princess? They got you on ice, don't they?'

" 'What's ice?' I asked."

Laura closed her eyes and smiled as the memories tumbled out.

"He played with me. Taught me songs and rhymes. Made me laugh. He taught me the capitals, the alphabet; he taught me to read. Every morning he'd wake me up singing 'Oh, What a Beautiful Morning.'

"Sometimes he'd leave me for hours. 'Gotta case the joint, kid. See what the Marshmallows are up to.' That's what he called Them: 'Marshmallows.' They knew he was there. They could hear him in my head. But when he knew they were listening, he'd say, 'Take a hike, Whitey!' And if they didn't leave he'd start saying the rosary. Boy, that would clear them out fast!

"He used to say, 'If they bug ya, Princess, say your prayers.' He said prayer was the only thing that kept him from going loony. He said prayers are like electrical current to the Holock. For some reason they jam the connection. I didn't even know what prayer was. The Memory Films never show it. All they can get is, like, the blueprint of a building. The rough sketch. The whole idea of religion— it's like a ballgame they can't get tickets to. They have to stand outside the stadium, listening to the roar of the crowd, smelling the hotdogs, imagining the game, the rules, the uniforms. It's a whole portion of your reality they can't record. That's probably why you feel safe here in the rectory, with Saul, beyond the fact that he petrifies them. Spirituality's like a wall they can't penetrate. He tried to teach me. But I couldn't 'get' it. All that talk about God and Mary and Jesus—it sounded like the Boogie Man to me. But that was before he came out of Dream Lock and started reading theology. He makes more sense now."

"What's Dream Lock?" I asked.

"Saul had a young Filipino chauffeur who did everything for him. A very devout Catholic. One day he called in sick. He said he hadn't slept for days; he was having 'evil' dreams. Saul went to take him to the hospital and got a shock: his hair had turned completely white. The doctors couldn't explain it. But the chauffeur told him of a native superstition about a race of people who lived in Dreamland. Saul stayed at his side for days until he woke up screaming from a nightmare. He died of a stroke. It shook Saul, as you can imagine.

"This was during the Cold War, right after the bomb, and everybody was paranoid about the Soviets. So Saul got this idea of using dreams as long-range weapons to infiltrate and destroy your enemies. He was a real patriot, you see. He got a government grant. He went to Tibet and studied Samadhi meditation with Buddhist monks. He practiced shamanism with Mexican Indians. He did Active Imagination with Von Franz in Switzerland. Then he built what he called a 'REM machine' that would induce alpha waves at an intense level."

Laura continued tracing circles on my belly. "There was an accident at his research lab in New Jersey. One of his assistants was electrocuted. I forget her name. They closed Saul down. After the Incident he couldn't get backing. They didn't believe in him. And they didn't see the applications; they won't for years. In the next ten years he lost most of his fortune on dream research.

"Finally, he used himself as a guinea pig. I know—it sounds like a bad science-fiction movie. He put himself on the REM machine and dreamed himself into the Holock's future. Somebody found him in his workshop in a coma. He hadn't eaten for a week. He stayed in the hospital for two years. Nobody visited him. When he finally woke up, he was kept under observation for weeks. They wouldn't release him. He had to pay them off, build a new wing onto their hospital before they'd let him go."

"He was with you for two years?"

"Yup. He was locked in a dream for two days, then he woke up—inside the dream. That killed the Holock who was sharing it. 'There's only one way to kill a Holock,' he used to say. 'Touching pesters them. Prayers scare them shitless. But you really want to nail them—you pull the plug. You wake up before they can get out of your dream— right in the middle of it—and you fucking send them into a seizure!' " She mimicked Saul making fish mouths; blowing smoke rings, and we laughed.

"After that, Saul was this uprooted consciousness floating around their world. He said he was terrified for a day. Then he started saying the prayers his assistant used to recite all the time. He found out he could scare the Holock. That was his hobby: haunting them. Eavesdropping. Watching their Memory Films. Sharing dreams. He was their resident ghost, interrupting their picture talk, putting pink elephants in their heads to freak them out. 'Roastin' Marshmallows,' he called it."

I told her she did a fair Saul imitation.

"You have a voice inside your head for two years, you don't forget it. But one day his voice started to get fainter. He tried to prepare me. 'I think I'm waking up, Princess. I can feel I gotta boner.'

"I begged him to stay. He said he'd dream about me. He said we'd meet again when I got bigger. You know, something you'd tell a child."

Looking at her eyes, I expected her to cry, but, evidently, this sorrow was too deep for tears.

"One morning he wasn't there," she continued. "For months I waited for his friendly voice between my ears. It never came. I thought I was lonely before, but I didn't know what I was missing. After Saul, I grew up in a very empty place. When they told me they were going to send me back, they made me promise to kill Saul. I told them I would.

"As soon as I got well, I tracked him down. I had a knife. I was going to make him pay for leaving me. But when I saw him, he said 'Princess! I've been expecting ya!' I couldn't do it. He was this little man with this crazy red bird perched on his bald head—nothing like I imagined him to be. It made me laugh. I'd forgotten how good it felt to laugh."

Every moment I spent with her made Laura's loneliness

clearer and clearer. I ached for her and the life she had spent. Or lost.

"Touch me," I whispered. "Here. And here."

She came to me, smiling.

When I woke up, she was gone. I found three twenties and a ten in the ashtray by my bed.

Twenty-one

We had three beautiful weeks. Even though this was Detroit in March—with its notorious gray pall, humid chill, and tiny sooty icebergs on every corner—nothing could have spoiled those weeks; we were marooned in happiness. Though I cannot quote anything but wisps of conversation, coos of pleasure and surprise, I distinctly recall our breath frosting before us as we walked arm in arm. And later, coming in from the cold, the way her chin and cheeks glowed like three red juggling balls, hanging in the air, in a frozen moment of time. It sounds so boring. We shopped, made love, ate out, made love, looked at antiques, and made love. Nights we'd walk under the quilted sky, through the muffled quiet of new snow, relishing an inward silence, as if all the important things had already been said. I even lost track of my beloved Pistons, and friends were stunned that I couldn't recite my usual stats and commentary. Our lives had shrunk into a private orbit. The pitiful world creaked on around us like a grandfather clock in the corner, unnoticed and unnecessary.

My memories of that brief interlude are hazy but warm.

Talking about them seems a betrayal, for they simply don't translate. Happiness cannot be described, merely connoted, like neutrinos, whose existence can only be verified by the trace patterns they leave in a particle pool. It's an insular state accessible only by clichés, a hobby that mystifies the unsmitten, a joke without a punch line. That's why it appears so dull to the outsider. How often have you wondered, What on earth do they see in each other? The silliness of love is the one consolation for the excluded. It is a secret place not open to voyeurs—you had to be there.

I've mentioned the last time we made love. The thunderstorm. The fear in her eyes. The strangeness between us. We laid together and counted the seconds between the flashes of lightning and the thunder.

"I have lied to you," she said.

"I know," I replied.

"Many times," she said.

I found this sudden candor touching. Like everything else in those charmed days, it seemed to deepen and amplify our love. "It doesn't matter."

"I'm going to have a baby," she whispered.

"I thought so. Boy or girl?"

"Shhhh," she said, rubbing my belly.

Far away: the thunder. Getting closer.

"There's one question I've been meaning to ask," I said, the way young lovers open doors, expecting ever new delights. We looked at each other: outlines of shadow in a dark room.

"Your questions," she sighed.

"When did you fall in love with me?" I asked, smiling, my body humming in the afterglow of our sex.

"Oh, John . . ." She looked away.

"The Truth," I said. I could feel her marshaling her strength. Her breathing quickened.

"The truth is . . . I wanted a baby."

I took this in, examined it like a sore tooth, until I arrived at the worst possible implication. I offered it to her, like something outrageous and unfounded, knowing she had to refute it.

"I could have been Dr. Stewart?" I asked, incredulous.

She nodded. "We thought you were. We knew it was a shrink. We knew about genes, blood type. We even knew what you looked like. But it's a big world."

I noticed she was saying *We.* She had always been scrupulous to avoid it, to call the Holock "Them." Not now. We seemed to pull away from each other, like a splitting amoeba. But it didn't feel like we were moving apart; it felt like we were growing back into ourselves.

She continued. "The problem was the name. The girl was adopted, you see."

I translated that into our time frame: she will be adopted. "What will you do with the baby?"

"Raise it. If it's a boy, they'll try to breed us. When he comes of age."

"If it's a girl?"

"Then we've won, haven't we?" She didn't mean "Us."

"You never intended to stay?" I asked, amazed.

"I don't belong here." Then she astounded me. "They need me, you see. Whatever else they've done, there's that."

I felt gutted, but you couldn't have told it from my voice. "The Truth, Laura." I touched her breast.

"Don't," she said, brushing away my hand.

"When did you fall in love with me?" I insisted.

She sat up in bed. Her body pale in the flashing light. Rivulets of shadow ran down her back like liquid tattoos. "You are a good man. I respect your intelligence, your sensitivity. We've had a wonderful five hundred hours."

It was rather shocking when she put it like that. I hadn't

been counting. Five hundred hours over the course of our months together. That's about three weeks. I probably spent less time with her than with most of my friends.

I reached up and felt the soft hollow of her back. "That's not an answer."

"John, you must know. I never intended to hurt you."

"I know."

Then she said it. "I have never loved you. It's not something I've learned to do."

I knew then, as I never knew before: she wasn't human.

Twenty-two

The next day I strode into Saul's room. He was saying the rosary with Jack. I sat down and waited for a break. Finally they both looked at me.

"What, Doc?" asked Jack.

I took my time before answering. "What is it, exactly, that you do, Saul? I mean, besides funding alien baby rings, indoctrinating people stressed out by guilt, and magic tricks with eggs. I mean, for a guy with enough funds to finance a lot of meals for the hungry, and enough faith to move mountains, how come I never actually SEE you DOING anything? Isn't there something in the Bible about no true faith without DEEDS? I seem to remember that."

"Geez," Saul said. "Who peed in your Wheaties?"

"And another thing," I said, gearing up. "Am I the only person in this cozy little sanctuary who's just a tad worried about what will happen if the police ever find a certain body in a certain dump?"

Jack fielded that one. "Do you have any idea how many missing-person reports they get a year? Thousands. We file more cases than we solve. That's just a fact of life."

I thought of all the parents of missing children. All the children with missing parents. That human phrase: I miss you. All the people who had passed through my office. All these hearts orbiting a vacuum, locked into a circle of hope and despair, continually reminded of what they've never had, never forgotten. Forever governed by the gravity of something missing.

"You set me up, didn't you, Saul?"

Saul smirked. "You think so?"

"All that Enemy shit. A Revolution-in-Consciousness crap."

He got up off his knees, lit a cigarette, and blew a smoke ring. "That was true."

"I bet it was. Hell, you're not working against the Holock. You're working *for* them."

Saul flicked his ash onto the floor and sat down. "Doc, you know what a Holock is? It's someone who's scared shitless all the time, who trusts no one. Someone who can look at something beautiful and not understand, who can listen to Beethoven and not GET IT. You hear what I'm saying? They don't have love, they don't have pleasure, touching makes their skin crawl. All they got is a Disneyland called 'dreams.' A place they can get away to where people hate and love and hope and wonder and do things differently every moment. A place where everybody is separate, everybody's different, everybody's a stranger. And everybody has their own little room inside themselves. With doors. So we can choose to let people in or not. They haven't got doors. Everybody is in everybody's head all the time. Think about that. No privacy. No secrets. No fantasy."

He took a deep breath. "All they got is Memory Films. You know what THOSE are like? Think about the best memory you've ever had. Everybody's got one. It's the best movie you've ever seen: a masterpiece. A five-hankie. Boffo Oscar stuff! The Holock will sit through a lifetime of memories, they'll put up with all the meals, the laundry, the toilets, and the traffic jams—just to find that one sacred memory. That one treasure that everybody carries inside without knowing it. They'll latch onto that and they'll play it. Over and over and over."

Saul lit another smoke. "I used to love to scare them. Boy, I was a real pest. But after a year or so, it wasn't fun anymore. They were *always* terrified; they didn't need me for that. Then, one day, I shared a dream with a Holock. A nightmare, really. Some poor little kid being chased down a road by a snake. And it dawned on me—that's what *I* do. That's what I've been doing for a year! I'd become their nightmare. And I enjoyed it. I was praying and scaring them and all the time I'm feeling like a Ghostbuster, a white knight chasing down dragons, punishing the wicked in the name of God. I was angry at what they'd done to my chauffeur. I was furious at what they'd done to Laura. And then I realized that I was no better than the Holock. I was doing to them what they do to us.

"The more I got to know 'em, the less they seemed like monsters. I couldn't hate 'em. They're the saddest creatures you can imagine. They can't sing, can't dance. They can't even smell a rose! All they got are these machines that open a door to a world they can never possess, or understand. A world they can only dream about."

For a moment I saw pain in his eyes. It appeared and disappeared, like a breaching fish. But I had been trained to appreciate such glimpses. And in that brief moment I caught a vision of the man behind the character. Saul's great secret was his almost unbearable guilt. What for? I wondered.

"We made them, you know," he concluded. "The Holock."

I wasn't buying it. "You felt sorry for them? So you decided to give them a little gift? A little baby they could feed off of. A little race of dreamers for them to suck on!"

Jack protested. "That's a helluva thing to say, John!"

"Ask him yourself," I spat. "Ask him if he wanted Laura pregnant!"

"I did," Saul confessed. "I'll tell you what I had in mind. Laura and you would have a daughter here. I thought the odds favored that. No World War Three. The Holock disappear as if they never existed. Which they won't. Everybody remembers their dreams."

"What?" I said.

"Didn't I tell ya? That's one of the fringe benefits. No more Dream Eaters, no more forgotten dreams."

"Wow!" Jack said.

"But I hadn't counted on the princess wanting to go back to them. She's changed a lot since I knew her."

"That's a pretty fucking big loophole!" I yelled. "What's the matter? Your clairvoyance slipping? Bullshit! You're a matchmaker. A collaborator!"

"You ain't got the Big Picture yet, Doc." He reached in a drawer and pulled out a spool of thread. "Imish?" he called. "Where'd I put that damn needle?"

There were noises in the kitchen. Then the cardinal flew out, landed on Saul's lap, and dropped a needle into his palm. "No," he said. "You already had your juice." Saul threaded the needle slowly, squinting with one eye. Then he looked at me. "Lemme show you something."

"Another trick?" I asked.

"Nahh, something Italian."

"I don't want—"

"Com'ere, com'ere, com'ere."

I sighed, got up, and walked across the room.

"Hold out your hand like this," he instructed. "Now make a fist." He held the needle at the end of a foot of thread, like he was showing me a necklace. With a flourish, he dangled it over the back of my hand. Then it began to move. It made one circle, then it swung back and forth like a pendulum. Then it stopped dead, as if my hand had magnetized it.

"What's it mean?" Jack asked.

Saul wrapped up the needle and thread, tossed it on the table beside him, and rubbed his jaw. "You know, I'm not sure."

"Nice little sideshow," I snickered.

"I mean, it could mean a couple things."

"Such as?"

"Laura's got twins."

"Jesus," I said. Then it hit me. "But she said *baby*. Singular. But how could she know?"

"She could know," was all Saul would say. "That's funny. The needle says you've got two kids. A boy and a girl."

I shuddered. Oh God. The best of all possible worlds. They're gonna breed them!

Saul put his hand over his head. He seemed troubled by this turn of events. I was practically beside myself.

"Come on, Saul! Make some magic! Say a prayer! DO SOMETHING, you stupid meddling squirt!"

His face was full of questions.

"I'll talk to her!" I said. "That's it! I'll talk to her." I was in my "long-shot" mode. You miss thirty free throws and, by God, you're Due. "I love her. That's got to mean something! Maybe I can get her to stay."

Saul looked up at me sadly. "You're too late, kiddo."

"Too late?" How many times had I heard that?

"They come for her tonight."

Jack whistled and I reeled on my feet.

"You mean she's . . ."

"She told you: one year."

I did a few clumsy mental calculations. I started pacing, weird thoughts ripping through my mind. She didn't say good-bye. She never loved me. World War Three. I have a son. I have a daughter. The image of the Dream Boy I met in Hart Plaza. Begging me. Pleading. "I don't want to be anybody. Not there." I swallowed. "Why you want to touch a woman like *that?*" he'd said. I knew what he meant now.

"Where?" I said. "Where'd she go?"

"It doesn't matter, Doc. You won't change her mind. *I* couldn't."

"Where is she, Saul?"

"You're wasting your time. What's done is done." His face looked defeated. "All we can do is pray."

"I don't believe that! Tell me!"

"There's no point."

I slammed my fist into his chair. And started walking around in circles. I noticed Imish watching me from the lampshade, warming his little behind on the bulb.

"IMISH!" I yelled. "You know, don't you!?" I held out my finger. He flew to it and roosted. I held him up to my face and smiled. "You're a smart bird aren't you, Imish? You know where Laura went, don't you?"

He nodded vigorously.

I looked at Saul and Jack. They knelt together. Saul crossed himself and took up his blue rosary. "The Third Sorrowful Mystery. Jesus is crowned with thorns . . ."

"Come on, pretty bird," I said. "Let's find her!"

We headed south down the Lodge freeway in Saul's

black Lincoln, me driving like a maniac and Imish clinging to the coffee cup on the dash like a Saint Christopher statuette. I promised him a gallon of Florida's finest if he led me to her. And he directed me with whistles and little leans to the right or left. Though I had to wonder when we started over the Ambassador bridge to Canada. We crossed the river at sunset, a purple April sky spread out above us. I turned on the radio, which Imish seemed to enjoy: he bobbed up and down to the beat. As we were approaching customs I realized that bringing a bird into a foreign country was probably taboo. Imish clearly resented my solution.

"Have you anything to declare?" asked a pimply young man.

I thought: I'm a dad. There's a magical bird in the glove box. I'm in love with an alien and I'm trying to stop World War Three.

"No, sir," I answered.

We were miles outside of Windsor when I began to think Imish was pissed at me about the glove box. It was cramped in there, and I had to scrunch him up against what looked like a pink telephone. "Are you sure?" I kept asking him. "This is the way?" He kept nodding. I will say this: that damn bird never lied to me. (I've trusted birds ever since.) We passed a sign, and something clicked. Something about a point. Saul had said "There's no point." Point. A mile later I saw a sign: "Pointe Peele, five km." Pointe Peele! That's where Dr. Stewart found her!

"Oh, Imish, you beautiful bird! I could kiss you!"

He looked at me with disdain.

I roared down the point, a thin V-shaped peninsula that stretches a few miles into Lake Erie. I came to a car parked haphazardly off the road. I parked and ran toward the shore. It was cold. The waves got louder as I stumbled through the underbrush. I could have used a flashlight, for when I got to the sand it was black as pitch. The only light was from the stars. When my eyes adjusted to the dark, I looked up and down the beach. I saw a pale figure about a hundred yards away, toward the tip of the point.

I could hear Imish flying beside me as I ran.

She was naked. And her skin seemed to pick up all the light of that night. She looked as white as a statue. "Laura!" I called.

I thought I saw her turn and look back over her shoulder.

"It's me!" I yelled, stopping to catch my breath. For a moment I thought she was walking back. But then I saw her body begin to disappear from the toes up, like she was pulling on a black dress. She was stepping into the water.

"Laura!" I screamed, running.

When I got to where she had entered the lake all I could see was her head bobbing above the black mirror that reflected the sky.

"Don't do it!" I yelled.

She turned around: her white face was the brightest thing in the night.

"I still love you!" I called.

I wanted to say so much, but I was out of breath. We looked at one another for the longest time. Imish lighted on my shoulder. I did not see it, but I felt as if she were smiling at me. Hope thundered in my chest.

I waded out into the black lake and Imish flew off. The water was so cold it took my breath away. It rose with my steps up to my waist, then shoulders. To this day, knowing how I felt about water, I'm amazed I made it that far. I stopped when I felt it lapping on my chin, my body numbing from the chill.

Finally, I yelled: "Laura!?" A question and a plea.

And her deep voice answered, strangely clear above the

crash of the breakers, in the way she had of always surprising me, always offering unheard-of alternatives, unconceived possibilities, unexpected choices.

"Come," she called.

I was stunned, overjoyed that she was even talking to me. Part of me wanted to hold her, keep her in my arms, never let her go, stay with her at all costs. I imagined for a moment this was a test—a test of how far I would go for her. Well, if it took that—so be it. I would trust her. Isn't that what love is? I'd take the plunge, dive into the surf. I'd let her take me to the tube. I'd convince her, protect her, change her; and we'd change the future together. Anyway, life with her and the Holock couldn't be any worse than life without her and alone. I loved her, dammit! I loved her. Anything was possible.

The other part of me looked on from a distance in disbelief—as if I had left it back on the shore. This was the woman I'd given myself to totally, sparing nothing. She couldn't leave. Didn't she know it would tear me in two? She wouldn't do that to me. I didn't believe her when she said she didn't love me. How could that be? And even if it were true—so what? She did a good enough imitation of love—that was a start. Time would take care of the rest. We had a child. And the chance for a life together after two lives spent mostly alone. How could she give up what we had for a future with the Holock? She couldn't. I loved her, dammit! I loved her. It wasn't possible.

I could almost feel her waiting for the right choice. The right words. The right promises. I had no idea what they were, so I laughed.

"I can't swim!" I called.

"I know," she replied and disappeared.

Twenty-three

I didn't sleep that night. I watched Imish snoozing on the rim of the vanilla lampshade, curling his beak down into his chest, his little body expanding and contracting like a red balloon. I kept expecting his claws to lose their grip, so that he'd topple down onto the mahogany desk with a soft *plut.* I figured it was inevitable. I worked out the odds in my head; I gave it a lot of thought. It never happened. By morning, the walls were closing in on me and I needed to talk. It took a lot of persuading, but I finally got Saul to leave the rectory for a walk. You'd have thought I was asking him to leap off a cliff, the way he paused at the top of the steps and blinked his eyes, taking deep breaths, like a man poised on the high board above a pool.

I touched him on the arm. "What is it, Saul?"

He looked at the dingy street, the brown and gray warehouses, the gang graffiti and the broken windows as if he were seeing something strange and wonderful. "I don't get out much," was all he'd say.

"In a lovely neighborhood like *this?*" I asked with a smile.

I took hold of his elbow and led him down the stairs, which he took one at a time, giving little grunts of anxiety after each one. I could feel the heat from his body, coming through his black mackintosh. We took little steps down the walk to the street. He flinched once, when a mail truck drove by.

"Jesus. Why are you so jumpy?"

He shrugged and wiped the perspiration off his upper lip with the back of his hand. It took me awhile to get it. "When's the last time you left the rectory?"

"May," he answered. "The twenty-eighth." He checked his golden watch. "Nineteen sixty-three."

It was easier after that. His stride lengthened. He even whistled a little. It was a blustery spring day, but as I told him of my trip to Pointe Peele the night before, the wind seemed to die down to nothing. So that by the end of the story all we could hear was the humming freeway traffic.

Then I told him I wanted to kill Laura.

We had stopped at a corner and I recited a long speech that I had rehearsed all night. I don't remember what I said. I wonder what anyone watching us might have made of the scene. A tall man with bags under his eyes, longish hair sticking up at weird angles, looking like he'd slept in his rumpled gray sweater and jeans, waving his arms, stamping his feet, raising his voice, talking down to some bald shrimp in a black coat: Mutt and Jeff. They might have picked up phrases like "World War Three!", "The HOLOCK can't win!", "Think of it as a psychic aBORtion!", "She LIED to me!" They must have concluded that we were two of those rejected souls who seemed to appear magically in the eighties, to wander the streets of urban America raving and wailing for Justice. Funny: I don't remember the homeless in the sixties or seventies. They seemed to arrive with the yuppies.

After my speech we were quiet a long time. I felt shy, like a man who has revealed too much of himself to a stranger.

"I thought you were a pacifist."

"No," I replied. "I'm a coward."

He looked at my toes. "You ever kill anyone?"

"No," I said evenly. If he doubted I could do it, he was wrong.

"Jack says you think it gets easier after you've popped your cherry—but it doesn't." He sighed. "I'm thinking how hard it must be to kill someone you love."

I saw a deep sadness in his eyes after he said that: another clue about his hidden guilt. "I don't love her," I said, twisting my mouth and shaking my head at such a ridiculous suggestion.

Saul looked at me. "You did twelve hours ago."

Just thinking about it made me wince, at how she had betrayed me, at how stupid I'd been. It would take a lot of rage before that wound would scab. And I could feel it spreading: an icy fury that set my teeth and put a fierce hum in my brain. Rage is usually such an ugly emotion; I always feel soiled afterward. But I felt clean, like I was shedding some skin, or rinsing off some scum. I'd forgotten how satisfying righteous rage can be, and I was a bit appalled by how resolved I was about it. Maybe contemplating killing was easier after watching Adrian die. Maybe I was still reeling from the night before, when my last hopes ran into a brick wall. But in the last twelve hours Laura had transformed from a woman I adored and desired into a sly predator, a poisonous creature who had conned me out of my deepest self, who, for that matter, threatened everyone alive. If anyone deserved to die, she did. So I loved her. So what? So fucking what?

"I've changed," I said.

Saul turned away from me then to look out over the skyline. A Great Lakes freighter was plowing down the Detroit River, its flags whipping in the wind. "She was just a kid," he said. "How'd they turn her into . . . that?" Saul took out a handkerchief and honked. When he turned I could see he'd been crying.

"I'll help," he said, shoving his lower lip up under his nose.

I could see in his face how much that decision cost him. I gave him a big hug. "It's the right thing, Saul."

"That's what I'm afraid of," he said into my shoulder.

We smoked our cigarettes for a moment, then headed back to the rectory. After a while I noticed he was frowning at his feet.

"What's the matter now?" I asked.

Saul looked up at me. "I take it you were thinking about using Dream Lock?"

"Of course." I figured if Saul could visit Laura in the future for two years, why couldn't I make a quick pit stop?

"That's a problem. I'm not sure where the REM machine is."

It felt like someone had dropped a cinder block on me. "Don't do this to me, Saul."

"That was years ago." He shrugged.

"Oh, geez," I groaned.

Saul began to tap a Camel on the back of his hand. "Lemme get a hold of Lenny. I think he's in Chicago." He winked and made a gun-cocking noise out of the corner of his mouth. "He owes me."

"He's got the REM machine?"

"Nyahh, but he might know where it is." He lit his cigarette with a lighter and was quiet. "Doc," he said, interrupting his thoughts. "I gotta warn you about something."

He took a deep breath. "Two things you gotta know about Dream Lock."

"Yeah?"

"What do you want first: the good news or the bad?"

"The good," I decided.

"It fucks you up with Time." He paused a moment. "It's hard to explain. Let me put it this way. Consensual Reality is something you take for granted—it's very comforting, very pleasant." He smiled ruefully. "I miss it a lot. But it's all rooted in Cause and Effect."

"Spit it out, Saul."

"Well, you kinda get untracked. Like, sometimes your memories seem a lot more real than what's happening two feet in front of your face. Sometimes I know what's gonna happen before it does. Like, you're gonna say 'Oh, fuck me' in about ten seconds. It's like once you step out of the River of Time, you can't really step back in. It's like, like . . ."

"Like what?" I said, eager to get on with it.

"Like this," he called from the porch of the rectory, about fifty yards ahead of me.

I looked down and saw his lit cigarette rolling on the sidewalk at my feet. "Oh, fuck me," I said. And felt creepier than I'd ever felt in my life. It's one thing to hear a prediction. It's another thing to act it out spontaneously. Now I understood why Saul didn't go out much. Didn't drive a car. Didn't much go anywhere. So *that's* how he did the egg trick, I thought. When I reached the porch he was sitting on the top step. I asked, "Did you have any control over that?"

"That's a cause-and-effect question, Doc. Doesn't really apply." He lit another Camel. "Long as I'm in the rectory, the 'Blip' is localized. It's the God Stuff. Seems to rein it in."

"Oh, Jesus." I sat down next to him. "Where did you go?"

"Hard to say. Could have been anywhen. I wasn't gone long, was I?"

"Barely a second," I replied.

"That was a short one. 'Course, it doesn't matter," he giggled. "I could have lived a decade in that moment."

"How'd you know it was going to happen?" I asked.

"I get flashes. I remembered it happening about three years from now. Fucks up your tenses." He smiled.

I shook my head. "I'd go nuts."

"That's something to consider." He nodded.

"So you know the future?"

"No, I live in it. I remember the present. I anticipate the past."

"Oh God." I cradled my face in my hands.

"Don't sweat it, Doc. In a few years you'll get used to it."

"I'll get used to it? What if I wanna get married? Have kids?"

"Not a good idea," he said, shaking his head. "You'll see their deaths. You won't be able to change it. Kinda puts a damper on things."

"You mean you can't change the future?" I asked.

"Not until it's the past."

"Why not? Isn't that what the Holock were trying to do with Laura's kid?"

"Not exactly. That's their past. You can change the past." When Saul noted the vacancy in my face, he said, "Look." He pointed to a tireless rusted hulk sitting on its hubs at the curb. "See that? Everyone's got this picture of Time in their heads. They think it's a tree."

I looked at him blankly. "A tree." Then I saw what he meant. Next to the wreck was a decrepit elm tree on the corner. Its brittle branches hung bare, ready to snap at any second. It was one of the few left standing after the Dutch elm disease epidemic ravaged the country in the sixties. There hasn't been a decent shady street in Detroit since.

"Yeah," he continued. "The present is the trunk and the future is all these probability branches shooting off in different directions. Understand?" I nodded. "They got it upside down. There are infinite pasts but only one future. One solid trunk."

I was juggling tenses, hunches. "You mean I could go back and stop Oswald from killing Kennedy?"

"Maybe. But then, he might not be elected president. Nixon might have beat him."

"What?" God, I felt stupid.

"Ripples," he said. "You change time and the changes go every which way. The past's changed, the future's changed. You drop a stone in a pond, the ripples go every way, the ramifications of change are infinite. The butterfly effect, right?"

"Huh?"

"Jesus, don't you know anything about science?" He shook his head. "Awww, forget it. All you gotta know is humans don't know shit about Time. It's not a constant, like the speed of light. It's fluid. A river full of tides, and twists and eddies and—" He stopped when he saw my face.

"I'm getting a headache," I admitted.

"Try living with it every minute. Now that's a headache. You wouldn't *believe* the shit I have to keep track of. You wanna know why you never see me 'DOING' anything? That's why. My hands are tied."

"It doesn't make sense."

"Who said it has to—?" Suddenly, Saul slapped his cheek with one hand. "Oh shit! You better sit down."

"I am sitting."

He looked at me as if I weren't there. "Oh shit!"

"What?" I stood up, looking around. I felt like a sniper had us locked in his crosshairs. "What?!!"

"I forgot to tell you the bad news," he said.

"Yeah?" I asked.

"The bad news is: you may not wake up."

That's when I fell down the steps.

As Saul gave me a hand, he said, "I shouldn't have warned you. It never helps."

Twenty-four

The trip to Chicago to see his friend Lenny was, to say the least, nerve-racking. I had to drive, of course; we couldn't risk Saul dematerializing at sixty-five miles per hour. But, even with that precaution, nothing could have prepared me for the shock of losing a passenger in mid-conversation. We were just outside of Detroit, and Blip: he was gone. For a moment I continued talking to him; I wasn't clear on the protocol of the matter. Twenty minutes later he was snoring in the backseat. When he woke he asked, "Where are we?" and I asked, "Where were you?" He didn't remember. The next time it happened was even stranger. I had assumed he was still lying down in the back when I saw him hitchhiking about fifty yards ahead. I pulled over and when he got in he introduced himself: "Hi, I'm Saul Lowe." "John Donelly," I said and shook his hand. "You look familiar," he said. "What year is it?" I told him and he cursed. "Damn! I'm twenty years early!" Blip! He was gone again and I spent two miserable, terrified hours driving alone until he Blipped back in midsentence just outside of Gary, Indiana.

"—you lay awake all night wondering if there *is* a Dog!" Saul cackled for about a minute. When he saw I didn't get it, he stopped.

"That was the punch line," I said. "What was the joke?"

"Oh." He fished out his pack of Camels. "What do you do if you're an insomniac, agnostic, and dyslexic?"

They say quantum equations work both backward and forward. I never thought jokes could do that, too. I laughed softly. Then I remembered: Johnny Carson did it for years.

Suddenly the glove box was beeping.

"It's for you," said Saul, and he pulled out a car phone. A strange car phone. It must have been the first prototype ever made. It had a dial. It was pink. And, I soon discovered, it was a lot heavier than it looked.

"Ma Bell laughed in my face when I tried to sell 'em this." Saul smirked as he pulled out an antenna so long you could have roasted marshmallows on it. "Idiots."

"Johnny? Is that you?" said the familiar befuddled voice of my brother.

"Gun? How'd you get this number?"

"What are you talking about? You dropped it off last night. Angie said you looked strange."

I looked at Saul. I looked at the phone. I definitely did not visit Hogan last night. My guts were curdling as I started imagining what this meant, so I pulled over and stopped.

"Johnny? You there?"

"I'm here," I answered. At least I think I am, I thought.

"You said some crazy shit last night. Angie said you'd been drinking." He chuckled. "Listen, next time you go to one of those bimbo wrestling dives, go home and change."

"What?" I snapped.

"At least wash the Jell-O off! What'd you have? A ringside seat?" He was taking big gulps of laughter.

"Saul," I croaked, handing him the phone. His hand was there to receive it. I opened my door and vomited on the shoulder. Saul handed me his red handkerchief and chatted a while with Hogan. "Nyahhh, he's fine. Really. He's just been extending himself." Saul chuckled at Hogan's comment. "You know what I mean. So'd you read that pamphlet? Yeah. Yeah. No, no, no. A sin of omission is when you should've done something and you don't. 'S'got nothing to do with sex. Yeah? Yeah, adultery's one of the top ten. Uh-huh. Uh-huh. Tell you what. You make a sincere confession. What? No, not to your wife! A priest. Right. Then you make a sincere act of contrition. How should I know? Give blood. Feed a homeless person or something. No, it doesn't have to do specifically with sex. It just has to be sincere. Yeah? What? I don't know. That's a toughie. I doubt killing an alien is covered by that commandment. Anyway, we're talking self-defense, aren't we? Don't worry about it. Nyaahh. Nyaah, she had it coming. Hold it—he seems to be coming around." Saul handed the phone back to me.

"Hogan." My voice quavered. "What EXACTLY did I say to you last night?"

Saul snatched the phone out of my hand and shook his head. "Not a good idea, Doc."

"What?!"

"I wouldn't if I were you." He leveled his eyes at me in warning.

"Give me the fucking phone, Saul!"

"It's your funeral," he said, handing it over.

I was determined to get to the bottom of this. Obviously I had gone into the Holock's future. I had felt the need to come back and warn Hogan about something. I wanted matters clarified. I was about to talk when Saul Blipped out again. I held the phone tightly with both hands;

it shook like a vibrator. I had a sudden vision: I had left my-self back in Detroit and was stuck in an extended dream from which I couldn't wake. I was not real; I wasn't even alive. Some impostor was back home in Detroit, living my life, sleeping in my bed, seeing my patients, and eating my favorite foods. I swallowed and took a deep breath. Maybe Saul was right. Maybe I'd better just cool it.

"So how's it goin', Gun?" I said as cheerfully as I could.

There was a pause. "All right, I guess. Listen, I just wanted to see if you're okay. I don't care about that other stuff. I'd forgiven you long ago."

"Yeah?" I answered, still shaking.

"You were a good brother, Johnny. The past is past. The buzzer's sounded. You can't change it. Anyway, that was a long time ago. We were kids. Okay?"

"Okay," I said, wondering what past deed I had apolo-gized for.

"So I wanted you to know—not to sweat it. If you have to go away, fine. I hope you don't, you know, and, like Angie said: we're gonna miss you. But I wanted you to know: the record's clear."

"Great," I said, biting my lip.

"I love you, Johnny," he said in a choking voice. "That was nice of you to say it last night. But you cut out so fast I didn't get a chance to tell you." He paused, then admitted, "Actually, Angie's been bugging me about it all day."

"Thanks, Gun," I said softly.

"Well, gotta go. The game's on. And bro . . . thanks for the alibi."

I listened to the dial tone for a long time.

I was thinking about how, for the better part of our childhood, my brother and I were at war. I was born 4 B.E. (Before Elvis hit the charts) and given my grandfather's name: John. My dad had once shared a putting green with

Ben Hogan, so when my little brother came four years later, he bore the brunt of my father's salute to his hero. I used to tease the poor kid about having two last names—a joke he despised because he didn't comprehend it for years. Maybe I never got over being dethroned from my position as the Only Child, but the day Mom brought Hogan home from the hospital, I resented the hell out of him. I looked down at that pudgy red doll wrapped in the blue blanket and asked: "Does he talk? Can he play? Then what good is he?"

'Course, he wasn't a total washout. I could always bounce balls of socks off his face and watch him gurgle. Or launch him in his Johnny Jump-Up and watch him carom around the doorway like a cartoon. "Here's a bee, Hogan," I'd say. "Step on it." And he would: barefoot. I don't know how many times I nearly killed him. "Jump, Hogan, jump!" I'd say. And he'd leap off the dining room table and land smack on his face. "This is a match, Hogan. Whatever you do . . . don't touch it." He could never resist that one. He'd bawl wordlessly, and Mom'd come and rock him in the chair and I'd hate him all the more.

I even had a name for this hobby: Operation Get Hogan. He always slept with his mouth open like a dead dog, so I used to wake him every morning wearing my Halloween zombie mask: a whiskered monstrosity with a loose eyeball drooping from the socket. I'd jostle him, cooing, "Hoooogun . . . Oh, Hoooogun." Boy, his face when he opened his eyes was priceless.

He always had this desperate stupid look that grown-ups found irresistible, but made me want to pinch him. It wasn't just that he was chubby and slow on the uptake. He'd always tag along with me, like a scab you can't scratch off. And he used to embarrass me in front of my friends— an unforgivable sin. So I'd always give him the sandy hot-dog. Always kick him under the table. Once I even badgered him into climbing a tree—he was terrified of heights—and left him there. Nothing worked. No matter how I abused him, he forgave me. And not once during this extended period of torture did Hogan ever tell on me. He was so thrilled for any crumb of attention I tossed his way—it made me sick.

This might have gone on indefinitely, but one day I had my first genuine crisis of conscience. Jimmy Schlitbeard was a smelly brat who nobody on the block liked, so naturally Hogan was the only kid who'd play with him. One day I found him picking on Hogan in the backyard sandbox. He had buried all of the runt except his head and, straddling his shoulders, was pouring glasses of water down his nose. I told him to knock it off, but he wouldn't. He said, "Make me." Now Jimmy was big for a seven-year-old, and loved to pick on younger kids like Hogan. But I wasn't about to let him get away with that with me: I was nine. "Get off him or I'll pound you!" I yelled. "You and what army!" he shot back. So I gave him a bloody nose and he ran off crying.

It was then I got a good look at my brother. A pathetic lump in the middle of the sandbox with a muddy halo around his head.

"Get up, you dope."

"I can't," he whimpered. It was his favorite admission of weakness. It always disgusted me.

Then I saw he was looking up at me with an adoration usually reserved for statues at church or superheroes on TV: I had saved him. I looked down at that loving face and I almost wanted to bury the rest of him so I wouldn't have to see it anymore. So trusting. So happy. I stared at my buried brother and realized that was exactly what I'd been trying to do for years: snuff him out. It helped that I had just seen *Premature Burial* at the Saturday matinee. Nightmares about being buried alive woke me up for a week: worms boring into your brains; tearing your fingernails off trying to dig out of the casket. For a moment I thought of all the gruesome tortures I'd wreaked upon this kid who worshiped me. I realized I was no better than Jimmy Schlitbeard. That was the lowest moment of my childhood. For about ten seconds, I felt pretty shitty.

Then I started to feel good. I had never rescued anybody before, much less Hogan. And the feeling of being admired and trusted and capable and honorable was heady stuff indeed. This is what Mighty Mouse feels. This is what Captain America feels. Not just the crunch of Red Skull's jaw against your fist. Not the armored muscle of a mutated body. But Respect. The Respect and Awe of lesser creatures who depended on your goodwill, your intervention, your rescue. THIS is what heroes feel.

"Are you gonna dig me out now, Johnny?" asked Hogan, interrupting.

"Hold your horses," I said. I reveled in the thunderous waterfall of feeling, drank every last drop of the newfound ecstasy of Doing Right. And when my transformation was complete, and only then, did I dig him out.

What had I said to Hogan last night? Why did I come back? Why did I give him Saul's car-phone number? Why was I covered with Jell-O? What the hell did he mean "alibi"? And how was I supposed to take Hogan's forgiveness when I didn't know what I had apologized for? It sounded like I was feeling guilty about our childhood, but I couldn't be sure. I began to comprehend just how dizzying life could be without the foundation of the One-Way Street of Time.

Then it came to me. I told him that I loved him. I don't remember ever saying that. It wasn't something that was done in our family. The occasional hug on Christmas, gifts, birthday cakes—sure. But that word was a currency we didn't exchange. It always made me uncomfortable when I heard my friends' parents say that word to them. It was embarrassing, like the kissing scenes in movies. "Love" was something you did in private, in the dark. You didn't talk about it. At least we didn't. I recalled realizing some time in college that this unspoken prohibition was odd and repressive. But it never occurred to me that I retained those values unconsciously. It was easy to tell my girlfriends that I loved them. I had always thought that empathy was my specialty. But when it came to my family there was a barrier, a gag order against blatant displays of emotion. So the unsaid thing became, by denial, something dangerous. Like that famous line about how alcoholic families cope with their sickness: "There's no elephant in our living room, and don't you DARE tell anyone!" Why hadn't I seen that before? I had never told Hogan that I loved him! Christ, was it that simple? Did I have to go to the future to figure that one out? What a dunce!

When I checked into the Chicago Hilton, Saul had still not reappeared. I had to explain to a nervous lady at the front desk that, yes, the reservations *were* for Mr. Lowe. I was Mr. Lowe's associate. Yes, I still needed a room with twin beds because Mr. Lowe would be joining me. (I hoped he would be, anyway.) Her eyes flinched slightly every time I said Saul's name. I finally had to put the room on my plastic before she'd give me two room keys and her trembling smile.

As I walked through the lobby lounge I noticed there were strange gatherings at various cocktail tables. Men in tuxedos were doing card tricks. A woman was turning a strand of rope into two and back again. A guy in a yellow sweater was rolling a quarter along his knuckles. A bearded Arab was pitching straws into a watermelon; they stuck out like the quills of a porcupine. Appreciative chuckles and mild applause greeted each trick. What the fuck? I thought. Then noticed a bulletin board by the concierge that read: "2 PM GRAND BALLROOM. OPENING ADDRESS: NAT. ASS. MAG." A magicians' convention? I thought. That's appropriate. Then directly below it: "COCKTAILS 7:30 PM ORCHID ROOM: INT. PAT. AND INV. CONF." Huh?

I had just unpacked and was removing the sanitized crepe paper seal on the toilet seat when I heard a familiar voice from the next room.

"International Patents and Inventions Conference," said Saul, answering the question I hadn't asked. "That's my gang."

I looked out and saw Saul straightening his tie in the mirror. "They're a bunch of misfits and hermits. But they know how to party."

"Saul. I'm having a hard time with this disappearing act of yours."

"Jesus. How do you think I feel? I shoulda brought my rosary. That could help." He opened up the drawers of our dresser until he spotted something. "Bull's-eye!" he yelled. He pulled out a blue leather book and held it in both hands. "Thank God for the Gideons!" He stuffed it in the pocket of his gray suit, where it made an odd bulge. He turned to me, buttoned his middle button, and held out his arms. "How do I look?"

"Like a midget Gorbachev," I replied, shaking my head at the sight. "With a boner."

He got a kick out of that, and started wheezing and giggling. "You'll like Lenny," he said as we headed for the elevator. "He invented 'Queen for a Day.'"

Twenty-five

Come on," said Saul as we reached the lobby. "The real action's in the bar."

I'd been in a lot of hotel lobbies, but nothing came close to this. It could have been a train station designed for the Third Reich: grandiose and scaled to intimidate. Gray marble columns towered into high white ceilings. Arching over the check-in desk was an extravagant historical relief of the Great Chicago Fire etched in marble. Muscle-bound firemen braced themselves against a snaky hose, spewing a plume of water on the tongues of flame that leapt from every window. The Hilton *H* motif was repeated everywhere: on the bouncy maroon carpet, on the lamp fixtures, on the coattails of the top-hatted doorman, even on the golden handles of the ballroom doors. We passed a long table where a host of white stick-on name tags lay in alphabetical rows. A few had been taken, leaving red gaps on the tablecloth.

"Jesus," I said, starting to read them aloud. " 'Liquid Paper.' 'Airwicks.' 'Frisbee.' 'Pacman'—this is a CLASS crowd. 'Torsion Bar Suspension.' 'Rotary Wankel.' 'Erasable Ink.' 'Krazy Glue'—gotta meet her. 'Silly Putty.' 'Super Ball.' "

I noticed Saul was bending over and writing on a few blank ones. "Free drinks with these," he explained.

"Look, Saul." I picked up a name tag and pretended to read. " 'Perpetual Motion Machine.' "

"Get outta here," he said, slapping my name tag on. I couldn't read it.

"What's it say?" I asked.

" 'Liquid Plumb'r'," he answered, looking up with a smile.

"Gee, thanks." Then I noticed his nametag. " 'Hold'?" I read. "What the fuck's 'Hold'? A color-fast detergent?"

"Come on, come on, come on," he said over his shoulder. "Lenny's expecting us."

On our way to the lounge I smiled at the nervous lady at the front desk who had checked me in. After about three seconds, she smiled back, as if she just remembered how. What was her problem?

Lenny Tolkien had seen better years. A thin man in a white suit two sizes too big for him. A California tan so dark it made the whites of his eyes shine. Hair transplants dotted the freckled dome of his head. He smoked tiparillos and smelled foul. When we shook hands I could feel all the bones in his. He had a voice that echoed Saul's, but was pitched higher, and with more nasal inflections. He'd be hell to listen to with a hangover. His name tag read: "Tickler."

"After Burbank, I went to San Francisco. They had a ripe underground industry, but it was kinda half-assed—no financing or production expertise."

"Movies?" I asked.

Lenny looked right through me. "Shorts, mostly. Art-theater stuff."

"Any I may have heard of?"

That look again. "Doubt it."

"*The Tickler?*" I offered, pointing at his tag. "That was a big horror film in the fifties, wasn't it?"

"Is he putting me on?" Lenny asked Saul. Saul shook his head and drank his orange juice. Then Lenny looked down at me with a withering stare and said, "The 'Tickler' is my project. My design. My invention. I believe you're referring to *The Tingler.*"

"That's it," I said. "Sorry."

That settled, he turned back to Saul. "We made a killing. The industry was just getting off the ground. Talent was cheap then. So was film. You wouldn't believe all the film people who came out of the woodwork. All these guys plugging away at industrials or hygiene films for grade-school kids. They were dying for a chance to direct." He smiled bitterly. "Big names now. Hotshots. Won't return my phone calls."

"Like who?" I asked, and he gave me that look again.

"So who's the hippie?" He jerked his head at me. My hair wasn't short and I was wearing wire-rimmed glasses, but it had been years since anyone had dubbed me a "hippie."

"This is John," said Saul with a head lean. "He's my doctor."

"No, I'm not," I interjected.

Saul smirked at me for spoiling his fun. "This is John," he clarified. "He's not my doctor."

Lenny beamed at Saul. "Your own personal physician! You always did go first class, Saul. My doc says my stomach can't take the hard stuff anymore. But who cares, eh? Like I'm gonna live forever, right? Let's have a drink!" He carried our drinks to a black vinyl booth by a window.

Lenny insisted he was paying for them, even though we knew they were free. It seemed important to him.

"I ever tell you about the squirrels? Biggest job I ever did. Free-lance for Disney. 'Hush, hush.' They didn't want anyone to know I was on their payroll."

"Why not?" I asked.

Now both Saul and Lenny were looking at me. I decided to shut up.

"Walt was into those dopey nature films, 'member? 'Wilderness' something. You know, cougars, bears, coyotes. Lotsa frolicking. One day he's watching dailies and he goes nuts. Blows a gasket! Absolutely livid! 'The squirrels!' he's screaming. 'What's with the goddamned SQUIRRELS! We CAN'T have THAT! Are you people crazy!!?' Nobody understands him. Turns out he's talking about the red butts of the squirrels. They got these little red behinds and every time they run away from camera they're mooning the audience! Walt says, 'America is not gonna sit there eating popcorn while a bunch of rodents run around with their assholes hanging out! Fix it!' Now, nobody at Disney will do the job. They're Animators. It's beneath them. So a friend of mine remembers I started in cartoons and knows my present circumstances and calls me up to beg me to do the job. So I spend two weeks airbrushing out the assholes of these fucking squirrels! Fun work, I'll tell ya. Only problem was, now all the squirrels look like they got little animated butterflies, following 'em around and sniffing their butts! Walt goes NUTS! 'I told you guys to fix it and you come back with this sick, perverted stuff!? Do something! I don't care what! Give the squirrels UNDERPANTS or DRESSES or SOMETHING, but fix it!' And they did! They put fucking tutus on those little rats to hide the evidence. That's how they started mixing live action and animation!"

Saul and I, by this time, were laughing so hard we were holding on to the table to keep from sliding to the floor.

"Different times," he said with a sad smile. "Used to be a quality business. Negligees and decent lighting. Heck, we used to have stories! Those kids could act! Now it's just hydraulics! Drugs spoiled it. We used to have fun."

"Hydraulics?" I asked.

"What medical school gave you a degree?" Lenny snapped, for no apparent reason.

I had had it. I'd been polite, interested, even. And the liquor was giving me a little edge. So I laid into him.

"Look, Stringbean," I said. "I don't know what your problem is—"

Lenny flushed and Saul put a hand on my arm.

"I ask a simple question—" And thank God I had enough gray cells left to kick myself in the head and add up the clues. Hydraulics. Negligees. Drugs. Tickler. Art theaters. I am a genuinely stupid human being, I thought.

I sighed. "Lenny . . . I apologize. I was out of line. Just forget it."

"What do you think we were talking about?" asked Lenny, shaking his head in disbelief. "Don't you know who I AM?"

It seemed a question he felt appalled to have to keep asking.

I was embarrassed. "Listen, let me get you a drink." Yet another dumb move.

"I'M buying the drinks," said Lenny. And left the table in a huff.

"*The* Leonard Tolkien?" I asked, when he was gone. "The Father of Porn?"

"Adult entertainment," Saul corrected. "Nothing like they got today. Lenny was an artist."

The thin man set the drinks shakily on the table and sat down. The mood had soured and for a few minutes nobody knew what to say.

"So Saul," Lenny began. "I heard you joined a monastery—what's wit all that shit?"

Saul shrugged. "Don't believe everything you hear."

"Doc," he said, turning my way, his cigar breath enveloping me, "do you have any idea who this man is?" He flung his arm around Saul. "This is THE MAN. SAUL FUCKING LOWE! This man invented the HOLD BUTTON!" He gazed at me as steadily as he could, waiting for the full impact of his words to register.

Saul gave a sheepish grin. I managed a whistle before I said, "How about that."

Lenny was not satisfied. He tugged down an imaginary one-armed bandit. "*Kerching!* Every time they build a phone! *Kerching!* We're talkin' monster residuals! What's the tab every day, Saul?"

Saul was embarrassed. "It varies."

"Varies MY ASS!" laughed Lenny. "Do you know how many cuckoos in this hotel would KILL for that patent!?"

Not a pleasant choice of words, I thought.

Lenny beamed at Saul. "This is THE MAN! My oldest living friend! My best friend in the WHOLE FUCKIN' WORLD!"

Lenny planted a wet kiss on Saul's head, gave him a big hug, and began to weep copiously. "They're KILLING me, Saul. I tell ya. The bean-counters of this world are KILLING ME."

Saul patted his back. "Take it easy, Lenny. You're due, you hear me? You're due!"

"Easy for you to say," he sniffled. "You're swimming in it. You can afford to live in a monastery. I have to bust my balls just to cover my nut."

"Lenny makes sexual aids," Saul explained helpfully, his red head poking up under his drunken friend's armpit.

"Lenny," said Saul, straightening his friend upright. "Listen to me. Are you listening? Listen!"

"I'm listening," he said, still pouting.

Saul pointed his pudgy index finger into Lenny's face; he got cross-eyed trying to focus on it. "I'm gonna say one word."

"One word," said Lenny.

"Are you listening?" asked Saul.

"Yeah, Saul."

"Jesus," said Saul.

"I'm listening," Lenny protested. "One word, you said."

"You missed it. That was the word."

"That was the word?"

Saul shook his head. "You're not listening."

"I swear to God, Saul!"

"Then what was the word?"

"What?"

"I told you," said Saul.

There was a long pause. Lenny looked pitifully at the empty bowl of trail mix. Saul gave him a warm smile. I downed my martini.

"I missed it," Lenny apologized.

"JESUS!" I exploded. "Jesus Christ! God Almighty! King of Kings! Lord of Lords! The Savior! CHRIST! Messiah! GET IT!??"

Everybody in the bar was looking at us. Lenny swiveled his head between me and Saul a few times, like he was watching a tennis match. Finally he frowned and said, "God?"

"God." Saul nodded happily.

"God! I need a drink!" I sighed. I turned and raised my empty glass to the waiter in the red vest who nodded and got me another one. For an hour I had to sit and listen to Saul proselytize a seventy-year-old Jew who manufactured sexual aids. I thought I would die. At last I moved to the bar and watched the inventors mingle. They mingled a lot. "Mood Rings" mingled with "Sausage Stuffer," "Teflon" mingled with "Velcro," "Baggies" was all over Miss "Legos" and "Ranch Dressing" was coming on to "Oil of Olay." God, it was loud. My ears were ringing; it sounded like a band was playing in the ballroom next door: "Somewhere Over the Rainbow" on tubas. I was staring at my ice cubes when I found myself being examined by a tall bespectacled man in a white turtleneck and a black sport coat. He wore a very large gold ring shaped like the horns of a ram. He smiled and said, "Strange group, eh?"

"I'll say," I said and drank.

He laughed. "Can't you just see all these guys growing up? Fiddling with their chemistry sets in the basement when all the other kids were out playing baseball."

"Exactly," I said. Thank goodness there was one sane person in this bar.

"I'm Dwight Fontaine. Doctor of physics at Loyola."

"John Donelly." I shook his hand. "I'm with a friend," I explained, wanting to disown myself from this crowd of weirdos.

He looked at me over the rim of his thick glasses. "A close friend?" he asked.

"You could say that," I replied.

"Maybe both of you would like to join me for drinks in my room?"

I looked him over. His name tag read "STEREO-CITY." Sounded like an appliance store. Didn't know you could patent those. His eyes were rimmed in red as if he'd been crying. His hair was blond and thinning. His fingernails were perfectly manicured. It could have been a friendly overture, but it made me uncomfortable.

"Think I'll pass. Thanks," I said with a cool smile.

He forced a grin and nodded.

"What's 'Stereo City'?" I asked, wanting to move on to safer ground.

"Ster-E-*Ah*-city," he corrected, pronouncing it as one word. He smiled broadly. "My Theory of Consciousness. Like to hear it?"

Anything was better than Saul's preaching. "Let me get a drink first," I said, looking for the bartender.

"Allow me," he said, laying one graceful hand on my wrist and signaling down the bar with the other.

After the drinks came, he began by apologizing. "It's not published yet. The physics are radical. But the first draft is causing quite a stir." He chuckled with relish. His diction was perfect; it fell just short of an English accent. Obviously, a man who made his living by talking.

"You better make it simple," I warned him. "What I know of physics I could write on this napkin."

He chuckled. "Relax. I'm a professor; I'm used to simplifying."

And then he began a speech that was astounding. I've always envied people who talked as if they were typing, words falling effortlessly into paragraphs. I could never organize my thoughts like that.

" 'Stereocity' is the phenomenon that activates Consciousness," he began. "Consider a pair of stereo headphones. Two sources of music that can create a third source, the phantom speaker that resides in the mind's eye, the center of the forehead. This effect or illusion results from identical signals of equal value being transmitted from both sources."

"So that's how they do that," I said. I'd always wondered about it.

"In a similar way, the waking mind achieves a rather remarkable balancing act—the two hemispheres work together, each supplying its own area of expertise. This harmony, if you will, creates an invisible overtone, as the signals from two plucked notes on a guitar overlap and create a third unplayed note. This, in a nutshell, is Consciousness: the invisible third speaker, the unplayed overtone."

It took me a while to process this. "Fascinating," I admitted.

"Thank you. Now, Consciousness"—he practically intoned the word as he began a pantomime with his hands. First he grasped his fingers around an invisible ball—"Consciousness does not exist without the operations of the two physical parts of the brain." These he weighed in his hands—"But it is far more than the sum of its parts." He clenched his fingers together—"And it exists apart from them because it is not physically tied to the brain." He unlocked his hands and spread them far apart—"Any more than radio waves are tied to your Sony receiver." He must have seen me watching his gestures, for suddenly he dropped his hands below the bar, tilted his head, and asked, "Clear?"

I was waiting for his hands to reappear, but took a moment to encourage him with a nod. "Sure." I was examining the dark wood of the bar. It looked wonderful.

He startled me by slamming the spot I was staring at. "THIS is why accident victims with brain injuries—as well

as different aboriginal tribes—'experience' the mind outside of its culturally consensual location."

I frowned. "Where's that, exactly?"

He looked at me. "Between the ears."

"Ah," I said. "Gotcha."

He lit a cigarette and said peevishly, "I'm not boring
you, am I?"

"Nooooo," I insisted. "This is good stuff."

He blew out his smoke and continued. "Comatose accident victims have been known to wake up and swear they
remember hovering in the corner of their hospital rooms.
They can quote you conversations that happened when
they were under. They can even describe who wore what
and where they sat."

"I've heard of that," I agreed. I thought I had, anyway.

"We all experience consciousness as substantive. And
we all find it necessary to localize it. But in fact *Consciousness has no location.* It is merely convenience and a desire to
overcome a certain psychic vertigo that make us place our
mind in the center of our heads."

"Wow!" I said, impressed and totally lost.

"This non-locality of the Mind allows it the ability to
reflect upon itself, to stand on the outside looking in. You
see, Consciousness evolved as vision did. Some animals
have eyes on opposite sides of their heads. Fish, for instance. They see in two dimensions. Put one hand over your
eye."

"Which one?" I asked.

"Either."

I did, slapping myself a little too hard in the process.

"See? Like that. As creatures evolved, their eyes turned
forward and their two overlapping fields of vision created
the hyperperception of depth—they activated a heightened

reality by adding a new dimension. Consciousness is that new dimension. You can take your hand away now."

He waited until I did, then went on. "It is the act of perception that triggers 'Stereocity,' the active engagement of the two sides of the brain simultaneously."

"That's quite a theory," I said, shaking my head. "But how the hell do you prove it?"

He waved his cigaretted hand to dismiss the suggestion. "I'll leave that to the Research Boys. I'm Theoretical." This struck me as pretty cavalier given the revolutionary nature of his ideas, but I let him go on.

"I call it the 'Theory of Metaphor.' Human language—as opposed to porpoises' or orangutans'—is essentially rooted in metaphor-making: the comparison of two things without the use of "like" or "as": i.e.: 'The sun is a chariot of fire,' 'He was a lion on the battlefield.' Follow? This basic human process reflects the paradigm of Consciousness: two signals harnessed together to create an invisible third. No wonder we feel so comfortable with metaphors in language! It is the way we perceive and think."

"Orangutans?" I asked. Didn't get that bit.

He went on as if my question were a stick in the road: he just drove over it. "Now here's the good part: the Animal Brain exists in the Now!" He jabbed the air before my chin. "Appetites are needy or sated Now!" Another jab. "Vision is on or off Now!" Yet another. Then he wrapped his fist around his index finger and beat them to individual words. "Senses. Are. Stuck." He released his grip and his hands floated above the bar. "In the Present Tense." I was damn near ready to applaud his performance. "Only Human Consciousness dreads and regrets, hopes and holds dear. Do you see? *Time* is created in the realm of Consciousness! Time is the resultant property of Stereocity."

"Hm," was my only comment. I was beginning to feel strange. "Hm," I repeated, buying time. He looked like he was expecting more, so I quipped, "I can see you really narrowed your topic."

He smiled with tolerance. "Broad issues. Broad ideas. You see the implications, of course."

"Of course," I bluffed. He wasn't going to lose me *that* easily.

"This ability to 'step out of time' allowed humans to develop morality—which is little more than the ability to anticipate needs being met or delaying gratification." He paused, sighed, and batted his eyes at the ceiling. "Actually, that's always been one of my problems."

I scowled. "Morality?"

"Delayed gratification." He widened his eyes and smiled—I believe the word is—*conspiratorially.*

Geez, I thought. He's wearing a lot of aftershave.

"Civilization itself springs from the objectifying properties of Stereocity. When humans discovered they had the ability to look at themselves from the outside, their lives became, in fact, STORIES. Consciousness became narrator. Thus myth. Thus history. Thus biography. Thus literature."

"Thus Spake Zarathustra!" I offered giddily, spitting all over his blazer.

His speech had reached a new pitch; I think his glasses were actually steaming up. I had the uncomfortable premonition that he was going to start talking about God.

"Indeed," he continued, raking quotations in the air with his fingers, "this 'outside' Consciousness, if you will, was most likely the beginning of a sense of 'the Divine.' For if Consciousness is experienced as anything, it is felt as 'Spirit': nonlocal, nonmaterial, hovering outside of things, observing, judging. It took a small leap to extrapolate from this basic human 'Spirit' a Greater Spirit, a higher omniscient mind, watching and recording the progress of the world. A surrogate for the Consciousness of the Human Mind. The Original Narrator. God." He took a long, satisfied drag on his cigarette, bent his head toward mine, and said softly, "Have you ever slept with a man?"

Saul was tugging at my arm. "Get away from him," he whispered. "He's a loony."

"Yeah," I agreed as we walked off. "But he's got great hands."

"You're drunk," said Saul with a sneer.

I looked back as Saul pulled me away. The professor had already turned to the poor guy next to him and was starting his spiel again. God bless him. God bless everyone. I felt wonderful. Saul had to prop me up against the mirrored wall of the elevator and hold my arm as he punched our floor button. I caught sight of my reflection: my shoulders were shaking I was giggling so hard. And all the way up he had to listen to me repeating: "Thus typology! Thus phrenology! Thus theology!" Then I noticed the name tag that Saul had stuck on my chest. Backward in the mirror it read: "sehsulF 0002." It took me six floors to decode it.

"You little prick." I glared at him, trying not to laugh, and pointed at the name tag.

Saul took his cigar out of his mouth and shrugged. "It just came to me."

Twenty-six

I woke up with a hangover so fierce it hurt to breathe. I managed to sit up and open one eye. All the blinds were raised; the room was full of piercing light. Saul's bed hadn't been slept in. The little red message light on my tan phone was blinking on and off; I could almost hear it. I called the front desk and got my friend, the nervous lady.

"Oh, good morning, Mr. Donelly," she said sweetly. "You have a message from a Mr. Kiefer. Would you like me to read it?"

"Sure," I groaned.

" 'Run,' " she said.

"Yes?" I answered after a moment. "Run? Run what?"

"That's the message."

"Run."

"Right. That's all it says."

It was too early to deal with this. "When did he call?"

"Two o'clock this morning."

I rubbed a sheen of grease off my face. "What time is it now?"

"It's eleven-oh-five."

"Thanks," I said and hung up. The word stuck in my aching frontal lobes like a ball bearing: RUN. Was I still drunk? Did Jack expect me to make sense of that message? I was sick of all this fucking intrigue. And I was sick to my stomach. I visited the toilet on my knees.

I was in the shower when it hit me. Where's Saul? Why didn't he leave me a note? Why doesn't he give me any notice when he's gonna Blip out? At least he left me three extra-strength Tylenols standing in a row by the sink; I popped them with gratitude. I had just gotten dressed when I noticed Saul's blue Bible lying in a pool of light on the floor next to the dresser as if it had been dropped: it stood balanced like a small tent on the carpet. It looked perfectly ordinary, but for some reason it scared the shit out of me. Run. As in Danger. As in get the fuck out of there. Run!

Oh *shit*, I thought.

That's when they broke down the door. Big men in black sport coats, white shirts, black ties, and crew cuts. They smelled very clean. They were very efficient. A blond man sat me on the bed and held one finger to his lips; it wasn't necessary. Another drew the blinds and started searching through my suitcase. He took out a knife and began to slit open the lining. A third went through all my drawers, running his hand under each of them, then started dumping their contents into a white garbage bag. Another ripped the phone cord out of the wall and wrapped it around his fist, then put the door back on its hinges. They all wore small black walkie-talkies on their belts. I saw no guns, though I expected to.

But it was the large quiet guy with the huge belly who made the biggest impression. The Fat Man in the baggy blue suit: my old shadow. He walked right over to the blue Bible on the floor, picked it up, sniffed it, and tossed it across the room to one of his colleagues, who made a perfect one-handed catch and dumped it in the Glad bag. Then the big man sat down and began cracking his knuckles. He didn't say a word. Just stared at me as if he expected me to give him something. His gray hair was trimmed close to his scalp, a very large head. He could have passed for a drill instructor. Everyone else stood; he sat.

When they had finished their chores they turned to him and waited. Finally he nodded slightly, and one of the big men said a single word into his walkie-talkie. "Secure."

My mind had watched it all from a stunned vantage point far removed from the culturally consensual location: somewhere two feet behind the back of my skull. I kept wanting to grab the remote and change channels. Any minute now there had to be a commercial break. I noticed a muscle in my thigh was twitching.

The blond young man who had put me on the bed began the interrogation. He had a Southern accent. He seemed very casual, very polite. Good Cop.

"If you wouldn't mind, we'd like to ask you a few questions, Mr. Donelly."

"About your mother," added the guy with the phone cord wrapped around his fist. His shoulders seemed to bulge at the seams of his suit. Everything he said from that point on was drenched in sarcasm. And he made sure his wrapped hand was always visible. Bad Cop.

"You were the last one to see her alive?" asked the polite one.

I nodded. My mother? I thought. My MOTHER? My face was puckered into an expression of profound confusion. Try it sometime when you have a hangover; it hurts.

"Did you know what your mother died of, sir?" asked the Southern man.

I looked at him a long time. "Cancer," I said.

"Would it surprise you to learn that she died of a broken spine?" said the bad cop, as if he relished it.

My jaw dropped. Then I clamped it shut. "That's impossible," I said through tight lips.

"This is a friendly interrogation," he said with a phony smile. "You're not a suspect. Not yet."

I wanted to spring on him and draw blood. I wanted to rip his nose off his smug know-it-all face. But I kept it in. Be careful. Be smart.

"What are you accusing me of?"

The bad cop said, "Would it be fair to say you had a stormy relationship with your mother?"

I didn't answer.

"I could understand a son wanting to spare his mother unnecessary suffering," said the good cop with a shrug. "Folks'd call it 'mercy killing.' "

The absurdity of it all finally got to me. "Let me get this straight. You think I broke my mom's back because I hated her, but I really loved her and I wanted to relieve her pain?"

The bad cop wound the cord so tightly around his fist that his fingers turned white. "Actually, we think it's curious that an eldest son who'd been written out of his wealthy mother's will was the last one to see her alive."

I know it sounds dumb, but until that moment the thought of a will had never crossed my mind. I knew Hogan was the executor; I assumed he would handle it. I expected there were funeral expenses, debts to pay, donations to her church and charities. I would never have characterized Mom as "wealthy." I hadn't gotten a penny from her in twenty years. I didn't expect any money. And the suggestion that I did irritated the hell out of me. I think I was more offended by being accused of greed than murder.

I glared at the bad cop. "If you're charging me, then arrest me. If you aren't—fuck off."

The good cop pulled out an eight-by-eleven glossy picture and laid it on my lap. "Mr. Donelly, do you know who this woman was?"

I grew very still. It was a photo of the only woman I had ever seen killed. I nodded. "How did she die?" I asked.

The bad cop smiled. "How do you know she's dead?"

"He—he just told me," I stammered.

"No sir, I did not," the good cop said. "She coulda changed her name. Coulda got married. When was the last time you saw her?"

My mind raced. "Last October," I managed to say. "What's this all about?"

Bad cop: "You left a Halloween party with her. Did she spend the night at your place?"

Mrs. Jordan. My neighbor saw us. I'd better fess up.

"That's right," I said and swallowed. Had they found the body?

Bad cop: "Ms. Adrian Jones disappeared in March. No one's heard of or seen her since."

"What's that got to do with my mother?"

The polite one answered. "Sir, we were hoping you could help us out on that one."

I said nothing. Did they know about Hogan?

"Like why was Ms. Jones's car seen several times parked in front of your mother's house?" asked the bad cop.

They found the car. Jesus, they knew about Hogan and her! I had to be very careful. A trickle of sweat ran down my chest.

"Mr. Donelly. Was your brother seeing Ms. Jones?" asked the polite one, looking at the shine on his black shoes.

"My brother's married," I answered stupidly.

"That's right," said the bad cop. "We're talking adultery, aren't we? Was he fucking her?"

"How should I know?"

"I hear your brother has quite a temper . . ." insinuated the bad cop.

"Sir, your brother was at the hospital when your mother died, was he not?" asked the good cop.

My head swam. My mother. Adrian. Hogan. What were they getting at?

The good cop looked puzzled and asked, "What's the connection between your brother, your mother, and Ms. Jones?"

Jesus, that was a tough one. "You tell me," I answered.

"All right, we will," said the bad cop with relish. "Hogan Donelly was having an affair with Adrian Jones when your mother died. He stood to gain a lot of money by her death. Did you know his dealership is filing Chapter Eleven? He could get his inheritance, pay off his debts, set up his dolly."

I smirked. "She could have died any second. Why the fuck would he break her back? Jesus, Hogan loved Mom!"

I swear: everybody in the room looked at each other as if I had just made the most incriminating statement possible.

"You think your brother killed her?" asked the bad cop.

I hesitated for too long. "No. He couldn't have."

Somebody in the corner wrote something on a notepad. What the fuck was going on?

The good cop had a manila folder in his hand. "Sir, were you aware that Ms. Jones was working for the government?" Then he showed me her dossier. Agent. Special Assignment. Undercover.

He took back the folder and it disappeared. I started to shake at the implications.

"Sir, are you acquainted with a Saul Lowe?" he asked.

I was totally lost by now. I had murdered Mom? Hogan had murdered Mom? Somebody had murdered Adrian? What did they think? Adrian was an undercover agent? What did Saul have to do with it?

"I know Saul."

"In fact, you live with him, correct?" asked the bad cop, moving a step closer.

"Yes."

The polite cop looked puzzled. "Sir, you left Detroit with him, rather quickly. Any particular reason?"

I said nothing.

"Why'd you come to Chicago?"

I said nothing.

"Where's Saul Lowe?" asked the bad cop.

I said nothing.

"Where's Saul Lowe?" asked the polite cop.

I said nothing.

There was a lot of silence in the room. The only sound was the lunch-hour traffic on Michigan Avenue twelve floors below. I felt like a punt returner surrounded by massive opponents, closing in, eager to take his head off; if I made a run for the door I'd get about five feet. My mouth felt like it had been blown dry.

"Where's Saul Lowe?" asked the man sitting in the corner, cracking his knuckles. It was the kind of voice that was hard not to answer, that seemed to promise serious consequences for such an affront.

I said nothing.

"Bring him in," said the Fat Man.

The bad cop snapped open his walkie-talkie and said, "Decoy."

The good cop went into the bathroom. I could hear him running the water in the tub.

There was a brief commotion at the door, then two cops whom I hadn't seen before dragged a tall, thin man into the room. He wore a T-shirt and pants. His bare feet were bound at the ankles with gray duct tape. His hands were cuffed behind his back. He was gagged with a white washcloth. His eyes looked as if they had been weeping. They sat him in a desk chair and faced him toward me.

We recognized each other at the same moment.

"What's *he* doing here?" I asked.

The Fat Man took his time answering. He cracked a knuckle and said, "I hear you two had a lot to say to each other yesterday."

"He's got nothing to do with this!" I protested. "He's some cuckoo inventor I met for the first time last night!"

The bound man grunted behind the gag. I got the feeling that I had said the wrong thing. There was an alarming stillness in the Fat Man's eyes when I said the word *inventor*. It was as if I'd said *spy* or *terrorist* or *homosexual*.

"Really, guys! You're off track here! Jesus, why do you have him tied up like that?"

The bad cop reached over and ripped the gag out of his mouth. The man winced for a moment, then started talking very loud and fast. "This is an outrage! I am a full professor at Loyola University! My dean chaired the President's Committee on Higher Education! My papers have appeared in scientific journals in Australia! I demand to call my attorney!" For a moment he ran out of breath. He looked around the room for a response. When none came, he whimpered, "These are pinching my wrists!"

Then they put the gag back in.

"Guys," I said, holding back a hysterical laugh, "this is getting crazy. He knows nothing. Understand? Nothing!"

The good cop came out of the bathroom folding a soaked towel neatly in half. I looked at the Fat Man. I looked at the good cop. I looked at Full Professor Dwight Fontaine.

"No," I said.

The good cop walked over and stood behind the man in the chair.

"No," I said.

The bad cop got down on his knees and braced both his hands on the feet of the man in the chair.

"Where is Saul Lowe?" asked the Fat Man.

I started to shake my head. "I don't know. I don't know. I don't know!" I pleaded.

The good cop flipped the towel snugly over the man's head and held it tightly from behind. The bad cop held down the kicking feet. I closed my eyes and listened to the noises coming from under the towel.

They seemed to last a long time.

When I opened my eyes they were carrying the body to the bathroom. I heard a splash when they dropped it in the tub.

The big silent man with the beer belly stood up slowly. Everyone stepped aside to give him a wide berth. He strolled over to my bed and stood over me.

I couldn't read his face. "You're not a cop. What are you?"

He leaned down and put his nose inches from mine. "I'm a man who wants some answers. What happened to Adrian Jones? Who murdered your mother?"

I felt if I moved I would be killed. I felt if I shut up I would be killed. I felt if I answered I would be killed. But all at once I saw a way out. A bright light that beckoned me—an alibi that could save Saul and everybody. The alibi that Hogan thanked me for. The perfect scapegoat.

"Laura Johnson," I whispered.

I had rolled onto the floor and started coughing before I realized he had slugged me in the stomach. From a distance I heard him say, "Stop the tapes! Strike everything after my last question!"

"What'd he say?" someone asked.

"Something about his son," the belly said. "Everybody out!" He barked. "Now!"

"But Colonel!"

"Now! You idiot! I want him alone. I need ten minutes. Log it anyway you like. Off the record. OUT!"

Footsteps. Door closes. I was picked up and laid out on the bed. A creak of bedsprings. When I opened my eyes, he was sitting on the edge of my bed. I thought the frame would break under his weight.

"Smoke?" he offered. I nodded and he lit one and put it between my lips; my hands weren't working yet.

"John, my name's Peter. You're right. I'm not a cop. I'm a colonel on special assignment for a branch of the government that doesn't officially exist. Judging from the political background in your file this should confirm your worst suspicions about—what did you call it in college? 'The Establishment.' "

I smiled weakly. It hurt to smile. He had hit me hard.

"You're a dangerous man, John. You're in the middle of it, but you have no idea what's going on."

I nodded in agreement. I felt a great urge to please him.

He cracked all the knuckles in one hand and looked at the painting on the wall above my head. He grunted. "Same picture in my room. Couple of fat ladies looking at the ocean next to a couple of beach umbrellas. Hell's that supposed to mean?"

"They buy 'em bulk," I suggested. He smiled. His were the deadest eyes I've ever seen in a human.

"Listen. You ever mention that person's name again and I'll put something into that punch. Clear?"

I nodded eagerly. I believed him.

"Let's cut to the chase. We want Saul Lowe. Where is he?"

"Why do you want him?" I asked, then regretted it—I was sure he was going to slug me again.

He shrugged. "We have a mutual acquaintance. Forgive the obscurity but it's regulations. They're our allies. We have a treaty. They have a very advanced technology, which they've been feeding us for quite some time. Stop me if you've heard any of this."

Horrified, I shook my head. This was worse than any dope-inspired conspiracy scenario I'd ever sweated through in the sixties. I had the dreadful feeling that the only reason he was telling me was that he knew I'd never get the chance to repeat it to anyone. If he promises me my freedom, I thought, he's lying.

"The catch is we've got to keep it secret. That's the condition." It sounded like the condition Laura put to me: "Tell no one. Absolutely no one."

"What sort of technology?" I asked.

He sighed. "It's all under the label of 'Star Wars.' But it's bigger than that."

"Bigger?" I asked.

"You don't need details. Let's just say we've leapfrogged our rivals by a decade." He put on what I'm sure he thought was a sincere face. "This is confidential stuff, John. I want to stress that. We're talking about the security of every American Child."

"What about the other children?" I wondered.

"What other children?" he asked, puzzled.

"Besides Americans."

"That's not my job." He shrugged.

Christ, I thought, he means it. He was a lifeguard who couldn't care less about the kids who were drowning on the other side of his buoy.

He looked at me out of the corners of his eyes. "You're smart enough to keep your mouth shut about this, I trust? Your freedom could depend on it."

I'm sunk, I thought. Saul, where are you? I prayed. Ashes fell on my chest and the big man brushed them off.

"Our mutual friends—" I asked. "They put you on to me?"

"They said you were trouble. Out to sabotage our defense."

"How was I supposed to do that?"

"You tell me."

Boy, there's nothing more dangerous than a man who knows everything. "Colonel. You told me what *we* get out of our treaty: the ultimate defense, right?"

He shrugged and the bed jiggled. "More or less."

"So what do our 'friends' get out of it? What's in it for them?"

"Classified," he said with a smile.

I discovered that when you're locked in a room with a crazy man who thinks he's a sane man and you're convinced you're a dead man, a strange kind of courage kicks in. There's nothing to lose. It also helps if you're hungover and everything anyone says pisses you off. I sat up in bed and shouted at him. "I'll tell you what's in it for them. Mr. Saul Lowe—that's what! The only fucking man on this planet who can kick them in the balls. The only man smart enough to know who the fuck our real enemies are!" I would have said the *H* word, but I was sure he'd slug me.

"Where is Saul Lowe?" he asked casually.

"I don't know!"

He took the cigarette from my mouth and stubbed it

out in the ashtray next to the phone. He seemed to be losing his patience. "Come on, John. You want your brother to spend the rest of his life in prison for murdering a government agent? How would his wife and daughters take it?" He breathed through his nose; it sounded like sandpaper scraping. "We could lock you up on manslaughter. Or we could confine you to protective custody for the remainder of your life for compromising national security. Someplace quiet and comfortable. Or we could tell our friends where you are and leave them the key. You want to die for Lowe? You're no hero. You want your brother to go to prison for Saul Lowe? Who the fuck is Saul Lowe? Some crackpot washed-up hustler from New Jersey? Are you a patriot— or are you too intellectual for that? No, that's right, you're a pacifist. You don't believe in dying for your country."

He looked at me for a long time. I figured I had one chance left. Before he gave up on me and called in his goons.

"You know, I always had a theory about guys who worked for the government. That they sort of fell into it 'cause they were too stupid to do anything else. That they operate on a missing cylinder."

He looked at me. "I have an IQ of one-forty-two."

"You got all the facts and the secrets and you don't know shit," I continued. "You'd fucking annihilate the world to make it safe for democracy! But let me ask you something, Colonel. What if our allies aren't our allies? What if they're just stringing you along? What if they want to guarantee our death, not our defense? Beware of Trojans bearing gifts, Colonel."

"Greeks," he corrected me with a smile. "It's 'Greeks bearing gifts,' Doc."

"You made one big mistake, Peter." I was buying time. Praying for Saul. Hoping that somehow I had the ability to wish him into this moment of time. "You shouldn't have left yourself alone with me." I was trying my best to sound menacing.

It took him a moment to get over being threatened. Then he burst out laughing and slapped his knees. "Watch a lot of movies, eh?" He laughed again.

The cavalry! I wanted to scream. Where's the fucking cavalry!?

"Doc, let me give you a piece of advice: Don't play poker." He began cracking his knuckles again. "Oh, I forgot. Only your patients call you 'Doc.' What's your degree in, anyway?" he asked sarcastically.

"Self-defense," I replied. Except the words didn't come out of my mouth. They came from behind the man with the huge belly sitting on my bed. There was the sound of a baseball bat connecting; then Colonel Peter's head slumped over to his shoulder and he fell onto the floor. Directly behind him stood a man holding a lamp like a club. He smiled crazily. It was me. Only I looked years older and I was covered from head to toe with green goo.

"Hi, John," he/I said.

I didn't move a muscle.

He set down the lamp and began pacing back and forth. "This is going to screw up the space/time continuum—but what the fuck! There's two guards at the door. Give me a head start. I'll run down the hall. You count to ten and run the other way. Saul's in the underground parking lot. Take the stairs at the end of the hall. Not the elevator. Got it?"

I nodded.

"I'm proud of us. That man has killed people. Close your mouth. You look silly." He turned for the door, then stopped and turned back to me, holding out a placating hand: palm down. "Don't worry. It's all going to work out. Watch out for Juan. See ya later!"

With that he flew out the door between two large men

and dashed down the hall yelling, "You're IT, motherfuck-
ers!"

I could hear them stomping away, yelling into walkie-
talkies. I counted to eight, then bolted off the other way,
knocking over a Hispanic waiter pushing a silver-domed
room service tray. His white plastic name tag read JUAN. I
left him cursing me in Spanish and headed down the stairs,
my heavy footsteps echoing.

Saul was in his Lincoln exactly as promised. He gunned
the engine twice and we headed down Michigan Avenue. It
started to rain. After a mile I realized I'd better drive, so
without stopping we changed places. Saul's size made that
easier than it sounds.

"Where to?" I asked.

"La-La Land," he answered. Then he started a robust
version of "CALIFORNIA, HERE WE COME! RIGHT
BACK WHERE WE STARTED FROM!" I had just
joined him, but he Blipped out before we got to the chorus.
Good thing, too. I didn't know all the words.

Twenty-seven

The skyline of Chicago was in my rearview mirror when the car phone started beeping. I nearly creamed a pickup trying to get it out of the glove box, so I pulled over. And went through the laborious process of opening the window and telescoping out the antenna. No wonder Ma Bell passed on it.

"Are you okay, Doc?" It was Jack. I could hear traffic on his end so I assumed he was in a phone booth. I told him about our getaway.

"Feds?" he asked. "G-men? Crew cuts and perfect teeth?"

"That's them," I confirmed.

"I tried to warn you. Didn't you get my message?"

"It was too late."

"Damn! I bet I clued them in to you! I tried to reach you on the car phone—Saul says this is an untraceable line—but I couldn't. I gotta tell ya—they raided the rectory right after you two left. Hauled me in for questioning. I told 'em shit. But watch your back."

"Where's Saul?" I asked.

"He just left. He said he knows where the machine is and he'd try to meet you in Saint Louie. Listen, Doc. Two things: Saul says the Holock got your seed. And they got wind of your plan. So you're expendable now."

"Great," I said. I'm a Wanted Man by the government and the Holock. Just great.

"The second thing?" Jack continued. "They know Saul's car. So you gotta make a switch."

"A switch?"

"You can steal a car if you like. Or you can borrow a buddy of mine's."

"I don't think I'm up for Grand Theft Auto, Jack."

"I figured as much."

Jack gave me directions to meet a pal of his in Evanston. Which meant I had to backtrack through the city and head north on Lake Shore. I felt like I was driving through the Valley of Death and any moment I'd be pulled over. Then it occurred to me that the last thing they'd expect me to do was head *in to* town. Our rendezvous point was the Baha'i temple, a gorgeous monument to that faith, built oddly enough in the middle of a suburb. Its pale stone dome is made of intricately cut rock, full of arabesques and gyres. Beautiful. Jack's pal pulled up in a rusty old black Chevy step-side pickup. He had three silver earrings and wore an old-style green cutoff field jacket over a black Chicago Bears T-shirt. A tall bearded man with dark circles under his eyes. Something told me he was a Vietnam veteran.

He nodded over his shoulder at the truck. "She's been turned over a couple times but she'll do ya right. What kind of car phone is that?"

"Prototype," I answered, a little embarrassed by the pink.

We stood there in the rain for a second, our breath frosting in the chilly air. He looked at me. "You look pale as a ghost. You got a jacket?"

"Naw. I was in a hurry."

"That's what the sarge said. There's a Bulls jacket on the front seat. Insulated."

"Thanks," I said. I was going to say something about parking Saul's Lincoln out of sight, but thought better of it. He was the kind of man who'd know about such things. "Thanks a lot."

"Registration's in the glove box. So's the insurance. Didn't have time to work up any I.D. But there's no reason you'd be pulled over if you drive sensible."

"I intend to."

"Well . . ." he said, and I gave him the keys. I watched him walk to the Lincoln. He had a limp, like one of his legs was shorter than the other. As he opened the door, I asked, "Why are you doing this?"

He looked at me a moment. "When I was nineteen the sarge saved my leg. I was wounded. He carried me on his back five miles. I like my leg. I like walking." He tilted his head back and gave me a challenging look. "You like walking?"

"Haven't given it much thought," I admitted.

He shook his head. "Nobody does," he said, then slid behind the wheel.

When the old pickup finally coughed into life he was gone.

I made good time. Around eight o'clock I pulled into a truck stop about fifty miles outside of St. Louis in Litchfield, Illinois. I was feeling fried and queasy from my binge the night before. I managed to scarf down a cheese omelet and some coffee. I was looking distractedly into my cup when I saw it was full of quivering concentric rings: my hands were shaking. The bedlam I had endured for the last year, and the shocks of the last few days especially, were taking a serious toll. I could feel the fatigue in my bones; my body was saying time-out. I realized then that I was very close to some sort of breakdown. The waitress was a chubby girl with shiny black hair tied back tight in a pony-tail. She seemed very attentive, though I didn't get a good look at her until she was giving me my third refill. "I know you," she said, deftly pouring.

I looked at her. Her features were vaguely Native American, smooth and solemn. She carried herself, I noticed, with the effortless poise you see in horses. "I don't think so."

She slid into the black leather booth opposite me and set down her pot. "Your name's John. You're a shrink." Her voice had a very pleasant Midwestern twang and a charming whistle of sibilance on every *s*. For some reason I wasn't alarmed by her insight. More tickled.

I smiled and shook my head. "Sorry. Bill Davenport. Schoolteacher."

She fiddled with the many turquoise rings on her right hand. Her arms were covered with black hair. "Don't worry. I'm good at secrets—all my friends say so." She put an odd spin on the word *friends,* as if it meant something special. Then she smiled. She had a nice smile. And sad brown eyes. There was a silver cross above her white uni-form and red apron. "You smoke too much," she said, looking at my Salem streaming in the ashtray. "You're run-ning from something. You're scared. And you don't know who to trust. There's a lot of that going around." It was a little joke, but it helped to lighten things up.

"Let me try," I said, and she seemed pleased by the sug-gestion. "You're twenty-five. Never been married. Boys are scared of you. Girls don't trust you. You were a loner in high school. You live with your parents. You're the best waitress this place has got, because you like to see people happy. What else? You're honest."

She nodded her head respectfully. "You see pretty good. Well, that's what shrinks are paid for. But I'm twenty-seven. Divorced. No kids. I go part-time to Blackburn College. Photography. And I get off in half an hour."

I laughed. "You don't fool around." She looked at me with a smile. "I mean—"

"I know what you mean."

She left the table and her scent lingered after her. Something simple and lovely. What was I thinking about? I had to get out of there. When I stood up she was next to me, sliding into a pink corduroy jacket. She scooped up her tip and slid it into her purse. "Twenty percent! Thanks," she said.

I paid the cashier and she was waiting for me at the door. I walked by her and she said, "Zip up. You'll catch your death."

I stopped under the awning outside the diner and looked at the big rigs parked in a row, massive machines armored in gleaming chrome. "Listen, I, this is, I'm not, I think . . ."

"I need a ride home," she said.

"Look," I said, trying to get her attention. "You don't want to know me. I'm a dangerous man."

She tilted back her head and examined me down her nose, through slitted eyes. "That's what the TV says: *dangerous.*" She passed me a gentle smirk. "I like that in a man."

She lived with her mother in an Airstream in a trailer park about a mile from the truck stop. Their home smelled like women: clean, delicate scents, shampoos and flowers, subtle wisps of fragrances I couldn't name. Her mother was in a wheelchair watching MTV—a bony woman with long white hair and thick glasses. "Hey, Ma," she said, flinging off her coat onto the couch. "This is John, or Bill. He can't decide." Her mother looked my way and I could see two TVs reflected in her bifocals.

"Bill," I said. "Bill Davenport."

The old woman's voice shocked me. Imagine a woman with the vocal chords of a bulldog. She growled: "John, Bill—doesn't make no difference to me."

"We just got cable," the girl explained, grabbing me with a warm hand and leading me down a narrow wood-paneled hall. My first impression was: a high-schooler's bedroom. There was school memorabilia hanging from the white wall: pennants, pompoms, a photo of a girls' basketball team under the heading "State Champs—1980." Girlish, I thought. Then I saw a wall covered with black-and-white photos: a bearded man in black leather on a BMW, a rocky waterfall, a horse looking over its shoulder, a naked baby asleep on a pillow, its tiny hands balled into fists, a totem pole whose top was swallowed by fog, someone diving off a cliff into a river, a black snake crawling over a bare foot.

"You did these?" I asked.

"Yeah. I didn't know enough about light then."

"They're very good," I said.

"Thanks, but—they're really not."

She took my shoulders and sat me down on her bed; it was covered with a multicolored patchwork quilt and it sank in the middle. "You're tired," she informed me. "And you shouldn't drink so much." She let loose her ponytail and looked in the round mirror on her dresser and fluffed at her hair. There were lots of pictures stuck into the wooden frame of the mirror. They were all postcards, nature scenes with no people. Who sent them to her? I wondered. What am I doing? I thought. I stood up and the bed creaked.

"I shouldn't be here. I gotta meet somebody in St. Louis."

She stepped over and pushed me gently back down on the bed. "He can wait," she said, and began taking off my shoes. "Everybody's in such a hurry. When's the last time you looked at a sunset? Pissed off a bridge in the moonlight? Watched a bird fly by? I tell you . . . people don't know how to use time." I lay on the bed and looked at the curved plastic ceiling; I could hear the rain pounding metallically on the trailer. My pants came off with a *whoof.*

"Give me your arms," she said. I did and she removed my jacket and snorted at the Chicago Bulls logo stitched into the back.

"Bulls fan?" she asked, flinging it on the yellow beanbag chair in the corner.

"Pistons," I mumbled.

"Bad Boys." She smiled.

Then off came my shirt; without removing any of the buttons, she pulled it over my head and tossed it on the floor. Then my T-shirt. She left my underwear on.

"Come on, Bill," she coaxed. "Get under the covers."

"I'd better not," I said, sitting up like Gandhi on the edge of her bed.

"Don't be contrary. You're catching a cold."

She was right: I could feel the stuffiness rising in my head, and my body was shivering. It was warm under the sheets and blankets and quilt. It felt like home. I could hear power chords coming from the TV. I watched her face in the mirror as she combed her hair, like she had something on her mind. There was a wooden cross on the wall at the foot of the bed, and stuffed behind it, a dry yellow frond of palm.

"You're Catholic?" I asked, pointing at the cross.

She looked at it. "I'm a lot of things," she answered. "I just like Palm Sunday. Now *that's* a holy day!"

I found this very charming even if it didn't make a lot of sense.

"You can watch if you want," she said.

I turned on my side, and resting my head on my hand, I watched her unzip her white uniform by reaching her arms crablike behind her: she was double-jointed. When she slipped it off I liked the way it hugged her high round butt, and I liked the crease showing just above her white panties. She bent over and stepped out of them. She unsnapped her bra and I could see the outline of it imprinted in red flesh. She turned around, held her hands at her side, and let me look at her. Her skin was remarkably like Laura's: sandy tan. But her breasts were much larger, her waist narrower, and she had something of a potbelly, which was nice. It was grooved by purple crescents: stretch marks. Would she tell me that story someday? I wondered. But then I was lost in the abundance of bright curves and shadows her shape took on in the dim light of her room. She looked at me straight on, almost proudly. "Not many people see this. I'm beautiful, aren't I?"

"Very," I agreed.

"But it's not magazine beautiful. Or TV beautiful. It's not the kind of beauty men give a double look to. That's *their* problem. But you see it, don'tcha, Bill?"

"Yes." I felt dizzy.

She stepped over to the bed and slid in, sighed, then pulled me to her. Her body was almost hot, but it felt pillowlike, comforting as it wrapped around me. Her hair was damp; it smelled like a kitchen. It's a dream, I thought. A very good dream.

"Shhhhh," she whispered. "You been running like a fool for a long time and you need a rest stop. That's what this is. There are places like that in the world. Gentle places. That quiet you down and restore you. We all need that sometimes."

"Why me?" I asked, taking deep breaths of the warm scent of her full body.

"You ask a lot of questions, don'tcha?" She squirmed, adjusting her position in the bed, putting a heavy leg over my thighs. "Your number just came up, I guess."

"Do you know about the Holock?" I asked, my muscles tensing at the thought.

"The who?" she asked, looking down at me. "Is that who you're running from?"

"That's one of them," I sighed.

"Well," she said, stroking my earlobe with her thumb, "let's put 'em on hold tonight."

I thought of Saul's invention: the hold button. That's exactly what I needed. My body felt fragile and spent. The last month of my life was catching up to me. How long did I think I could go on like that? But I was here now. In the arms of a kind and beautiful woman who was going to let me hold her. Put it on hold. Hold off a little. I was drifting off to sleep when I snapped to and asked, "What's your name?"

I could feel her body shaking, holding back a giggle. " 'Bout time you got around to that. Well, Bill," she said with a small laugh, "my name's Suzie."

"John," I said. "John Donelly." I looked up into the brown eyes in that soft round face. "Why do I trust you, Suzie?"

"Same reason I trust you." She smiled, and rubbed a smooth palm over my belly. "You deserve it." She pinched my nipple and reached behind her and turned off the lamp beside her bed.

"Your mother?" I asked.

"Leave her out of this," she said in the dark. "Rest up, now. You're too darned tired for sex tonight."

Well, nobody's right all the time.

That night I dreamt I was swimming in a cold black lake. Laura was teaching me how to swim. She was bald and giddy. "It's this way," she laughed. And I dove and followed her down a bright yellow tube that turned into a whale that swallowed us whole. "Don't worry," said Laura, taking my hand. "She doesn't bite." I was so happy. I was in love.

The next morning we slept in and her mother made us pancakes on a very low stove. The whole trailer, in fact, seemed scaled to her wheelchair. I noticed the living room couch had no legs. She called me "John Bill" and talked at length about MTV. "They're stupid, those videos. Like a salesman talking so fast 'cause he's got nothing to say. Not a damn one of them makes any sense!" In general, she objected to dances involving pelvic thrusts: to her, dancing was something done above the waist. Suzie was quiet but kept tickling my leg with her chubby toes under the table. I was smiling a lot, at nothing in particular. Her mom sipped her coffee with both hands and asked coyly, "How was your evening?" Suzie replied with a mouthful of pancakes, "None of your business, Ma."

Suzie and I were doing the breakfast dishes and her mother was flicking through channels with the remote when she called out, "Hey! John Bill! You're on TV!"

Suzie and I exchanged glances, then walked over to watch. It was a newscast from Chicago.

"Professor Dwight Fontaine was found suffocated in the bathtub of the suspect. Authorities say the suspect"—here my high-school graduation photo appeared above the newscaster's shoulder—"a Detroit psychologist, has no previous criminal record but is believed to be armed and dangerous. Both the suspect and Professor Fontaine were attending a conference at the Hilton in downtown Chicago. Donelly left suddenly, without paying his bill, and he may be driving a black 1952 Lincoln."

"That's a LIE!" I yelled. "I prepaid!"

Suzie's mom looked at me, then turned to her daughter and said, "He's innocent."

I left the trailer with an itchy new butch haircut, courtesy of her mother, and a new pair of shades Suzie had scrounged up. "Well," she had insisted, "if you're a fugitive from justice, you need a disguise."

I dropped her off at the truck stop for her shift and she kissed me and gave me a self-addressed stamped postcard. "Send it to me?"

Tasting her cherry lipstick, I looked at the card. The picture was the same one Tim Buckley had used for his last album cover, *Greetings from L.A.*: an airplane shot of the smoggy brown city. I hadn't told her I was going there. For a moment I tapped it against the steering wheel. I was thinking about the dresser mirror in her bedroom, rimmed with similar postcards. Then I looked at Suzie and some devil made me say, "You get a lot of these?"

She looked at me steadily for a few seconds. Whatever I was laying on her she wasn't buying. But I could see her step back into herself, and the disappointment floating just behind her eyes, ready to surface.

"I got a lot of friends," she said. "So?"

I was immediately embarrassed. "So nothing." I shrugged. "I'll send it." I smiled. "Promise."

In a moment the tension passed. She touched her fingers to my lips. "You sure you're gonna be all right?"

I nodded and said, "If you're ever in Detroit . . ."

She frowned and smiled at me at the same time. "Ahh, what's a psychologist gonna do with a waitress?"

"I've got a few ideas," I said with a leer.

She laughed. "I bet you do." Then she looked at me gravely for a moment. "Careful, John. I take invitations seriously."

I was a little hurt by her warning. "I meant it," I protested. "I'd like to see you again."

She looked through the windshield for a second. It had started to rain. "Well, that's nice. I'll think about it." She turned to me. "You, too. Don't forget the postcard." I watched her pitch her coat like a tent over her head and dash into the diner. I liked the way her body moved when she dodged the puddles on the blacktop.

I made it to St. Louis in the late afternoon. I parked behind a Dumpster in a hidden corner of a cobblestone lot where I could see the arch. I waited. And waited. It was chilly, so I started the truck, turned on the heater, and flicked on the wipers against the rain. It still hadn't let up. I yawned deeply and laid down to sleep.

In my dream I was still driving Saul's car. Imish hung upside down from the rearview mirror like a souvenir. It was a sunny day and I had to squint against the light. I wanted music, so I started punching buttons on the Delco. A pompous newscaster's voice came on: "Today's headlines. NATO nuclear treaty in jeopardy. Renewed border disputes in South America. Ragunian rebels have overrun government positions outside the capital. She's back, Doctor Donelly. And you're out of time." I frowned down at the radio and a tiny hand turned the knob off. The boy in the red sweater was sitting next to me on the seat. He smiled

and said, "Step on a crack. Break your mother's back."
Then he snatched Imish and jammed him into his mouth.
His eyes irised in and out and tiny red feathers fluttered
down to his lap. Then he was gone.

I woke up screaming. It was morning. My wipers were
screeching on the dry windshield, and I could see the arch
of St. Louis silhouetted on the pink horizon. Saul wasn't
around.

Fuck it. I couldn't wait forever; I had to get moving.

I was just out of Joplin, Missouri, when it hit me. If *I*
didn't break my mom's back—and *Hogan* didn't break her
back—who did? I didn't want to think the obvious. I didn't
think it until Oklahoma. Laura. I slammed down the accelerator and headed toward Amarillo. I would take great
pleasure from her death. I would get a real kick out of it.

Twenty-eight

This leg of the trip was so hot that the steering wheel burned and I had to switch hands every mile. I would have killed for air-conditioning. That old black pickup seemed to suck up every bit of heat and sun available. The back of my shirt soaked through and stuck to the vinyl seat. It was miserable. And still no sign of Saul. In the middle of New Mexico I decided to take a detour south to Alamogordo, the site of the first atomic test blast, the true beginning of the twentieth century, where man finally proved he didn't need God to end the world. I'd heard of the White Sands national park, which lay at the heart of an enormous missile range, but I wasn't prepared for the sight of a white Moby Dick beached on the horizon twenty miles away, looking like the Pontiac Silver Dome, where the Detroit Lions play. It kept getting bigger and bigger until it became a sea of white snow in the middle of this red desert, some twenty square miles of gypsum. I drove into the park at high noon and followed the white road as it curved around fifty-foot-high white dunes. A beautiful desolate place. There was absolutely no shade and I could feel every pore working overtime; it felt like someone had spritzed my body with warm water. The heat didn't seem to bother the other tourists, though. Kids scampered up the dunes, traced their names with their shoes, and rolled down laughing, their hair and clothes salted with the gypsum—like chicken parts rolled in Bisquick. I imagined they looked like Holock children. A thermometer on a wooden plaque read 110.

I sat down on the bumper and got a scorched ass. The dunes formed a valley around us so that anything anyone said was muffled and insubstantial, and seemed to dissipate in the surrounding quiet: a thick foreboding that was broken suddenly when two jet fighters screamed by in close formation; they were almost out of sight by the time I saw them. Death Machines. The roar of their afterburners echoed for a good thirty seconds after they had disappeared. I noticed everyone, including me, was watching the sky.

I headed southwest toward Tucson, driving at night when it was cool, sleeping in the shade during the day. Ugly daydreams about Suzie being held down and raped by strangers dressed like Pete Townshend in white jumpsuits. If they had been nightmares I would have freaked and called to warn Suzie to watch out for the Holock. As it was I was scared enough to stop at a religious goods store in Wilcox, Arizona, to buy a magnetic transparent statue of Mary full of holy water. I was taking no chances. Driving under the limit. Dodging the Marshmallows. I no longer expected Saul to show up. All I knew was I was heading to L.A., to the machine, to the Holock, to kill somebody who deserved it.

I got in the habit of talking to myself, and more than once I noticed somebody in a car next to me, usually a lady, giving me a look. It was a pretty redundant conversation because it always came down to one question: "Why?

Why'd Laura kill Mom? That's the last thing I'll ask her before I snuff her. I'll wait for her answer. Then I'll catch her dreaming, enter the dream, and wake up. Bingo. Laura all gone."

I knew I was talking like an idiot. I couldn't help it.

When I saw the sign welcoming me to Arizona, I remembered I had friends there. Two Deadheads who tended a ski resort on Mt. Lemon north of Tucson. It was a perfect life for them, some nine thousand feet up, clean air, beautiful view, and they only had to baby-sit the lodge during the off season, which allowed them plenty of time for their main hobby: joining the throng of pilgrims who followed the Grateful Dead across the country, from concert to concert, for months at a time. They were leftover hippies who couldn't care less that the world had passed them by. And, like most of the Deadheads I had met through them, they were incredibly decent, open-minded, and generous people. Sphene was an ace carpenter and cook. June was a former geologist who earned a decent living running a licensed mail-order business specializing in Dead memorabilia: concert bootlegs, posters, T-shirts, rings, books. When I pulled up to the circular drive of the empty resort—it resembled a smaller version of the Overlook Hotel, the one Jack Nicholson caretakes in *The Shining*—I yodeled: our old password.

"Donelly?" a man's voice called down from above me.

I squinted up at the sun and saw Sphene—a bronzed blond Norseman straddling the rooftop, in mountain boots and white cut-off jeans, a leather tool belt around his waist, a hammer in his hand. I waved.

"Thor! God of Thunder!" I called.

He gave me the whitest smile. "Ring da bell. June's in da office."

The small tan woman who opened the door wore a tie-dyed granny dress. She yelped and leaped into my arms, wrapping her short legs around me and kissing me on the mouth.

"Johnny!" she said. I remembered how much I missed her beautiful blue eyes.

"Hey, June." I gulped. I hadn't expected to be so choked up, maybe because I hadn't counted on such a reception. When she released me, she leaned back and looked me over. "Jesus," she said. "Your hair."

"I'm traveling incognito," I explained. "The government's after me."

I had expected her to laugh, but instead she nodded, taking my quip for fact, which, of course, it was. I'd forgotten the paranoia of her politics. Maybe I'd forgotten it wasn't a laughing matter.

She was showing me around when Sphene practically tackled me, saying, "Yo, bro! What kept you? You said you'd be here yesterday."

"I did?"

"Well," June said, "Sphene said it was a bad connection."

My friendly doppelgänger, I thought. Watching out for me.

"Where's your luggage?" June asked, looking at my truck.

"I'm wearing it, like the Buddha."

"You smell like it," she giggled.

After my first bath in days I threw on one of Sphene's kimonos and sat down to a feast by candlelight. Good wine raided from the resort's cellar. Fresh bread with a crunchy buttered crust and warm insides that steamed when you tore it open. The main course was a goopy dish that was red and green and yellow (I don't know vegetables) and sprinkled with cheese. It tasted so good nobody said anything the whole meal. When we were sufficiently stuffed we sat back at their pale wooden kitchen table and passed each other contented smiles. Their apartment was in the highest spot in the hotel: right under the main roof. It seemed to go on forever, following the arched ceiling that V'ed over us. Every gable that ran adjacent to the long attic held one of Sphene's wood carvings, which he periodically shipped off to a New York gallery where they would be displayed and sold for what June called "an obscene profit"—which she made sure he invested in various ecological causes. Skulls and skeleton posters abounded, but like all vestiges of the Dead, they were never ominous, usually whimsical and weird.

"So who is she?" asked June, when our tongues were finally through tasting Sphene's gourmet dinner.

"Huh?" I answered cleverly.

"You met somebody," she insisted.

"Well, yeah," I admitted.

"Dat's goot," grunted Sphene, rubbing his belly. "You on a rock." It was one of his charming lapses into non sequitur that sprang from his less-than-perfect grasp of English. I think he meant "You're on a roll."

"I don't know," said June, scrunching up her nose as if she could read me by my scent. "I'm getting vibes good and bad."

"Maybe because it's two women." I explained as much as I could about Laura without saying anything that could endanger them. Then I mentioned Suzie.

June caught my reticence about Laura and didn't press it. But Suzie intrigued her. "I like the yellow beanbag chair, and the fact that she's Indian." June nodded. "But she doesn't really sound like your type."

"What's 'my type'?"

"Straight," said Sphene, with a smile.

It was something of a joke between us. My lifestyle was infinitely unhip to them, too tied into the materialism of the System: Urban, White-Collar, Nine-to-Five. And while they granted that my career was contributing a healing energy to the overall renewal of the planet, psychology itself was suspect. Sphene thought most neurosis could be traced to bad diet and chemicals. June respected psychology as a newborn science, but thought it too theoretical and too reductive: childhood trauma became the excuse for everyone's suffering. "Really," she said once, "it's all a newfangled way to talk about sin. To blame someone. It's straight thinking. Stimulus/response. Newtonian physics. Old World." We had covered this many times; they accepted my vocation while merrily regarding it as misguided.

"No, what I mean is," she continued, "she's not difficult enough for you."

"What?"

"All your girlfriends have been a challenge in one way or another, Johnny. Tough ladies. Critical. Argumentative. Suzie sounds . . . accepting."

"You know," I said, "I haven't any idea what you're talking about."

She gave me an impish smile and lit a joint. "I know."

" 'Seventy," said Sphene. "Da peace rally."

"Exactly," said June, passing the jay to Sphene and waving out the match.

"Da march," said Sphene, crossing his legs lotus-style and toking.

"The Commons." June nodded, closing her eyes.

"Uh, guys . . . ?" I interjected.

Sphene thought I meant the joint. He took a quick toke and held it toward me.

"No. Thanks," I said. "Actually, I was wondering what—"

June exhaled and the cloud hovered over the table. She took a deep breath and recited a monologue that had no punctuation. "The first time I ever saw you was before the march when you argued for a half hour with that suburban chick with the Indian headband about why we shouldn't be shoving dandelions down the barrels of the National Guardsmen because it was humiliating 'put-down theater' you called it and the whole point was to confront them with love as people not as drones of the state but you were shouted down and when we were marching and the soldiers charged you just stood there and watched them pummel those kids around you standing on the Common your hands in balls at your hips standing there weeping as they bashed heads and pulled girls by the hair and you're so helpless and enraged but mostly disappointed Johnny you got something on your chin you thought if we were calm and cool and righteous and fair everybody would see it our way and the bombs would stop dropping on the children and Nixon would resign and everybody would be nicer to one another but you couldn't deal with the fact that we were just a bunch of spoiled kids children of affluence clenching our fists and holding our breaths and messing up our rooms until we got what we wanted a new world and it hurt you I know."

After a time I said, "Who'd have thought a bunch of suburban hippies could scare the shit out of a militia of working-class part-time soldiers with words like *peace* and *love* and *freedom?*"

"They were scared," June agreed.

"Ya," said Sphene. "Me, too."

"I'd never seen anyone so angry," said June. "Maybe 'cause you couldn't do anything?"

"I was angry with myself," I admitted. "For being so stupid. I couldn't fight those bastards. I couldn't rescue anyone. I was afraid if I moved I would be hit, and if I was hit I'd have to kill something. I felt awful. Hypocritical. Furious. Cowardly." I shook my head. "Fucking pacifism. I hated them. And I just stood there."

"Until I grabbed you and dragged you to the student center," she said.

June offered me the last toke and I declined. Dope fucks up my emotions, makes everything unreal. I didn't need any more of that.

Sphene picked it up from there. "I was looking for June for hours. We got separated after da charge. I called da jail. Da hospital. Then I yust walk de campus, feeling like someone sock me in the stomach. Then I see my girl sitting with a guy who looks like Yon Lennon, holding his head in her lap, and for a minute I'm wishing maybe it'd be better if she was at da hospital. HA!"

We all laughed disproportionately. It was needed.

"Poor Johnny," sighed June, after we had recovered. "It's so important for you to be right."

That night, I got a hard-on listening to June and Sphene make love at the opposite end of the attic; their pleasure sounds made me very lonely. I thought of Suzie straddling me in the gray moonlight in the trailer, eyes closed and head to one side as we rocked together. I was dozing off when I heard the plaintive howl of a coyote. It echoed off the mountain like the sustained roar of ocean surf or the aftermath of a bass drum recorded with tons of reverb. For some reason I thought it was her, calling me back to that greasy truck stop in Litchfield, Illinois. Reminding me not to forget.

The next morning after a breakfast of stewed tomatoes, poached eggs, navy beans, and homemade plum jam on toasted bread that crackled when you chewed it, June directed me to a path that led up the mountain behind the resort. She said I'd know the place when I saw it, and that I was to leave something there, something that mattered to me, because the Spirit Tree always gave something to anyone who visited. I was used to their counterculture rituals by now, and I retained a grudging respect for June's sensitivity to the necessity of myth.

I walked up the steep and winding path under thick spruces. The wind coming over the mountain and pouring through the trees sounded strangely like traffic. I heard a bird call and saw what looked like a hawk with rust-colored wings making slow spirals down to earth. Hawks always made me think of God: a magnificent predator with perfect eyesight, seemingly effortless speed—at the same time beautiful and ruthless. Then I heard the faint tinkling of bells. I followed the sound to a small clearing, which looked like it had once been the bedding place for a family of deer. There, on the low branches of a blue spruce, was a makeshift shrine. Its centerpiece was a wooden triptych nailed into the bark at eye-level. Orbiting about it on the sagging branches were various incarnations of wind chimes. There was a string of copper bells corroded green and shaped like acorn caps. A piece of driftwood swayed lazily: an upside-down *Y,* like a divining rod, looking for water in the sky. The busted strings of Sphene's guitar dangled together from one branch, making almost inaudible metallic sounds when they randomly collided. Suspended on a rope there was a section of two-by-four that had been perforated by termites, who left their perfect tunnels bisecting the handiwork of man: nature tamed, nature reclaimed, two types of dwelling in one. There was a bone chime made of three thigh bones—a large animal by the size of it: a moose or deer; when they knocked together it sounded like the clucking of a tongue. Above the triptych a gray deer antler hung inverted on a broken nub of the tree. There was something hypnotic about it all. The combination of animal remains and human totems gave it an aura of magic and shamanism. I stood there for a long time watching. Then I stepped up to the three-piece wooden artifact at the apex of the Spirit Tree.

It was the size of an old tabletop radio, but flatter. Copper hinges bound the three parts together: the center piece was a Gothic arch, and it was flanked by two half arches so that when it was closed it would once again become one. Behind the center glass was a picture of people dancing. I recognized it from their apartment in Ann Arbor: the audience at a Grateful Dead concert shot looking down from the balcony. You could not tell the women from the men as the aperture was left open for more than an instant and their dancing blurred into a whirlpool of motion. Sphene had taken that on his first acid trip. The right side was Magritte's picture of a nude woman's torso straining at the frame that contained it, like a body against a girdle. The left frame was the ditch of children from the My Lai massacre. I stepped back a bit at that one. It was the only repulsive part of this hippie altar in the woods. Then it occurred to me: perhaps no more repulsive than a crucifix. Innocent victims of man's fear and folly. The massacre. The body straining to be itself. The Dance.

I don't know why, but I began to cry.

The only thing I had to leave was a postcard from an Indian woman who had said she trusted me. I memorized her return address and impaled the City of the Angels on a point of the antler. When I got back to the lodge June was working at her Apple, updating her mailing list. I gave her a big hug from behind and she leaned back into me.

"Worth it?" she asked.

"I don't have the words," I said gratefully.

"Sphene said you got a phone call."

"Dat's right," he called from one of the gables down the way. I walked over and found him sanding a wood sculpture, something abstract.

"Dat's a pretty pink phone you got dere, Johnny," he teased.

"Who called?"

"Somebody named Sul. Said he was in yale."

"Yale?"

"Prison," he clarified.

"Christ!"

"Said to tell you he'd meet you at da Lows on da Ocean."

"Da Lows?" I asked. Sphene nodded. Trust Saul to be obscure. "Did he say he was gonna make bail?"

"Nah. But he said he'd be dere. 'Da details are handled. Get into da Big Picture.' "

That was Saul, all right.

"You in trouble, Johnny?" called June from down the way. Sphene stopped sanding to look up at me.

"Better you don't know," I said. There was a moment of silence. They had too much respect for the boundaries of others to pry when not invited.

"A very, very pretty phone," said Sphene with a grin. Then he turned back to his sanding.

I hated to leave that place. The company. The food. The vibe. They packed me a knapsack of extra clothes and gave me some cash. At the pickup, Sphene cried. Then we had one of those three-way hugs that seemed endless because nobody wanted to break it. Finally, June slapped me on the butt and said, "Don't lose the Indian."

"Ya," added Sphene. "But remember da Alamo."

Another one of his non sequiturs. But as I drove down the dusty mountain road, I thought that, for some reason, it made sense. As a synchronistic reference to Alamogordo:

the bleached lifeless dunes, the Genesis of the End, the playground of men who still believed the enemy was outside themselves. Or maybe it was just a multipurpose warning. Or a reason for revenge. After all, I reminded myself, I had someone to kill.

Twenty-nine

I drove straight to Phoenix. And right through it. It's a strange town in the middle of the desert, and once you're out of it, it just stops. There's a suburb, then there's a road, and then . . . nothing. Nothing but red mountains and red desert as far as you can see. And that's practically all I saw until I made it to L.A. about eight that night.

It was beautiful, twinkly, and remarkably smogless—it had rained that morning. I missed the legendary rush-hour gridlock, cruised down Hollywood Boulevard, and saw a man pushing a poodle in a shopping cart—that's when it all came back to me. The psych conference I had attended a few years before. The blue pools that, seen from the air, dot the brown landscape like sequins. The pool cleaners in white vans making their rounds like bees from flower to flower. The unemployed actors giving eccentric performances as waiters. The Mexicans at stoplights, selling oranges, bananas, papayas. The would-be rock stars strutting in outrageously colored spandex. The hoards of homeless, sleeping under viaducts, toting their possessions in Glad bags. The palpable wealth—car phones and Jaguars and three-hundred-dollar jogging shoes. The seductive vortex of opulent architecture. The perfect malls. The cheerful abundance of drop-dead gorgeous bodies. The full-time sun, the dazzling aura of available dreams. On a tour bus at Universal Studios the guide interrupted his spiel to announce, "The Monkees are reuniting for one and one show only—with THE Mike Nesmith!" That's Hollywood in a nutshell: the trivial, the hyped, and the inspired.

It's the one place I know that can accurately be compared to a drug. You feel sort of giddy at first, then a huge bliss swallows you and you lope around with a silly smile. Then the sweet hangover of perfect, sun-stroked days. Finally the irreality of it all hits home and you begin to get paranoid—these people don't really like me; they just want a fucking TIP! Then you can't wait to GET OUT. Get Home. Get off this mad rudderless Disney ride and get back to where people shovel snow and cook their own meals and don't plot their lives around their next impression, audition, lunch, break. The cool ambition of L.A. spoils the party. Everyone is so poised for that moment when destiny hoists them out of life and says: "YOU are the Next One!" They never quite connect; you never feel they're really present to you, but always gazing somewhere, just over your shoulder, to a horizon that will someday appear behind the turdish haze.

I headed straight for Venice Beach and caught the last show of the famous chain-saw juggler. A line of girls on Rollerblades skated by. There was a redheaded hippie in a tux who looked like Ginger Baker playing ragtime on an upright piano on castors on the sidewalk. I requested Monk and he laid a tasty version of "Well, You Needn't" on me. I gave him a five and asked if he had ever heard of "The Lows on the Ocean"—my translation of Saul's chosen rendezvous point. He turned and pointed down the coast at what looked like a gigantic dock on pylons jutting out into the Pacific. I could make out the twirling lights of a Ferris wheel in the distance.

"Pink hotel," the piano player said. "Just hug the ocean; you can't miss it."

"Thanks."

"You're staying *there?*" he asked, looking me up and down.

"Meeting somebody."

He seemed relieved. "For a minute I thought you were rich."

The "Lows" turned out to be a contemporary luxury hotel right on the beach, a short walk from the Santa Monica Pier: a huge Coney Island boardwalk with a rather crummy full-time carnival. I pulled into the circular cobblestone drive right next to a fleet of Mercedes and Porsches. The Hispanic valet reluctantly took the keys to my weathered pickup and the doorman in a white military uniform tipped his hat as I entered. Jesus, I thought, passing through the automatic doors into the main lobby. A spectacular atrium rose eight stories above me, pale green steel buttresses looming over the vast marble floor below doing a contemporary take on a Gothic ceiling, except there was no ceiling, only huge panes of tinted glass. The color scheme was pink and green. A real harpist was playing, but I couldn't see where; there were too many plants and flowers and fountains full of albino koi fish and guests wearing flipflops and high hemmed white robes with golden *L*'s stitched into the breast. I strolled to the front desk, feeling very out of place in my T-shirt and black jeans.

"My name is Donelly. A Mr. Lowe is expecting me. Did he leave a message?"

She beamed at me like I had just given her a raise. "Of *course,* Mr. B! Your suite is all ready!" She rang one of those service bells and its echo embarrassed me as all the guests turned to see who was checking in.

"Mr. B?" A Hispanic bellhop in white greeted me and led me to my room. Or should I say *rooms*. Everything was white and pink and looked like it had just been featured in *Architectural Digest*. There was a bowl of fresh fruit and cheese and a bottle of champagne on a table by the balcony. A white fan turned under the arched ceiling. A bed as big as a diving raft. A living room with big screen TV and VCR. A kitchenette. A dining area. A sitting area. An office equipped with computer and fax. A full bar. A sunken tub surrounded by mirrors. As he was turning on the lights and showing me around he told me that the chef had a very fine crab pasta in cream sauce that he could personally recommend. Before he left he assured me that if there was anything he could do to make my stay more pleasurable—anything at all: a masseuse, manicure, haircut, driver, concert tickets—just call him at the bell desk. His name was Enrico. It was a delight to make my acquaintance, Mr. B.

Christ, I felt guilty tipping the guy a dollar.

I lay down on the bed and noticed a fresh pack of my favorite brand of Salems open on the table next to the phone.

I had a long, hot bubble bath, watching myself in the mirrored walls, smoking and drinking the bottle of champagne. The hotel's trademark calligraphic *L* was embossed everywhere. On crystal ashtrays. On the bottom of the tub. On the hair-dryer fixture on the wall. On every single towel and washcloth. Even the vanilla soap—except it spelled the full name out. L-O-W-E-S.

Lowes?

I said it aloud, looking at my shocked face in the mirror. "LOWES!! Christ! Saul OWNS this fucking joint!"

"Ya comfortable?" a familiar voice asked from the adjoining room.

"Obscenely!" I called back, and was rewarded by his trademark chuckle.

"I taught cha would be," said Saul, appearing in the doorway in the same gray suit in which I last saw him. He lit a fat cigar and looked at me.

"You all right?" I asked.

"Fit as a fiddle."

"I missed you in St. Louis."

"I was detained by various law-enforcement agencies. Couldn't be helped."

"Where?"

"Let's see. After I left you I was with Jack at the rectory. Then I Blipped into Las Vegas. Somebody recognized me at the craps table. Next thing I know the feds got me in this suite at the top of the Sands. Handcuffed to a toilet. Asking questions."

"Did they hurt you?"

"Nyaahh. Chickenshits."

Our voices took on a strange echo in the grand bathroom. Our sentences lasted a few seconds longer than usual, and we had to wait for the silence before we could talk. "You called me in Arizona," I said.

"They had me in some rinky-dink jail somewhere, waiting for a helicopter to take me to Washington. I insisted on my one phone call."

I wanted to kiss him on the head. "It's damn good to see you, Saul."

"You're getting sentimental on me. Oh, I see: champagne."

He left the room and returned with an ashtray and one of the pillows from the couch. He laid it on the floor and sat down, then reached for one of the five phones in the suite, ordered two pastas and a pitcher of orange juice. "I expect you got a few questions."

"Only about a hundred."

"Shoot."

"Where's the REM machine?"

"It's in town, at one of the studios. I'll take you to it tomorrow."

"Am I too late? I mean, can I still stop Laura?"

"Not sure, Doc." He rubbed the lit end of his stogie on the rim of the ashtray. "Like I told you, the Holock got your seed now. As far as they're concerned they've clinched the deal. Settled their future. See, they only had that small window of time when you were vulnerable. One year when they knew you'd have a child. It's passed now, but that doesn't necessarily mean we haven't got a chance. Any bad dreams?"

"One awful one," I remembered.

"They're tracking ya." He nodded.

I told him about the holy water Mary statuette I bought.

"Good thinking. Probably put them off your scent. Where is it?"

"In the truck. On the dash."

He reached for the phone. "Enrico? This is Rocky. Would you be kind enough to go down to the garage and get Mr. Bullwinkle's luggage? And Enrico—grab that statue on his dashboard and bring it up. Yer a peach."

"Rocky and Bullwinkle?" I asked.

He waved his cigar expansively. "Hey, this is Hollywood. Stars do it all the time."

I took a long swig of champagne.

"Take it easy," Saul admonished. "You've got a long trip ahead of ya."

"Saul? Who's my double?"

"You mean yer better half?" He chuckled.

"You know who I mean."

"Well, it's *you,* of course. But beyond that—who knows? My best guess is he's from an alternative past. And he's visited Laura. That would explain the goo, eh?"

"It doesn't make sense," I said.

"There you go again," he said, shaking his head.

"So what's the government got to do with all this?"

"Dream deprivation," he said with a solemnness he usually reserved for religious topics. He tapped his cigar against the ashtray. "That's the weapon the Holock sold 'em. You know we can't survive without sleep or dreams? Let's just say there's a bunch of very cranky defense engineers around the world these days."

"So why do the feds want you?"

" 'Cause the Holock want me. Arms for hostages," he smirked. "I learned a lot by their questions. What they did and didn't ask me. The government cooperated with the Holock to help Laura find you. Files, I.D., birth certificates. You're a pretty well-known guy. I'm surprised you made it this far."

"I see." I swirled the bubbles around a bit and lit another cigarette. "Adrian was an agent."

Saul nodded.

"Laura was an agent?" I asked.

"More like a highly placed diplomat with special immunity."

"Did you know she killed my mother?"

Until that moment, I hadn't thought Saul was capable of being surprised.

"SHE WHAT?" His cigar dropped out of his mouth and he retrieved it, patting the ashes off his lap.

"Killed my mother." I was examining my wrinkled toes above the froth of bubbles.

He frowned deeply and shook his head. "I don't believe it. No way."

As I explained, he covered his eyes with one hand. Then he sighed.

"Doc," he said at last. "I'm sorry I dragged you in to this."

I'd never seen Saul so serious. His skin was turning white. "Hey, Saul!" I said, alarmed. "*You* didn't do anything! This was all the Holock's idea."

He looked sadly at me and blinked several times. "Right. What I mean is . . ." The thought seemed to trail off as he spoke and he stared away for a time, at nothing in particular. "I never knew my mother," he said. "She died when I was very young." He caught himself, blushed, and looked back at me. "What was yours like?"

"She was . . ." I contemplated the mirrored ceiling above the tub. ". . . a bitch."

"Oh."

The mood had gotten a little dark for me, so I teased him. "You mean to tell me there are things you actually don't know?"

"Hey, I'm Chronoscient. I'm not omniscient."

We laughed together and the mood passed. Finally he said, "Tomorrow we'll set up the machine and you'll meet Wanda."

"Wanda?"

He blew a puff of smoke at the ceiling. "My assistant."

"Didn't know you had one."

"I just hired her. But we go back a ways."

"Saul, can we be found again?"

"I don't think so. Our suite here doesn't have a number. And here . . ." He handed me the phone. "Ask if Mr. Donelly has checked in yet."

I asked.

A woman purred back the answer. "There are no reservations for anyone under that name."

Saul whispered, "Ask if there are any messages for Mr. Bullwinkle."

There weren't any.

The next morning we had a delicious breakfast of crabs Benedict and fresh raspberries on our private patio overlooking the ocean. A cool fog lingered over the breakers, obscuring the sky. We took the truck into Hollywood and picked up Wanda at a small adobe house with an orange tree in the front yard. She looked like a gangster moll gone to seed. Poufed-up silver hair and tight silky black stretch pants, a spangly rhinestone blouse that emphasized her top-heavy figure. She took little baby steps down the walk to the car—maybe because her pants were so tight.

"Howdy, Natasha!" Saul said lustily.

They smooched and she slid in next to him. "Hello, Rocky!" she giggled. Then she fluttered her lashes at me. "You must be the moose! Isn't this fun!?"

I had a strange, incongruous feeling when Wanda chirped that. Strange because I was feeling pretty rested, quite pampered in fact, glad of the company after my lonely road trip. The sun was everywhere; the oranges on her tree were ripe. There was nothing that could have reasonably triggered the stab of dread I felt. I looked at Wanda and her piled-up tinted hair and I felt she was going to die. Horribly. Quickly. I tried to discount the feeling as an intuition set off by being in the Movie Capital of the World. You know how you can always tell the expendable types in films? The ones that serve as fodder for the plot? They're usually eccentric, cheerful, trusting. They make you grin. Not handsome enough to be the leads, not interesting enough to steal the show, they're the fall guys, the character actors who do their shtick and are promptly dispatched in the first reel. Walloped by a madman or a monster. Wanda was perfect casting.

Then I saw her inspecting us with amusement and I knew just what she was thinking: how much our nicknames matched our body types: me, lanky and bony; Saul, squashed and round.

"Moose un Squirrel!" she said with a perfect Russian accent.

And we all laughed.

Saul steered me to the new Paramount Studios. A vast film production complex full of old and new soundstages. "Used to be MGM. Louie Mayer played tennis with me. Cheated, too."

The old guard at the gate gave Saul a big smile and waved us through. We parked and walked onto the lot, Wanda giving little oohs of recognition wherever we went. I concluded she must have worked here.

All the soundstages were painted manila yellow—they looked like airplane hangars: wide sliding doors, convex corrugated roofs, and beside a regular-size door, a prominent red light. When it was flashing, Saul explained, they were filming and no one was admitted. A man in a brown jumpsuit walked by carrying a prop: a volcanic boulder as tall as he. People in golf carts puttered by, delivering costumes on hangers to their sets. A man in a gorilla suit was leaning on a wall, holding his hairy head in one hand and smoking a pipe. We climbed a steel staircase, entered a door, and stood at the rim of what looked to be a rusted old soup bowl about fifty feet in diameter. Overhead was a network of girders and walkways. The bowl was full of green-blue water and it was circumscribed by a narrow wooden walkway. Not a very smart design—no one had even bothered to put a guardrail around it! Why, any toddler could just trip into it and—

"Ahh, memories," Wanda sighed, lacing her arm into Saul's and leaning on him.

Keeping well away from the edge, I saw it was some vast swimming pool with concave sides that narrowed to the bottom. I could make out tiny square portholes about halfway down. It looked about thirty feet deep. No, actually, it looked about a mile down to the bottom. "What is it?" I asked.

"Esther Williams's pool."

"Memories," sniffled Wanda.

"She was an artist." Saul nodded.

"She was a star!" said Wanda, openly weeping now.

I remembered overhead shots of swimsuited girls doing Busby Berkeley patterns in a pool. I wanted to hear all about it. I wanted to examine this tidbit of trivia from every possible angle. "She was the one who did that water choreography?" I asked.

They both looked at me like I had belched in a cathedral.

"It sounds so cold when you say it like that, Mr. Bullwinkle."

"Sorry," I told them, stepping back from the pit and leaning on the railing that encircled it.

"Well?" said Saul. "There it is."

I saw his look. "What?"

"The machine."

I looked around. "Where?"

"At the bottom."

Wanda was on her knees, looking into the pool. "I can see it, Rocky!"

Keeping a solid grip on the rail, I leaned over. "Where?"

Wanda snickered and pointed. "Right in the middle, Silly. Squint!"

I craned my neck and squinted. I could just make out the vague outline of a long rectangular object. This annoyed me. "What the hell's it doing down there?"

Saul lit a cigar and tucked a thumb into his belt. "It's as safe as any place. Lenny hid it good, all right."

"At the bottom of a pool?" I said. "How we gonna get it out?"

"You mean how are YOU gonna get it out?" Saul replied. "My swimming days are over, Doc."

I looked at Saul. I looked at the pool. I looked at Wanda.

Saul frowned. "You dive. You unscrew it. You bring it up. Nothin' to it. Wanda? You got it?" She pulled a socket wrench out of her hefty purse and held it out to me.

I backed away, thinking, the Irony of It All. Damn, was this ironic. It's unbelievably ironic! We come all this way for nothing. Ain't that a bitch! That just burns my socks. Well, as Hogan says, what are you gonna do? I peered down into the depths of Esther Williams's pool and had a newfound respect for her talent and her bravery. I looked around. "Hey! I got an idea! Maybe we can hire somebody!" I smiled eagerly, looking around for help.

Saul snickered. "What are you, nuts? This is top secret!"

"How top secret can it be!" I shouted. "It's in the middle of a pool in Burbank!"

"It's only thirty feet down!" Saul replied, resting his fists on his hips. "You can hold your breath underwater, I assume!"

"Forget it!" I snapped.

"What's wrong with you?" said Saul.

"I can't swim."

Saul gave me an exasperated look.

"Everybody can *swim!*" Wanda scoffed. "We *came* from the *ocean!*"

"It's only water!" Saul said.

"Then *you* do it!" I said.

"I can't believe you," said Saul. "You come all this way and you can't even—"

There was a big splash that drenched my ankles with cold, cold water. We looked over the edge to see Wanda porpoise-kicking down to the bottom, her red pumps set together by her purse at the edge of the pool like Dorothy's ruby slippers.

"What a woman!" said Saul.

She must have been under for two minutes. Little streams of bubbles seemed to take forever to get to the smooth surface of the pool. We could see her twisting the silver wrench. I was getting a little nervous when she came up for air, shockingly fast. Her perm was ruined. She took a couple deep breaths, then she dove back down.

"She was one of Esther's girls," Saul explained.

"She's something else," I admitted.

She came up again. "Seven-sixteenths," she said, spitting water at us. I could see she had the wrench in her hand. Saul fished into her purse and pulled out a shiny socket and handed it to her. "Mooses can't swim," she smirked, and went under.

It seemed to take longer this time. When she finally came up I got my first glimpse of Saul's time machine. She tossed it on the deck and Saul pulled her out. I don't know what I had been expecting. But it sure wasn't a World War II stretcher with tiny stilts and a soggy built-in headrest. It looked like it was made out of canvas and aluminum.

"This is it?" I asked.

Saul glared at me and wrapped his suit coat around

Wanda. She sat at the edge of the pool, quite out of breath. "I left the wrench down there. Sorry."

"Fuck the wrench, Natasha. Ya done great!" he said, patting her shoulders.

"You sure did," I said, and they both looked up at me with withering contempt.

"I still got it," she said, trembling and jamming her purple lips together. "Don't I, Rocky?"

"You never lost it, babe," said Saul, kissing her dripping silver hair.

Thirty

When we got back to the hotel we had a guest. A cheerful red bird sitting in a golden cage in the corner. "God bless that Enrico!" said Saul, letting the bird out. Imish was so happy to see us he flew circles around the room, nearly decapitating himself on the ceiling fan. After he scolded the bird, Saul introduced him to Wanda, who had changed into some pink sweats at her house, and he seemed to approve: he sang to her. He spent a lot of time on my head, his tiny claws gripping my hair, like he was afraid to let me go.

We set up the machine in the middle of the bed—Saul assured me that, soggy or not, it was still in working order. I sat next to it, trying to figure its mechanism. There were no exposed parts. It could have easily been a World War II Hollywood prop: green canvas, silver tubing. The only incongruous thing was the headrest. It looked like a soft brick of clay wrapped in aluminum foil.

"Don't you have to strap me down or something?" I asked.

"Not to worry," Saul said. "You ain't going anywhere. Wanda?"

Wanda had brought a doctor's black bag and was rummaging through it. She pulled out the longest syringe I had ever seen and smiled sweetly at me. "Bottoms up!" she said.

"Now wait a second," I said, standing up. "What's with the needle?"

"It's procedure," said Saul, changing his wet pants in front of all of us. He wore boxer shorts and those weird sock suspenders. "You have to be completely still when you go in. This'll help you reach alpha stasis." He saw my face. "What are ya? Chicken of needles *and* water?"

"We never talked about this . . ."

"Listen, among other things, Wanda here's a nurse. So you're in good hands."

Wanda squirmed with pride at the compliment.

"Can we talk about this?" I said. "Can we? I need a moment here to"—I swallowed—"to get into this."

Saul pulled on his pants and looked at his watch. Wanda sighed, slumped down into a chair, and turned on the TV with a flick of the remote. Imish stayed perched on my head as I sat back down on the bed and started taking deep breaths. I eyed the contraption next to me. It didn't look like much.

"So, how's it work?"

"You wouldn't understand." He shrugged.

Yeah, I probably wouldn't. "Shouldn't I have, like a trial run, or something?"

"What for? Listen, I'll make sure the machine gets you there. You go; you find her; you wait till she sleeps; you enter her dream; you wake up. Simple. Clear?"

"Yeah, fine. It's just . . ."

"Just what?" he asked, irritated.

I finally said what had been on my mind the whole trip back from the studio. "If I don't wake up. Tell Hogan . . . I said good-bye."

"Sure thing. Geez, you make it sound so dismal! The odds aren't so bad. I'd say, maybe, ohhh—one outta ten—you're deep-fried, or you're stuck there. You can't get odds like that in Vegas!"

I thought: This must be what it feels like before you go into surgery. "What's it going to be like?" I asked.

"Like a dream," Saul answered. "Exactly like a dream. Except you'll be awake." He walked over and put a hand on my shoulder. "John. I've done it myself. And I didn't have anybody to watch over me."

I nodded.

"It works. I made it myself. Anyway," he said, straightening up, "this was *your* idea."

I nodded. The sun was setting through the drapes, casting an orange glow into the room. I thought of Laura, particularly the time she lifted me up by the collar and knocked me senseless. It pleased me to think that now she had something to fear from me. I couldn't wait to see the look on her face.

"You want me to tell her anything for you?" I asked.

He turned his back to me and was quiet for a moment. "Nyahhh."

"Then let's do it," I said.

"Right," said Wanda, reaching for the needle.

"Imish!" called Saul. "Cage."

The bird bent over my forehead and looked me in the eyes upside down.

"Don't worry, little friend," I said. "I'll be back."

With that he launched himself off my head, dipped down to the floor, and swooped up to make a perfect landing in his golden cage.

"Take off your shoes," Saul said. "And bend over the bed."

I did as I was told and Wanda pulled down my pants

and gave me a very nasty jab in the ass. "URM!" I grunted.

"Help him lie down, Wanda," Saul instructed.

"Relax, Moose. I'm not gonna let anything happen to you," she cooed.

It felt like I was in a dentist's office, about to go under the gas. Wanda was the efficient assistant, Saul the impatient doctor.

"Take off his belt," Saul said. It came off with a whisk.

I watched the ceiling fan spinning. I tried to follow one of the blades all the way around. It made me dizzy. I closed my eyes.

"Take it easy," Saul told me.

"You're supposed to say: 'This won't hurt a bit,' " I quipped.

Wanda gently grabbed my wrist and took my pulse. After a moment, she said, "Descending."

I could feel the damp canvas soaking through my pants. "My butt's getting wet."

"Shhhhh," said Wanda, placing a cool hand on my forehead.

I opened my eyes. It was the only time I ever saw Saul look anything like frightened. He covered it immediately with a smile.

"T-minus thirty and counting, Doc."

"I don't feel anything yet."

"Feel this?" asked Wanda.

I felt nothing. "Nope."

"I just pinched your big toe," she said with a smile.

"Oh," I said. "That means?"

"You're on your way, Bullwinkle."

"Shhhhh," said Saul, and we were quiet.

Now I could definitely feel a deep, relaxing wave creeping up my body. It started in my shins: like I was stepping slowly into a warm bath.

"I feel it," I said.

Wanda took my pulse again. Her hand was very cold.

"Extremities," she said.

I opened my eyes suddenly without remembering closing them. Saul was leaning over me, doing something to the headrest. "Suzie," I said.

"It's Wanda," said Wanda.

"Quick. Write this down." I told her Suzie's address and what to say if anything should happen to me. My tongue was having trouble moving against my teeth. It felt very heavy.

"Mark," said Wanda.

"It's John," I said.

"He's under," said Saul.

"No, I'm not," I said.

"Yes, you are."

My eyeballs started shaking in their sockets: a very odd sensation.

"REM," said Wanda.

"But I'm not even sleeping," I said.

"Yes, you are," said Saul.

"Jesus," I said. "Let's not argue about it."

"Sweet dreams, Doc," Saul said, his voice echoing slightly.

"Full alpha," said Wanda.

The laws of physics punched out and my body sank into the bed like a stone into a vat of vanilla pudding. For a moment everything went white and it felt like I was falling from a great height toward a giant lake of milk. There was a low humming sound: like the prop of a Great Lakes freighter straining against the current.

All at once I could feel I had a steering wheel in my hand. I opened my eyes and found myself sitting in a Chevy dealership behind the wheel of the original Corvette: the classic white ragtop with the screens over the headlamps, no door handles on the outside. I thought to myself: It's 1953. I was just born. Muzak oozed into the showroom from hidden speakers: a syrupy version of Percy Faith's "A Summer Place." It seemed a bright summer afternoon. White light streamed through the huge glass windows that filled three walls of the showroom and bounced off the polished linoleum.

I heard a giggle and turned to find my dad and mom leaning against a Chevy wagon. They wore loud yellow matching golf clothes. They were kissing passionately. I thought: I must be dreaming. I jumped out of the 'Vette and walked over. "Hi, guys."

Dad goosed Mom and she squealed and slapped him on the shoulder. They leaned on one another and laughed like kids.

"Uh, guys?"

Still wrapped around each other, they turned and beamed at me, beamed at each other, then beamed back to me. I was beginning to feel peripheral.

"You're looking fit, Johnny!" said my dad proudly.

"Doesn't he, though!" Mom agreed.

Then they both stood there. Mom was wiggling her butt like Dad was getting funny in ways I couldn't see.

"How are you?" I asked.

"We're dead," they said together.

"I know, but . . ." This was not easy. I wanted to ask a lot of questions, but they kept jumbling into nonsense the moment I tried to speak. Finally, I said the first thing that came to mind. "What's Heaven like?"

"Well," said my mother, crinkling her forehead and thinking hard. "There are seven levels. First—"

"Rose," Dad interrupted, in a way he never would have dreamed of doing when he was alive. "Let me handle this."

That seemed just fine to her. "He's all yours." She smiled.

"Johnny," he said striding up to me and spreading his legs like John Wayne. "Hold your arm like this." He held his straight out from his shoulder. I did the same.

"Now hold it there. That's right. Hold it." He smiled an encouraging smile. We stood opposite each other like mirror images. My happy mother looked on. It wasn't long before my arm started aching. After a time, he said, "That hurts, doesn't it?"

"Yes," I said.

"It doesn't hurt in Heaven." He let his arm fall to his side. His smile was warm as he stepped back to my mother and gave her a peck on the cheek.

For some reason, I kept my arm suspended in the air. "I can't stay long," I apologized. "I have to kill someone."

"We know, dear," said my mother with sympathy. "It won't be easy, but we've got a lot of faith in you. Your father would be very proud," she said, as if he wasn't right next to her, goosing her butt.

"You can do it, Johnny. But try to enjoy yourself," he added.

"I will," I said.

Then they were gone and I was left standing in the middle of a Chevy dealership with my arm in the air. It was turning out to be one of those dreams that was either very important or very dumb.

"Howdy, Doc!" a voice called from behind me.

I turned to find a tall pale man in a baggy red sweater walking toward me, extending his hand. I felt as if I should remember him. An old companion of Dad's at the dealership? A golfing buddy? Damn, I hate when that happens. I knew this guy! I put down my arm, shook his hand, and took a closer look. His blond hair was trimmed short; he reminded me of a German actor who always played U-boat commanders. He had the stature and bearing of an Englishman, but was dressed rather casually for a salesman: khakis, canvas boat shoes—typical Grosse Pointe leisure wear. His name tag rang a bell: "Max Stillner." What was he saying?

"See anything you like?"

"I was just browsing."

He laughed like I'd just said something very witty. I noticed he still had a grip on my hand. He wouldn't let go. Then, so quickly it made me dizzy, he swung me to him and wrapped an arm around my shoulder. Still holding my hand, he walked me over to a black hearse parked in the corner of the showroom. "Rockabye Baby" played on a music box somewhere. It kept sliding out of tune, as if the prongs needed straightening.

"Now this baby is tailor-made for you! Notice the genuine wood grain. The brougham lights. And this," he said, kicking the quarter panel, leaving the dusty jagged imprint of his sole. "This is a six-foot finish!"

It looked like a reliable car. Why, I wondered, would he want to kick it like that?

"Sorry," I said. "I'm not in the market. I was thinking of something less . . . permanent." That's not what I wanted to say, but that was how it came out.

"Really?" He wouldn't let go of my hand. He looked the hearse over to see if there were any obvious flaws. "Geez, I thought you'd like it," he said, disappointed. "Sure you don't want to lie down and give it a test-drive?"

"No thanks. Listen, would you let go of my hand?"

He removed his arm from my shoulder and, still keeping a firm grip on my hand, he dusted the dandruff off my shirt. Then he stepped back and smiled with his lips as if he had just made a very sweet chess move. "We've been looking everywhere for you, Doctor Donelly. You must have moved. So where are you living now? Got to update the old prospect list."

When I didn't answer he gave me that showbiz David Letterman smile, and his baggy red sweater and teeth seemed to glow brighter the tighter he squeezed my hand. "You know, we're all very proud of you. I tell everybody at the dealership: that doctor's one smart boy. One. Smart. Boy." Mischief twinkled in his eyes. "In fact, I've always thought of you as a son."

That's when I got lucid. It was exactly as Saul had promised: both real and unreal. I was dreaming; I was awake in the dream. And I knew exactly who this salesman was.

"Let go of my hand," I said.

He looked surprised.

"Let go of my hand."

He smiled wider as if I were teasing him and his eyes began to iris in and out.

"Well . . ." I said. "Don't say I didn't warn you."

I swung from my knees and hit him flush in the throat. His head snapped back and he tried to let go of my hand—I wouldn't let him. I pulled him to me and kneed him in the gut, and when he bent down I chop-chopped the back of his head.

Then I let go of his hand.

I grabbed his ears and pulled him to his knees. "Hail Mary full of Grace," I began.

I kneed him in the face and heard his legs crack as he flipped over onto his back. "The Lord is with Thee."

He lay there, a smear of black running from his nostrils to his ear. "Blessed art Thou amongst women."

His eyes went wide as I straddled his body and stood over him. "And blessed is the fruit of thy womb Jesus."

Kick in the stomach.

"Holy Mary Mother of God." Kick in the face.

"Pray for us sinners." Kick in the face.

"Now and at the hour of our death." Kick in the face.

"Amen."

I was actually pretty good at this. Better than I expected. I'd been rehearsing it in my mind for the longest time. He lay there whimpering and moaning on the floor. It was beautiful. I picked him up by his heels, dragged him over to the 'Vette, and dumped him in the passenger side: his head on the floor, his feet sticking up against the seat.

"Let's go for a ride," I said, leaping in and grabbing hold of the wheel.

Thirty-one

Homing," I heard Saul say.

I felt silent bubbles dancing on my skin, like that tingle you get when your leg falls asleep.

Then I found myself riding on the back of a great white whale. Her head was a torpedo: she had no eyes. The Holock was behind me, his hands around my waist, like we were riding a Harley-Davidson. The whale's skin felt warm and slippery; I had to hold on tight to her hippo ears because we were diving furiously fast. Dark water swirled about us as we swam round and round in tight descending spirals.

I was not surprised when the white whale spoke to me in a great aching basso voice. This was, after all, a dream. And her words were beautiful: they rolled out from the depths of her massive body in a haunting song, or chant, or poem that vibrated through my legs as I rode her. It didn't matter that I didn't understand it. I could have listened to her forever.

My children have no dreams
They live a Maybe Life

No dreams
No way to touch the Dreamer
The One who dreams the Dream we swim
You the Chooser
Will you let my children sleep
The long last sleep
Where they can meet
The Dreamer
Will you eat
The Maybe Man
You would be were?

In a blink of time everything went black.

I found myself rising out of a dark tunnel, which shrank downward to become the earhole of a pale head, a bald head, a still dead head with eyeballs frozen open. It smiled. The Holock I had just killed lay like a Chinaman in an opium den—languidly curled into a fetal position on a green floor, enfolded in a green cloud that oozed and twinkled around him, then faded away. Saliva hung in a long silver strand from his mouth and pooled on the floor of the "Dream Room."

He was just as Laura described—his white skin seemed to glow in the green light—a pale translucence that reminded me of the pictures of saints on holy cards you get at funerals—upturned suffering faces—like they all had the flu. He was naked, bald, with earless concave swirls on the sides of his head. But there was one detail she hadn't mentioned. His buttocks were unusually high; he reminded me of a male ballet dancer in white tights, thin and muscular. I recognized the loud humming sound I had heard before: it Dopplered loud and soft, like the song of a gigantic mosquito dancing around my ears.

I felt terrific. "One down, one to go."

Though I imagined that everything would feel slippery and smell of pungent salt like the ocean, there were no smells or touches in this dream. And to be deprived of these senses made me understand how important they are. Why should I be able to hear without ears, see without eyes, but be unable to smell or touch?

Then I realized: I had no body, just a point of view. It was one of *those* dreams. That was strange until I thought of myself as a camera. A Steadicam in a slumbering drift, I moved outside the Dream Room and roamed. After a while I felt like a scuba diver exploring the bowels of a sunken ship. Then, as I became more adept, I began to imagine myself a ghostly shark cruising for prey, sliding through walls and floors and Jell-O with ease.

This world of the Holock was, as Laura had said, "one long dream." It was a world of green: not the green of a lima bean, or a Granny Smith apple, not dark like spinach. I could only compare it to the green of the sun seen through a maple tree in summer, the glowing underside of leaves: radiant and rich. The perpetual sunlight cast a warm shimmer upon everything: the network of transparent domes and tunnels, the flat streams of bubbles that swirled beneath their pliant walkways and ceilings like liquid insulation. All was in motion—not the pitch and keel of a boat, but the dance of seaweed in the gentlest current, bending to the flow. Their whole home swayed. Yet despite this, there was a great stillness everywhere—a pervasive feeling of permanence. Each chamber I passed through felt as though it had been there forever. It seemed to be a restful place. Laura had said it was weird. Saul had said it was spooky. Neither had told me it would be beautiful.

A shadow passed over me and I looked up to see a great white serpent coiling hypnotically above the domes. Slow bubbles danced away from its tail. This was what they called "Mother." It was the only evidence of the two species of water creatures Laura had mentioned. Apparently, some of what she said was true.

As I watched, two Holock swam up slowly to greet her. They each grabbed hold of her middle as if she were a log floating down a river. Then something so marvelous and unexpected happened that even as I watched it, I didn't believe it. The white serpent stalled midswim in the green Jell-O, then curled back onto herself to make the letter O. She bit her own tail and encircled the two Holock so that, for a moment, they looked like two kids floating naked in a swimming hole, grasping onto a white inner tube. Her body expanded as if it were filling with air and, at the same time, it began to spin, faster and faster until she became a wobbly white blur, like a ring spinning on a table. The rotation accelerated, her skin glowed brighter, and all at once she catapulted straight up—leaving a tornado shaft of light behind her. It lingered and glowed, like the afterimage of a flare against the retina, then faded gradually, from the base up, until the Jell-O was green and quiet again, as if it had always been that way. I stared for a minute at her point of departure. If I could have, I would have shaken my head. Yet, as strange as what I had just witnessed was, it also felt faintly familiar, like I had seen it all before, as if it had been a memory, but one I had forgotten. I recalled what Laura had said about flying saucers: "They're not discs, they're tubes . . . like a kid rolling down a hill in an inner tube." Christ, I thought. That's it. That's their flying saucer. Not a machine—but a creature. A living thing! The Dragons are Time-Taxis!

Then I saw a Holock walking down a green corridor. He moved as if he had given it a lot of thought, like a person who had someplace to go and was in no hurry to get there. He reminded me of a lion in the jungle: a graceful, stately animal who ambled fearlessly, for he had no natural predators.

I followed him down a passageway flanked by slits about shoulder height. Upon these shelves were row upon row of what looked like white Hershey bars. He snatched one en route and devoured it in one bite, apparently without pleasure, eating as he walked.

He led me to a room full of machines. I hesitate to describe them, because I doubt I can do their beauty justice. Imagine the pipes of a huge organ in a Gothic cathedral, fanning out like the tail of a peacock. And made of glass. Now imagine different shades of green fluid pumping ring-shaped bubbles up and down the length of these transparent cylinders: tubes striped at irregular intervals by pale green, almost yellow bands. How ironic that the machines of a race that didn't understand music resembled instruments: calliopes lacking only a keyboard. Silent and beautiful, as if an isolated tribe had tried to fabricate an organ from a picture in a *National Geographic* they'd found washed up on their island shore. How they operated was a mystery; I never saw the Holock touch it. But I watched him stand beside it with folded arms, gazing with an intent that bordered on rapture.

I attached myself like a parasite to a passing Holock, riding in his mind. It felt like I was tuning to the police channel on a shortwave radio: different voices came and went, each whispered, each distinct. Though the thoughts of the Holock were childlike in their simplicity, they lacked the energy or enthusiasm of children. There was much repetition, as if everything they'd ever thought had been thought of before and needed no expansion. This might have seemed intriguing had it not been so dull. "I will go." "He is sleeping." "Let us go." "It is working." "We are working." "He will sleep." "Nothing more." "Dreaming?" "Long dreaming." Some thoughts were rather mysterious. For example: "They do the Mouthing thing." But most were brief, clipped phrases: telepathic shorthand. I guess I had expected a mental eloquence, but perhaps it was unneeded. Like any language, the cultural implications imbedded in timing and delivery were no doubt rich in ways I couldn't fathom. But they struck me as the most boring creatures alive. Like drones inside a hive. Everything was rehearsed to perfection. Realizing this, I had a peculiar feeling. The beginnings of a sadness rose up in me, a pity for a race that had no juice, no joy, nothing to live or hope for.

Between these moments of bland vanilla thoughts I was surrounded by a silence so absolute, it made me nervous. Think of how our lives are awash with sound: traffic, planes, TVs, radios, appliances—even our breathing and heartbeats or the sound of our swallows punctuate our daily lives with noise. I could only compare this silence to a twilight I had spent in New Mexico, on one of those legs of our trip that Saul had "sat out." It was on a red desert split by an empty highway. I had pulled over to pee. It was a windless, lifeless, barren place, and after I shut the engine off, the silence was so pure it was almost a physical presence. It was suffocating. I was sure that if I said anything my voice would be swallowed by the land; it would disappear three feet in front of my face. I felt as if I were a ghost. I remember thinking at the time: "You don't belong here."

I felt it now. I did not belong here.

For a while I rode in the Holock's mind, eavesdropping. And as long as I was quiet, the Holock didn't notice me. But the first moment I allowed myself a thought or a silent comment, he wrenched violently away as if I were a bee that had lighted on his head. The experience was disorienting. I found myself hovering a few feet before him, watching his shocked white face squirming in alarm. Then he made a gesture like a claw and "thought" a fascinating phrase.

"Get behind me, Soul Man!" was what I thought I heard him think.

Then something very odd happened. The phrase "Soul Man" was passed on and echoed through their home like the ripples cast outward from a stone, repeating itself in various voices in all directions, near and far. For a moment, I imagined rows and rows of slaves lying side by side in the black hold of an eighteenth-century ship bound for the Carolinas. Their thickly accented voices whispering the same frightened words in the dark: a code, or a warning, perhaps when the ceiling of their cell opened to a harsh shaft of light, revealing the boots of a man descending. "Captain!" I thought. "Here comes the captain!" Repeated with reverence and terror as their dark lord descended from his throne above to judge their fitness for life or death.

Maybe I mistook it for black jargon, because their thoughts had never suggested any emotion. Then I realized what he had actually thought was "Get behind me, Saul Man!" It was that note of flagrant fear that made me wonder at the impact Saul must have had on the natives of this world.

I wandered on through green walls and floors, sometimes swerving out into the Jell-O and back into their home, watching them saunter upside down through the network of green shafts and bubble/domes that spread out as far as I could see. At the center of the complex I noticed one bubble that was much larger and brighter than the rest. It seemed to be filled with light. An egg, I thought.

I floated into it and found it was empty except for a rectangular green bed. A rather large lump in the middle.

Bed?

I moved closer and found a bald head lying on a pillow. The figure sighed and turned to lie on her back; her full pregnant belly pushed down the light green blanket, exposing the square nipples on her breasts, which rose and fell to the rhythm of her breathing.

I watched her sleeping for a long time. She was as beautiful as ever. Even with her head shaved. Her sandy skin took on a translucence under the light of the domes. Her room was empty but for a wide-screen TV of sorts on one wall. I looked at her and looked at her until I could feel the rage humming behind my eyes. I could have entered her dream and gotten it over with. But I had a few questions. I moved down to her ear and said, "Laura."

She sat up so fast it startled me. I pulled back to the ceiling and watched her swivel her head back and forth like a frightened bird. It was very amusing.

She scratched her belly and yawned and lay back down.

I waited till she had closed her eyes again. This time I spoke in her other ear. "Laura."

I was watching her profile against the green pillow. She opened her green eyes.

"Who's doing that!" she yelled, sitting up again.

Boy, this was going to be fun.

A Holock unzipped the chamber door like a Velcro tent flap and poked his head in. He was upside down, a white bat looking around a curtain.

I heard him think: "Something you want, Mother?"

Mother?

"Did you call me?" she replied aloud.

"No," he answered telepathically.

"Where's Suki?" she asked.

"In the Dreaming," he replied.

"When he wakes . . . tell him to see me."

He pulled his head back; the wall zipped up. And I

wondered: Was Suki the one I had killed? Was Laura's Holock father the Boy in the Red Sweater? What had his name
tag read? "Max Stillner"? Boy, oh boy. I was on a rock.

She folded her arms around her legs and rested her head
on her knees.

I positioned myself about a foot from her face. "Laura,"
I said. "It's me."

Her eyes went wide and she leapt out of the bed and
huddled naked against the wall. I followed.

"It's me, Laura," I said, nearly laughing.

Perhaps it took her awhile to recognize my thoughts.
Until then, she had only heard my voice. But soon enough,
she knew. She tried to smile; she couldn't. She tried to be
casual; she couldn't. She tried to act pleased to see me again.
She couldn't get close to that one. Finally her face attained a
rictus of terror. I could see the muscles twitching involun-
tarily under the skin, under the frozen mask of the woman I
had once loved.

"You!" she said.

Thirty-two

How did you get here? Where are you?"

I toyed with her. "Wherever I want to be."

I moved behind her head and said, "I'm here." She turned around. Then I slipped up to the ceiling and said, "Up here." She looked up. I moved down to peek over her belly. "Down here," I said, and had the pleasure of watching her look with horror at her full womb, as if her unborn child were addressing her.

"Don't," she said, putting her hands over her ears. "I won't listen!"

"Yes, you will," I said, moving to hover before her face. "I'm going to ask you some questions. You're going to answer them. And then, I'm going to kill you."

When she realized it was useless, that, try as she may, she couldn't lock out my thoughts, her hands slid down to her face and she began massaging her temples with her fingers. With a weary grunt, she looked down at her belly. "You can't kill me," she said. "You're just a voice."

Let her think that. I was going to enjoy this little interrogation.

"Tell me, Laura. Why did you kill my mother?"

She was quiet for a moment, then began to scratch her forearms. She stood abruptly, walked back to her bed, and sat down. "Leave me alone. You're nothing but a bad dream."

"Why, Laura?" I repeated.

Her green eyes jumped tensely to and fro; she was working out possible replies, weighing the options. Her lips were jammed together so tightly that all the color had left them, and for a moment, she resembled an old crone who had lost her dentures. "I don't know what you're talking about."

"Laura," I pressed her. "Tell the truth and I'll make it a quick death."

"You don't understand," she whimpered. "They forced me. I *had* to do what they wanted!"

This sounded both plausible and false: a fudged confession bucking for a reduced sentence of manslaughter. Even then I might have believed it, had I not remembered that Laura stopped calling the Holock "Them" as soon as she had my seed. Red flags went up. I concluded: whenever she was lying about the Holock, she used the third person.

" 'They'?" I asked, doing my best imitation of Nancy cross-examining. "They're your family, Laura. You give them orders, don't you? You're the one they call 'Mother.' "

"It's just a superstitious title."

"Bullshit!" I snarled. I repeated the question and she closed her eyes and slammed her bald head against the wall behind her; it yielded and framed her face in quivering green Jell-O. When she sat up, she left a perfect imprint of the back of her skull in the wall. Then, with a viscous *pop,* the depression was gone.

She opened her eyes and sighed. "It was the only way they could be sure the 'Fertile Year' began. They knew you would sire a child after your mother died. I didn't have much time. She was already terminal; I just sped up the process."

Her face was empty; her tone: half-hearted. That was three excuses when one would have been enough: she was padding. I decided to test her. "Did the government know it was you?"

She paused a beat or two, then absorbed this into her alibi. "Sure. It was part of our agreement."

"Bullshit," I spat. "They thought *I* did it!"

She started squinting, and scratching her bare head, lathering it with an invisible shampoo, leaving dark streaks in her scalp.

"Why did you kill my mother, Laura? I want the truth!"

She thought about it a long while. "Truth?" she said at last, rising to her knees, shedding the blankets into a pile around her and bracing her hands on the bed, like a cat ready to pounce. "You want the truth?" This was the calm Laura. The aloof Laura. The Laura I remembered. Until that moment, I had only seen a woman of uncanny composure. Now I saw the cruelty behind the cool.

She sprang out of bed and stood before the big green screen on her wall. "Target Donelly," she commanded. "Pre-Genesis. Profile."

It startled me when the screen came alive into a high-speed mosaic of detailed graphs and charts. They scrolled upward as weird mathematical figures danced across the frame. I couldn't imagine the megabytes involved. There was a lineup of naked men who resembled me. We all had erections. The camera zoomed into the third in line: myself.

The interrogation in my dream of a year ago was replayed almost word for word. But it was sped up and all my answers sounded chipmunky.

But how could this be? She had told me they couldn't record dreams! Then I realized that this wasn't the actual dream, but my vague recollection of it. This was a Memory Film. The quality was poor: full of jump-cuts and muffled dialogue, like a worn sixteen-millimeter print that had been shown too many times. Laura stood silhouetted before the projection, her hands on her hips. I could just make out her features in the green glow of the room.

"The truth is you could never have fallen in love with any woman as long as *she* was alive. Your psych profile revealed how profoundly you were linked to her. Your dreams were a mess of unresolved mother issues. You had to act out this conflict with all your mates. Project your power struggles on to them. Declare your independence over and over. No woman was ever going to have control of you again."

This rang brutally true. Which means I experienced it as an attack. I felt my body stiffen as my mind dashed about, desperate for any escape into denial. It found none.

Then, without warning, the screen began a fast-forward review of our therapy sessions. Through Laura's eyes I watched as we acted out a frantic insect pantomime: me slapping cigarette after cigarette into my mouth; white clouds blossoming above me and fading like smoke signals, Laura crossing and uncrossing her legs, her hands gesturing into blurs before her eyes, the sun in the window dragging itself down into dusk. Laura counting money money money into my hand. And if that wasn't odd enough, all her memories were pixilated, as if I were looking through the eyes of a bug. I thought: This is how they see!

She continued with the offhanded authority of a coroner reciting an autopsy. "I became what you needed. A totally dependent woman. A victim who craved just one thing in the world: you. Your belief. Your trust. Your love. I mirrored what your mother always wanted from you. And let you project yourself on to me. Countertransference, eh?"

At the flick of her hand the screen froze on a close-up of my flushed and angry face. "We argued all the time. I let you win. I let you be what your mother never would: the one with all the answers, the one in control, the one with the final word, the one who knew best: the doctor."

I was furious. How dare she play with my life like this? She had no right!

Then I watched as my adult face flipped over and morphed into the features of a baffled child, holding back tears, hanging upside down—from monkey bars, perhaps? He was bracing himself against—what? I felt a sick mounting dread in my gut. What was that child looking up at with so much fear and despair? She showed me: the upside-down towering figure of my mother, her voice slowed into a growling nonsensical harangue. I shuddered at this memory I did not recall.

"And why a doctor?" she asked, her voice rising a bit in pitch: winding up her opening remarks. "Because Mystery is the one thing you cannot abide. Because you understand nothing. Because you must explain everything. Because you have never known who she was and why she acted as she did. Right, Doctor?"

Laura clapped her hands once and said, "Genesis."

The screen cut to a high-angle hidden-camera shot of Laura and me making love on my bed at the rectory, our bodies thrusting onto each other. It was hard enough to see our sex so clinically displayed, to watch my surrender to this repulsive beautiful creature. Two people sharing a lie—if that wasn't pornography, what was? But that wasn't what

I found most disturbing. It was the whisper of panic that seemed to grow louder in the back of my brain. Something I had forgotten. Something important. Something very dangerous. Something like this:

Where was the camera?

"So I gave you your favorite mystery," she went on. "The Mystery of Love. I invented a mystery woman so you could dance your lifelong dance, only this time with the illusion that you were leading, you were calling the steps, you would get to the bottom of the mystery.

"I disrupted your tidy ego again and again. Fed you enough implausibilities to fracture your belief in your own senses. And once you doubted your reality, you were able to enter mine. You could make the transition into the Believer. The Pawn. The Victim. Something you swore you'd never be again. But, in truth, something you always wanted."

Laura turned from the screen and smiled. "And when I finally won your precious 'love,' when your fragile persona cracked, you crumbled. You were no longer your mother's good obedient boy—you were mine."

This was the truth I had asked for. Cold. Ruthless. Merciless. Laura had ripped open my psyche and left it raw. It shook me deeply. But still, in some part of my mind, the nagging thought persisted: Where was the fucking camera? How did they get these shots? And if this was a Memory Film—whose memory was it? We were alone, dammit! There was nobody in that room besides Laura and me.

Suddenly, my mother's young upside-down face leaned over me and froze, haloed by the summer sun. Laura wrapped her arms around her breasts and stared as the face on the screen match-dissolved to a close-up of the same woman, right-side-up, forty years older, golden, suffering, dying. "The truth is, I snapped her tailbone."

Through her pixilated eyes I saw it all. My mother squirming on the bed.

"Isn't that what you always wanted to do? Put her out of your misery? But you were so terrified by your rage you squelched it and inflated it into pacifism, and your grandiose schemes to save the world one victim at a time." Laura chuckled. "You really think you can kill me? You never had the guts to kill anything!"

Laura whistled sharply through her teeth. This cued a montage of human atrocities: death camps, torture, beheadings, napalm, and Nagasaki. Bones broke, faces melted, bodies shattered. Through the eyes of hundreds of murder victims, I saw their last living sight. There are no words to tell you what I felt. If I could have, I would have closed my eyes.

"Anyway, life is sacred, remember?" she continued, pointing at the screen, heating up her argument with indignation. " 'Thou shalt not kill'? You starve thirty-seven thousand people a day. (That's just a ballpark figure, mind you.) Over thirteen million a year. Mostly women and children. You exploit a permanently impoverished underclass. You oppress strictly according to skin pigment and gender. You devote a third of your resources to weaponry. To 'preserve the peace' you've perfected the technology of genocide. And you swear you'll never use it. But you already have! Twice. You have never failed to tyrannize the weak and stupid. Your history is written by madmen who raped women and wore gold. You are a planet of criminals who claim to be innocent. And you believe in Love."

She did something with her hand and the screen switched to black and white and played a strange amateur travelogue featuring the monuments and houses of worship of every faith in the world. The shift in detail was remarkable: everything had gone a bit out of focus. Cold stone structures, graveyards, empty minarets, ruined temples, bombed synagogues, eroded Celtic crosses, rotting idols. It struck me that they never went inside. It was as if religion were some mysterious archeological find—the remnants of an ancient culture whose rituals were utterly obscure. For the Holock, faith was architecture; churches and mosques were abandoned houses; hymns were white noise. They lacked the Rosetta stone! Religion was the Holock's blind spot. Music they could not hear or play. Symbols that had no meaning.

Laughter was brimming in her voice as Laura continued; she was putting forth preposterous data. "Every one of your religions claims the same doctrine: 'Love one another.' All your forms of culture have this 'love' motif. Love songs. Love scenes. Love stories. And you believe it! You really believe this 'love' exists! Do you think, perhaps, if you repeat it often enough, you'll make it come true?"

I realized that Saul had once made a very similar speech to me. But he'd been talking about Enemies. I had a strange thought: It was as hard for humans to imagine a world without enemies as it was for the Holock to imagine a world with love. I'm sure this part of the program was supposed to be a devastating indictment of humankind. It had the opposite effect on me. It made me feel how flawed and dense the Holock were—and how alone. Saul had told me: prayer jams the connection, breaks the bond. So maybe all the Holock knew of spirituality was the isolation they felt when humans pray or meditate. Maybe that separation hurts them because it is exactly like their daily life—linked with each other but unable to touch.

Suddenly the screen showed a young woman holding a naked child by one ankle over the opening of a stone well. Its head swung gently back and forth, and below him, the only light came from a round mirror at the bottom of the well that reflected the sky, the woman, and the boy. She was talking to him very calmly, in words a five-year-old would understand. "Will you be a good boy? Will you be a good boy?" Watching this, a scream rose in my throat, caught in my vocal chords, and ripped into my mouth. I wouldn't let it out. This was a wider shot of the scene I had witnessed before.

It was my mother. It was me. I wanted to die.

"Do you know how many of your children have nightmares every night? We do. Do you know where they come from? Your loving mommas and poppas who daily torture them 'for their own good.' With utensils. With fingers, fists, feet, and words. You breed your own destruction and call it 'love.' That is your legacy. The legacy that created the Holock. You are the monsters, Doctor. You are the nightmares. Not my people. We are your children. *That* is the Truth."

The screen faded out. Laura leaned against the green wall and crossed her legs.

"My daddy should have warned you not to play doctor with me."

"Suki?" I asked with glee. I could hardly wait to tell her.

"No, my Earth Daddy," she answered, smiling.

I snickered. "The one your enlightened race kidnapped and took the samples from?"

"That was a lie." She smiled a scary smile. "They didn't just take samples, Doctor. They fucked him. I wonder what that little squirt felt like between their legs—humping away like a squirrel in heat. Suki said he liked it."

I almost passed out then.

"Convulsions," I heard Wanda say.

"This was his idea, wasn't it? One last-ditch effort to

talk me out of it? Daddy doesn't like to think about the little baby he gave to the Holock, does he? Or didn't he tell you about his Biggest Deal?"

Somehow my eyes were shuddering as Laura started to trace a big circle on the wall; her finger left a dark green indentation that slowly oozed back into flatness and disappeared. "Remember? I told you. The Cold War. The Red Scare. Daddy contacted the Holock and proposed an exchange. Arms for hostages. He'd give them his seed. They'd become the perfect weapon, an unstoppable invisible mind sabotage: Dream Deprivation. He traded me for it. Soon a lot of the Soviet scientists were having breakdowns, losing memories, becoming insomniacs. We wouldn't let them keep any of their dreams. We'd eat them all. Their work suffered accordingly. Their science grew sloppy, mediocre, while American research leaped forward. We won the arms race for you."

She made a cross on the wall that quickly faded. "You don't buy all that religious crap, do you? That came later, after Daddy realized his folly. He thought the Russians would surrender. He hadn't foreseen your race's hunger for overkill. That it wasn't enough to be capable of destroying the world ten times, fifty times, a hundred times. Winning isn't good enough for you. You must annihilate. It is your way.

"And when he discovered the whole reason we agreed to the exchange was because 'our future' depended on you destroying yourselves, he was too late. He wormed his way back in Dream Lock and tried to kill us all, one by one. He couldn't do it! The Father of the Ultimate Weapon took pity on us. On me especially. So he tried an alternate plan. He thought he'd change the future by changing the past. Lure me back and get me pregnant and keep me there. As if any sane Holock would ever want to remain in Your Time!"

She laughed heartily for a minute. "Ahh, Poor Daddy. Such a dreamer! Such a saint! Saul the Holy Man. The man who sold his daughter for his country. What did he tell you? That this was all a Holock plot?" She giggled a bit. "*He* started it! It was his plan. Me. You. All of it."

At this point, I was not entirely sane. Thoughts babbled away in my skull; anguish I had never allowed myself to feel coiled in my gut and left me trembling; images no one should have to reckon with flashed relentlessly against my inner eye. Yet in some dark corner a part of me had survived the devastation and was gathering itself for the aftermath, when time would once again resume and life would have to go on. That tiny sane part of me couldn't help thinking about the camera. Where was the fucking camera? There was no camera! There was nobody in that room but Laura and me. I was stuck on that thought like a skipping needle on an LP, afraid to leave that puzzling groove.

Laura and me.

Laura and me.

Laura and me and a quiet little red cardinal, sitting on the lampshade in the corner of the room.

Imish saw everything.

Imish was in the hotel room now.

Imish was watching everything.

They were watching everything. Through his memories.

They were watching Saul. And Wanda.

And me. Sleeping on the bed.

They knew where we were.

"I'll kill you!" I said.

She stepped forward. "You can't even *touch* me. You're dreaming, Doctor. You have no power here."

Laura strolled back to the bed, sat down, and began to pinch the nipples on her breasts, toughening them, no doubt, for lactation. A long laugh came out of her nose. "You know what you are, Doctor? You're a figment from a possible past that ended when you joined me at Pointe Peele!"

"God, you'll say anything!"

"I said 'come' and you came. I took you and the unborn child back in the Mother Whirl. And now you are one of us."

"I never . . ."

"Yes, you did. You loved me, remember? Even after all the lies. Even after I *told* you they were lies! 'I still love you!' you said. You followed me into the water. You *drowned* and we revived you. You're not real. You're just a dream from a possible past that didn't come true. We've won, Doctor."

"It's a lie!" I cried.

"You can't change the future. Didn't Saul tell you? You can only change the past!"

"It's not TRUE!" I screamed.

"I'm afraid it is," said a voice at the door.

I turned to see my double again. Dressed, I realized, in the same clothes I wore at Pointe Peele. Smiling sadly. Covered with Jell-O. Older, too, as if he had made a long, long journey through time.

Thirty-three

I did go with her. I couldn't help it. I loved her."

My double strolled over and took her into his arms. Is that how I walk? I wondered. That stooped lanky amble? I look like someone ducking under doorways all the time.

"Go back," said Laura over his shoulder. "Haunt someone else, you stupid ghost!"

"You're a Shape Changer!" I said to him. "You're a Holock. You could be anybody!"

He turned and nodded. "Actually, that's very astute of you. It's not true, but it could be." He smiled. "Really, John . . . I'm you."

"Prove it!"

"How?" he asked.

After a minute or so, I realized I couldn't think of a single way to prove beyond a reasonable doubt that he was me. Then it struck me that, if the tables were turned, even I wouldn't be able to put forth enough evidence to convict me of being myself. I had to admit, though, he *felt* like me. Our dialogue was very much like a conversation you might have with yourself in a mirror. And there was the peculiar corroborating fact that, unlike Laura, my double seemed to have no trouble knowing my exact "location." Whenever I spoke, he looked directly into "my eyes."

I watched as he led Laura to the bed and tucked her in. He gently laid a hand on her belly and she covered it with both hands. "Sleep, my love," he said. "I'll speak with him."

"Don't give him the satisfaction!"

"Hush, now," he said softly. "You'll upset the child." With that he bent down to kiss her forehead.

She looked out at the room then, her eyes roving about, imagining where I was. She held her full belly in her hands like a trophy.

"Our child," she said triumphantly.

The tableau of mother, father, and unborn child held for a moment, like a bizarre yet sentimental portrait by an artist with a limited palette of greens. It was the last time I saw Laura: a bald mother-to-be, with no eyebrows. Her green eyes, which had been so striking in my office, had lost their power amongst the many green hues of this underwater world: green skin, green sheets, green walls, floors, and ceilings. It felt like I was looking through a cheap pair of children's sunglasses.

They seemed a happy family. Who was I to spoil it? For a time I entertained the idea of drifting off, going away, letting it be. What right had I to tamper with their joy? Anyway, this *was* a dream. Maybe Laura was right. Maybe I had no power here. I certainly felt powerless. I had come to that place where any choice, any choice at all—stop/go, left/right, up/down, yes/no—seemed meaningless and tiresome and futile. It didn't much matter to me, at that instant, whether or not I woke up, killed Laura, or simply hung out here for a while, letting things slide. I felt that numb heaviness I used to feel when stoned. Yeah, sure, I could get up, walk across the room, and change the channel on the TV. But, whew—what a bother! Besides, this was okay. This wasn't bad. I could sort of glide around here for a while— roast a few marshmallows if I got bored. Saul could handle things. Aww, fuck him—he got me into this; let him get me out. So Imish was watching us—so what? I wasn't going to get worked up about it. If they got your number, they got it. So maybe the government bashes down the door to our suite and pulls the plug on me and hauls Wanda and Saul away. Big deal. There's only so much a man can take.

I floated backward through the door and sailed listlessly down the corridor like a lost balloon.

"Hey!" he called from behind me.

I wandered on.

"HEY!" He ran after me. And when he caught up he grasped me between his hands—don't ask me how—and held me before his face like a crystal ball.

"John?" he said. "John!"

"What?" I answered, annoyed.

"Snap out of it! You're acting like a Holock!"

"What are you talking about?" I whined. "Leave me alone!"

"Stop it!" His words slapped me alert.

"What do you want from me?" I asked.

"Your attention. Okay?"

"Okay, okay," I groaned.

"Follow me," he said. He released me and headed down the corridor, then led me through a flap to a small domed Dream Room. I watched him sit cross-legged on the floor: it swished and jostled beneath him like a waterbed. He seemed to be waiting for me to get comfortable, so I hovered before his face.

"This is a stupid dream. I wanna go to sleep."

"Don't!" he yelled.

"You won, you bastard! What else do you want from me!?"

"That's better," he sighed. "For a moment I thought I'd lost you." He looked around. "It's this place. You've got to fight it every second. Like a sleeping sickness. I've only been here a month and I still catch myself drifting— Hey!" he said suddenly. "Hey!"

"What?" I realized I'd been nodding off.

"Watch it! You go to sleep on me and you'll ruin everything!"

I laughed and groaned at the same time. It felt like one of those all-nighters I used to pull in college. Studying for my finals. My roommate torturing me with textbook questions. What was his name? Oh, yeah. Timothy. A big guy from Grosse Pointe. Used to write all his papers stoned. I could never do that. I'd always slide into silliness or fall asleep and—

"STOP THAT SHIT!" he yelled, and I snapped out of it.

A Holock poked his head in the room and my double growled at him. The creature's eyes went wide and he quickly withdrew.

"God!" He shook his head. "They're like waiters who won't let you eat in peace!" Then he turned to me. "John? I want your full and total attention."

"Why? This is just a dream!"

"Yes. It is a dream. And it'll be your last dream if you don't listen to me."

I sighed. "I could use a cigarette."

He nodded, commiserating. "I know what you mean. What I wouldn't give for a Salem."

"Hey! *I* gotta question!" I said.

He raised his eyebrows. "What?"

"If this is how it ends . . . why'd you bother to come back to warn Hogan and rescue me in the hotel?"

He smiled. "I haven't yet. Whether I do or not depends on your answer to a question. It's a trick question, so take your time. Take all the time in the world."

"What?"

"Do you love me?"

"Ah, Jesus." I hated these kinds of dreams.

"It's not as stupid as it sounds."

I tried to pass it off. Then I thought—what the hell? I considered it. You know what? I didn't know. I felt if anyone could answer that question, I could. But I couldn't. Did I love me? I was stumped.

"I don't know," I admitted.

"I do," he said gently. "You don't. You have never loved yourself. You disappointed the first person in your life who loved you. And you never forgave yourself."

"Mom?" I laughed. "Oh, come on! She's the one who never forgave me!"

"But she did. She apologized. On her deathbed. Remember?"

I recalled the Egyptian tomb. Her golden skin. Her icy hands and the last time she ever called me by name. Her chilling final words that seemed to cost her all the energy she had left. "I'm sorry, John."

"*That's* what she meant? She was apologizing for holding it against me?"

"Yeah: It," he said. "All of It. She had a lot to be sorry for."

I remembered the well and shuddered. "Why would a mother do that to a child?"

He sighed deeply. "She was sick. Who knows why?"

"I—I never remembered that."

"No. But it stayed with you all your life. It made you who you are. And you never even knew it. But I'll tell you something, John . . ."

"What?"

"I remembered it. I'm all the things you've forgotten. I'm the life you don't remember living. And I know how that child endured that moment at the well. It was the only way he could handle that much terror and pain and betrayal by the one person he needed to trust and love." He crossed his hands over his chest. "He blamed himself."

"Come on! I was five years old!"

"It's how kids cope. You know that, John. 'Magical thinking.' Somehow that boy thought, 'If I never do another naughty thing, I won't ever be this afraid, this hurt, this helpless.' It was a bargain, see? 'If I'm never bad, I will never be unloved.' "

I couldn't remember any of this, but it felt true. "Must have been when my Religious Phase started," I said bitterly.

He nodded sadly. "It was a cruel standard to live up to. No wonder you had to take it out on someone." He looked at me.

"Hogan!" I said immediately.

"Right. He was the only safe object of your rage. To everyone else, you were the Perfect Boy. You could only show your shadow to your brother."

"God, I'm fucked up."

"We sure are," he agreed. "You lived the rest of your life trying to be perfect. It was the only way a person who felt as worthless as you did could justify his life. And when you gave up being the perfect son, the perfect seminarian— you put on the role of the perfect doctor. The man with no problems. Why? Because you have always considered yourself a failure. And you are." He smiled. "As is every perfectionist."

"Wait a second! I'm not a perfectionist! Geez, one look at my office will tell you that!"

He shrugged. "So part of you knows it's impossible, and you make messes in protest. And you continually arrive late just to prove how unfair it is."

He had me there. I was just about to mention my tardiness.

"Remember how repulsed you were by the smugness of Dr. Stewart—your look-alike?"

"Yes."

"That was projection. The part of you that you cannot face on the inside. Only on the outside—where it can be safely rejected. So you devote yourself to convincing your clients that they are ultimately lovable. Don't misunderstand—it's an important vocation. It is your gift. Because you know very well what it is to feel unlovable. To attempt to live up to impossible standards. But, on some level, you think by healing others you will heal yourself. You can't. It doesn't work that way. You need to let yourself off the hook, John. You've got to forgive yourself. Then you can love yourself."

Therapy-in-a-Dream. This was a new one for me. I wondered what he charged: a therapist in the future. Given inflation it had to be somewhere in the neighborhood of a thousand bucks an hour. Maybe—

"John!" he snapped.

"All right, all right," I sighed. "I recognize the truth in what you say. So what? What does it have to do with anything? Laura. Saul. The Holock. Our child."

He clapped his hands and smiled broadly. "*Now* I've got your attention. I'll tell you in a minute. But right now I've got to warn Hogan, save you from the feds, and call the Deadheads in Arizona." He grinned. "But not necessarily in that order."

He Blipped out and I was left alone in a bubble about the size of a pup tent. It did make sense. That's why I was so bugged by Nancy's criticisms. I had projected on to her my Critical Self. That's why it was so easy to empathize with my patients. I had projected my unloved victimized child on to them. I was giving myself a break. And that's why I fell so hard for Laura. The Ultimate Victim. It was true! I *was* a perfectionist. Why hadn't that occurred to me before?

My double Blipped back and startled me.

"Well, that's that!" he said, standing in the middle of the room and dusting off his hands.

"So soon?" I asked.

"You still don't get this 'time' thing, do you, John?"

I smiled and wondered if he knew it.

"Listen, I gotta tell you something," he said as he reassumed his former position. "I had to kill Imish."

"What?!"

"I'm sorry. I had no choice. Another few minutes and the Holock would have figured out where you and Saul were. And they would have notified the government and— I know," he interrupted himself. "I know. I'll miss him, too. Don't tell Saul. It'll break his heart."

"Didn't he see you?"

"He was in the john."

Growing up I'd never had a pet. Mom always said they were intolerably messy. I didn't realize how attached you could get to them. I remembered the way he clung to my hair. The miniature helicopter sounds he made when he flew around the room. I smiled recalling the way he gurgled when I'd scratch him under the chin. Do birds have chins? I didn't know.

"John!" he said. "You're drifting."

"Sorry," I said. "He was a special bird."

"He sure will be," my double said.

"Will be?"

"Oh, that's right, you don't know. Imish is one of the Awake Birds from the future."

"Awake?"

"Genetically altered. His cognitive functions were rerouted nanotically through his enlarged cerebellum. Saul rescued him on one of his time Blips."

"Rescued?"

"Imish was one of the tampered creatures they used as lie detectors in the Shing Crisis of 2330."

"Shing?" I said, and immediately felt like a monosyllabic straight-line feeder.

"Aliens who could mind lie." He shrugged. "Don't worry. The good guys win."

I made a great attempt to assemble a thought composed of at least several coherent words. "Why did Saul rescue him?"

"He was being attacked by other birds. One of the unfortunate side effects of the tampering. He became an object of revulsion to his own species. Sort of a traitor. Ordinarily he wouldn't be allowed outdoors—but he'd managed to escape and Saul found him under a swarm of birds. Wounded. Left for dead." My double didn't look like he was too happy to have finished the job.

"He was like a little Saul," I said. "Crabby. Touchy. He had an attitude."

He gave me a strange look. "Yes. He was. Very much like Saul."

I realized how easily we had slipped into the past tense—and was saddened. He seemed to pick up on this and, for a time, we stared at the floor. "I always wondered how he could communicate his moods without words."

He looked up. "Part of it's chemical: scents. Another part has to do with his peculiar intelligence: why they called birds like him 'awake.' His consciousness is akin to that of a lucid dreamer. Aware *in* his thoughts rather than 'thinking' them." He stopped short, closed his eyes, and sighed. "It's kind of gruesome talking about Imish like this. Especially because, right now, you gotta kill somebody, too."

I was shocked. It took me a moment to recover. "You *want* me to kill Laura? But you said you loved her!"

"Not Laura, John. This is the hard part." He started twirling his hair. "You can't just forgive yourself. And it's not an abstract issue you can talk out in therapy. You've got to kill that perfectionist."

"You want me to kill myself?"

"No." He folded his arms and looked at me. "I'm the Perfect One. Not you. I was arrogant enough to rationalize sleeping with a patient."

"Wait a second! I slept with her, too!"

"No, you didn't."

"Yes, I did!"

"No, you didn't."

"YES, I DID!" For a second I was embarrassed by this exchange.

"Trust me on this," he said finally. "You didn't. I went to bed with Laura in the rectory that night. You stayed down in the living room and fell asleep in the chair."

"I don't remember that!"

"Of course not. You were sleeping."

"But we had *weeks* together! I remember them."

"You do?" He smiled. "What happened?"

"Well ... I ... we ... hmph." The memories were foggy. Shopping. Walking. Talking. For the life of me I couldn't recall making love to Laura! I didn't have any recollection of it at all. And I wouldn't until later. Those were *his* memories I've written about. "I don't remember ..." I admitted wonderingly.

" 'Cause it didn't happen. I'm the possible past that slept with Laura. I was foolish enough to chase her that night at Pointe Peele, even though I couldn't swim. You didn't go in the water, remember?"

"Yes." I saw myself waiting on the shore in disbelief.

"I was stupid enough to think I could still save her—by love alone. You weren't. I'm the romantic, John, not you. I've spent my life justifying the warped love of a sick woman by trying to be perfect. I was naive enough to buy the idea of pacifism, to think that you can survive in the world without reasonably defending yourself. By being good and passive. The bravest thing I ever did was coldcock Colonel Peter at the Hilton. I don't think I could have done it if you weren't here. But that was easy compared to what you gotta do."

He reached out and "touched me" with his hand. "You gotta help me. I'm not strong enough to do this alone. You've got to be everything I'm not, John. You've got to be ruthless. Like a wolf who bites off his leg to free himself from a trap. I'm a trap, John. I'm not your better half; I'm your worse. The part of you, the choices you made—habitually, unconsciously. The part of you that has to die."

"You want me to kill you?" I asked, incredulous.

He nodded. "Please. It's the only way. Remember what the Great Mother said? 'Will you eat the Maybe Man you would be were?' That's me."

I cringed. "You want me to eat you?!"

He laughed. "That's just Holock talk. They only die when they're eaten. They're so literal. Do you know: They don't have metaphors? They compare nothing; everything just 'is.' I've spent a month here and they drive me crazy! All their ritualized repetition and control. It's like binary thinking or something: On/Off. Either/Or. They make no intuitive leaps. They can't create anything new. They can only revise and amplify. All their machines are built from leftovers of the last war. You know what these Dream Rooms are?" He held out his arms and looked at the top of the dome. "Models based on Saul's REM machine! They're like *mandelbrot* sets: doomed to replay the same shapes over and over to infinity. Sure, it's pretty here at first. But after a while . . ." He sighed, disgusted. "It's like being stuck in a world monopolized by a fast-food franchise. McReality!"

We laughed.

"Poor bastards. They're like stupid sharks. Perfectly evolved creatures who haven't changed in eons. 'Cause they can only imitate, they can't create. They're master mimics, hollow chameleons. That's why they need us. If they didn't have human dreams—they'd have nothing to think about."

"They seem smart enough to me," I offered.

"Nahh, they just got bigger libraries. Trust me. Laura's smarter than all of 'em put together."

"Is she?"

"Well, she came from genius stock, didn't she?"

I winced, thinking of Saul's deal with the Holock. Saul mating with Suki.

He looked me in the eyes, imploring. "Kill me, John. Do it."

"How?"

He held out his hands. "Wake up."

"Wake up?"

"That's all." He nodded.

"But what good will that do? You're not dreaming."

"You are." He stood up and gave a huge yawn. "You wake up when a Holock's sharing a dream and *he* dies. That's how it works for them. But if you wake up while I'm in *your* dream, I die. That's how it works for humans. Our link is as strong as an umbilical cord. Cut it in the womb and the child will die. Wake up, and none of this mess will have happened. Me. Laura. The Holock. It'll all be over. Just a possible past that didn't pan out."

His explanation had the resonance of dream-logic. It made perfect absurd sense.

"You want to kill the Holock and Laura, too?"

"I want to save the earth from a fate it doesn't deserve. And keep this wretched race from ever happening."

"But the child! What about our child?"

"Don't worry. There's always Door Number Three." He smiled as if he held a secret. "You know, everything Laura said about humans is true. Believe me, I've heard it many times. But it misses something that everyone knows on some level."

"Like what?"

"Laughter, poetry, Coney dogs, rock and roll, sex, circuses. They seem to know everything about humans. Everything but what makes life worth living."

"I hate Coney dogs," I said.

He ignored me. "Didn't you feel it as she talked? Didn't you keep thinking, yes, but . . . True, but . . . It's like a tourist describing the skyline of New York without mentioning the Statue of Liberty. You know what I mean?"

"Not really," I said.

"Never mind." He frowned. "They remind me of Hogan's daughter. The one with the learning disability?"

Jesus, I thought. He likes Coneys and I remember names. "Janice," I said.

He nodded. "They can hear the sounds and they can recognize the symbols, but they can't put the two together. They can't read. They don't get it."

"It?" I wondered. Do all Time Travelers talk like Saul?

"It's the Holock's blind spot," he concluded. "They're too practical for miracles."

"Christ!" I gasped. "You're a Believer!"

"No," he laughed. "I'm the Doubter. I have to have everything proved. You're the Believer."

"This is a dream," I said.

"And it's real, too." He smiled. "I told you it was all going to work out in Chicago."

I didn't know what to say.

He reached out and once again held me in his hands. "Do it, John. Spare Laura her childhood. Spare your son his miserable life. Spare me my perfectionism. Spare Saul his awful guilt. Spare the earth World War III. Spare us all, John. All you have to do is wake up. And I'll be a harmless collection of memories that never happened." He withdrew his hands.

"True?" I asked.

"True," he answered. "Do you love me enough to do that?"

Maybe I did. Maybe I just did at that. I saw he was twirling his hair in the way I always used to. He was really quite a likable guy, this me. I would miss him.

Thirty-four

I woke up after lingering in one of those dreams that blend the noises of the day into their soundtrack. I was watching the pendulum of a grandfather clock swing to and fro; its chimes were the sweet trill of a bird. I was annoyed by the incongruity, and after it had started to fray my nerves, I turned to the mirror and said to my image, "Would somebody PLEASE fix that damn clock?" I watched as my reflection lifted one hand and gave me a farewell salute, then wobbled and dissolved before my eyes like a mirage in the desert. And as I turned back to the swinging golden disc I heard Saul praying "The Glory Be." Then the bright light of morning flared against my eyelids and I woke to see him in his Scrooge robe sitting beside me on the bed in my room at the Lowes.

"Hiya, Doc." He smiled. "Sorry about yer ear."

I noticed my ear throbbed as if it had been pinched.

"I thought I lost you," he said.

At that moment, I wasn't glad to see him. I wasn't even glad to be awake or alive. In fact, I resented being woken. I wanted to get back to the dream. For I was overcome by a nagging emptiness, something forgotten, something important I had to remember. Something left undone. Why did he wake me?

Saul touched my leg. "I know, I know. It'll pass."

I coughed long and hard, my lungs seemed full of phlegm. "What?" I asked.

" 'The Empty' is what I call it. Hit me like a ton of bricks when I came out. It's like the bends; your psyche's still underwater. Don't sweat it. Another half hour you'll be as good as new."

I swallowed hard. It felt as if I were about to cry. "Sadness," I managed to say. "It feels . . . like sadness."

"Like you just lost your best friend." Saul nodded. "I know. First time it happened to me I thought it'd last forever. I thought: A few days of this and I'll blow my brains out. 'At's why I made sure I was here when you woke. Trust me . . . it passes."

I started sobbing silently. Saul held my leg. It didn't help. My body grieved and grieved for something I'd never had, but whose absence was irrevocable and heartrending. How is it possible to miss something you've never lost? After I'd calmed down a bit Saul got me a glass of water and explained.

"It's the Empty. They breathe it like air. But they haven't got a name for it. They don't know what they're missing . . . but you do."

I nodded.

Saul continued. "That's the despair of the Holock. Dream addicts with a dwindling supply of dreams. They had to choose between their extinction, or the loss of the one thing that made their lives bearable."

Saul put a hand on my head. "No fever. 'At's good." He patted my arm. "I called Hogan. He's flying in tomorrow."

That cheered me a little. It'd be good to have family around. "What's tomorrow?" I asked.

"Good question," Saul answered.

A sudden wave of nausea swept over me and I shuddered. "God, this must be what cold turkey's like." After a moment I asked, "Where's Wanda?"

"Wanda?" Saul frowned.

I looked at him. He seemed to be remembering something that happened long ago.

"The nurse," I prodded.

"Wanda," he said. "I don't remember telling you about her."

"Saul!" I laughed. "Stop it. She was here. She put me under."

"Oh, shit," said Saul, scratching the back of his neck.

"What?"

He looked out the window. "Wanda was a woman I nearly married. Seems like a lifetime ago."

"She was in this room, I'm telling you!"

"Maybe. Maybe that was a possible past."

I felt like throwing up. What happened when I was under?

"She was the assistant that died in my lab. Electrocuted. Accident, of course. I used her as a guinea pig. I was . . . reckless." Saul sniffled and blew his nose.

My premonition had been right. Wanda was expendable, in some possible past. What the fuck *is* Time? God's idea of a practical joke? We can't get enough of it. We save it. Spend it. Dread it. Fight it. Lose it. When we run out of it, it's the only thing we want. Saul had said it: Change time and the ripples go every way.

"I miss her," I said, remembering her feistiness and envying her ability to swim.

"So have I," said Saul, tamping a Camel on the back of his hand. Suddenly a tiny red bird landed on Saul's shoulder and peeked out from behind his ear. He seemed apologetic.

"Imish!" I said. "What are you doing here!"

The cardinal lighted on my head and cooed.

"Give the man a break!" scolded Saul.

"No, it's all right," I said, giving the cardinal a scratch under the beak.

"He got nervous when you were under so long and nabbed ya on the ear. He's a pest!"

"Nooooo," I said. "He's a good bird, aren't you, Imish?"

He looked at me resentfully. I've since learned he cannot stand being condescended to.

I started to giggle. So maybe Time worked both ways. You win some. You lose some. Maybe the same changes that eliminated Wanda rescued Imish. Maybe it wasn't a joke. Maybe it was just another mystery.

"I wanna show you sumpin'," Saul said. He tossed a yellowed magazine on my lap. A defunct weekly from the fifties, like *The Saturday Evening Post*. "Page twenty-two," he said. The book smelled musty, like it had been tucked away for a long time. On page twenty-two I read: "The Wooden Leg: A Reminiscence by Saul Lowe."

"What's this?"

"Read it," he insisted. "Reading helps."

Saul watched me as I read, blowing smoke out of the corner of his mouth. And for the rest of the story he tapped his ashes on the carpet and ground them into the rug.

I'll never forget the day my father took me to get his new leg. He never explained why he needed it— whether this was a regular thing like visiting the dentist or getting your car tuned up. I always wondered: Did wooden legs rot? Had some family of termites bunked down some night as it lay beside his bed, like a pet, always there in the morning, always ready to be of service? I imagined they tunneled out a network of passages that eventually caved in one morning as he thumped his way down the stairs. I imagined they had adjusted to the tempo of his walk—the thump/squeak and swing. They must have gotten used to it. I recall how natural it was to walk beside him, next to his good leg, how obvious it was that anyone dumb enough to take the other side was going to get clipped as it arched wide like he was mowing the weeds that poked up through the sidewalk cracks. Sometimes I'd listen to his leg from the other side, as I held his fingers: the rhythm: the normal step, the pause (or hiss if we were walking on grass) as it swung about, and the big thump/squeak that completed the cycle, a sort of loose beat that I sometimes catch myself hearing today in certain jazz tunes. It'll stop me and I'll listen, wondering where the hell I've heard it before and why I find it so comforting. Then I smile and remember the crisp smell of burning leaves on the day my father walked me downtown to get his new leg.

He wasn't much of an explainer. So I didn't bother asking. Even when I finally figured out that other fathers didn't wear their left legs, didn't have a ritual of leather straps they belted and buckled every morning, didn't have the red bands of puckered flesh when they removed it every night, or the raw and scarred stump at the end of a pale thigh (which never held much mystery for me). Even when I understood that my father was, in one particular way, different from my friends', I never thought to ask. I used to drive him crazy with questions.

But I tell you, when he did give me answers, they were showstoppers. He had this way of explaining the world that made you believe mystery was everywhere. Unfortunately, that's the last thing he wanted me to believe. He hated that stuff. He called it "whimsy." Yet his answers always left me with the impression that the architect of reality had the showmanship and timing of a magician. They knocked me out. Like he was explaining sex over and over for the first time.

That's how I learned that man was once an ape and lived on green bananas and swung from tree to tree on vines. He taught me the wonders of the opposable thumb, which made possible Dizzy Dean and Mozart. He taught me that ice freezes from the top down, not from the bottom up. That earthquakes were the result of hard plates of stone under the soft crust of the earth shuffling like cards on a green felt table. I learned the fastest thing in the known universe was the speed of light and that had one enough power and the appropriate vessel it was possible to abolish time. That's a funny one. I learned that no dinosaur had ever seen a man. That frogs sleep all winter in the mud. That women bleed regularly between their legs. That breasts make milk. That his starched white shirts were constructed from plants with fluffy white blossoms like the hair of Einstein. And, when I told him my dearest dream was to fly above the treetops, I learned in no uncertain terms that levitation was bunk.

Now my mom was a different fish. I only know her from Kodaks. Strange, that all my memories of her are from his stories and her pictures. I learned secondhand that she was the mystic of the family. My father used to say "Your mother was a gullible skeptic. She was never satisfied with the obvious explanation for anything." She believed in ghosts, St. Anthony—the Patron Saint of Lost Causes—precognition, and the appearances of the Virgin Mary at Fatima (though not at Lourdes)—a distinction my father relished, as it so perfectly impugned her ideas. I gathered from his stories that she put a lot of stock in dreams. A suggestion he felt compelled to repeat with scorn. Later, I learned that she had, in fact, kept a journal of her dreams for some thirty years until the morning she was struck by a speeding taxi. I never saw this journal until I was cleaning my father's house in the days after I had moved him into a nursing home. The last entry predicted her impending departure, my present career, the invention of self-cleaning ovens, contraceptives, and a plastic prosthesis which would render obsolete my father's wooden leg. She also reminded him of his one and only adultery. She wasn't mad. She rebuked him for his prolonged guilt. "You really ought to forgive yourself, dear. I have." And then she wrote, ". . . after all, she was a widow . . . just like you."

He told me something that fall morning as we walked to get his new leg. I was tired. And I had complained aloud, wondering why we hadn't taken the Ford with the specially designed accelerator pedal in the shape of a footprint. I recall him stopping then in the middle of a block. A huge blue church bus swam past and stirred the leaves in our path, so that, for a second, I thought something momentous was about to happen to us. I heard the metallic scrape of a rake on cement, a distant yelping dog. Somewhere around the corner two kids were yelling: Was not, was too, was not, was too. He looked down at me and said, "I've had this leg for ten years. I got one more walk left on it. Don't spoil it." And that was fine; that was a perfect answer. I was content with the knowledge that wooden legs lived for ten years.

I was surprised when we stepped under the familiar green canvas awning of Drexal Drugs. It was where my father took me for chocolate Cokes in conical paper cups mounted in an odd holder: a pewter contraption that was funneled at both ends like a tornado siren, so that the cup could be fitted into either side. They'd jam it against a dispenser that looked like a stack of dunce caps and the top cup would come off—untouched by human hands. I thought it was a great idea. But my father insisted it was "self-explanatory."

We didn't stop at the black marble soda fountain with the swivel stools. We strode past the pharmacy, which I always thought was a ticket booth to Never Never Land: the glass partition with the opening, flanked by those weird teardrop jars filled with blue and red and green water. These, too, were fitted with ornate metal braces, which held them up for everyone to see. They had no visible openings, and it made me curious: How'd they fill 'em? What were they for? When I asked, my father just looked at me as if the question was too absurd or the answer too obvious. That was how he said he did not know. We walked under the lazy fans, past the magazine racks with blindfolded women on the covers on the bottom row, and back into the shadows where the Leg Man worked.

It was in a shady side room off the pharmacy—you had to step down onto a hardwood floor—and looking up I saw pinned against the far wall the outline of half a man. His other half was a puzzle made mostly of wooden parts: a full leg browned by the sun and notched at the knee on a steel pivot, the lower half molded in a perfect concave to receive the thigh. There was a foot with red painted toes covered with a thick coat of dust. His forearm was an ivory tusk tipped with a gleaming claw of steel. There was a shoulder that resembled a piece of football armor, and hovering above it, a marble half-jaw like a small boomerang, and a full set of dentures (the only complete part, I mean the only one that had the other half). The whole figure was proscribed by a dotted white line, painted with great care.

I stared at that for a long while, and then began to take in the other fixtures of the shady room. There was a whole wall of legs and arms. They hung in order of size from child to fullback and under each was stuck a coded tag. Having not yet learned my alphabet I imagined at the time that they were the names of their owners, that they said things like "Joe" and "Maddy." Under them, stacked closely like bikes in a rack, were vehicles of transport: white padded stretchers, wheelchairs with tall woven straw backs, aluminum chairs collapsed upon each other that only very thin people could ride, chairs with openings big enough to hold a goldfish bowl—I wanted one very badly. There was a line of wooden crutches hanging on a long peg and each had a clean red rubber tip that had never touched the earth.

There were no windows in the room. The light came from a few green rectangular canopy lamps that hung from the pressed-tin ceiling on chains. They cast green light against the walls, bright light on the floor.

It was here I figured out that a great many people were missing a great many things.

My father let go of my hand and I explored the room, hunkering down to find the discarded treasures that lay below adult eye-level. Behind a glass counter was an army of dentures dressed in full smile. Then I saw a black-and-white spotted cat, or rather, I saw its thin tail drift around the corner. I followed. It turned to give me a bored look. Fat cat. Sagging belly. Yellow eyes. As I followed it I pocketed a buffalo nickel, found a sprung copper mousetrap behind a file, and a spray of tiny nails near the black claw foot of a safe. I twirled the combination lock until I realized the door was open. There, inside this cool chamber, in a golden shoe box, I discovered a squirming pile of baby kittens: pink, no hair, squinting at the light. The cat brushed against my leg and I could feel the purring of its body. We looked at her children together, the proud mother and I.

A sudden whirring sound startled me. The cat bounded away.

I followed the sound to a small room that smelled of oil and sawdust. One whole wall was jammed with shelves of unfinished wooden feet, like a Dutch shoe store. Thick white canvas belts ran up to the dark ceiling and disappeared, and under them, a bald man in a blue apron with many pockets was carving a hunk of wood on a lathe. My father sat behind him on a stool, rolling up his pant leg.

The man would turn the electric motor off and on with a foot switch, scrutinize, then press a sharp stubby tool against the spinning chunk. The shavings showered down like sparks upon his boots. Curly lengths of wood grew out of his working and stood up for as long as they could, then tumbled gracefully to the floor. He stroked and shaped the wood until it looked like a baseball bat. My solemn father sat inspecting the newly carved foot. He seemed pleased by its form as he ran his thumb along the arch. He noticed me and said with a smile, "Kootchy, kootchy, kootchy."

Then the Leg Man pulled a triangular fragment of mirror from his pocket and ran it up and down to put the final polish on my father's new leg.

That was the moment I knew I wanted to be an inventor when I grew up.

I remember he had woken late that morning, yelling, "Where's my DAMN LEG!" I had been for some time doing an experiment. Trying to get the damned old thing to stand up by itself. It had fallen over so many times that our neighbors in the flat below must have thought I was repairing something again.

"I'm almost done!" I yelled from the living room.

"WHA'?!" he called from the bedroom.

Thunk went his old leg, refusing once and for all to stand at attention.

I carried it back to him like a log in both arms and I offered my conclusion: "Legs need people."

"Wha'?" he asked, beginning to strap it on.

"Can't stand up by itself."

"Me neither," he informed me.

I followed his baggy white boxer shorts into the bathroom where he lathered up with Burma Shave as I hung from the sink and swung to and fro: my morning ritual. I was waiting for him to deposit the used blade in the rusty slit in the medicine cabinet behind the mirror. I had reasoned that someday this dark space would be stuffed with razors and my father would have to remove the mirror and a wall full of Gillettes would topple into the sink. I didn't want to miss that. But that tiny slit seemed to have an infinite capacity for razors. So that I came to believe that behind the mirror in our bathroom was a void of vast proportions, a black pit from which nothing escaped.

"Daddy?" I asked.

"What?"

I always knew I had gone too far when he put the *t* on. So I proceeded gingerly. "Are you working today?"

He swirled his razor in the sink then tapped it on the porcelain. "Not today. Why?"

"Could we go see Momma?" I meant her grave.

"Why?"

"It's her birthday."

He swirled it again for so long that I thought something must have been wrong with the binding mechanism. I stood on my tiptoes to get a closer look. He watched me out of the corner of his eye over his whipped beard.

"The radio said it's Monday," I explained. "You said she was born on a Monday."

"There's lotsa Mondays. There's fifty-two Mondays every year."

I received this news gravely and pondered it.

"And I'll tell you something funny. Her birthday's on a different day every year." He smiled through his lather.

This level of math was too much for me so I resorted to the tried and true method of repetition. "So, can we?"

"That's what I'm trying to say. It's not her birthday."

I listened as the razor scraped whisker.

"Is it her deathday?" I asked.

"Nope," he said.

"Is her deathday on a different day every year?" That's how my mind worked.

He stopped shaving, reached out, and held my face between the fingers and the thumb of his dry hand. "No, Saul. That's always the same day."

After he had toweled his face dry and slipped the blade through the slit, he paused, looking down at the driblets of water he never felt falling on his dark old wooden leg. He seemed surprised to find it had the stains of many mornings.

"Do I always do that?" he asked.

"Every day." I nodded.

He looked at me then, and I saw something moving in his eyes: an unfamiliar thought, or something he was trying to remember.

"I got an idea," he said.

THE END

I put the magazine on my lap and looked at the little man on my bed.

"Saul, you didn't write this."

"It's my story," he protested.

"But you didn't write it," I pressed, cocking my head at him.

"No, I commissioned it. But it's all true. I just needed a writer to schlep the words."

"Who?" I asked.

"Some unemployed screenwriter. Blacklisted. Needed the work."

"It's good." I smiled.

"It better be," he smirked. "I paid two grand for it."

"The beginning's at the end," I noted.

"Yeah, that was his idea. I thought it was a pretty screwy way to tell a story. On the other hand . . ."

"Yeah," I agreed. We were talking about Time. We knew better than anyone how chronology can get shuffled.

I closed my eyes and remembered my last image of Laura. She glowed with that vitality certain women have when pregnant. Holding her ripe belly like a basketball: the way Wilt Chamberlain used to shoot free throws. I must have drifted off for a second, for when I opened my eyes Saul was standing by the blinds, looking over the freeway, fingering a blue rosary.

"I did it," I said sadly.

Saul clung to the beads in his hands. He glanced at the bird on my head. "You hear that, Imish? Laura's dead." He turned to me and forced a smile. "That bird never liked her. Always was a better judge of character than me."

I watched him for a moment, then said, "You never told me she was your daughter."

He didn't move a muscle. I glimpsed then in his face something I had only seen before in the features of my mother. A fierce desolation: a hopelessness so deep and daily fed that it required constant absolution to be tolerable. I understood then, as I never had before, Saul's religion.

"Saul?" I asked, after a time.

"I was getting to it," he explained. Then his shoulders started shaking up and down. And he wept bitterly, silently, for five minutes.

I'm sorry, but I won't go into the next hour I spent with Saul, except to say he confirmed everything that Laura had said, and he bared his soul to me. It was a confession as brave and wrenching as any I've witnessed. He started by saying he was "the worst man in the world." After an hour I believed him. It was extremely personal; and, frankly, it's nobody's business—not even yours. After all, he's my client now.

Suffice it to say, everything that Saul had held on to, held down, held against himself, came pouring out. He had finally released his hold button. And I felt, as I listened and listened to this stranger I had grown to love, that for the first time in his long life, Saul had begun to extend to himself something he had always promised to everyone else: forgiveness.

Thirty-five

Wednesday morning we burned the Time Machine. That afternoon, at a bar in Santa Monica that overlooked the ocean, Hogan and I sat on the cool patio, ordered some Guinness, and munched on yellow popcorn that overflowed from a coffee filter in the middle of the wooden table. A grungy homeless man with a gray garbage bag was collecting empties on the khaki beach. Hogan signaled him, and when he walked over, gave him all the change in his pocket. "God love you," he said hoarsely, and staggered away toward one of those beautiful California pink sunsets; the pollution index was high that day. Beyond the waves maroon beds of kelp sagged on the surface of the rich blue water like oil spills, and every now and then the black head of a sea otter would poke up through their tendrils. The sound of the breakers made an envelope of white noise around us, which seemed to encourage intimacy and the telling of secrets. I told Hogan all about Dream Lock and Laura. He listened attentively. Then he said the most outrageous thing.

"Well, you had your turn."

366 | Patrick O'Leary

I looked at him. "My turn?"

"Sure. At least you had a shot. That's more than some people."

What did he mean? My experience with Laura was a "turn"? An opportunity?

"Like Mom and Dad," he continued to flabbergast me. "At least they had each other."

I wasn't going to let this go. "Hogan, did they kiss in front of us? Hug? Did you ever see them exchange any affection, act happy to see each other?"

He thought about it. "They played pinochle." I snickered and he blushed. "Marriage isn't fireworks, John."

"Hey, I'm not fourteen. I've lived with a few ladies." I read his look. "All right—so maybe I haven't had the greatest luck." He smiled. "All right," I conceded, "so maybe I don't know much about it."

We watched two bouncy blondes in Day-Glo thongs jog by, scattering the gulls on the beach.

"You're just an idealist. Like Mom," said Hogan.

This shook me. "Hogan. In my entire LIFE . . . no one has ever accused me of being like Mom."

"It's not an insult! I'd say she batted five hundred."

"Name me one thing, ONE WAY, that I'm like Mom."

He didn't even have to think about it. "You're too hard on yourself."

I laughed. "What are you talking about? Mom was hard on everybody else!"

"Don't you remember? She always said 'I never ask anyone to do what I'm not prepared to do myself.' Well?"

"Well what?"

"Well, you know how hard she was on people . . . Imagine how she was on herself. *That's* why she couldn't forgive anyone. I mean, how could she? She never forgave herself for marrying Dad."

Hogan was telling me things I'd never heard, that I wasn't sure I wanted to hear. It gave me a strange feeling, as if I was about to take a detour into a dangerous unexplored frontier. It was almost fear, but not quite. Like it could go either way. "She told you that?"

"Dad did." Hogan nodded. "You remember how he used to embarrass her. The way she used to go on about how loud his clothes were? 'Your clothes are too loud, Robert.' I couldn't figure it out; I went in his closet once to listen to them." He smiled, remembering. "And that noise she made when she dusted the dandruff off his blazers."

"Tsch," I said automatically. I could still hear it.

"Tsch," he echoed. "She had to keep reminding him he was beneath her. He was her ticket. But she never forgave herself for buying him."

"Buying him?" I had no idea what he meant.

"You remember the stories. How poor they were in Dublin. No hot water. Outside toilet. Sharing a bed with her sisters."

I remembered. Her past always sounded gray: gray walls, gray streets, gray sky. And all her memories seemed to have the same point: that we had "no appreciation of our circumstances."

"She was proud of that," I said.

"She was proud she got away. She hated it, 'member? All her other sisters got married. She thought she'd never get out of her parents' house. Then along comes this dashing Yankee G.I. on R&R, and he's her ticket. Just like you were."

"*I* was her ticket?" I asked in disbelief.

"Yeah." He smiled and shook his head. "And you thought she was out to *get* you or something."

I sputtered for a moment, "Well, she was! The moment I stopped being her boy . . . I was a Nobody."

"Because *she* was a Nobody." Hogan drank, then cleaned the foam off his upper lip with his lower: exactly as my father used to. "Dad said it's an Irish Thing. See, as long as she had a priest for a son, she was okay. You know, as long as she was the mother of *Father Donelly,* she was special. When you dumped that idea, she was just a wife. Dad's wife."

"And your mom," I reminded him.

He dismissed this with a shake of his head. "I was Dad's. You were Mom's. Mom liked me. But she loved *you.*"

"Come on! I was her property, her personal pet. That's not love!"

"It's something. It's more than we had." Sadness settled into his face like a familiar friend. He smiled through it and his eyes watered.

I gripped the wet glass of stout in my hand like I was going to throw it at him. I laughed. "I'm listening to the insights of a college dropout! A man whose idea of literature is *Reader's Digest!*"

Hogan looked at me and sighed. "Stop it, Johnny."

I held out my hands and looked around, pretending to include the rest of the diners on the patio in the absurdity of it all. "A man who sells Mazdas for a living—who gloats about manipulating people into spending sixty dollars extra on floor mats—is giving me morality lessons!" I was getting hysterical.

"Floor mats are optional," said Hogan, jutting out his chin. "And there's nothing immoral about Mazdas!"

I couldn't stop myself. "A man who fell in love with an alien is trying to lecture me—" I stopped myself. Look who's talking, I thought. I knew I was derailing, possessed by a mood I had no control of. Why was I acting like this?

Why was it so critical to discredit what Hogan was saying? What's it mean when a patient gets this rattled, John? It means something has hit the mark. I lit a cigarette, took a fierce puff, and pointed a finger at him, and whispered, "You're telling me I'm supposed to be grateful because I was the suffocating obsession of a mother who regarded me as 'a ticket'?!" I took off again. "What's with all these tickets? Is her life a travelogue?!"

"Johnny, don't," he said softly.

I took a long drink of stout. "Hogan, don't strain yourself with these in-depth analyses, okay? And don't tell me how lucky I was to be the target of Mom's affection! It was no treat. Believe me, you wouldn't have wanted to be her favorite son."

"I couldn't have been." He shrugged.

"That's right," I agreed bitterly. "You were Dad's. I'm supposed to feel blessed?" I said the painful thing. "I never even felt like he was my father."

"He wasn't."

"That's what I said. I couldn't compete with Dad and you. Your mutual admiration— WHAT DID YOU JUST SAY?"

He shrugged. "He wasn't your father. You weren't his son." He saw my face. "What? What?"

I put down my glass and leveled my eyes at him. "Hogan, I'm not adopted. I've seen my birth certificate."

"No, you were like Jesus," he said, looking out over the ocean, then back at me with his dull blue eyes. "You know, Joseph had to raise him as his own."

I'd had a lot of rugs pulled out from under me in the past year. Ever had your world pulled out from under you? I was in L.A. once during a small earthquake: 4.5. One moment you're standing on something you've always trusted, always assumed to be solid, the next moment—you're falling. The room shudders; the windows rattle; the trees do an upside-down hula dance.

Rock is liquid.

There's no place to go.

And you think: Will it ever end?

There was a free-fall moment of wonder when I realized I had no idea who I was. And then . . . a weird unexpected glimpse of freedom, a sense of open possibilities to know my mother comprised only half my genetic makeup. It was almost a relief: I'd felt something like this all my life, some gut-level cognition of not truly belonging, not truly being wanted—I suspect, My Dear Reader, you might know what I mean.

For a minute all the sounds faded out. I watched the bubbles pop on the tan head of my beer. A gray gull landed on the railing of the patio and looked at me. And I saw the familiar sight of my mother in her blue Sunday dress at the top of the stairs, straightening all the family pictures on the way down. Suddenly she was a person I didn't know. Questions ricocheted in my mind. When I recaptured the ability to speak, I said, "Dad . . . ?"

"Married Mom when she was pregnant," Hogan said simply.

"When did he tell you this?"

"Just before he died."

"Why didn't you tell me?"

"I promised not to tell till Mom died."

"Did he know she was expecting me at the time?"

"Nah."

Appalled, I asked, "She tricked him?"

Hogan shifted in his chair. "Well, I guess. But it was okay by him." He shrugged with his mouth. "He loved her."

I remembered my dad on his hospital bed. His feeble breath steaming on the plastic oxygen mask. His last words, which seemed so inadequate then, were suddenly full of love and wisdom and kindness: just what I needed to hear—and I hadn't really heard them: "Have fun." My father was a person I didn't know. In one moment my respect for him took a quantum leap. "It didn't bother him? Raising someone else's child?"

"He didn't regret it," Hogan answered. "He said, 'That's why they invented erasers. People make mistakes. Mom had a problem; I was an eraser.' He told me, 'She was the hardest sell I ever had; I could never quite close that deal.' " Hogan wiped the sweat off his glass with a thumb. "He said she was ashamed of herself. For getting pregnant. For using him. She thought if you were a priest it'd wipe it all out. You wouldn't be a sin; you'd be a gift from God. I don't get that part."

Stunned, I said: "That's what she used to call me: 'God's gift' to her."

Someone at the bar started a fresh batch of popcorn; it perfectly complemented the new feelings dribbling around inside me. Confusion. Shock. Sadness. Grief. Wonder. I finally settled on the most comfortable, my old standby: Anger. "Geez, that's sad. That's really sad. The Holiest Woman in Detroit screwed around, got knocked up, married a man she didn't love, and made our lives miserable 'cause we couldn't live up to her standards. That's really sad."

"Oh, grow up," said Hogan quietly.

"What?"

"Grow up, big brother. Stop whining. You're just like her!"

"In no way am I—"

"Remember how Mom was about the house? Mopping,

waxing, polishing? How she'd throw a fit if we didn't take our shoes off when we came in? Nothing was ever clean enough for her."

"That's right."

"That's you. Life is messy. If you weren't so hard on yourself you'd accept that. If you weren't so hard on people, you wouldn't have to *fix* them all the time. Well," he admitted, "that's what Angie says, anyway."

It was the most stinging summary of my career I'd ever heard. I didn't say a word for about five minutes, just stared at the empty coffee filter. When I looked up the gull was gone and Hogan was smiling.

"All that God talk you and Mom did around the kitchen table. Like it was never settled. Like you had to keep convincing yourselves. You could never believe God really loved you." He chuckled softly. "Dad and I used to listen to you guys and hold our guts, we were laughing so hard."

This would have been funnier if it wasn't so annoying. "Hogan, you're making me feel like shit."

He rolled his eyes. "There you go again," he sighed.

I was rubbing my forehead with my fingers and thumb, like I was trying to pull something out of my brain. When did Hogan get so smart? Or did I need to feel superior to him for all those years, to justify my mom's adoration, to feel like I deserved it, when actually it had nothing to do with me? I felt like a white man raised by Indians who had just been told he wasn't an Ojibwa. It seemed I had grown up in the company of strangers. Mom. Dad. And Hogan. He sat patiently across from me, scratching his potbelly, waiting for me to catch up.

"Jesus, you just did for me in twenty minutes what usually takes five years with a patient!"

"Client," he corrected. "You're supposed to call them 'clients,' right?"

"Right."

"Angie says, 'Doctors have patients; Johnny has clients.'"

"Right," I repeated. I couldn't begrudge him this small victory; he seemed to enjoy it too much.

"I don't know what to say. Hogan, you just told me some Serious Truth, and I haven't even thanked you!"

He considered this, then offered: "If it'll make you feel better, you could give me some money."

Then he broke into that irresistible smile of his, and we had one of those truly great laughs. The kind that leaves you clean and exhausted. The kind where everyone around you has to stop a moment and check you out; they haven't any idea what's so funny but, eventually, they can't help but smile.

When we settled down, Hogan yawned. "You know, you're taking this *really* well. You wanna another beer?"

Thirty-six

The next day, Hogan, Saul, and I were booked on a morning nonstop back to Detroit. So I asked the front desk for an early wake-up call to give us time to pack and get to LAX. But I rose out of a sound sleep before it came. I sat up in bed. I was wide awake. Hogan was snoring on the sofa bed, Imish sleeping in his cage. Saul could have been anywhere, or anywhen. I walked naked to the window and watched the gray surf crash under the foggy Santa Monica Pier. I felt as though I had remembered something important—but I couldn't place it. My mind seemed strangely full, teeming with odd recollections and detail. I remembered the lineup of the 1968 Pistons. All of my grade-school teachers' names. Conversations I hadn't thought of in ages. It was a little scary. After years of being misplaced, someone had uploaded my past. I distinctly saw the view from my crib, the cracked yellow ceiling. I recalled my first words. My imaginary childhood friend. My old gym locker combination. I remembered who borrowed and never returned my copy of *Astral Weeks* twenty years ago. For some reason I forgave him. I saw my first girlfriend, hunting crawfish at the lake; their eyes glowed like red coals in the flashlight beam, and she lifted her Notre Dame sweatshirt to show me her tiny breasts. I remembered her name; I remembered I had hurt her. And most surprising: I recalled trivia I had no desire to remember. Dates. Times. Places. How tall Ringo was. Who wrote "The Bird Song" from *Easy Rider*. Who else died on JFK's deathday. All my clients' numbers. Even the phone number of Nancy's parents.

On a whim, I called them to help track her down. She had moved out of state. I called her long distance. Before Nancy had a chance to say anything I apologized for being such a whiny prick. I told her I still liked and respected her. I took full and total blame for messing things up. I was sorry. I told her I'd been giving it a lot of thought and that if anybody was responsible for our breakup it was me.

"I know that," she agreed, disconcertingly.

"No hard feelings?" I asked.

"No," she said. "Actually, it's kind of funny. I can't think of two people more ill suited for each other."

We laughed about that.

Then she said she had some "important news." She thought I had the right to know. I was a father. We had a daughter.

I was speechless for about fifteen seconds. "But, Nancy, that's impossible! You were on the Pill!"

"I went off it."

"Why?"

"You remember! My doctor was very pushy about the side effects. She had that strange new assistant of hers fit me with that Swedish thing."

"I don't really—"

"Honestly, John! I told you all about her. The weird nurse who kept sucking on a grape jawbreaker the whole time? 'Adrian' something."

Christ! I *did* remember her mentioning something about an unusual nurse. The Waker was trying to sterilize Nancy before I even met Laura!

"But I ended up taking it out after a day," Nancy said. "It felt funny. But that nurse called me once a week for months. I just told her it was working fine. What a pest!"

"But," I struggled to recall, "forget birth control. We didn't make love in our last six months together."

"Sure we did."

"Nancy, I'd remember it."

"You would, eh? With *your* memory? The end of July when I came back to the apartment to pick up some of my stuff? You were smashed on martinis and babbling about your mom and the Church. You were in bad shape. I felt sorry for you. So I tucked you in, and bang."

"Bang?" I said. "What'd I do—force myself on you?"

She made that snorting sound I always hated. "Hardly. I was horny. And . . ." She sighed. "I was leaving town. I didn't think I'd see you again."

"I'm sorry, Nancy. I don't remember."

"That's okay, Walrus. I was a little drunk, too. To get my courage up. If you had asked, I might have stayed. It was a dumb idea."

Funny that the Holock never picked up on that, I thought. I guess I never dreamed about Nancy. She's not the sort of woman you dream about. Or did my "babbling about the Church" that night jam their connection? And my blackout make the Memory Film unrecordable? That was more likely.

"So anyway, congratulations, Dad."

I thought of Saul's Italian needle trick. A boy and a girl, he'd said. The boy, I knew, was gone. But I had a daughter. I'm a dad, after all. I'm a dad. For a long minute I watched a cloud roll by, oozing beautiful and slow, like it had all the time in the world. When I snapped out of it, I asked: "What's her name?"

Nancy wouldn't tell me. Privileged information.

"What are you saying? You don't want me to see my own daughter?"

"She's safe, John. I don't even know what state she's in. Any further contact is up to her when she reaches the age of consent."

It took me a moment to understand. "You put her up for adoption?"

"Of course." It seemed the most sensible thing to do, given her lifestyle. And how important her work was. The birth was uneventful. She was sedated. She wasn't into that sixties' natural childbirth crap. She got to nurse her once.

After that there was little left to say. She asked if she could keep a few of my Jung volumes she hadn't returned. I said I didn't mind. Then we talked of all those silly little things we thought we had forgotten, those scattered grace notes of harmony in the bum arrangement of our love. We laughed a lot.

When we had wished each other well and hung up, I had a sudden daydream that made me unreasonably happy. A little blonde girl with Nancy's eyes coming to my door selling candy bars for her school; they were dark and hard on the outside, soft and bright white on the inside. From this day on, I thought, every little girl I see on the street, at the market or the ballgame, could be mine. I was taken by a wondrous new feeling: I felt gifted and had no one to thank.

These days, as Hogan says, I'm "back in the lineup." I've got a new practice—or should I say: I'm "still practicing"? But all my clients have had to adjust to my erratic timetable: I see them on a last-come first-served basis.

I often think about Laura when I'm "between appointments": those ten missing minutes from every hour, when the healer recuperates. I still have the photograph she gave me of herself, the one I promised to destroy. It hangs on the wall of my office next to my diplomas. A reminder to always make room for mystery. It's a Polaroid of an empty doorway, which I've dubbed—you probably guessed—"Door Number Three." And there's just enough room in the frame for a woman to stand, a woman who once was, or may have been, or still could be. In a possible past.

I still see Jack and Saul occasionally. They run a food program and shelter for the poor downtown, and I'm happy to say that their business is plummeting. Suzie's mom is their chief cook. But I moved out of the rectory and set up housekeeping with Suzie on a houseboat on the Detroit River. We like the water. She's teaching me how to swim. And every Fourth of July we've got a ringside seat for the fireworks. But they scare the shit out of Imish: our first mate. A very opinionated bird, but charming, nonetheless. We've got an understanding. He doesn't let anybody else know how smart he is, or how dumb I am.

I'm learning to live with mystery one day at a time. It's like the feeling I get after I've finished my Sunday *New World Times* and I leave a treefull of paper in a pile at my feet and go wash my hands. My soy-inky fingers make a black-water whirlpool in the white sink. And I always end up feeling none the wiser, but vastly informed. I will admit, though, that I do sleep well, and I have one great consolation. I remember all my dreams.

We all do now.

What we call the "Changes" were vast, abrupt, and astounding: the equivalent of a Revolution in Consciousness that happened overnight. The implications of Dream Retention were manifold. All dreams became "Lucid Dreams." And it was discovered that a dream lucidly experienced and flawlessly remembered was as ecstatic as any drug—no wonder the Holock were addicted. Dream inspirations were no longer lost. Dreams were confirmed to be linked to memory storage, and once the transmission lines were unblocked, that is once they weren't secondhand dubs of the Holock's Memory Films, everyone's past burst into vivid clarity. Oddly, this additional burden of data did not register as a sensory overload. It was as if a natural capacity, which had been dormant for eons, finally awoke. The software was already in place, waiting for the proper command.

But the most profound repercussion of Dream Retention was also the most mysterious: an exponential leap in empathy. Some psychiatrists dubbed it a "Phobia Deletion." Some scientists called it an illusion triggered by "Stereocity." Politicians of every persuasion concluded it was an inevitable evolutionary step that validated any number of agendas—which meant they didn't understand it either.

Saul says this new empathy remains a mystery because it is not something that can be quantified; it is literally something missing. The hub of a wheel, the crucial ghost at the heart of all metaphor that allows two unlikely things to be compared. The absence of the Holock freed us all to cross the no-man's land that separates every human, the synapse gap between our fortified impenetrable skulls, to find communion—our natural state. And when our most intimate boundaries were no longer violated by the Holock, when our psyches were no longer occupied territory, our siege mentality was no longer relevant. What were we thinking? we thought. Why did I hate? What good did it do me? No one could remember.

To most of us, it was an embarrassing revelation. For it was found that, in the place we all dream, the urge to scapegoat, tribal snobbery, "Us and Them" thinking—in fact, every stone of the vast wall of human prejudice—crumbled like an overwhelmed levee. And any notion of bigotry, discreet or inflamed, was shed as an overcoat in the desert. It wasn't just useless anymore; it was downright ridiculous. It was as if a world of slave owners had awakened one day to find themselves abolitionists.

For if we learned anything we've learned that it isn't so much the total recall of dreams that matters, but the healing knowledge that lies at the center of all dreaming, the secret that our forsaken children, the Holock, so desperate to touch their parents of the past, had unwittingly stolen from us. The secret was in the remembering of the places where we are most human. There, in our deepest hidden selves, we discover we are not alone; we are truly family, truly the same, all born from the same womb, all sharing the same fears, all living the same dream. It was a timeless knowledge that once recovered could not be lost again.

All this yielded a simple truth, which the eminent chronologist B. D. Wyatt put so well in her landmark holodance on Dream Theory, *There Is No Enemy:* "Pain shared with another creature is lessened; joy shared is increased."

But perhaps here I go too far.

Or "Beyond Here Be Dragons."

Or, as the Wizard said to Dorothy: "Come back tomorrow!"

You've got enough to fret about in your own Now. Besides, knowledge may be power, but, as Saul says: foreknowledge is as useless as a three-pronged plug for a two-jack outlet. Even he couldn't have predicted the weirdness of this future. Suffice it to say that once the aftershocks of the Changes had settled, it seemed possible that a New Age of Humankind had dawned and that the old demons of want and war might at long last be expelled. We found it wasn't that simple. "The New World" has new problems that no one could have foreseen, that even now seem insurmountable.

Which goes double for Time Travelers like me. I have yet to find the controlling mechanism that can moderate my time-blipping. Prayer doesn't help me as it helps Saul; neither do religious artifacts. I seem to drift in a world where effects cause causes and time has its own agenda. I'm not complaining. It's not really that different from what everyone has to go through. Nobody knows what's going to happen next; I don't know *when*'s going to happen next.

I do miss a few things. It's hard to get worked up about basketball anymore. I seem to experience most games from the final buzzer backward—the points subtract themselves into equal zeroes. But I find that knowing the ending before you've read a book doesn't necessarily spoil everything; it depends on the book. Sex is interesting. Sometimes I start at the climax. I suppose a lot of women would say: So what else is new?

My biggest grief is that I find it nearly impossible to sustain friendships. True, my warped calendar doesn't allow for much of a social life, but there's more to it than that. Wryly I record how irritating it was when Saul ditched out on me in midsentence. I record how annoying his non sequiturs were. However charming and amusing—and I love him dearly—Saul is exhausting to be around. If I spend too much time with him I get resentful. Time Travelers seem to have that effect on people. We are notoriously unreliable. We miss birthdays, break dates; we seem destined to disappoint those closest to us. Like fortune-tellers who can tell your future, just not the parts you're curious about.

Luckily, I am blessed with a patient lover.

Suzie says she knows when I've been gone. I get this look on my face, like I've just come out of the dark into a room full of light and I need a second to adjust. She says I do it a lot. When I tried to explain what it's like, she said: "Oh, you mean like those videos in the eighties? Jump-cuts, nonlinear editing, and all that gratuitous choreography?"

God, I love her.

But time-blipping isn't like that. It's not like anything, really. I've had to face the fact that a reality that doesn't obey the rules of time will not be explainable to people who do. It's sort of like describing sex to a preadolescent.

I've had to learn to live with that kind of isolation.

When I told Saul about this I discovered that he doesn't even remember that wild year the same way I do. He told me Hogan remembers even less. But he did understand, and he suggested I write. Somehow writing your life in some semblance of chronology helps establish a psychic gravity, a link to a continuity, a harbor to dock into. A home.

But there's another reason.

I miss my daughter.

The experience of missing someone you've never met, I suspect, is peculiar to me.

I think about you a lot.

I hope you are happy.

I wonder if we've met.

Imish thinks I'm getting sentimental. He's been reading this story from the beginning. He likes to perch on my head and watch the blue letters stacking sideways on the gray holoscrim. I've had to discourage him from the actual typing (a job he loves but for which he's physically ill equipped—his orange beak gets very sore after a page or two and his spelling is atrocious). But that doesn't stop him from commenting on its progress.

Fuck 'em. Let him write his own book.

This one's for you.

I'm leaving it on the Libnet: someplace where Saul says

you'll find it. I hope it helps explain something about your missing father. And what he was up to. And why.

And I want you to know that I'm so very proud of you. From what I know, you are or will be someone whose life will change the world. You mustn't be frightened of this. Because, My Dear Daughter, it happens to everyone.

But then, you probably know that, as by the time you read this the Changes will have begun. Or perhaps you still exist in one of the infinite possible pasts that hasn't yet had its course corrected. Don't sweat it. The Cavalry is coming. It may be tomorrow, or the next day. It may be now.

I don't know, myself.

I live in the future. I remember the present. I anticipate the past.

If we could read the secret history of our enemies,
we should find in each one's life
sorrow and suffering enough to disarm all hostility.

—Henry Wadsworth Longfellow, *Driftwood,* 1857